Paper Boats

Paper Boats

DEE LESTARI

Translated by Tiffany Tsao

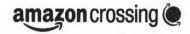

Text copyright © 2004 Dee Lestari
Translation copyright © 2017 Tiffany Tsao

Previously published as *Perahu kertas* by Bentang Pustaka & Truedee in Indonesia in 2004. Translated from Indonesian by Tiffany Tsao. First published in English by AmazonCrossing in 2017.

Published by AmazonCrossing, Seattle

www.apub.com

Amazon, the Amazon logo, and AmazonCrossing are trademarks of Amazon.com, Inc., or its affiliates.

ISBN-13: 9781503943582
ISBN-10: 1503943585

Cover design by Adil Dara

Printed in the United States of America

Paper Boats

Paper
Boats

CHAPTER 1

THE WINDING ROAD

June 1999

It made no sense to leave Amsterdam in summer. This was the best time of year to cycle around the Leidseplein and Dam Square, to enjoy the sunshine that turned the city into paradise on earth. He wanted to sit on Bloemendaal beach with his canvas and paints, or at a café in De Negen Straatjes with his sketchbook, sipping milky *koffie verkeerd* from morning to sundown.

As he cleared the last of the books from the shelf beside his bed, the same thought he'd been having all week repeated itself: *I'm only eighteen and I'm already too tired for this.*

The door behind him creaked open.

"*Nee*, Keenan," his oma said. "Don't weigh down your suitcase with books. When you get to Jakarta, I'll send it to you."

Keenan gave his grandmother a tight smile. *So much for packing,* he thought, his heart sinking. What Oma had said made it seem as if he were never coming back.

Keenan always knew this dreaded day would come. Only a miracle would prevent him from having to return home to Indonesia now. For years, Keenan had hoped and prayed for such a miracle, but it never came—just phone calls from his mother praising the sketches he had sent, without any mention of him being able to stay in Amsterdam. He should stay. Oma was too old to be living by herself, and she refused to move into a nursing home. Here, he would sit on a bench in Vondelpark and paint. Here, he would grow up to join the city's multitude of artists, whom he so admired.

Living here was a miracle in itself for Keenan, but it had reached its expiration date. Six years, no more. His parents had argued for an entire week before finally agreeing to let him, their oldest child, live in a foreign country. Keenan didn't feel like a foreigner, though. Sure, his father was Indonesian and his name was Gaelic—a gift from his mother's late father, in tribute to a distant Irish ancestor—but his mother's family had lived in Holland for generations. This was the city where his mother was born, and where she had become a painter—until she had moved to Indonesia to study art, met his father, and given up painting entirely. Keenan didn't know what had happened exactly, but he still wondered how his own mother—the source of the artist's blood flowing through his veins—could now want to suppress the very talent he had inherited from her. Or rather, he wondered why she hadn't stood up more to his father, who had worried that Amsterdam would awaken the artist inside his son.

"What are you scared of?" Keenan had asked him.

"You're too smart," his father had answered. "You shouldn't waste it by becoming an artist."

Keenan had even contemplated getting lower grades at school to change his father's mind. But luckily, his parents had come to an agreement. His father would let him attend school in Amsterdam for six years, and six years only.

Now, over two thousand days had passed, and Keenan felt the six years had gone by in the blink of an eye.

"Maybe you should bring these ones with you, child," said Oma, handing him two books. *Preparing for the Indonesian National University Entrance Exams: 2500 Exercises*, volumes one and two. "So you can study on the plane."

"*Ja*, Oma," said Keenan. He took the heavy books from her, planning to hide them under the bed once she left the room.

"I'll be waiting for you at the dining table." The old woman stood, smoothed the wrinkles from her paisley-print blouse, and refastened the clips in her hair, which was white but still abundant. Then she smiled. Her wrinkles did not lessen the beauty of her features. Oma looked a lot like his mom. Suddenly, Keenan felt a pang of longing. Maybe going back to Jakarta wouldn't be so bad after all.

"What did you make for dinner, Oma?"

"*Bruinebonensoep* and *kaasbroodje*. That's what you wanted, wasn't it? Oma *vergeet dat niet*, child—your oma doesn't forget. I always keep my promises."

One night during Keenan's first winter with his grandmother, the heater had broken. Oma had wrapped him in a thick blanket and held him, and they had stayed huddled together like that on the sofa until morning. It was the first time they had felt so close, like two friends looking after each other. That night, Oma had promised not to cry when the time came for Keenan to return to Indonesia. And Keenan had made a promise not to cry as well, though he hadn't known how hard it would be to keep.

Keenan watched his grandmother through the crack in the door as she headed toward the dining table. The corners of Oma's mouth were always turned upward, giving her face a perpetual expression of warmth. And her steps were still strong and sure, though slower than they had been a year ago. Keenan watched Oma smooth out the table-cloth, which didn't really need smoothing out, and sit in front of the tureen of brown-bean soup, its steam wafting into her face. And without her knowing, he saw her old eyes glisten before she swiped at them.

Keenan closed the door. Soon, the whole room became blurry. No matter how many times he blinked, his own tears wouldn't stop flowing.

July 1999

The petite young woman was a flurry of movement—skipping and sometimes leaping or kicking. In preparation for her big move from Jakarta, she was packing books into a box—that was all. But she had decided to throw in some dance moves as well.

New wave music blasted through her earbuds, courtesy of her older brother's music collection. It had been a month since Kugy had graduated from high school, but her taste in music was that of a high school student from fifteen years ago. Everyone liked to say that Kugy wasn't just not up-to-date—she was completely *out* of date. She always responded to this observation with a disregard that bordered on pride. Kugy remained adamant that the music of the '80s, the fashion sense of the decade notwithstanding, was pure genius—the epitome of cool.

As Kugy sang and danced to Culture Club's "Karma Chameleon," she fanned herself with a book and tried her best not to look directly in the mirror. The blur of motion that was her reflection already made her want to burst out laughing. *Simply awful,* she thought, shaking her head in dismay.

Her younger sister, Keshia, was knocking on the door. She waited a minute, and when there was no response, she began banging.

"Kugy! *Koo-gee*! Hey, Koogster! Someone's on the phone for you!"

"*Koogster?*" said their mother. She looked up from her book, eyebrow raised. "Also, it should be *Kak* Kugy." Their mother never tired of reminding Keshia that she should use the proper term of respect for an older sister: *kak*, short for *kakak*. The problem was, her older sister's behavior wasn't exactly befitting of a *kakak*.

Suddenly, the door, which was plastered over entirely with stickers, opened, and out poked Kugy's head, an earbud dangling from one ear. She wasn't in any hurry to answer the phone, and looking at her mother, asked, "Mom, what if I change my name to Karma? Your kids' names would all still begin with *k*, so it wouldn't change anything."

Keshia looked at her mother in exasperation. "See what I mean, Mom? She's such a weirdo."

Kugy continued. "It's not like Kugy is a normal name, anyway. What were you and Dad thinking? If you ask me, Karma sounds way better."

Their mother shrugged and resumed reading. "I already have trouble keeping the names of my five children straight and I'm not even senile yet. Go ahead. It won't make a difference—Karma, Karno, whatever you like."

Keshia was speechless. She was beginning to understand where Kugy got her weirdness from.

Affecting a heavy British accent, Kugy went to the phone and answered, "Karma Chameleon speaking. Who is this?"

A few seconds passed before the voice on the other end spoke. "It's Noni. Who did you think it was? The queen of England?"

Kugy's eyes brightened at the sound of Noni's voice. She and Noni had been friends since they were little, and Noni couldn't wait for Kugy to finish packing so she could join her in Bandung, a few hours southeast of Jakarta. Noni also couldn't resist busying herself in preparation for Kugy's arrival, which she looked forward to with the same excitement a small village might exhibit in anticipation of a visiting dignitary. It was Noni who had found Kugy a room in the same student boarding house where she was staying. It was Noni who had arranged to pick her up from the station. And it was Noni who had put together an itinerary for Kugy's first week in Bandung. In short, Noni had designated herself as Kugy's personal assistant.

"So, you *are* coming, right? If not, I'll let someone else take your room!" Noni's voice sounded shrill, especially in contrast to the smoothness of Boy George's voice in Kugy's other ear.

"My dear Madam Noni, try to relax. I haven't even sent the official copy of my high school transcript—"

"Seriously? Everyone else sent theirs in centuries ago!"

"'Centuries ago'? *Someone* needs a history lesson."

"But when will you be done packing? And don't bring your gajillion books with you. They won't fit in Eko's trunk. Just bring your clothes, okay?"

"Has anyone ever told you that you're fussier than three of my mothers rolled into one? Seriously."

"I don't care. Be in Bandung by next week. I've already told Eko to take Fuad for a tune-up so he doesn't break down when we pick you up at the station."

Fuad was the name of Eko's Fiat, which had seen better days. Eko's friends had dubbed it Fuad because of the sound people made when laughing at it: *"Fua-ha-ha-ha."*

Noni continued, "From the station, we'll go buy everything you need to settle in. I've been cleaning your room since yesterday so it'll be all ready for you."

"Has anyone ever told you that you're more industrious than three maids rolled into one?"

"You're crazy."

"And rude, too," Kugy added.

"You're right! You *are* rude!"

"What are you going to do with me? I'm such a pain!"

Noni burst out laughing. "See? Even *you* get angry at you."

Kugy began laughing, too. "I'm getting angry at me to help you save your energy. You'll wear yourself out taking care of me, Eko, and that broken-down yellow Fiat of his."

"Tell me about it. Sometimes when we go out, we use a motor scooter instead of Fuad. I don't know which happens more often: Fuad breaking down or Kombi getting busy."

Kugy couldn't stop laughing. Noni and her boyfriend, Eko, had a pair of hamsters named Komba and Kombi. Together, Komba and Kombi had produced so many litters that Noni and Eko had started a hamster-selling business on the side.

"That bad, huh? If only Fuad could reproduce. Then at least you'd be able to breed Fiats."

"So I'll be expecting you next week, okay?" Noni continued. "And don't forget: get the official copy of your transcript, pack, send your books, and bring that travel umbrella I lent you a while back—and my denim jacket. You still have them, right? What else . . ."

Kugy held the receiver away from her ear as she turned on the TV and flipped through the channels, waiting for Noni to finish talking.

"Kugy? Are you writing this down?"

"Yes!" Kugy answered hurriedly. "See you next week, okay?"

She chuckled as she put down the phone. Noni was really something else. In terms of getting her ready to go to college in Bandung, there was practically nothing left for her own family to see to. Noni had willingly and thoroughly taken care of almost everything. Such had been their relationship, ever since they were little. Although they were the same age, Noni had always taken care of her as a big sister would.

Noni, an only child, and Kugy, one of several siblings, had been inseparable since kindergarten. Both their fathers had started out working for the same company, and the relationship between the two families had been tight-knit since the day they met. Their fathers were even often assigned to work together on the same projects. It was as if it had all been planned.

So Noni and Kugy had grown up together, living in the same housing developments and moving from city to city: Ujungpandang, Balikpapan, Bontang, and finally Jakarta, where they finished elementary school together and where, for the first time in their lives, they'd had to part ways. Noni's dad was the first to retire, and he decided to live out the rest of his days with his wife in Subang while Noni went to boarding school nearby in Bandung. Kugy's father, on the other hand, decided that their family would remain in Jakarta.

Although Noni appeared to be the more mature and organized of the two, Kugy's seemingly chaotic disposition belied a determination that Noni lacked. Kugy always knew exactly what she wanted, ever since she was a child. And when something really mattered to her, she transformed into a completely different person.

Her decision to major in literature stemmed from her ambition to become a fairy tale writer, and she was attending university in another city because she dreamed of being financially independent and living on her own. For all her spontaneity, Kugy had charted her life's course with great thoroughness. Every step had a good reason behind it, and when it came to seeing her dreams through, Kugy was all business.

Kugy had been diligent about saving money since elementary school, and she invested all her savings in children's books, starting with cheap picture books and graduating to expensive volumes of fairy tale classics. She used these books to start a library, complete with membership and lending fees, and turned a profit, ensuring her books would continue to increase in number. So it was that Kugy became the youngest library owner in the housing development, not to mention the fiercest. Like a predator in a jungle, she hunted down delinquent library patrons on her little bicycle until she had cornered them, leaving them no choice but to return their books in order to stop her from chasing them down again in the future.

Anything and everything Kugy believed would help her achieve her dreams, she carried out with zeal. In middle and high school, she was editor in chief of the school newspaper. She earned a reputation as a pioneer, always coming up with fresh story ideas, and she worked hard to set up interviews with well-known public figures that she conducted with a meticulousness worthy of any professional before turning them into hard-hitting articles.

She entered every writing contest she came across in magazines and worked as hard as possible to win them. It got to the point where Kugy knew who would most likely be on the selection committees and what their reading tastes were.

Not everyone thought becoming a fairy tale writer was a worthwhile pursuit. Kugy knew this. As she got older, she became increasingly aware that the kind of career that people did deem "worthwhile" was one that earned a lot of money. Being a storywriter wasn't one of them. So to prove them wrong, Kugy had tried her whole life to show she could in fact earn a living from her writing.

Holed up in her room, which led to the lending library in the attic, Kugy constructed her lifelong dream, block by block. She knew where she was headed—even if the road she would have to take was a winding one.

CHAPTER 2

MOVING TO BANDUNG

August 1999

"Where's Keenan?"

The man asking the question was tall—and sturdy for someone in his early fifties. He was wearing running shorts and a plain white T-shirt, and had been pacing back and forth for some time now.

"Probably still sleeping," his wife replied. She was preparing two cups of milky coffee, and the task appeared to be taking up most of her attention.

"How can he sleep at a time like this? We're more nervous about his exam results than he is," the man complained.

His wife heard a sound at the front door. "Oh! I think the paper's here!"

The two of them scrambled to open the door, then the newspaper, turning the pages until they came to a long list of names.

"Here he is! He got in!" his wife exclaimed, almost choking with emotion as she pointed at the page.

There it was. Clear as day.

"Let's wake him up," he said.

"Oh, let him sleep as long as he wants. Poor Keenan. He's been staying up late every night." His wife's tone was gruff, but then her face blossomed into a smile. "He's done well, and now we can relax."

But Keenan had heard the news. It was impossible not to in their cozy cottage. They lived in East Jakarta, and though the size of the property was considerable, his father had asked the architect to keep the house small to make the most of their lush green surroundings. As he lay in bed, he curled up into a ball, hugged his knees to his chest, and asked himself whether it was wrong not to feel as happy as they did. Wasn't he content that he had succeeded, and that his success had brought happiness to others? And hadn't he grieved long enough over the betrayal of his own dreams?

Keenan's eyes remained fixed on the blank canvas next to his bed, its emptiness the only answer he received.

———

There was a stream a few blocks from Kugy's house. Its water was a muddy brown, but unlike most of the other streams in the city, which were congested, its current ran smooth. When Kugy had first moved to Jakarta, she'd realized that every place she had ever lived had flowing water nearby. It was as if something, or someone, wanted to make sure she continued doing what she did—writing letters to Neptune.

Kugy remembered how it had all started. At the time, her family had been living in Ujungpandang. Their house had been near the ocean, and she had spent most of her days at the beach. It was Karel, her oldest brother, who had first told little Kugy that she was an Aquarius. The water bearer. Little Kugy had imagined that she had been dispatched by the god Neptune to live on dry land. As it was a spy's duty to routinely report to headquarters, Kugy began telling Neptune about everything that was happening in her life.

She sent the first letter as soon as she had learned how to write, folding it into a paper boat and setting it out to sea. From then on, Kugy stopped by the beach almost every afternoon, sending Neptune letters filled with stories or drawings.

When it came time for their family to move, Kugy had protested, for it meant they couldn't live near the beach anymore. She only stopped sulking when Karel explained that wherever they were, as long as there was flowing water, Kugy would still be able to send these letters. All water flows to the sea. That's what Karel had told her as he wiped the tears from Kugy's cheeks.

"All rivers flow to the sea?"

Karel nodded.

"All reservoirs flow to the sea?"

Karel nodded again.

"All gutters flow to the sea?"

Karel continued to nod.

Only then was Kugy satisfied. Even though they never lived near the ocean again, wherever they moved, their house always happened to be near flowing water of some sort. So Kugy was certain her letters would continue to reach Neptune wherever she lived, including the house they lived in now.

She sent fewer and fewer letters over time. Now that Kugy was older, she knew that Neptune didn't really exist. She knew that by the time her letters made it to the ocean, all that would be left were meaningless microscopic shreds. She knew they probably never even made it to the ocean at all. Yet, though she couldn't explain why, in her heart of hearts, Kugy still wanted to believe it was true. Nor could she explain why the sight of those paper boats, carried out on the water, set her soul at ease.

That morning, she was standing by the stream. There were street kids playing in an alley nearby, and their shouts rang in her ears. But Kugy didn't mind. She gazed at the current of brown water flowing in

13

front of her. Carefully, she took something out of her pants pocket. A paper boat. Kugy couldn't remember the last time she'd set one afloat from there. She had neglected her duties as a spy for the underwater kingdom for too long. For some reason, her upcoming departure for Bandung had moved her to write to Neptune once more—this time a short letter containing only a few sentences.

> *Nep,*
> *I'm moving to Bandung. I'll find my stream. Until we meet again.*

The street kids spied the paper boat. Amidst a hail of stones, fish-hooks, leaves, and anything else they could get their little hands on, it sailed on, undisturbed.

———

A curly-haired boy wearing a middle school uniform ran toward the cottage, opened the white wooden gate, and hurried inside. The boy's features were strong and well defined, and his skin was fair, though its sunburnt ruddiness made him look like one of the tourists who came to surf at Kuta Beach in Bali.

He looked around anxiously, but when he saw his parents' car still parked in the garage, his breathing relaxed. There was even a spring in his step as he opened the front door.

"Mom! Keenan hasn't left yet, has he?" he asked as he entered, just to make sure.

His mother smiled and shook her head. "No, he hasn't. But if you want to come see your brother off at the station, you have to take a shower."

Keenan emerged from his room and, at the sight of his grubby, sweat-drenched little brother, he grinned. "Disgusting, isn't he, Mom? And all the girls still fall for him."

Jeroen's face reddened. His thoughts flew to the letters and photos that the girls at school were always slipping into his bag, and he tried to guess how many of them Keenan had discovered.

"You're lucky you're leaving," their mother joked. "I feel like his personal receptionist. Every time I answer the phone it's for him."

Quietly, she regarded her two sons, six years apart in age. She was struck anew by how different they were. Jeroen—extroverted, athletic, and agreeable—loved organizing activities and attending social events. He was a carbon copy of his father. Keenan, on the other hand, was introverted and gentle. He hated crowds and preferred to spend his time painting. He was a carbon copy of herself. Nevertheless, Keenan and Jeroen looked out for and admired each other. They were inseparable, like two magnets. Jeroen looked up to Keenan, and Keenan alone. And Keenan loved Jeroen more than anything in the world. Keenan's departure for Amsterdam had devastated Jeroen. It was as if someone had broken his heart. And now he had to let his brother go again, this time to attend university in Bandung.

"Mom, c'mon, let me skip school today," Jeroen pleaded. "I want to go to Bandung, too. I want to see Eko." His request had already been denied out of hand by their father, and now he was trying his luck with their mother.

No dice. His mother shook her head. "No can do, Jeroen. You have to go to school."

"Mom, are you sure Eko's going to pick me up?" asked Keenan.

"Yes, yes. I've already spoken with him on the phone. What's the problem?"

"I don't remember what he looks like. He probably doesn't remember what I look like, either. We were in elementary school the last time we saw each other."

Jeroen seized his chance. "See? That's why I should go, Mom! I can help him find Eko."

It made their mother smile to see the two of them working together to make her change her mind.

Eko, Keenan's cousin, had been living in Bandung since high school. And now both of them were going to attend the same university. When Keenan and Eko were in elementary school, before Keenan had left for Amsterdam, they'd been close. But this would be the first time they had seen each other since then.

"I see where you're coming from, Keenan," his mother answered, giving Jeroen a sideways glance. "But I've already told Eko to carry a sign with your name on it. You'll find each other, even if you don't recognize each other anymore."

They heard their parents' bedroom door open, and out stepped their father. Even though he'd gotten permission to miss work in order to see Keenan off to Bandung, he wore his usual dress shirt and tie.

"Is everything packed?" he asked, picking up the car keys from the table.

"Yes, Dad," said Keenan, standing beside his one bag.

"That's it?"

"We're mailing the rest," answered Keenan's mother, glancing at the boxes of painting supplies stacked in the corner.

Keenan's father took a deep breath. It was impossible not to notice the change in his expression. Keenan saw it all too clearly. At that moment, it was if a cloud had descended on the room. One by one and without a word, they began loading the car.

———

It was Kugy's firm belief that there was nothing better than curling up under a warm blanket in one's room on a rainy day. She finally felt settled in her new room in Bandung, and it was her mission to spend the afternoon in bed, dreaming sweet dreams. Unfortunately, she had forgotten to lock the door.

A ray of light from outside briefly illuminated the dark room, followed by a flurry of footsteps and a shrill voice breaking the peaceful stillness in which Kugy had been cocooned.

"Kugy! Wake up! Let's go!"

The mound underneath the blanket failed to stir.

"Eko's already outside. Fuad will stall if he turns off the engine. Hurry up!"

Kugy mumbled, forcing Noni to take more drastic measures. With one swift motion, she pulled off the covers and sprinkled her friend with water from a glass beside the bed.

Kugy recoiled and sputtered. "I'm being attacked! This is an invasion of privacy!"

"Oh, don't be so dramatic. Come on, get up!"

Kugy forced herself into a sitting position, eyes squinting, hair a mess. "Since we're going to be living next door to each other for four more years, I'd like to establish some ground rules. Number one: my afternoon nap is sacred. *Especially* when it's raining out. You should have entered this room on your knees. You should have kowtowed at the foot of my bed . . ."

Noni ignored her friend's sermonizing. "Let's go. We're picking up Eko's cousin from the station. His train arrives at five. I'll get out your clothes. What do you want to wear?"

Kugy opened her eyes. "Hold on, hold on. Eko has to go because it's his cousin. You have to go because you're Eko's girlfriend. But why get me involved in all this?"

"Well . . . Fuad's been having problems again. If it stalls, he'll need a push. And if he needs a push, we'll need more manpower."

Kugy's jaw dropped. "So you roused me from my hallowed slumber to enlist me as reserve manpower in case Fuad breaks down?"

"That's about the shape of things." Noni shrugged. "Can't be helped."

"This is rude! Just plain rude," Kugy grumbled as she got out of bed. "Who do you think I am? Treating me like some car-pushing coolie—"

"So what are you going to wear?"

"This!" Kugy pointed to the clothes she had on: a pair of faded batik bermudas and an oversized T-shirt with the words "Lake Toba" printed on it. The fabric of the T-shirt was so stretched out and thin that it looked more like a cleaning rag.

"Hey, you're not mad, are you?"

"No, no. I'm just dressing the part, that's all," replied Kugy, grabbing a denim jacket from a hanger. "I'm a coolie, aren't I? Come on, let's go!"

Noni regarded her friend with concern. A clump of Kugy's shoulder-length hair was sticking up, as if she'd tried to arrange it in a bouffant but given up halfway. Her T-shirt really was on the verge of falling apart at the seams. It didn't help that the denim jacket she was wearing was way too big for her—Kugy had snatched it off Karel seconds before boarding the train for Bandung. There was also the plastic Teenage Mutant Ninja Turtles watch she never took off her wrist. And completing the spectacle that was Kugy's outfit for that afternoon was a pair of electric-pink flip-flops, which she also wore when using the boarding house's communal bathroom.

Nevertheless, out Kugy strode, ready to take on the world. She was immediately greeted by Eko, who doubled over with laughter at her appearance.

"Great! You look like you've gone broke *and* insane," he exclaimed as he rummaged in his backpack for his camera. "Ready . . . one, two, three, and *pose*!"

Without missing a beat, Kugy adopted a weightlifter's stance and flexed her arms.

"Perfect. I'll print them out in 5R and post them all over the bulletin boards on campus."

"You mean *10*R, Eko. Magazine quality. Come on."

"Crazy people are so happy when you humor them," said Noni, pointing at Kugy, who was examining herself in the windshield. "Look at that face. Positively ecstatic . . ."

Upon realizing just how strange she looked, Kugy chuckled appreciatively.

As he watched her, Eko began to look as concerned as Noni. "Hey, you know how much gas costs, right? And I can't turn off the engine because I'm afraid it'll stall. But *if* you really want, I'll give you five minutes to change."

"Instead of wasting five minutes' worth of gas, just use the money to buy me a drink. Being a coolie is thirsty work! Let's go!"

With that, the matter was closed and off the yellow Fiat 124S sped, through the wet streets of Bandung.

———

In the station, a sea of passengers had been surging past them for ten minutes now, and still the three friends hadn't found the person they were supposed to pick up.

"Are you sure he took the five o'clock train? Why isn't he here?" Kugy asked Eko, who was frantically scanning the crowd.

"I'm sure he was on this train. The real problem is I don't know what he looks like."

"*What?*" exclaimed Kugy and Noni in unison.

"And you didn't think about making a sign, Grandpa?" Noni asked, slugging him on the shoulder.

Eko gave an embarrassed grin. "I forgot to bring it."

"Why didn't you say something?" Noni exclaimed. "I would have gone looking for a pen and paper!"

"Relax. My cousin's face is very unique. I just don't know what it looks like, that's all."

"When was the last time you guys saw each other?" asked Kugy.

"Elementary school," Eko answered, half-mumbling.

Kugy and Noni exchanged glances. While Noni resumed scolding Eko, Kugy took off for the station entrance.

She was already at a considerable distance when she turned and yelled, "Eko! What's your cousin's name?"

"Keenan!"

"Keenan?" she repeated. At that exact moment, a horde of passing people cut them off from each other's view. Kugy hoped she'd heard him correctly. "Keenan . . . Keenan . . . ," she repeated to herself as she walked.

Not too far away, Keenan thought he heard someone calling his name. The sound seemed to be coming from a young woman who looked his age and was moving in his direction. Keenan studied her with great interest. He was sure he didn't know her. He'd never met anyone so strange looking in all his life.

Hesitantly, Keenan approached her and fell into step beside her. She took big steps for a person with such tiny legs. She was fast, too. "Excuse me . . ."

Surprised by the young man who had suddenly appeared at her side, and who was now blocking her path, Kugy stopped.

Keenan studied her again. She was petite, only as tall as his chin. She looked as if she could be in middle school. She had no fashion sense. Her hair gave the impression she'd been electrocuted. Her eyes were wide, almost menacing. Keenan suddenly regretted approaching her at all.

"What do you want?" Kugy asked loudly.

With great effort, Keenan suppressed a sudden urge to smile. So, here he was face-to-face with a kitten attempting to act like a lion.

"Never mind," said Keenan, flustered. "I thought you were someone else. I thought . . . ummm . . . sorry." He flashed a wide smile and beat a hasty retreat. Yet, even as he did so, he knew in his heart he would never forget that face.

Kugy nodded curtly and resumed walking toward the information kiosk. Once she was sure she had left him far behind, she let out a deep breath. She didn't mind being mistaken for somebody else. But the guy she'd just met was the most attractive creature she'd ever seen—at least, since the introduction of Therrius in the Candy Candy comic book series. Still, Kugy told herself, one should always be wary of strangers, especially friendly ones. She refocused her attention on finding Eko's cousin. *Poor guy,* she thought, and tried to put the stranger out of her mind.

CHAPTER 3

MOTHER ALIEN

Noni and Eko had given up hope. Abandoning their spot, they started for the veranda in front of the station. The crowds had begun to thin, and only a few people remained.

"I'll try calling my aunt," Eko said. "Who knows? Maybe he did get on a different train. Noni, give me your cell phone. I don't have enough minutes."

Scowling, Noni was about to hand him the phone when they heard a familiar voice booming over the station's loudspeaker.

"Calling Keenan, recently arrived from Jakarta on the Parahyangan train. Again, calling Keenan, cousin of Eko Kurniawan. Your cousin is looking for you and matches the following description: hair, crew cut with a cowlick like the cartoon character Tintin; height, five foot nine; skin, light brown. Big eyes. Long eyelashes. He's wearing a Limp Bizkit T-shirt and is with two good-looking girls . . ."

Noni's and Eko's jaws dropped. They turned around. Kugy was at the information kiosk manning the microphone. Before long, a station employee hurried over to take care of the situation—a punk kid who'd taken the opportunity to get up to no good when he'd taken a break to go to the bathroom.

Noni and Eko weren't the only ones witnessing all this. Not far off a young man also stood gawking. And this young man was now sure that the strange girl whom the station attendant had just shooed away was the same girl he thought had been calling his name before.

Kugy was laughing as she approached Noni and Eko. "It's his own fault, leaving his post like that."

Just then, the three of them saw a young man walking toward them.

Keenan was about to say, "Excuse me," when it struck him. "Eko?" he asked.

"Keenan?"

They looked at one another in amazement. Their minds ran down their respective corridors of memory, all the way back to nine years ago. Keenan remembered Eko as a big-boned boy bordering on plump, with a cheerful disposition and long curly lashes that made him look like a girl. Eko remembered Keenan as a boy with Caucasian features and brownish hair, skinny and long-legged with downcast eyes. Even though he had rarely spoken, he had always had a smile on his lips. And now here was Keenan towering over him, tall and strong. His hair, which was tied back in a ponytail, was no longer brown but pitch-black, and hung a little below his shoulders. Only the expression in his eyes hadn't changed—the same expression that made Keenan seem older than he was, even when he was a little boy. Keenan also wouldn't have recognized his cousin if it weren't for his two round eyes fringed by curling lashes. They had always been Eko's most distinguishing feature and had earned him the nickname Pretty Boy. But now his cousin was no longer round like a ball. On the contrary, he looked as if he could be a fitness instructor.

Those nine years seemed to melt away when they embraced each other. Laughing, they realized that they'd practically been standing next to each other the whole time.

"Your mother was right. You do look like a real artist!" Eko exclaimed, thumping Keenan on the shoulder. "Keenan, this is my girl, Noni. And this is her friend . . ."

Kugy looked flustered, her face red as she extended her hand.

"Hi. I'm Kugy . . ."

Keenan grinned as he took the small hand and watched her duck her head in embarrassment. She really was just like a kitten. "Hi. So, we're properly introduced at last."

"Have you two met?" asked Eko, seeing the odd way they were looking at each other. Kugy had gone limp, like a prawn cracker someone had drenched in water, while Keenan looked guilty, as if he'd been caught red-handed.

"No!" they both answered at the same time. Exchanging glances, they laughed.

"Yes!" they said at the same time again, correcting themselves. And again, they laughed.

"What's going on?" asked Noni. She and Eko were beginning to wonder if this was all a setup.

"We must have known each other in a past life," Kugy answered quickly.

"Yup," Keenan added with a straight face. "And let me tell you, she sure was fierce."

Eko tilted his head, wondering whether they were serious or joking, and whether it mattered. "Did she dress this badly in her past life?"

"Oh, always!" Keenan grinned.

Kugy guffawed with delight. She felt her confidence returning. For an instant, the four of them felt a closeness that transcended time and space, as if they had all been friends for a long time.

Soon, it began to pour again. In the parking lot of the train station, a bright-yellow Fiat was trying its best to exit. Noni sat behind the wheel while her three friends pushed the car from behind, Kugy in the middle, flanked by the two men. Kugy looked small, but it was obvious from the sound of her loud voice that she was the overseer. Yelling with all her might, she spurred them on until finally the Fiat began running again on its own power rather than theirs.

———

The telephone in the corridor of the student boarding house had been ringing for some time. Finally, there came the pitter-patter of running feet and Kugy yelling, "Don't pick it up! It's for me!"

She snatched up the receiver and breathlessly greeted the person on the other end. "Hello?"

"Hi, darling."

"Hi, Josh."

"Did you just come back from jogging or something? That's unusually athletic of you."

"Not jogging. Pushing. A car."

"What?"

"In the rain, too. *Pouring* rain."

"*What?*"

"Oh, it's nothing. Fuad's sick and Eko had to pick up his cousin from the station. The one from the Netherlands. So they needed me to push the car in case it stalled. Ugh. It's just like Fuad. He *really* stalled this time."

"Is Eko crazy? Why couldn't he find someone else? There must have been lots of coolies at the station. He should've just paid one of them to help instead. You'll catch a chill being out in the rain like this. Eko and Fuad can't sub for you if you have to miss class."

"Josh, it's not a big deal. Eko and his cousin were the ones really doing all the pushing. I just pretended—for moral support."

"But it *was* raining, right?"

"Well, yeah . . ."

"See?" And with that, the floodgates opened, releasing an unceasing torrent of rebuke.

Kugy grimaced, waiting for it to end as she wrung out the hem of her T-shirt. Josh had been her boyfriend for two years, and when it came to arguments she could never win. If Kugy had to pick a phrase to describe their dynamic, it would be "opposites attract." Not a single one of their friends believed it when they had first become a couple—not hers, and not Josh's. They were different in almost every way. Clean-cut, basketball-playing Josh was a favorite among the girls at school thanks to his good looks, his cool car, and the manners of a born Prince Charming. Opening doors, buying flowers, taking her to candlelit dinners at expensive restaurants—for Josh, this was all standard operating procedure. Kugy was popular at school in her own right since she was very social and participated in a variety of activities. But she was his polar opposite. They called her Mother Alien because she was considered the head honcho of all the weirdos at school. Nobody knew what to make of it: How on earth did Prince Charming and Mother Alien end up together?

No one knew the answer. Not Josh. Not Kugy. Maybe Josh had been smitten with Kugy because she was so unlike the other girls he had dated. Kugy was so relaxed and unafraid to be herself. In contrast, other girls were always falling over themselves to get him to take them out just once for dinner or a movie. Kugy hadn't taken Josh's advances seriously at first because of the glaring differences between them. What Kugy hadn't realized was that this had piqued Josh's interest all the more.

Kugy would never forget the day they had officially become a couple. The rain had been coming down that afternoon with the same force it was coming down now. And Josh had taken up Kugy's challenge of taking public transportation to get to her house. He had arrived at the front door, drenched. His hair, usually so neat, was limp with rainwater. And his bouquet of white roses was a mess, having been crushed against the backs of the other passengers on the Metromini bus. It was then that Kugy saw Josh in a new light—not as a spoiled brat, the apple of the school's eye, but as someone who was willing to make sacrifices for the person on whom he had set his heart. And in the end, Kugy had decided to set her heart on him as well.

They had been going out for almost two years, and they still remained two completely different people. But to Kugy, Josh—so careful and fussy—functioned as someone who gave her life structure, who brought her back down to earth whenever she lingered too long in the realm of imagination. To Josh, Kugy—who couldn't care less what other people thought and did whatever she liked—served to remind him that he should relax and welcome the surprises life had to offer. They'd learned to adapt to each other. One trick Kugy had learned whenever Josh lapsed into nagging was to hold the phone away from her ear and busy herself with something else—as she was doing now, wringing the hem of her T-shirt with great enthusiasm.

"Kugy? Are you listening to me?"

Quickly, Kugy returned the phone to her ear. "What? Sorry, you were breaking up just now."

"I said, in the future just take a taxi. Don't rely on Fuad. You've been taken in by that car one too many times."

"Eh. Taxis are expensive. Besides, whenever I push Fuad, Eko buys me something to drink."

Josh took a deep breath. It was useless. "All right. Whatever. Change your clothes or you'll catch a cold. Oh, also, when are you going to buy a new cell phone? Do you really want to keep using the communal phone at the boarding house? Wouldn't it be nicer if you could talk to me in your room?"

The screen on Kugy's cell phone, a secondhand model from four years ago, had stopped working. She'd resorted to "relying on feel." As a result, Kugy was always running out of minutes because she kept dialing the wrong number. She also couldn't avoid unwanted calls because she couldn't tell who was calling her.

"I have to save up first, Josh. I'm too embarrassed to ask my old man for money. And if it's for a cell phone, I don't think he's going to give it to me. But I'm writing a short story and sending it to a magazine. There's prize money involved."

"What's the story about?"

"Oh, it's just a love story. If they publish it, I'll get enough to buy a new phone."

"Of course they'll publish it. You're amazing. After all—"

"And guess what else? I'm writing a fairy tale about vegetables! Get this: the protagonist is Prince Radish from the Kingdom of Root Vegetables. And the villain is a witch named Madam Turmeric from the land of Spice . . ."

Whenever Kugy began yammering away about imaginary worlds he didn't understand, Josh had his own trick. He would hold the phone away from his ear and busy himself with something else. He began flipping through the stack of car magazines in front of him, his mouth opening occasionally to utter an "Oh yeah? Hmm. Uh-huh. Is that so?"

"Cool, huh? Awesome story, right, Josh? Hello?"

Josh quickly pressed the phone to his ear again. "Wow! Crazy! Very cool! Okay, you should go take a shower. I'll call you tomorrow, okay, darling? Bye!"

"See ya!" said Kugy. She was about to stand up when a towel landed in her lap.

Noni was standing in front of her. "Josh chewed you out, huh?"

"Yeah, what else is new? He's basically the male version of you." Kugy cackled.

"Eko's taking me out for dinner later. Come with?"

Kugy gulped. "Will we be taking Fuad again?"

"Fuad's dead. We'll take him to a mechanic tomorrow. The plan is for Eko and Keenan to come here by bus, and then we'll all walk to look for something close by. Or we'll order takeout."

"Woo-hoo! Free food! And I don't have to push anything!" Leaping happily to her feet, Kugy disappeared into the bathroom.

CHAPTER 4

THE SACRED CIRCLE

An empty cardboard pizza box lay open on the floor in the communal living room at the boarding house. The TV was on with the volume low, but no one was watching. Around the pizza box, four people sat on the floor, chatting and laughing.

"Your turn, Kugy."

"Okay," said Kugy, clearing her throat. "Each member of this sacred circle must share the weirdest thing they've ever done. Full disclosure!"

"Sorry, but I don't think this is a good idea," said Noni, raising her hand. "Nothing is 'weird' to Kugy."

Everyone laughed, including Kugy. "Bad news for you. And good news for me."

Noni thought for a bit. "When I was in elementary school, I was in a play. And I was cast as . . . Pak Raden from the TV show *Si Unyil*. Complete with a false moustache."

Everyone giggled.

"Physically speaking, you were miscast."

"But character-wise, very fitting."

It was Keenan's turn. "Hmm. I once did a lip sync of a *dangdut* song by Meggy Z. Complete with a *joget* dance."

Keenan's confession was greeted with silence. Everyone's mouth hung open as they imagined Keenan crooning like an old-fashioned *dangdut* singer, swaying his head and hips from side to side.

Seeing their reaction, Keenan felt he should elaborate. "My school in Amsterdam was having a talent night, and because they knew I was from Indonesia, they asked me to perform something uniquely Indonesian. That was the only thing I could think of. But they loved it. The whole school danced along."

"Which song?"

"'Toothache.'"

More silence. And then, Eko started to clap. It wasn't long before everyone joined in.

"Thank you, thank you." Keenan stood up and took a deep bow.

It was Kugy's turn. She thought hard. Noni was right. Almost everything she did tended to be weird. It was hard to choose.

"Hurry up. You're taking too long," Eko said.

"Hold on, hold on," mumbled Kugy. "This is really tough." She screwed up her face and thought long and hard.

"Do you need help?" Noni offered.

"If you please."

"Kugy likes to send letters to the sea god, Neptune," Noni said, suppressing a laugh.

Keenan knitted his brow. "How?"

"Simple," Kugy said. "When I used to live near the beach, I set them out to sea. After we moved, I set them out wherever there was flowing water. All water flows to the sea." She was sitting up straight now, explaining herself with great energy.

"So what was your purpose in sending the letters?" Eko asked.

"Friends, it's high time you all knew. I'm actually"—Kugy took a deep breath—"an alien."

The silence this time was even deeper than before—stifling, to be exact, rendering them all speechless. Eko was trying so hard not to burst into laughter he felt like he was going to die.

"I actually work for Neptune, and I have been sent to Earth as a spy," Kugy explained. "And, *by sheer coincidence*, I'm an Aquarius. Amazing, isn't it?" Her eyes were shining.

"Same! I'm an Aquarius, too," said Keenan.

"Yo! Brotha!" Kugy shook Keenan's hand, then placed two fingers on either side of her head and waggled them. Keenan did the same.

Eko buried his head in a pillow. He was shaking with laughter. "I feel like I'm in an alien nation right now!" he exclaimed from the pillow's depths.

"See, I was right. This challenge isn't challenging for Kugy at all," said Noni. "Come on, Eko. It's your turn."

"I say this with all due respect, but the weirdest thing I've ever done was . . . to have a crush on Kugy."

Keenan guffawed, followed by Kugy, who proceeded to roll on the floor with laughter. Meanwhile, Noni's mouth hung open. "You had a crush on Kugy? W-When?"

"When my classroom was next door to hers. Second year of middle school. Good thing you'd moved from Jakarta to Bandung by then, darling. You didn't have to watch me embarrass myself." Eko patted Noni on the shoulder. "Don't worry. I regretted it immediately. I used to go to Kugy's library all the time. Every time I saw her, she was reading a book. But once she opened her mouth . . . it was all over!" Eko began laughing as well.

Keenan pointed at Eko, then at Noni. "So how did you two end up together?"

Eko's expression turned serious. "Noni is the love of my life. I mean it. I've had my eye on her since the first year of middle school."

"Liar!" Noni sputtered. "We didn't even know each other back then! You only met me after I'd moved away. And even then, we met at Kugy's house, didn't we? I bet the only reason you were such a faithful library patron was because you were still trying to get to know Kugy. Huh! You have some nerve, pretending we were close, pretending you had your eye on me since the first year of middle school, even though you didn't know me at all."

"Whoa, take it easy," said Eko with a grin. "Just trying my best. Who knew you had such a good memory?"

"So Kugy played matchmaker?" asked Keenan.

"As if!" chimed Eko and Noni in unison.

Kugy shook her head. "Sorry. I'm staunchly against matchmaking and all attempts to set people up," she said coolly.

"I'll say. This idiot is actually the one who most opposed it!" Eko exclaimed. "She even told Noni that I was a dangerous species of human being! Would you believe it?"

"I based my analysis on your record of not returning your books. And on what kind of books you borrowed. No offense."

"See? She's too much! Imagine! Ruining my prospects just because of a library record."

"What kind of books did Eko borrow?" Keenan asked.

"In two years of membership, all he borrowed were books from the *Captain Shadow* comic series. And he checked out the title *Children of Satan* more than ten times. In the end, he never even returned it. Why wouldn't I be suspicious?"

This was greeted by an explosion of laughter from Keenan and Noni. Eko's face turned red. This time, he could offer no defense.

Kugy cleared her throat. "So you see? I can't be a weirdo, because everything that has anything to do with me is awesome. Eko—whose claim to weirdness rests on falling for and associating with a weirdo—isn't weird after all, because the weirdo he likes is actually awesome. Noni, your fake moustache pales in comparison to Keenan's Meggy Z impression, meaning the winner of the sacred circle this time around is . . ."

"Keenan!" the three of them chorused.

The evening concluded with Keenan lip-synching "Toothache" by Meggy Z.

———

"Hi. Can I come in?"

Kugy had been working on her computer in her room with the door half-open. To her surprise, she saw Keenan standing in the doorway.

"Hey, you're still here?" asked Kugy, glancing at her watch. It was already past ten.

"Yeah. Eko's my ride home, but those two lovebirds need some time to themselves. I don't know what else to do."

Kugy stood and opened the door all the way. "Come in, my good sir!"

Keenan looked around. He seemed impressed.

"Surprised? My room is neat, unlike its occupant."

"Yeah, I'd never have guessed," Keenan answered. His eyes came to rest on a framed photo of Kugy's family.

"There are a lot of us. We call ourselves 'The K Family.' Five kids, and all our names begin with *k*. This is my oldest brother, Karel, and my older sister, Karin. This is my older brother, Kevin—he's only a year older than me. And that's my little sister, Keshia."

"Your name is the most unique one, isn't it?"

"You mean the strangest!" Kugy laughed. "Seems like my parents had run out of ideas. I guess I'm lucky they didn't name me Kryptonite or something."

"You're the prettiest one, though."

Suddenly, Kugy felt her throat close up. To change the topic, she hastily pointed to the shelf where she kept her comics and fairy tales neatly arranged in rows. "This is just a small part of my collection. There are more in my room at home."

"Eko said you like writing fairy tales."

"Yeah. It's been a hobby of mine since I was little."

"Have you written a lot?"

"Quantitatively speaking, yes. But I don't have a readership. And isn't that what makes writing meaningful? Having people who read it?" Kugy chuckled. "So far, the only one who gets any enjoyment out of it is me."

"How come?"

"Who wants to read fairy tales?" Kugy laughed again. "If I want readers, maybe I should become a kindergarten teacher. At least I could make them read my stories in class."

"A lot of fairy tale writers managed to become famous. And they didn't have to teach kindergarten to get readers."

A small smile appeared on Kugy's face, as if in reply to that one perpetual question—the answer to which she already knew by heart.

"Keenan, I'm eighteen. I'm majoring in literature. I want to become a serious writer and to be taken seriously as a writer. I'm surrounded by people who want to win writing contests in magazines for 'grown-ups,' or who want to win the Jakarta Arts Council Novel Competition. That's how you prove you're a real writer. And in the meantime, my head is filled with characters like Prince Radish, Fairy Celery, and Madam Turmeric the Sorceress. At my age, I should be writing love stories, or stories for teenagers, or stories for adults—"

"A lot of fairy tales have love in them."

"My point is, none of it fits together—my age, my major, my ambitions, what I need to accomplish in order to prove myself, what's going on inside my head . . ."

"I still don't understand." Keenan folded his arms across his chest.

"When I was little, wanting to become a fairy tale writer sounded cute. But now that I'm grown up, it just sounds unrealistic and stupid. At the very least, I'll have to become a serious writer first. Then once

I've established myself and people begin to see me as a real writer, I can write all the fairy tales I want."

"So you want to first become something that you aren't in order to eventually become who you really are? Is that what you're saying?"

"Yes. If that's the path I have to take, then why not?"

"And you really think those two things fit together?" Keenan asked.

"In case you didn't know, there are only a handful of writers who can make a living from writing full-time. Most writers have other jobs—as journalists, or professors, or copywriters at advertising firms. Imagine if you're an aspiring fairy tale writer! I may be serious about my love for fairy tales, but being a fairy tale writer isn't a 'serious' occupation. A girl's gotta eat."

"You just ate pizza. No problem there, right? You'll be able to eat."

"I have to earn my own living, have a steady income. And then . . . *we'll see.*" Kugy's voice was rising in pitch. "I don't know what planet you've been living on all this time, but on Planet Reality those are the rules of the game."

Keenan was quiet. In his mind's eye he saw the rolled-up canvases that he'd left behind in Amsterdam—his paintings. "You're right. Those are the rules of the game," he mumbled.

The two of them fell silent—long enough for the atmosphere in the room to grow awkward.

"Maybe I'll go wait outside. Eko might want to go home soon." Keenan walked toward the door.

"Wait," Kugy blurted. "I want to lend you something." She opened the small cupboard in her desk and took out a thick bundle of A4 paper bound with metal rings.

Keenan took the bundle. Written on the front cover were the title and author: *A Collection of Fairy Tales from the Chest of Wonders* by Kugy Karmachameleon.

"My brother Karel once gave me an old-fashioned chest, the kind that looks like a treasure chest you see in comic books. He said it had been retrieved from a shipwreck and that it once contained scrolls—historical manuscripts—that had been damaged after being underwater for so long. I was so happy to have that chest. And I was determined to fill it with my own manuscripts, so that the chest would be full again. I wrote with all the energy I had. This went on for years. And here is the result. I'd like you to read it. You can return it whenever you're done."

Keenan looked at Kugy. He was at a loss for words. With great care, he stroked the front cover.

"I've never given it to anyone else," said Kugy slowly. "I don't know why I feel I should lend it to someone I just met."

"Thank you. And sorry if I was—"

"Only a few years ago I found out that Karel and my father bought the chest in an antique store on Jalan Surabaya in Jakarta. It wasn't a treasure chest. And it wasn't from a shipwreck, either. Just like nonexistent Neptune. And my letters . . . the fish probably got a kick out of them. Or they contributed to all the garbage clogging up the rivers." Kugy gave Keenan a pointed look. "And those are the facts of life on Planet Reality."

Keenan found himself at a loss for words again. And once again, the room was enveloped in silence.

But there was a question nagging at Keenan. "Your full name is Kugy Karmachameleon?"

"No. It's Kugy Alisa Nugroho."

"They're not even remotely similar!"

———

That night, Keenan stayed up late, immersed in the world of Kugy's imagination. It swept him far away to the Land of Antigravitia, which hung suspended in a layer of the atmosphere just one step away from the moon. He was taken underground to the home of Joni Sewer, the excavating antlion. He was introduced to the world of vegetables, where Carrotina became a famous ballet dancer.

Keenan knew the value of the bundle in his hands. Each page breathed such energy, such strong conviction. Kugy had used a computer for most of the manuscript, but she had written much of it by hand as well. On some pages Kugy had even tried to illustrate her own characters.

Keenan felt a pang of pity when he beheld Kugy's efforts. *The kid's a fantastic writer, but she can't draw at all,* he thought. He got out a new sketchbook and his art supplies, which he hadn't unpacked yet, and began drawing with great zeal. All night long, Keenan sketched dozens of drawings, one after another.

Only when he heard a rooster crowing in the distance did Keenan stop. He realized it was the first time he had ever drawn that much for anyone, much less someone he'd just met yesterday afternoon.

CHAPTER 5

A BANANA

September 1999

Even at a distance, Kugy could recognize him anywhere—that towering frame, the long hair pulled into a ponytail. He wore a maroon backpack with the letter *K* emblazoned on it in black. Of all the new male students, he was the only one with long hair. The others had shaved their heads in keeping with tradition for freshman orientation. He'd decided not to attend orientation rather than lose his ponytail. It was the only real memento he had left from living in Amsterdam. That's how he saw it.

"Hey, K!" Kugy called.

"Hey! Another K!" Keenan gave a loud laugh as he ruffled Kugy's hair. "Just took a shower, huh?"

Kugy made a face. "Is it that obvious?"

"Oh, very. Your hair is still wet and you look a bit shinier than usual."

Kugy made another face. "I never thought I'd run into you on campus. If the four of us didn't go to the midnight movie every Saturday, I don't think I'd ever see you. You must be busy."

Keenan cast a glance around and gave a small shrug. "I'm only on campus when I need to be. I don't really like hanging out here."

No wonder, Kugy almost blurted out. She walked past the economics building, where Keenan attended class almost every day. And almost every day, she craned her neck as she passed by, looking for that maroon backpack with the letter *K*. Kugy was beginning to suspect that Keenan was taking classes by correspondence.

"What about lunch on campus? Would you be up for that?" asked Kugy.

"Depends on who's coming."

Kugy shook her head. "Wrong answer. It should be, 'Depends on who's paying.'"

"So lunch is on you?"

"There's one place that you have to try. It's your duty. You can't call yourself a university student if you haven't eaten there."

"The food's that good, huh?"

"No. The food's that cheap."

"Oh. No wonder it's on you," murmured Keenan, chuckling softly.

———

The bamboo-walled *warung* was packed to bursting. The people in line were selecting from an assortment of dishes served buffet-style. Keenan paused to read the sign hanging on the front door: "The Hunger No Longer Hut."

Once they had gotten their food, Kugy and Keenan sat in a corner near a window, next to a hanging bunch of bananas.

Keenan was astonished at the mountain of rice on Kugy's plate, so high it was on the verge of toppling over. "How can someone so little eat so much?" he commented.

"Studies have shown that along with pedicab driving and ditch digging, jobs involving creativity and writing consume a lot of calories." She detached two bananas from the bunch near her head.

Keenan shook his head in astonishment as he watched her. "You really are a surprising creature."

"Oh! And I have another surprise! Hold on . . ." Kugy reached into the front pocket of her backpack. "Ta-da!"

Keenan squinted. "A cell phone?"

"It's new!" Kugy laughed. "I paid for it with the sweat of my brow! My story got published. The money was enough to buy a new phone and to treat you to lunch."

"Wow, and yet another surprise! Congratulations," said Keenan. "Can I read the story?"

Kugy looked bewildered. She felt nervous all of a sudden—though the only reason she had passed Keenan's building so often was because she had wanted to give him a copy of the magazine with her story in it. She'd been carrying it around with her every day. Kugy fished around in her backpack and handed him a rather creased-looking magazine. "Here. I kept one for you."

Keenan took it, his eyes shining. "Kugy Karmachameleon . . . a real author. Wow."

Kugy laughed. "Actually, I've asked my mom if I can change my name to Karma. No response yet."

"Can I tell you something? I think you're a wonderful writer."

Kugy's face turned red. "You can't say that. You haven't even read it."

"I'm not talking about your short story. I'm talking about your fairy tales."

Suddenly, Kugy didn't know what to say or do. She realized that something rare was occurring: she felt embarrassed. She really had no idea how to respond. Finally, she detached a third banana, peeled it, and munched with gusto.

"When are you going to finish eating?" he asked, shaking his head.

"I like your paintings."

"You've seen them?"

"No. But I already like them. Imagine how much I'll like them when I do see them." She tried to laugh, but felt her face growing hotter and her speech more nonsensical.

"In that case, let's go to my place after lunch so you can see them."

Kugy nodded. She couldn't help but smile. All of a sudden, she was grateful for blurting out what she had. She couldn't wait for lunch to end.

————

Keenan's boarding house was quite far from campus. It was an old house, built during the Dutch colonial era, and surrounded by leafy trees. In contrast to Kugy's and Noni's house, which was very crowded, Keenan's only had a few residents. The rooms were spacious and the ceilings were high.

Kugy gasped when Keenan opened the large door and flicked the light switch. Wire railing crisscrossed the ceiling above them, and from the railing dangled little halogen lights that illuminated the places where Keenan had hung his paintings or propped them against the wall on the gray-tiled floor. The room felt desolate because of the small amount of furniture—there was a bed, a small cupboard for clothes with a mini compo stereo system on top of it, and a large desk with Keenan's art equipment neatly arranged on its surface.

"You should be majoring in visual arts, not economics," murmured Kugy as she slowly stepped inside. "And this is more like a gallery than a room in a boarding house."

As if they were at an exhibition, Keenan took Kugy around the room to look at his paintings. "This one is called *Sunset from the Rooftop.*

This one is called *Heart of Bliss*. This is *The Shady Morning*. And this one—*Silent Confession*. And this—"

"Is the weirdest-looking one," Kugy finished, pointing to a painting that consisted only of gradations of color and fine lines like wisps of cotton. "The others all have people in them. But not this one."

"Guess what it's called."

"*Mission Impossible*. Come on, you're crazy. How am I supposed to guess what it's called?"

"With this painting, you can't think. You have to feel. What do you feel when you look at it? That's the title."

Kugy studied the painting closely, then closed her eyes for a long time. Keenan heard her exhale and in a half whisper she uttered, "Freedom."

It was Keenan's turn to be amazed. Slowly, he picked up the painting, which was sitting on the floor, turned it around, and pointed to the title printed on the back.

Kugy's jaw dropped. "*Freedom?*"

"I swear . . . I never thought you'd guess it." Keenan scratched his head. "What a strange coincidence."

Kugy shook her head. "I don't believe in coincidences. It must be because we're both Neptune's envoys equipped with telepathic powers. But before we were sent to Earth, our memories were erased. Just to make it all even cooler." She spoke confidently.

Keenan nodded. "It's a plausible theory."

"I do have a question. And I don't want to use my telepathic abilities . . ." Kugy grinned. "What *is* this a painting of?"

"It's from the perspective of a bird flying through the air. It sees no limits. It sees no barriers. There's nothing tying it down to earth. It's free. Completely free."

Kugy's gaze had been fixed on the painting, but now she turned slowly toward Keenan. "When did you paint this?"

"After I passed the state university entrance exam."

"You're . . . you're being forced to attend university, aren't you?" She was unsure whether it was appropriate to ask the question, but she couldn't stop herself.

Keenan returned Kugy's gaze, a bitter smile spreading across his face. "Nothing fits together," he said curtly. "What I'm passionate about, my ambitions, my parents' wishes . . ." He shrugged. "Maybe I have to do what you were talking about. Maybe we do have to become something we're not so we can be ourselves one day."

Kugy's thoughts returned to that moment in her room at the boarding house. Only now did she understand that Keenan had actually been talking about himself. And once again the same silence was present in their midst.

"And because you successfully guessed the title of this painting, I have a present to give you." The expression on Keenan's face was warm once more.

"That wasn't a guess, you know. Are you saying you don't believe we have a telepathic connection? Because—"

Kugy's chatter suddenly ceased. Keenan was holding out an open sketchbook. She took it from Keenan's hands and flipped through page after page. "This . . . ?"

Keenan pointed to the drawings one by one. "Prince Radish . . . Fairy Celery . . . Carrotina . . . Madam Turmeric . . . Joni Sewer . . . Hopa-Hopi . . . and this is the valley where they live . . ." Keenan sounded excited as he explained. Suddenly, a drop of water splashed onto the page. Keenan looked up to find Kugy in tears.

"Oh gosh. Sorry," said Kugy, hastily wiping the tears from her cheeks. "The drawings. They're perfect, aren't they? Sorry . . ."

"No, no. Don't be sorry. Are you sure you're okay?" Keenan sounded worried.

Kugy sobbed, half laughing, half crying. "I'm such a softy. But never in my life has anyone illustrated my fairy tales. And they're so beautiful, too. I-I don't know what to say . . ."

Keenan smiled. "It's your stories that are beautiful. They're inspiring. They're what moved me to make these sketches."

"Can I borrow this?" Kugy held the book to her chest hopefully.

"The book's yours. Take it."

Nothing could have prevented Kugy from hugging Keenan. The sudden embrace lasted only for two seconds before Kugy drew away, her face bright red. "Thanks," she whispered, her voice barely audible.

The two of them were quiet, partly out of embarrassment and partly because they didn't know what to do, until at last, Kugy broke the awkwardness by reaching into the pocket of her baggy pants.

"For now, all I can give you is this."

Keenan took what Kugy was offering him—a banana from the Hunger No Longer Hut. "Okay. I think we're even," he said with a small smile.

CHAPTER 6

A SWORD OF ICE

It was Saturday night in Bandung, and the yellow Fiat jockeyed with the other cars traveling up Jalan Dago. Kugy and Keenan were in the backseat. Eko was driving, and Noni sat beside him, talking to someone on the phone.

Noni looked relieved as she ended the call. "Guys, Mr. Itok managed to get four tickets. They're near the front, but it's better than nothing."

"As professional midnight-movie goers, it's important to have connections like Mr. Itok. Long live Mr. Itok!" cried Eko.

"Long live Mr. Itok!" Kugy repeated from the backseat.

Ten minutes later, the car pulled into the parking lot of Bandung Indah Plaza. The four of them got out and hurried to the top floor.

They were greeted by a skinny bespectacled man in his early thirties. It was Mr. Itok, who worked at the video rental store Eko frequented. Buying movie tickets on commission was a side business of his. "These are for you," he said, giving two tickets to Eko and Noni. "And these are for Keenan and his girlfriend."

The four of them exchanged glances and burst into laughter. Mr. Itok took his commission and left, wondering what the group had found so funny.

"Careful," said Eko, amused. "If we keep watching these midnight movies together, the four of us may end up double-dating after all."

"Amen!" said Keenan.

The four of them laughed again. But Kugy felt a little disturbed by Keenan's response. She cast a sideways glance at him as he walked beside her, searching for something—a sign of some sort. Exactly what kind of sign, she didn't know. Then suddenly, Keenan glanced back. Quickly, Kugy turned away to look at something else, and found a safer object to study in the popcorn machine.

"Want some popcorn?" Keenan asked.

Kugy felt she had no choice but to nod.

"You two go ahead," Keenan told Eko, who was walking in front. "Kugy and I are going to buy popcorn."

"Sure!" Eko answered, and he and Noni continued strolling toward the theater.

"Come on," Keenan said lightly. Then he took her hand.

Kugy wasn't sure whether Keenan was aware of the change that had just occurred. She hoped the hesitation in her step and the tension in her hand had escaped detection.

October 1999

Keenan's mother had been standing alone beside the telephone in the living room for a long time. She held an open address book, her fingers trembling. *I wouldn't be doing this if it weren't the right thing to do,* she thought. Decades had passed, yet this was still difficult for her. Swallowing, she summoned her courage and began pressing buttons: 0 . . . 3 . . . 6 . . . 1 . . .

She heard the voice of a teenage boy on the other end. "Hello?"

"Good afternoon. May I please speak to Mr. Wayan? This is Ms. Lena, calling from Jakarta."

It wasn't long before she heard the voice again, more faintly, calling Wayan by the affectionate nickname his nephews and nieces had given him. "Poyan! There's someone on the phone from Jakarta."

She heard the receiver being picked up again, and this time, a man's voice greeted her.

"Wayan?" she asked.

There was a brief silence. "Lena?" The man's voice sounded unsure.

"Yes, it's Lena. How are you?"

"I'm well. I wasn't expecting you to call." Each word he uttered sounded stiff and formal.

"I want to talk to you about Keenan. His semester break is coming up, and he really wants to visit you in Ubud—"

"Yes, Keenan told me a while ago," said Wayan, cutting her off. "We've been talking about it since he was in Amsterdam."

"Still, I felt uncomfortable not asking you for permission directly."

The man's tone became firm. "Keenan is like a son to me. This is his home, too. He can come here whenever he wants. I'll always be happy to have him."

"Hopefully he won't be too much trouble—"

Again, the firm voice cut her off. "Keenan is never any trouble. On the contrary, my whole family will be happy to see him."

Lena took a deep breath. "If that's the case, then thank you."

"There's just one thing I want to be sure about. Keenan's father has given him permission to come, right?"

"Yes. Adri's given his permission."

"Are you sure?"

Lena paused. "Of course."

"All right, then there's no problem."

Silence again. And with that, Lena knew the conversation was over.

Keenan bounded up the escalator two steps at a time, working his way past the other riders. Eko and Noni were already there when he arrived, holding up three tickets.

"My man! Right on time!" Eko greeted him. "They've opened the doors, but the film hasn't started."

"And I got us drinks and snacks," said Noni. "Relax."

"Sorry I'm so late. I fell asleep," said Keenan, still panting. Suddenly he realized something. "Where's the little one?"

"Kugy has an important guest from Jakarta, as usual."

Keenan frowned. "An important guest? What do you mean?"

"Her boyfriend, Josh, is visiting. So she won't be joining the midnight-movie gang this time," answered Eko.

"Knowing Josh, they probably went out for a candlelit dinner."

"Yeah. It's the one opportunity Kugy gets to rise above the Hunger No Longer set." Eko chuckled.

Keenan was quiet for moment. "I didn't know Kugy had a boyfriend. In Jakarta?"

Noni nodded. "Her high school sweetheart."

"He's fierce," Eko added. "Fiercer than the whole Student Army Regiment."

"Are you speaking from personal experience?" teased Noni, punching Eko's shoulder. "Because Josh can detect which guys are secretly crushing on Kugy."

"You're not bringing that up again!" Eko laughed.

Eko's and Noni's exchange continued as they entered the theater. Keenan followed behind them, saying nothing.

———

"Keenan!"

He knew that voice. He would have recognized its cheerful ring anywhere—and the distinctive pitter-patter of those scurrying feet. But this time, for some reason, Keenan felt reluctant about looking behind him. He took a deep breath before finally turning around.

"Hey, Kugy."

"Hi hi! How was the movie on Saturday? Was it awesome? Noni said she had dreams about it. Sorry I couldn't join. Have you eaten dinner yet? Let's go to the Hunger No Longer!" Kugy prattled energetically.

"I'm not hungry," Keenan answered curtly. "And I have to get home. I have a lot to do. I hope that's okay."

"No problemo," said Kugy with a wide smile. "Actually, I just wanted to chat. But it's okay. Some other time."

"About?"

"Mmm . . ." Kugy paused for a bit. "It's been two weeks since I gave you that magazine with my short story in it. But you still haven't told me what you think." She gave a little laugh and smiled. "No pressure. Just curious."

Keenan took another deep breath. "Can I be honest?"

"Of course!" Kugy exclaimed.

"I don't like it."

She felt like someone had taken the spark in her heart and doused it in cold water. Snuffed it out. She tried to remain composed, but her expression betrayed her.

"To someone who doesn't know you, the story is good," continued Keenan. "But I think your fairy tales are far more authentic. More original. And they reflect who you really are. I couldn't find anything of you in that short story—just a writer clever with words, but lacking in soul."

Kugy froze. It was as if Keenan's words had transformed her into a statue. She gulped as if she were swallowing a meatball whole.

"Sorry. But if you really want me to be honest, then that's my opinion, plain and simple."

Kugy gave a little nod. "Thank you for your honesty," she said slowly.

Keenan said good-bye and left Kugy standing there to contemplate what he had said. Each word had pierced her like a sword of ice—painful and chilling all at once, rendering her speechless and helpless.

———

Kugy lay awake in her bed for a long time that night—on her back, staring at the ceiling, the wheels of her mind turning round and round and her heart churning. She didn't understand why Keenan's remarks had made such an impression. She also didn't understand why she had been so anxious to hear what Keenan thought—as if his opinion mattered the most. Ironically, all the people closest to her, including Josh, had liked her short story and had praised it. Only Keenan—who had spoken so decisively, without sparing her feelings—had said he did not.

Kugy kept asking herself where she had gone wrong. How could Keenan say she was clever with words but had no soul? She'd worked her butt off writing that story. She had chosen each word with great care and precision. She had been meticulous in putting together the plot. Every conflict appeared right on cue. She had read books on how to write a good short story and knew all their formulas and theories by heart. Maybe there was something wrong with Keenan's taste, not her writing.

Kugy sat upright. She opened the magazine to her short story and read it from start to finish. Then she turned on the computer, opened one of the documents containing her fairy tales, and read it closely as well. As she did, she began to realize something. With the fairy tale, it felt as if she were running free, wherever her heart desired. With the short story, it felt as if she were walking on a tightrope, carefully and with great control. And there was another difference between the two that seemed so clear to her now. She had written the fairy tale for her own satisfaction. She had written the short story for the satisfaction of others.

Her mind returned to her encounter with Keenan, and again she felt the sting inflicted by his words. But this time, Kugy felt their truth.

CHAPTER 7

THIS MOON, THIS JOURNEY, AND US

December 1999

The boarding house, which already felt deserted, was even quieter now that almost all the residents had gone home for the semester break. There were only a few people left.

Keenan put the last of his things into his bag before closing it and securing it with a small padlock.

His door, which had been ajar, suddenly opened wide. It was Bimo, his fellow boarding house resident, carrying a travel bag. "Hey, do you need a ride back to Jakarta after all? There's still room in my car for one more."

Keenan shook his head. "No, thanks. I'm catching the train later this afternoon. I already bought a ticket. Say hi to the others for me."

Bimo was just about to go when he stopped midstep. "Oh yeah. Congratulations."

"What for?"

"The others told me you got the highest GPA in the class this semester. They don't call you the campus specter for nothing. All you do is stay here and shut yourself up in your room like a bear." Bimo chuckled.

Keenan gave a brief smile, unsure whether it was a compliment or an insult. But he liked the nickname enough. *The campus specter.*

———

Keenan was waiting on the front terrace when the yellow Fiat pulled up. He walked around to the back of the car and put his bag in the trunk. Only when he opened the door did he notice someone inside whom he hadn't expected to see.

"Kugy? You're going to Jakarta today, too?" Keenan asked.

"I swapped tickets with Eko," Kugy answered brightly. "He's staying with Noni in Bandung a little longer to keep her company."

"Oh, okay," Keenan said curtly.

Suddenly, a strange feeling crept into Kugy's heart, confirming the suspicions she had been harboring for the past month. She had assumed Keenan was keeping to himself because he was studying so much, as evidenced by his getting the highest GPA in their class. But now, Kugy felt that there was another reason. She felt Keenan was avoiding her.

Without saying much more, Keenan threw himself into the backseat. Because of his long legs, his knees were practically pressed up against the seat in front of him. Kugy watched him out of the corner of her eye. She noticed that his sneakers looked like they had just been cleaned, and he was wearing the long-sleeved denim jacket that he had worn the night he held her hand at the movie theater. She took in the shampoo scent of his wet hair. Kugy noticed—and remembered—all of it. She didn't understand why. Nevertheless, all of it stuck in her memory, haunting her, and she was powerless to do anything about it.

———

Keenan shut his eyes ten minutes after the train pulled out of Bandung Station. He was woken by a parching thirst and what seemed like an unnaturally long silence. When he opened his eyes, he found that the train had stopped at a small station and that Kugy wasn't next to him anymore.

From the murmurs of the people around him, Keenan concluded that the train had been there for a while, and that the delay was making many of the passengers nervous.

He decided to get off the train and ask a station attendant what was going on.

"*Muhun.* Another train got derailed, *Cep,*" the station attendant explained, his speech sprinkled with Sundanese. "We'll be here for half an hour, maybe more. We don't know yet." Above his head hung a sign: Citatah Station. The train wasn't even halfway to its destination.

The sky was growing dark. The clouds, which had been hanging low for a long time now, began to release a light drizzle. Even though he'd been advised to wait inside the train, Keenan wasn't in a hurry to return. He glanced around, looking for something to keep him occupied, and his eyes came to rest on the front veranda of the station.

"*Cep!* Don't go too far!" the attendant called after him.

Yet Keenan felt as if something were beckoning his feet to head out into the village—out toward the muddy road dotted with coffee warungs, which were beginning to light their kerosene lanterns to greet the darkness of night.

Keenan stopped at one of them. The assortment of fried snacks on display looked enticing, not to mention the ripe yellow bananas hanging in bunches from the tent's wooden poles.

The old woman at the warung greeted him warmly. "*Mangga.* Come in for coffee, *Den.*"

Keenan was just about to sit down on the wooden bench when he noticed someone's head moving into his line of sight, followed by two tiny hands reaching for one of the bananas.

"Kugy?"

"Hey! You're awake! What are you doing here?"

"Neptune radar, perhaps?" Keenan exclaimed, both amused and amazed. He sat down beside Kugy and ordered a cup of hot coffee, and the two immediately began talking and laughing, shaking their heads at how they had wound up in the same place.

"Wait, wait," said Kugy. She looked alert, as if something were about to burst into view.

"What is it?" Keenan began looking around as well.

"That smell. You smell it, don't you?" Kugy sniffed the air.

"Did you fart?"

"No!" Kugy scowled. "It's the smell of the rain falling on the earth. Don't you smell it?" She inhaled deeply, her expression ecstatic. "Wonderful . . . ," she murmured.

Keenan sniffed the air, too, then inhaled deeply as well. "This, combined with the fragrance of the coffee . . . Amazing . . ."

Kugy snatched up a banana peel. "And combined with the fragrance of these bananas . . . Wow . . ."

The two of them were so busy sniffing this and that, they didn't notice that the warung owner was looking worriedly in their direction.

"A light drizzle, the smell of rain falling on the earth, coffee, bananas . . . What an incredible combination. I'll never forget this." Kugy grinned, the gleam in her eyes made even brighter by the lamplight.

"Citatah Station, this warung, these lanterns . . . and you. I'll never forget this, either."

Kugy fell silent. She felt compelled to say something, but her tongue wouldn't move. She wanted to ask whether her instincts had been right—whether Keenan had been avoiding her, whether something strange had indeed happened between the two of them, though she didn't know what. But she didn't know where to start.

They sat quietly. Keenan took slow sips of his coffee. Kugy did the same with her hot tea. But this time, it wasn't an awkward silence. Every second that rolled by had a freshness and solemnity, like the drops of rain falling outside, one by one.

"You were right about my short story," said Kugy, breaking the silence. "I wasn't being myself. I just wrote it for the money, for the recognition . . ."

Keenan lifted his head and looked at Kugy, who was watching him closely.

"Thanks," she continued. "I wouldn't have realized it if you didn't have the courage to be honest with me. It doesn't mean I'm going to stop writing short stories altogether, but now I can see who I really am—my weaknesses and my strengths."

Keenan's face broke into a warm smile. "The road before us is a winding one, but someday—who knows when—we'll be ourselves. Someday, you'll be an amazing fairy tale writer. I'm sure of it."

Kugy took a deep breath. Her gaze wandered. "Raining, painting, writing . . . someday we'll be ourselves," she murmured slowly, as if she were spelling something out, as if she were reciting a prayer.

In the distance, they heard someone announcing that the train was about to leave. Then, together, they set off. They took their time, picking their way through the mud with care. And just before the train began moving, they hopped onto a car.

They made their way back to their seats, stopping for a moment between cars on a narrow, shaky platform. Kugy could feel Keenan close behind her, could smell the aroma of his cologne emanating faintly from his shirt, could feel Keenan's face brush against her hair.

Though it was noisy, Kugy heard Keenan whisper something into the strands of her hair, which fluttered in the wind. She didn't know if Keenan was whispering it to her, to himself, or to the both of them. But she heard his words very clearly: "This moon . . . this journey . . . us . . ."

Only when they were back in their seats did Kugy realize that the moon was shining brightly. Kugy couldn't bear it any longer. Her eyelids felt hot and her vision blurred. She wanted to take the words Keenan had whispered, wrap them up, and store them away in her heart—words she didn't fully understand, but knew she was experiencing at that very moment. This moon. This journey. The two of them.

———

Josh had been waiting in the café for an hour. He had ordered all kinds of drinks and donuts from the menu and his stomach felt full to bursting. Then, at last, he heard a booming voice announce that the Parahyangan train from Bandung had arrived. Kugy's train. He took off immediately to wait at the station entrance.

He recognized her tiny figure from far away. Her shoulder-length hair hung loose, and it swung against her backpack, which was so enormous that it seemed to overwhelm her small frame. She was also wearing a denim jacket—obviously borrowed because it was too big for her. She was a fashion disaster. And yet there was something about her that made her stand out wherever she went. Even at this distance, Josh could see the life radiating from those two eyes, could feel the warmth of her presence and her laugh, so open and carefree . . . Suddenly his brow furrowed. His eyes narrowed. There was someone walking beside Kugy. Someone he didn't know. Josh scanned them closely. The furrows on his brow deepened.

"Josh!" Kugy waved at him, then broke into a half jog.

"Hi, babe," Josh greeted her, grabbing her around the waist and kissing her on the cheek. In one swift motion, he took the large backpack from Kugy's shoulders and slung it over his own.

"Josh, this is Eko's cousin . . ."

"Keenan." He extended his hand and gave a friendly smile.

"Hi. Joshua." Josh shook Keenan's hand, keeping his other around Kugy.

"See you next semester, Kugy. Happy writing."

"Happy painting. Don't forget . . ." Kugy held her index fingers to her temples, like antennae.

Keenan let out a low laugh and did the same. "Neptune radar."

Josh kept his eyes on Keenan, even after he'd said good-bye and was walking away. Josh's own radar had picked up a signal. A signal indicating something wasn't right. And he felt uneasy.

CHAPTER 8

START SMALL

All but one of the four chairs at the dining table were occupied. Even though it was just the three of them—Keenan, Jeroen, and their mother—the mood around the table was bright. The two brothers talked nonstop, their mother occasionally chiming in or joining in their laughter.

They heard the front door open, and someone came in and seated himself in the fourth chair.

"Hi, Dad," Jeroen and Keenan greeted their father.

"Sorry to keep you all waiting. A meeting with a client went late."

"It's okay." Lena smiled, pouring hot tea into her husband's cup. "Keenan has an announcement for us."

"Oh? What is it?" asked his father, sipping his tea.

Keenan glanced at his mother. He seemed reluctant to speak. "Well . . . my GPA for this semester was a 3.7."

"The highest in his class," Lena added, beaming. A 3.7 at Keenan's university was certainly no easy feat.

"Very good," his father answered evenly, nodding a little. He couldn't help but look pleased. "I told you an economics degree would be a good fit for you. Another point three points and you'd have gotten a perfect GPA. But there's always next semester, right?"

"I suppose," Keenan answered.

"Whatever you need—a new computer, textbooks—just let me know. I'll buy them for you."

"What I really want is some time."

Keenan's father set his cup of tea on the table. "What do you mean?"

"I'd like to request an extra week before starting the next semester." Lena tried to explain. "He wants more time in Ubud—"

"I know what he wants," Keenan's father said sharply. "You want permission to skip class for a week. Is that it?"

Keenan nodded.

"You must prioritize your studies. You've shown what you can do, and now you're asking I reward you by letting you *skip class*?"

Keenan nodded again.

"Ridiculous." His father shook his head. "You've just said you're going to raise your GPA to a 4.0. How is that going to happen if you miss a week's worth of classes?"

"I didn't promise anything about my GPA, Dad. I only said, 'I suppose.'"

"Don't you get smart with me."

"I'm not asking for a lot. I'm not asking for a car. I'm not asking for a new computer. I'm not asking for any books. All I'm asking for is an extra week at Uncle Wayan's place." Keenan had raised his voice.

"But skipping class—that *is* a lot to ask for. A whole extra week! Why do you need to spend so long in Ubud?"

"I already gave you six months, and now all I'm asking for is one week—"

"You think you're studying for my sake?" his father yelled.

Keenan didn't answer. There was no point. He sighed.

The playful laughter, which rang so brightly just seconds ago, seemed to evaporate without a trace and was replaced with tense silence—four people sitting stiffly without saying a word.

"I'm sure Keenan will be able to catch up," Lena said at last.

"Do whatever you want," her husband answered, half mumbling. Then he got up and left.

———

All of Keenan's art supplies were packed and ready to go. Jeroen was also ready to go and had been for two days. He was going to spend a few days in Ubud with Keenan before joining his friends, who were on a school excursion in Kuta. He declared he might die of boredom in Ubud—it was such a quiet town—but he was willing to sacrifice a few days of his vacation in order to spend time with his older brother.

There was only one more thing Keenan wanted to do before leaving for the airport. He opened his address book and searched for a name.

"Hello." He was greeted by the voice of a teenage girl.

"Good morning. May I please speak to Kugy?"

He could hear a lot of noise on the other end, with lots of people talking in the background. "Kugy! Phone!"

"I think she's in the bathroom!" a female voice answered.

A male voice chimed in. "Kugy! How long are you going to be in there? Are you taking a dump? Phone call for you!"

Then he heard the pitter-patter of feet. "All right already. I'm upstairs, you know! Hold on!"

"So who's in the bathroom then? Why does it smell so bad? Phew! Did someone fart? Own up!"

At last he heard Kugy's voice greet him. "Hello?"

"Hi, Kugy."

"Keenan?"

"Yeah. It sounds really busy at your house. Is something happening?"

"Oh, no. It's like this every day." Kugy chuckled. "You—how are you? Why are you calling all of a sudden?" She chuckled again. "Not that you're not allowed to. It's weird, that's all. I mean, not weird. Just . . . yeah." Kugy was beginning to feel awkward.

"I'm going to Bali for a month. I just wanted to say good-bye."

"Oh . . ."

"I'm calling Eko and Noni after this to say good-bye to them as well," Keenan added hastily. "What do you want as a souvenir?"

"Hmm . . . what *do* I want?" Kugy thought for a while. "I already have five *barong* shirts, three beach sarongs, and a miniature surfing board."

"Salted peanuts? They're a Balinese specialty."

"Oh, I know!" exclaimed Kugy. "Something that can't be bought."

"So, something stolen?"

Kugy laughed. "No. Something handmade."

"Okay." Keenan smiled. "Something handmade. I promise."

It felt like something was coursing through her blood. She felt warm. And it felt like something was tugging at the corners of her mouth. She felt like she couldn't stop smiling. Then Kugy caught a glimpse of her reflection in the closet mirror and felt like an idiot.

"I gotta go. Sorry I can't talk for long. Take care of yourself, okay? See you next semester."

"Sure. See you next semester." And she heard him hang up. Slowly, Kugy put down the receiver. Then she sat there for a long time. The phone conversation hadn't even lasted two minutes, but it felt as if time had dropped anchor and come to a standstill. Then gradually, Kugy hoisted the anchor and returned to her family's living room and its usual state of pandemonium.

The compound was located in the village of Lodtunduh, quite a distance from Ubud's town center, but everyone knew the place. Wayan and his enormous extended family lived there on almost twelve acres of land filled with hills and valleys and traversed by rivers. All the members of the family were well-known artists. There were those who painted, who carved, who sculpted, who danced—and there were even some who made jewelry. It was as if every one of Bali's art forms was each represented by at least one person among them.

Even though it was Keenan's first visit to Lodtunduh (he had only seen it in photos Uncle Wayan had sent him), he fell in love with the place immediately. One month would be enough to satisfy all his artistic yearnings and keep him going for a long time. He wished he could spend the rest of his life there.

His mother and Uncle Wayan were old friends, and Keenan had known the man since he was little. Whenever Uncle Wayan had an exhibition at a gallery in Jakarta, his mother would make a point of stopping by. Little Keenan would tag along and pepper the artist with questions as she smiled and watched, occasionally saying something herself.

This was the first time Keenan had seen Uncle Wayan since returning from Amsterdam, though they had stayed in touch. Keenan was always sending photos of his paintings, and Uncle Wayan did the same. Keenan also corresponded with several of Uncle Wayan's nephews and nieces who were the same age, and he felt as close to them as siblings, even though he had never met them in person. Coming here almost felt like returning to his hometown to visit relatives.

Keenan didn't paint every day. Sometimes he felt content watching the family members going about their different art-related activities. He had spent all day following Banyu, one of Uncle Wayan's nephews, who was working on a commissioned wooden sculpture. Keenan squatted next to Banyu to watch him work as Uncle Wayan stood nearby.

"Do you want to learn how to sculpt, Keenan? You look so serious."

"I'm just impressed, Poyan, that's all. I've never tried it. Do you sculpt?"

Uncle Wayan laughed and spread his palms. "These fingers are made for brushes, not chisels. I'll leave the sculpting to Banyu and his father."

"Give it a try," Banyu chimed in. "Who knows? You might be good at it."

Keenan looked around at the chisels and knobs of wood lying strewn about. His face began to show signs of interest.

Uncle Wayan fanned the flames. "Come on, what are you waiting for? Luckily, Banyu's father is around, too, so you can ask him questions. You know, their work is highly regarded in the village of Mas, and Mas is famous for its sculptures."

"Okay, okay," said Keenan, smiling, "but I'll just watch for today." Then he returned to his devoted observation of Banyu.

———

As evening approached, Keenan returned to the woodworking studio. This time he was alone. The studio belonged to Uncle Wayan's brother, Putu, and it was where Uncle Putu and his son Banyu usually worked. It was only two lots away from the studio where Uncle Wayan did his painting.

Many different types of wood of all sizes lay in piles. Keenan recognized a few of them. There was Indian rosewood, frangipani wood, suar wood, belalu wood, and ketapang wood, as well as other kinds of material, like roots, fibers, and twigs. Finally, after much deliberation, Keenan found what he was looking for—a piece of teak with a beautiful wavy pattern on it.

Start small, he thought. Keenan found a spot to work, got out the tools that he needed, and began carving. He stayed late into the night.

CHAPTER 9

THE MATCHMAKING PROJECT

Kugy had something new to keep her occupied these days. It was as if she were a child again, working on arts and crafts projects for school. She photocopied all of Keenan's sketches and cut them out into squares. The small printer in her room whirred continuously, printing out all her fairy tales. Once everything was ready to go, Kugy began to match the text of her fairy tales with Keenan's sketches to produce a handmade book. And she worked on every detail with all her heart.

A particular date had inspired her to make the book, and she kept it in mind as she labored away. She had even circled the date in her calendar. It was only one day away from her birthday.

New Year's Eve 1999

Keenan had decided to emerge from his cave in Ubud and descend the mountain. Tonight he was going to Kuta with Banyu and Agung to celebrate New Year's Eve. He was excited about what it all meant—a new year, a new century, a new millennium even. A fresh start. Jalan Legian was packed, and the traffic was at a standstill. Nearly every café was overflowing with people who spilled out onto the sidewalk. The three friends had to yell at each other just to be heard.

"So, where are we going?" bellowed Banyu. They had parked at a nearby house and decided to walk on foot.

Keenan shrugged. It was so busy, it already felt like they were celebrating just standing on the side of the road. Truth be told, he couldn't wait to get back to Lodtunduh and the compound.

Agung pointed at a café on the corner, just a few yards away. "Let's just go there! It belongs to my friend Parta. We'll definitely be able to get a table!"

They moved toward the dimly lit café, which was decorated with Buddha ornaments. But Keenan slowed when he saw a small telephone warung wedged between two stores.

"Agung, Banyu. Hold up. I won't be five minutes!" Keenan yelled as he went in. There was one booth available. Keenan took out his wallet and searched for the little piece of paper he'd slipped in it.

The cell phone number he dialed went straight to voice mail. He tried another number.

"Hello?"

Keenan recognized the voice. It was the same one that had answered the last time he called.

"Hello. May I please speak to Kugy?"

"Hold on," the voice said sweetly. And once the receiver was held away, the sweet voice transformed into a piercing shriek. "Kugy! It's for you again! I'm so tired of picking up the phone for other people all the time! Why hasn't anyone called me?"

"That's the way it is! Just accept it!" someone answered.

"Ugh. Typical teenager," said someone else. "Wait till you get a bit older. Then you'll be sick of answering the phone."

"I don't have to wait till I'm older if all the calls I pick up are for everyone else. I'm sick of it now."

Then he heard the pitter-patter of footsteps. A moment later, the telephone changed hands. "Hello?"

Immediately, Keenan smiled. It was just a "hello," but it was enough to make him feel happy again.

"How far away is your room? I hear you stomping down the stairs every time I call."

"Keenan? Hi! How are you?"

"I'm good. I'm in Kuta, celebrating the New Year with Uncle Wayan's nephews. I thought of you, so I wanted to call. But I figured you wouldn't be home. You don't have plans?"

"A lot of invites, but I turned them all down." Kugy chuckled.

"Are you having a party at home?"

"Nah. I have work to do."

Keenan's eyes grew wide. "Important enough for you to skip New Year's Eve altogether?"

"Yeah, I guess," Kugy answered. She glanced at her fingers, still coated in dried glue from all the pasting she'd been doing for the past few days.

"We're ahead by an hour here, and it's going to be midnight in a little while. So . . . Happy New Year, Little One! Don't grow up too fast. You're pretty cool just the way you are."

Keenan said it jokingly, but for some reason, Kugy felt very touched. She swallowed. "Thanks. Happy New Year to you, too."

"I actually have a lot to tell you. But I never know what to say over the phone. Maybe later, when we meet up again in Bandung, okay?"

Kugy felt a pang of disappointment. It looked like their conversation was going to be over in less than two minutes. "What about my souvenir? You haven't forgotten, have you?"

"A *barong* shirt, right?" Keenan teased. This was greeted by a peal of laughter from the other end. His mind drifted to the object which, for the past few days, he almost never let out of his grasp—the object which caused Uncle Wayan and Banyu to shake their heads, wondering at the earnestness with which Keenan scrutinized it and polished it daily to perfect it further.

"Hey, you owe me a lunch at the Hunger No Longer if you end up bringing me a *barong* shirt, or a beach sarong, or a miniature surfing board . . ."

"What about salted peanuts?"

"Well, salted peanuts *would* make me pretty happy."

"I'll bring all of the above, plus something I'm making right now. So, we're still on for our date at the Hunger No Longer, right?"

"Right," said Kugy cheerfully.

Soon afterward, they hung up, and the conversation replayed in Kugy's mind. And once again time dropped anchor and stood still. And once again Kugy found herself tethered to a moment, preserved like all their other moments in crystal.

January 2000

The trio brought their plates of food to their usual table and sat down. They also brought their respective stories about what they had done over the semester break.

Eko began by recounting the recent operation Fuad had undergone. "Fuad had his engine replaced. It's like getting a new soul. Fuad is only a 124 in body now. Inside he's a Mirafiori."

"In plain language, this means . . . ?"

"The odds of Fuad stalling in the future are low, and life is going to be a lot easier for you two," Eko summed up.

"Hooray!" Kugy exclaimed as Noni said, "Thank goodness."

"What'd you do, Kugy?" asked Noni.

"Mostly hung around the house, wondering what will become of me."

Eko tilted his head. "Nothing better to do?"

"I'm also making . . ." Kugy faltered, thinking better of it.

"Talk about building up suspense!" Noni exclaimed.

"What did *you* do, Noni?" Kugy shot back to divert attention.

Noni's face instantly brightened—as if she was about to convey some spectacular piece of news she'd been dying to share. "I've already told Eko about this, and he agrees that it's an absolutely brilliant plan."

Kugy's eyes began to shine as well. She sat up straight. "It must be something pretty amazing," she said in anticipation.

"Let's be systematic!" exclaimed Eko. "Provide some background for the problem at hand."

"All right—some background." Noni cleared her throat and began to elaborate. "Something's missing in our gang. You have a boyfriend, I have a boyfriend. Keenan's the only single one. And from the looks of things, that kid is too antisocial to find a girlfriend himself. So . . ."

Kugy held her breath.

"So Ms. Noni here wants to try her luck as Madam Matchmaker," Eko finished, touching the tip of Noni's nose.

"I have a relative," Noni continued. "Not a direct cousin, but we're pretty close. She's been living in Melbourne, but she's taking a break from her university studies and coming back to Indonesia to intern at her dad's company. She's planning to visit Bandung next week—right when Keenan gets back from Bali."

Kugy could feel herself tensing up. "And then what?" she asked.

"And then we should introduce them to each other. That's what," said Eko.

"You really want to set Keenan up like that? I don't know," said Kugy. She couldn't force herself to sound enthusiastic about Noni's project.

"They're not going to know about it, of course. It has to happen *naturally*. We're the only ones who'd know they'd been set up."

"Oh, you two just go ahead without me," Kugy answered weakly. "I'm no good at matchmaking. I have a zero percent success rate." Her spine, so straight just moments before, slumped, and she returned to leaning back against her chair.

"Why so pessimistic?" asked Eko. "Imagine! Then we could triple-date! Me and Noni, you and Josh, Keenan and . . . What's her name again?"

"Wanda."

"And Wanda. How cool would that be?"

"Yeah, I appreciate your optimism, but enough already. They haven't even met. They might not click. Don't talk about triple-dating just yet." Kugy was barely able to suppress the edge that had crept into her voice.

"Strange," commented Eko. "Aren't you the one who's always been the professional dreamer?"

Noni chuckled. "If it's a matter of clicking or not, I'm positive they'll click."

"Oh yeah?" Kugy asked.

"Just wait and see." Noni gave them a satisfied smile.

———

It wasn't just their conversation at the Hunger No Longer that afternoon— Kugy had been feeling there was something wrong with her for the past few weeks. She felt it was on the tip of her tongue, yet she still couldn't explain what was happening. Not even to herself. She felt the time had come to talk to someone else about it. If she could at least work up the courage to speak about it, maybe she could get an explanation. That was her hope.

Noni's door was ajar. She knocked. "Noni, are you busy?"

Noni was in the middle of talking to someone on the phone, but she motioned for Kugy to come in. Kugy sat on the corner of the bed and waited.

"We're definitely confirmed for next weekend, right? Do you need a ride? . . . Okay. Me and Eko will pick you up and take you to the hotel, then we'll all go out together. Yeah, some of my friends will be coming, too. Okay. See you later! Take care. Bye!" Noni put down the phone. "Sorry, that was Wanda. What's up?"

Upon hearing Wanda's name, Kugy felt uneasiness spread through her body again. She felt even more like something was wrong. She looked at Noni, who was looking back at her expectantly. For some reason, Kugy suddenly felt that Noni wasn't the best person to discuss this problem with after all.

"What is it?" Noni asked again.

"Never mind. I forgot what I wanted to talk about. Sorry." With a nervous laugh, Kugy got up to leave.

"Are you sure?" Noni studied her friend's face. "It feels like you've been on the verge of saying something all day."

"Maybe it's time for me to repent and do more good works," Kugy blurted randomly as she hurried away.

"Crazy girl," Noni said with a grin before shutting the door.

CHAPTER 10

THE YOUNG CURATOR

By the time Kugy got back to the boarding house it was past five o'clock. She had just returned from a meeting for the Youth Mentoring Club, which had invited her to be a teacher at a volunteer-run elementary school. The Sakola Alit—"Little School" in Sundanese—would be situated outdoors in the hills of Bojong Koneng. They didn't have enough funds to rent a space, so they would have to carry out their educational activities in flimsy thatched-roof shelters in the fields or under the trees.

"Can you believe that in a city as developed as Bandung there are nine- and ten-year-olds who can't even read or write?" Ami had asked Kugy at the meeting.

"So where do we start?" Kugy asked.

"We'll divide them into classes according to their abilities. The lowest class will focus only on reading, arithmetic, and drawing—what they would learn in kindergarten. But the ages within each class may vary, ranging anywhere from four years old to ten."

Kugy listened quietly as Ami spoke. She kept looking at the photos of the children they were going to help.

"Think about it first," said Ami. "We're committed to teaching them four days a week, so it'll take up a lot of time."

"How many volunteers do you currently have?"

"Two, including me."

"And how many children are there?"

"Twenty-two."

Again, Kugy was quiet. "Okay. I'll let you know sometime this week."

All the way home, Kugy couldn't get those children's faces out of her head. Her attention was diverted only when she opened the door to her room, switched on the light, and saw the pile of gifts on her bed. Her eyes grew wide. "Noni!" she called.

She heard a voice call out from the room next door. Before long, Noni appeared in the doorway.

"Was Keenan here?" asked Kugy.

"Yeah. He and Eko stopped by. He was looking for you, but you weren't here. So he gave me these souvenirs for you. You saw them, huh?"

Kugy nodded. She looked at the white shirt with the mythical lion-like creature on it and the black patterned sarong, both neatly folded. On top were a miniature surfing board and a box of salted nuts.

"Later tonight, Eko and I are going over to his boarding house. Do you want to come?"

"Yes! Yes!" Kugy answered, almost shouting, unable to hide how excited she was.

Once Noni had left, Kugy opened her desk drawer—just to take a look at the book she had made. It was finally finished. She felt something blossom in her heart. She couldn't wait for evening to come.

———

"Hey, are you ready?" Noni poked her head into Kugy's room. Behind her was Eko. "Wow. Why so dressed up?"

"What? Nah, not really." Nervously, Kugy adjusted her black knee-length dress. It was the nicest piece of clothing she had ever owned, and it was so special that she had never taken it out of her closet. Abruptly, Kugy snatched up Karel's denim jacket and quickly put it on.

"And . . . you're back to being a mess," Eko said with a laugh. "But it suits you better."

Suddenly a woman she didn't know appeared behind Eko and Noni. She walked elegantly, and her lithe body was clad in tight jeans and a tank top. Her trendy-looking high-heeled wedges matched the tiny purse she was carrying. Her long hair looked perfectly styled, like she'd just come from the salon. Every time she moved, Kugy caught a whiff of floral perfume. Kugy froze.

"Let me introduce you," said Noni. "This is my cousin, Wanda."

"Wanda." The woman repeated her name in a melodious voice that reminded Kugy of a receptionist's.

Kugy shook Wanda's hand and saw that her nails were painted a metallic blue, which gleamed in the lamplight. Then Kugy realized that Wanda's eyes were a similar bright blue. She must have been wearing contact lenses. It was as if every square inch of Wanda's appearance had been carefully planned—something that Kugy felt utterly incapable of.

Wanda turned to face Noni. "Shall we?"

"I'll be out in a bit. You guys go ahead," said Kugy. After they left, she threw herself onto the bed. Her emotions were in turmoil. She felt so anxious she almost couldn't bear it. Everything about Wanda, Noni's plan, and all the possible scenarios that might play out left her paralyzed. Finally, Kugy came to a decision.

She ran out front where her friends were waiting in the car and made up an excuse so she wouldn't have to go to Keenan's place. Instead, Kugy spent the whole night curled up in bed.

From his room, Keenan could hear Fuad pulling up. Then he heard the sound of footsteps approaching. Immediately, he rose and opened the door. He could feel his heart beating faster.

Noni and Eko stood there, grinning from ear to ear.

"Where's Little One?" Keenan asked.

He heard the click of high heels approaching. "Sorry, guys," someone said. "I lost one of my contacts. Good thing I found it."

Keenan was astonished to see a tall woman walking in their direction, blinking rapidly. Then he looked at Noni and Eko, searching for an explanation.

"Keenan, this is Wanda, my cousin from Melbourne. You've heard of the Warsita Gallery in Menteng, right? Wanda's father owns it. She likes paintings, too. I mean, she knows a lot about art-related stuff. I told her that painting is your hobby, and she said she's on the lookout for paintings here in Bandung." Noni prattled on like a peddler promoting her wares.

Keenan greeted Wanda with some awkwardness. Behind her, Eko widened his eyes, signaling for Keenan to invite them in.

"Oh, sorry. Please come in," stammered Keenan as he opened the door wide. "Sorry it's a bit messy. I haven't had the chance to clean up since returning from Bali—"

Before Keenan could finish, Wanda barged in, already transfixed by the artwork throughout the room. She examined painting after painting with great care, as if she were a professional curator. She was so focused that it seemed as if everything else had vanished into the bowels of the earth, leaving her alone with Keenan's paintings.

Keenan watched in confusion as Wanda ogled the paintings appreciatively. At the same time, he saw Eko and Noni standing in a corner, smiling. There were a lot of questions hanging in the air that evening.

"Have you ever exhibited your work?" Wanda asked, her eyes still fixed on one of his paintings.

"Not yet."

"Have your paintings ever been shown in a gallery?"

"Not yet," Keenan said again, shaking his head. "Painting is just a hobby. I do it for fun."

"Ah. Such a shame," said Wanda, a faint smile on her face. "You are very, very talented."

"Really?" Keenan raised his eyebrows. "In your opinion, are these paintings good enough to be shown in a gallery?"

"'Good enough'?" This time, Wanda looked at him and chuckled softly. "You should be a professional painter."

Keenan's expression instantly changed. He stepped closer to Wanda, all ears.

"You're a wonderful portrait painter. You bring all your subjects to life in such detail. Your strokes and lines are sure, precise. And what's especially unique is the way you bring portraiture and the abstract together in one frame. Your abstract-painting abilities are also very strong. Usually, a painter's strengths lie in one area or the other, but you're strong in both. Impressive." Wanda shook her head in amazement.

Keenan swallowed. This was the first time anyone had commented on his paintings with such seriousness. This visit had suddenly gotten interesting.

Noni and Eko ended up resorting to pizza delivery for dinner. Wanda and Keenan were having so much fun chatting about art that they didn't even notice Noni and Eko trying to get them to leave the house.

As Noni raised a slice of pizza to her lips, she extended a hand toward Eko and gave him a surreptitious handshake. Mission accomplished.

———

Kugy had been lying awake for a while now. She'd tried distracting herself, but in her mind she was riding in Fuad toward Keenan's boarding house, coming up with a thousand and one possible scenarios for what would happen that night. *No normal guy wouldn't be attracted to Wanda. But Keenan might be different—he values different things. Then again, guys are guys. But Wanda might be boring and bland, and maybe they won't click. Still, if you're that pretty, who cares if you're bland and if you don't click* . . . And so Kugy's mind rambled on.

When she heard the door to Noni's room open, Kugy leapt out of bed and stood in the doorway, trying to look nonchalant.

"Still not asleep?" asked Noni as Kugy yawned and scratched her head. "I thought you said you had a lot of work and a stomachache, and that you wanted to go to sleep early."

"Just about to go to bed. I was doing a bit of writing." Kugy yawned again. "So how did our Madam Matchmaker's debut go? Was it a success?"

"On a scale of one to a hundred, I scored a ninety-five," Noni declared confidently. "I fell short by five points only because I didn't wait around to make sure that Keenan and Wanda weren't struck by amnesia."

"You're certainly the optimist. Do you really think Keenan would want to go out with a Barbie girl like Wanda?"

"Kugy, darling, Wanda is a young curator in the making. Her old man owns the Warsita Gallery in Menteng." Noni issued her explanation with a triumphant smile. "True, Keenan had a bit of an allergic reaction at first, but once Wanda began commenting on his paintings, it was like he was bewitched! The two of them were so busy talking that they lost track of everything else. We had to cancel our plans to eat out and ordered pizza instead. And then Eko and I ended up taking refuge in an Internet café. So much for being matchmakers—wallflowers, more like it. Crazy, huh?"

Kugy laughed, too—an empty, fake-sounding laugh. Her tongue felt too dry to offer a response. In the end, she said she was going to bed.

Something had shattered in Kugy's heart, and it felt like the fragments were spreading throughout her entire body. She grabbed her bolster pillow and clutched it to her stomach in agony. All the restlessness and confusion she'd been feeling came to a head and exploded. She could no longer contain her misery. One by one, the tears began trickling down her cheeks.

Briefly, Kugy raised her head to glance at the book of fairy tales she had made, which was lying on the desk. She frowned. Suddenly she felt so stupid. The book looked awful. She buried her face in the pillow, disgusted at her handiwork.

Then she realized: she had fallen in love with Keenan.

———

When Kugy woke up in the morning, her eyes were puffy and swollen. She had to wrap some ice cubes in a handkerchief to use as a compress. With one eye open, she looked up a number in her notebook and dialed it.

"Ami? Hi, it's Kugy. I've made my decision. Yeah, I'd like to be a teacher at the Sakola Alit. Can I start right away? . . . Yeah, I'm ready."

After the conversation ended, Kugy breathed a sigh of relief. She had to do something, anything. She had to keep busy. She would do whatever she needed to take her mind off this pain. And Ami's offer had suddenly become her best ticket out.

Then she remembered something—something handmade and neatly wrapped in blue paper. Kugy took it out of the drawer. She opened her closet, where she kept a few small boxes of assorted knickknacks. Then she opened one of the boxes and hurled the object in. Still not satisfied, she buried the box in a pile of other things. As she did so, Kugy wished she could forget the object—and the way she felt.

CHAPTER 11

THE SAKOLA ALIT

The *angkot* they'd flagged down was an old Colt L-300, and it climbed the hills with great difficulty, finally dropping the three of them off at the beginning of a footpath. It was good to feel the warm morning sun on their faces after being trapped inside the van for so long.

Kugy, Ami, and Ical exchanged glances before setting off down the dirt path. This was officially their first day teaching at the Sakola Alit. They had no idea what lay in store. Toting small chalkboards and shouldering backpacks stuffed with books and writing implements, they descended down the path, shaded by clusters of bamboo to their left and right.

After walking for half an hour, they arrived at a mosque. Lots of small children were running around. A man wearing a felt *peci* on his head was sitting smoking. He quickly stood up to receive them.

"*Neng* Ami." He extended the tips of his fingers toward Ami in greeting. "*Kumaha? Damang?*" he asked in Sundanese. "How are you? Well, I hope?"

Ami introduced her friends, then explained, "Mr. Somad helped us round up the children from the village."

"*Muhun,*" answered Mr. Somad. "That's right. We've managed to get fifteen children today, *Neng.* The rest will probably come tomorrow or the day after. We hope you understand—a lot of them have work to do as well."

"It's all right. We'll go ahead and start. Where do we go?"

"Oh, *mangga, mangga. Diantar ku Bapa.* This way please. I'll show you." Mr. Somad hastily put out his clove cigarette and called the children, who were scattered all around the mosque. Before long, they were walking in a boisterous group toward a large shelter located beside a field of chili pepper plants.

The children were divided into three classes. Ami's class got the big shelter, Ical's a rather small shelter about a hundred yards away, and Kugy's was to meet under a tree.

Kugy scurried around getting her "classroom" ready. She spread out the plastic tarp for the students to sit on, propped her chalkboard up against the tree, and handed out books, pens, and pencils. Sitting before her were five children, ranging from four to nine years old. All of them admitted that they couldn't read or write. Kugy took a deep breath and tried to figure out where they should start.

"Good morning," Kugy greeted them as sweetly as she could. No one responded. One of them was enthusiastically checking a friend's hair for lice. Another had torn pages out of a book and was making them into paper boats. Another was busy calling to a friend in the shelter nearby. And the last one sat frozen to the tarp, staring at her as if he'd seen a ghost.

Kugy broke into a cold sweat.

———

In Menteng, Central Jakarta, a middle-aged man was heading to his office. He was dressed simply, in loose-fitting pants and a collared linen shirt. This was what he usually wore to work. His "office" was a room sectioned off from the rest of the gallery, which was spacious indeed—for the gallery he owned was the largest in Jakarta. He ran it with the help of his friend Syahrani. She had been an art collector for several decades and had ended up marrying a famous artist, whose sculptures now graced several corners of the gallery.

"Good morning, Mr. Hans," his secretary greeted him.

"Morning, Mia. Is Wanda already here?"

"Yes, sir. She's been here for half an hour."

The man glanced at his watch. "Wow, she's on top of things. No wonder she left the house right after breakfast."

"Morning, Hans. Morning, Mia." A bespectacled middle-aged woman approached them. She had hardly any makeup on—just the faintest smear of dark-red lipstick—but her face looked radiant. A batik *selendang* was wrapped around her neck like a shawl.

"Morning, Ran," said Hans. "How was Teguh's exhibition in Germany?"

"It was wonderful," said Syahrani with a light laugh. "They loved it, those strange Westerners. Teguh's work always does much better abroad. So, how's our beautiful young curator? She rang me last night. She sounded very excited. Said she found a lot of fabulous paintings in Bandung."

"She's acting a bit funny this time," said Hans, shaking his head. "She didn't even want to give me a sneak preview. Just this morning we were eating breakfast together at home, and then she vanished. It turns out she arrived before I did—by a whole half hour no less."

"Oh really? Let's see what she has for us, then." Syahrani smiled and rubbed her hands together.

Opening his office door, Hans stepped inside with his colleague.

Wanda greeted both of them with a grin. It looked like everything was ready to go, including the projector, which was already on and connected to her laptop. She went over to Syahrani and embraced her. "Auntie Rani, I've missed you so much."

"I've missed you, too, dear. Your dad has been telling me that you're very excited about your presentation this morning." Syahrani gave Wanda's cheek a playful poke.

Wanda nodded earnestly and, without further ado, showed them the slides she had prepared. She began with works by more established painters and made her way through photo after photo, until she arrived at the last batch. She took a deep breath before launching into her commentary. "These are by a young artist. In my opinion, he's extremely gifted. His work is fresh, authentic. Under good management, I think his prospects are extraordinary."

"What's his name again? Keenan?" asked Syahrani as she read through the files that Wanda had placed on the table.

"Yes. He's a friend of Noni's, Dad," said Wanda as she glanced at her father.

"Has he had any exhibitions for his work before?" he asked.

Wanda took another deep breath. She knew this question would come up. "Not yet."

Syahrani joined in. "Which galleries have shown his work?"

That was the second question she was expecting. "None yet."

Syahrani and Hans looked at each other. "Well." Hans cleared his throat. "If it's a matter of whether he's talented, I agree with you. Authentic? Yes, I suppose. But it looks like this young man is still developing. He hasn't reached his full potential as a painter. From what I see, it seems like he's still trying to find his identity. Give him one or two more years. Maybe then he'll be ready for us to show his work."

The expression on Wanda's face changed as her lips formed a pout. "But Dad, I'm positive he has a certain something. He's like a raw diamond."

"Exactly," her father answered. "Raw. Good—but raw."

"I agree with you on every point, Hans," Syahrani chimed in. "But there is another factor we should take into account, and that's Wanda's perceptiveness in spotting new talent. Of course Warsita is famous for its collection of works by established painters, but there's no harm in providing opportunities for new painters. If this painter turns out well, it'll be a credit to the gallery."

Hans smiled a little. "We've had dozens of new artists lining up to show their work here, and we've turned them all down. Why should we make an exception for him?"

"Because he's different, Dad," Wanda stated firmly.

Syahrani examined Keenan's file again. Attached was a photo of Keenan standing next to one of his paintings. "Because," she said, "I think our Wanda likes him."

Wanda's face turned bright red. She opened her mouth, but nothing came out.

"I'm joking, darling," Syahrani added quickly. She chuckled gently. "This young man is definitely talented. I think he deserves to be given a chance."

Hans gave a light shrug. "Fine. We'll see how he progresses."

Wanda breathed a sigh of relief. She was still unnerved by what Syahrani had just said, but she couldn't suppress the smile on her face.

February 2000

His feet were beginning to feel sore—an indication he'd been standing there for a long time now. Keenan considered giving up and going home, but he looked around once again, examining the faces of everyone who passed by. Finally, he caught a glimpse of the person he had been looking for—with her shoulder-length hair worn loose, the same denim jacket she wore almost every day, and the backpack, disproportionately large in relation to her small frame.

"Kugy!" Keenan shouted.

Kugy kept on walking. Keenan had to chase her down and tug at her arm.

Kugy closed her eyes before turning around. Her face assumed an innocent expression. "Hello, fellow agent! What's up?"

Keenan looked at her in disbelief. "Where have you been? You know I don't like being on campus, but I've been hanging out here in the same spot every day looking for you, and you haven't shown up once. Are you really that busy?"

It was the first time Kugy had heard Keenan sound so emotional.

"Yeah. Pretty busy," said Kugy, almost mumbling.

"It was your birthday," said Keenan with regret.

"Yours, too," said Kugy quietly. "Hey, sorry I didn't get the chance to wish you a happy birthday. But I told Eko to wish you a good one on my behalf."

"You couldn't tell me yourself?"

Kugy swallowed. Keenan had asked the question politely, but did so with an accusatory gaze. "It was when Wanda was in town and I didn't want to bother you. The four of you had your own plans—"

"And I invited you, too," Keenan said. "I never said it was meant to be just the four of us, did I? Kugy, you're my friend. I would never—"

"Sometimes good friends have to know their place. Like I said, I really didn't want to bother you, so I—"

"Are you mad at me? Is that it?"

"Mad? About what?" asked Kugy uneasily.

Keenan shrugged. "Dunno. But as far as excuses go, 'I didn't want to bother you' is kind of lame."

Kugy was quiet. *How can I tell him the truth?* she thought. When it came to being lame, her real excuse took the cake.

"Actually," Keenan said. "I have something for you. I wanted to give it to you for your birthday."

"It's okay. Some other time," Kugy answered hastily, trying to smile.

"We're going to the midnight movie showing this week, as usual. Why don't you come? Mr. Itok has been asking about you."

"The . . . four of us?" asked Kugy, cautiously.

"Probably five. I think Wanda's coming to Bandung again this weekend."

"We'll see, okay? I'll try," said Kugy, trying to sound nonchalant. *There's a 200 percent chance I'm not going,* she added to herself.

"The Warsita Gallery is going to show my work," Keenan added. "That's why Wanda's been in town so much."

Kugy's eyes widened. "Wow! Congratulations!" This time, she really meant what she said. "Keenan Aquaneptuniamania . . . a real painter. Fantastic!"

Keenan laughed. "Since when has my name been Keenan—what did you call me? Kleptomania?"

"Aquaneptuniamania. You've been officially dubbed so." Kugy grinned. "Really. I'm so happy for you. Your work deserves to be shown in a place like that. It was only a matter of time."

"Come on, let's get lunch together. My treat. The Hunger No Longer?"

Kugy took a deep breath. Her stomach had been rumbling, and there was no one else on the planet whom she liked to eat lunch with more than Keenan. "Um, sorry. I've got to go. I'm meeting with Ami from the Youth Mentoring Club. Some other time, okay?"

Keenan was silent for a moment. "That's the second time today you've told me 'some other time,'" he said slowly. "There won't be a third, I hope."

Kugy didn't have the courage to look Keenan in the eye. The sense that she was being accused of something seized her. "Good-bye," she mumbled, then left as fast as she could. She took big strides and kept her eyes fixed on the asphalt. *Kugy, if you don't do this now, you'll never break free.* She repeated the words over and over, until it became her mantra.

CHAPTER 12

GENERAL PILIK AND THE ALIT BRIGADE

March 2000

The bespectacled man stood at the ready, with four movie tickets in hand. Several more tickets were tucked away in his back pockets. This was now how he usually spent his Saturday nights. Since Eko started commissioning him to buy tickets for the midnight showing, many of Eko's friends had begun using his services as well. It had gotten to the point where he had to enlist the help of others.

"Mr. Itok!"

He turned toward the escalator as Eko and his friends rose into view.

"Here you go," said Mr. Itok. "These are for Eko, Noni, Keenan, and . . . Keenan's new girlfriend." He handed Eko and Keenan each a pair of tickets.

The four of them burst out laughing.

"My name is Wanda, but you can call me Keenan's new girlfriend if you like," said Wanda. She glanced at Keenan, who was standing next to her, his face turning red.

"Kugy never comes with you anymore, Keenan. You officially broke it off, then?" Mr. Itok's eyes gleamed, eager for gossip.

"Mr. Itok, don't be such a weirdo," Eko said uncomfortably. "Your job is to buy us movie tickets."

"Keenan is really something, huh?" continued Mr. Itok. "No trouble getting girlfriends, thanks to his good looks. All pretty ones, too."

They hurried away before Mr. Itok could pry into their affairs any further.

"So you and Kugy were going out?" Wanda asked slowly.

Keenan only shook his head. He didn't feel like providing a long explanation.

"Kugy and Keenan were going out only as long as Mr. Itok was under the impression they were," Eko chimed in, chuckling. Keenan knew his friend's words were in jest, but they troubled him all the same.

"Kugy is really busy these days," Noni said. "She started teaching at a school run by volunteers, and she's there almost every day. She always gets back late and stays in her room for the rest of the night."

"Strange," Eko chimed in again. "Does she really teach that late? Do they have a projector and outdoor screen running at midnight in Bojong Koneng? She may be busy, but no one can be *that* busy, if you ask me."

"Keenan, are you okay?" asked Wanda.

Keenan was startled by this question, and he realized Wanda had been studying him closely. In lieu of an answer, Keenan flashed her a smile.

Wanda touched his hand. "Let's buy some popcorn."

It was as if he had been hurled into a time warp. It felt like déjà vu. He recognized this scene—this night of the week, this place, this popcorn machine. The only difference was that last time, it had been Kugy holding his hand.

April 2000

Josh had been lying on the carpet, watching his girlfriend, for some time now. Her hair had grown out, and her "Lake Toba" T-shirt—her favorite bedtime attire—had become even more worn. She wore wrinkled batik shorts, and her big eyes pored over an excessively thick book by J. R. R. Tolkien. Josh had once joked that a book that thick was better suited for fending off ferocious dogs than for reading. Josh could never imagine reading even 10 percent of all the books Kugy had read—not even if he spent his whole life trying.

Sensing she was being watched, Kugy looked up. "Do you want to read something, too, Josh? I have some Donald Duck comic books."

Josh shook his head. Kugy returned to her reading. He returned to his watching. The room returned to a state of silence. Minutes passed.

"Kugy?"

"Hmm?"

"Are you okay?" he asked.

Kugy looked at Josh. "Yeah. Why?"

"You've been quieter than usual recently. Is something on your mind?"

Kugy looked troubled by this question. But hastily, she smiled. "Not really. Except for Alit-related business, maybe. We have more students now."

"That school keeps you so busy."

"I really like teaching there. Those kids . . ." Kugy shook her head in admiration. "Sometimes I feel like I'm the one who's learning from them."

"But you have to take care of yourself, too, you know. You're losing weight."

"I still eat like a horse."

"Yes, but you've gone overboard with your activities. You have to rest. At some point your body is going to give out."

"Nah. It's just that the anaconda in my stomach is getting larger."

"Kugy, I'm serious."

"Josh, *I'm fine*. Okay?" Then Kugy immersed herself in her book once more, and again the room fell silent.

"Kugy."

"Hmm?"

"You need a vacation."

"What vacation?"

"C'mon! Let's go to Singapore. Just for the weekend. My uncle bought an apartment near Orchard Road. We can stay there."

"Don't have the money."

"I'll pay."

"Don't want to."

"You work with those kids from Monday to Friday. All I'm asking for is one weekend. You *really* can't give me that?"

"It's Saturday night and I'm spending it with you, aren't I? What's the difference?"

"You're not spending it with me," said Josh. "You're spending it with Tolkien!" And with that, he rose to his feet and exited the room, leaving Kugy in stunned silence.

———

Josh didn't usually wake up early, but he had plans Sunday morning to meet Noni, who went jogging every morning around Gasibu Field in front of the Satay Building. So Josh dragged his body out of bed and drove over.

He was hanging out by a drinks stand while he waited for Noni to finish her last lap. Before long, Noni ran up to him and began gulping down the bottle of mineral water he had waiting for her.

"You're amazing. How can you go to a midnight movie and still go jogging the next morning?"

"I still need to lose weight, Josh. Five more pounds. I have a target to meet."

Josh tilted his head. "There'll be nothing left of you. Women . . . I don't understand you at all. By the way, your best friend has lost weight and she doesn't even jog."

"You mean Kugy?"

"That's what I want to ask you about. Why else would I go through the trouble of getting up at the crack of dawn?" Josh's expression grew serious. "What's up with her, Noni?"

"Why? What's wrong?"

"You're the one who sees her every day. You don't think there's something funny going on?"

Noni thought for a moment. "Well, it's true she rarely goes out with us now, but she's so busy with Ami at the Sakola Alit. She's probably just too tired at the end of the day. She doesn't even talk to me that much anymore—only if something really important comes up."

"You don't think there are any other reasons, apart from the Sakola Alit?"

Noni thought about it some more, then shrugged.

"She . . ." Josh seemed reluctant to continue. "She hasn't been seeing any other guys, has she?"

Noni's brow furrowed. "Other guys? Not as far as I know."

Josh deliberated whether he should mention the particular matter that was troubling him. "How about Keenan? She's not—"

Noni burst into laughter, almost choking on her water. "Oh no! So you've come down with whatever Mr. Itok has, too."

"Who's Mr. Itok?"

"Never mind," said Noni with a wave of her hand. "As far as I know, they're close, and they get along, but there's nothing going on. In fact, Keenan's got his eye on my cousin from Melbourne."

"Oh yeah? So they're a couple?"

"Not yet, but it's only a matter of time." Noni chuckled. "I'm their matchmaker, don't you know?" she added with some pride.

Josh felt somewhat relieved, but his concern didn't disappear altogether. "Keep an eye on Kugy for me, okay? If there's anything, let me know."

"Relax, Josh. The Sakola Alit is probably taking up all her attention. You know how that girl is. If there's something she's really involved in, she likes to be left alone."

But Josh's thoughts returned to that night in Gambir station. The look in Kugy's and Keenan's eyes and that inside joke about a "Neptune radar"—whatever that was. In his heart, Josh knew he was never wrong. *His* radar was never wrong.

———

It took eight sessions for Kugy to win the hearts of her students, who now numbered eleven. Only a few were fluent in Indonesian. Almost all of them persisted in using Sundanese—and Kugy couldn't speak any Sundanese. But after two weeks, both sides began to learn from each other. Now, more of the children were willing to speak in Indonesian, and Kugy had picked up a few Sundanese terms—with the result that Kugy's broken Sundanese became a great source of amusement.

Apart from becoming the butt of their jokes, Kugy finally found another way to get them to read. Initially, she had brought a stack of classic fairy tales with her, along with her enormous collection of Donald Duck comic books. But to her surprise, she found that the children had never even heard of Thumbelina, Snow White, Cinderella, the Tin Soldier, or any other classic fairy tale characters. Even Donald Duck and Mickey Mouse were only familiar to them as pictures they had seen on T-shirts. And she realized that her childhood and that of the children at the Sakola Alit were worlds apart.

In the end, Kugy came to an agreement with them: every time they succeeded in moving to the next reading level, Kugy would make up a fairy tale about them. The cast of characters would be drawn from the children themselves, complete with details from their everyday lives.

"Ms. Kugy! I want to be a general!" said one of the children, raising his hand and puffing out his chest when Kugy told the class of her plan.

In her heart, Kugy shouted for joy. The boy, Pilik, was the oldest, and the other students looked up to him. He was nine and still couldn't read or write. During the first week, Pilik had thoroughly hazed Kugy. He interrupted her constantly, laughed loudly, and talked about Kugy in Sundanese. She didn't understand, but she knew she was being made fun of.

Although she was annoyed, Kugy knew that the boy was actually very smart—a natural-born leader. So it was no surprise that Pilik greeted Kugy's idea with the most excitement, with one stipulation: he had to be the main character—and he had to be a general.

"It's a deal, General Pilik! Who else wants to join in?"

When the others saw Pilik's enthusiasm, they immediately began raising their hands. And so it was that General Pilik and the Alit Brigade came into being—and also Hogi the Saintly Rooster, Palmo the Stubborn Goat, Gogog the Amazing Swimming Dog, and various other animal characters adapted from their pets and livestock. Every day after school, Kugy returned with them to their village to play. And every day, she wrote about their adventures in a notebook. They read slowly and haltingly, but still, the children always cheered and clapped encouragingly for each other as they took turns reading tales about themselves. From that day on, Pilik was her faithful friend. And Kugy was a hero to them all.

Late that afternoon, after all the students had gone home, Kugy sat in one of the shelters to write about the adventures of General Pilik and the Alit Brigade. She heard a rooster crow in the distance, loud and long and clear. "That Hogi . . . ," mumbled Kugy. Immediately, she began drawing a handsome rooster, arrayed in glossy black feathers. She stopped. "Huh. It looks like a stegosaurus," she muttered.

"Whatcha doing, Kugy?" a voice asked from behind her.

She jumped in surprise and turned to look. "Oh, it's you, Ical. I thought it might be Mr. Somad checking on the shelters." Kugy laughed. "I was trying my hand as an illustrator. But . . . total fail."

"Yeah, Ami said that story method of yours is a great success," said Ical with admiration in his voice. Then he glanced at what Kugy had drawn. "But don't feel the need to add visuals as well."

Kugy laughed. "That's one area where I know my limits. Let's keep this Jurassic chicken a secret between you, me, and God."

"I have a friend who's amazing at drawing. Maybe we can invite him to teach here once in a while."

"A visual arts major? Does he go to the Bandung Institute of Technology?"

"No, he goes to our university. He's majoring in economics and lives in the same boarding house as my friend Bimo."

Kugy felt like she'd been skewered through the heart.

"I'll try to get in touch with him through Bimo. Who wouldn't feel sorry at the sight of that drawing?" said Ical, amused.

Kugy was smiling, too, but it was a smile that had gone sour. She knew who Ical meant. She had tried her hardest to flee, to avoid him and immerse herself in this new world. But suddenly, there he was, being invited to take part in it. If that were to happen, Kugy didn't know where else to run.

CHAPTER 13

WANDA'S BIG PLAN

May 2000

Kugy couldn't escape this time. She was going back to Jakarta, and because she was getting a ride in Fuad, who could now handle out-of-town excursions, she couldn't refuse when Noni suggested stopping by the Warsita Gallery.

"What's the point of going?" Kugy protested. "To buy a painting? We can't afford it. To see Keenan's paintings? We've seen them already. Why go?"

"It's called support, dear," said Noni. "We have to show Keenan we're behind him. This is a big day! It's the first time his paintings are being shown in a gallery—and an important one to boot! Most painters his age don't get this kind of chance. We're his friends and we should be proud."

Though her face didn't show it, Kugy knew in her heart that Noni was right. But she didn't want to deal with what she would see. It would be too painful.

"We're just going to drop by for a little while, right? We'll look at the paintings he has on display and then get going?"

Eko cleared his throat. "Well, you see . . . the gallery's holding an afternoon high tea to debut their newest acquisitions, including Keenan's art. There'll be painters, journalists, collectors, curators . . ."

Kugy turned pale. "You guys are so mean! Why didn't you tell me? I look like a fugitive on the run!"

Eko turned his head and looked at Kugy. "You're the most confident person I know and you never care what people think. You're really scared of an event like this? It's nothing big. Wanda said they only invited around fifty people."

"Fifty?" Kugy was practically shrieking. "I'm definitely waiting in the car!"

"Don't be silly. You look fine—"

"I do not!" Kugy said. "You two go in, I'll wait in the car. Period."

Unfortunately for Kugy, it was not to be. When Fuad pulled into the gallery parking lot, they were greeted by Wanda and Keenan, who had also just arrived.

"Hi, guys," Wanda said. "Thanks for stopping by." This time, she was dressed entirely in silver, with the purse, shoes, and nails to match. Her makeup was flawless. She looked like a singer about to go onstage.

Kugy quickly glanced at her own outfit and felt a pang of regret. If only she'd known they would be dropping by the Warsita Gallery on the way home, she would have put more effort into her appearance. But this was not to be, either. She would just have to resign herself to the fact that she was wearing a T-shirt she had gotten for free from organizing a Fun Bike event. Never mind that the design on the front was faded. Never mind that Josh had officially designated it a potential car-washing rag and was ready to steal it from her closet at any moment.

Keenan immediately went over to her. "Kugy!" he said brightly. "I didn't think you were coming."

"Me, neither," said Kugy with a forced smile. She wished she were an ant so she could escape—from Wanda, who looked like some glamorous artiste about to give a performance, from Keenan, who looked so handsome in his collared shirt, from the sight of Wanda's fingers wrapped around Keenan's arm, from Noni and Eko, who were beaming with pride at the success of their matchmaking project. But this was also not to be.

————

In the corner of the gallery was a large table bearing all kinds of teas and other beverages, and replete with little cakes arranged prettily on silver trays. Kugy set up camp there, drinking cup after cup of tea and filling her stomach with cake.

"They shouldn't let you eat for free. The organizers will lose money."

Kugy turned around to find Keenan standing beside her. "This is the starving college student's modus operandi," answered Kugy with some difficulty, her mouth full.

Keenan gazed warmly at her. "I'm glad you came."

Kugy couldn't help but smile. A freshness flowed through her whenever she saw that look in his eyes. "I saw your paintings. They're amazing. If you ask me, they're the best ones here." Kugy spoke earnestly. "But then again, I don't know much about art. It's probably just a matter of personal preference . . . and well, you *are* my friend," she added with a smile.

Keenan smiled back. "You don't need to understand art to like it. Just listen to your heart."

Kugy took a deep breath. "You're right. Listen to your heart," she said slowly.

"Mr. Itok thinks we've broken up."

Kugy had just taken a sip of tea and it almost came spraying out of her mouth. She laughed uneasily. "Mr. Itok is the only person in this whole wide world who knows about us being a couple. Even we don't know about it."

"Now he thinks Wanda and I are going out."

Kugy continued laughing, but her laughter grew flatter and flatter, until it petered out entirely. "Who knows?" she said. "Maybe Mr. Itok is psychic. Maybe he can predict the future . . ." Kugy swallowed. "You . . . aren't interested in Wanda, are you?"

In lieu of answering, Keenan looked over at Wanda, who was standing at the far end of the room, deep in conversation. Kugy followed Keenan's gaze, and they both watched her.

"If I were a guy, I'd be stupid not to like Wanda," murmured Kugy.

"There are stupid guys," Keenan murmured back.

Kugy felt the blood pounding in her veins. Her heart leapt. "So . . . you—"

Keenan's gaze shifted. "My family's here. Sorry, I have to go."

Kugy had no choice but to nod and swallow what she was about to say. Keenan hurried to the entrance. She had seen Keenan's family in photos, but this was the first time she was seeing them in person. His mother, a Dutch woman, looked more beautiful than she had in the pictures. She was dressed all in white, her long hair in a bun. His father was tall, like Keenan, and looked handsome in his navy-blue jacket and jeans. With them was a teenage boy with curly hair. His face was like Keenan's, but darker. "Jeroen," Kugy whispered to herself.

At that moment, somebody joined Keenan's family, greeting each of them with a pretty smile. *Wanda.* Kugy frowned.

She felt someone tugging at her arm. "It's Keenan's mom and dad. Here, I'll introduce you," said Eko, who had appeared at her side, along with Noni. "Auntie Lena! Uncle Adri! Jeroen! How are you?" They approached the group.

"Hi, Eko," said Lena, hugging her nephew. "Hi, Noni."

"Auntie, this is Kugy," Eko said. "She's a friend of Noni's."

Lena turned to Keenan. "Oh, so *this* is Kugy."

Eko, Noni, Kugy, and Wanda exchanged puzzled glances at her peculiar tone.

"Keenan's told us a lot about you, Kugy. He says you like to write stories."

Kugy grinned, partly out of embarrassment, partly out of happiness. "Yes, ma'am . . ."

"Keenan is very impressed with your stories."

Kugy cleared her throat. "*Ehm.* I'm glad he's a fan. Unfortunately, he's my only one." She laughed.

Everyone else laughed, too—except for Wanda. "Please, let me show you around," she said to Keenan's parents. Tugging at Keenan's arm, she forced the whole group to follow along. Kugy couldn't help but stare at Wanda's silver nails. They were fastened around Keenan's arm like an iron chain.

They came to a stop in front of Keenan's four paintings, which were hanging on a panel, beautifully framed and presented. The halogen lighting gave them a certain sheen. Lena gasped and her eyes filled with tears. But her husband only stood there, saying nothing.

In an instant, Lena was hugging Keenan. *"Ik ben zo trots op jou,"* she whispered to him in Dutch. "I'm so proud of you, *vent.*"

"What else is there? Where to now?" Keenan's father asked Wanda.

Wanda regarded him in confusion. "There's . . . nothing else. Please, feel free to look around. Perhaps you two would like a drink? We have tea, wine—"

"Sorry," said Keenan's father. "I can't stay long. Lena, we'll leave in fifteen minutes, all right?"

"Mom can come home with me later," snapped Keenan. "If you need to leave, please go ahead."

Tension filled the air, infecting everyone.

"Jeroen, are you coming with me?" asked his father.

Jeroen looked confused. "I . . . I want to walk around with Eko first, Dad."

The awkwardness of the situation was relieved when a waiter appeared, offering food and drinks. Eko, Noni, Kugy, and Jeroen immediately engrossed themselves in the act of chewing.

"You go ahead, Adri," Lena said to her husband. "I'll come later with Keenan. I want to look around a little longer."

"How will you get home? Does Keenan have transportation?"

"We'll take my car," Wanda answered quickly.

Kugy stopped chewing altogether.

"Fine. Up to you," said Keenan's father. And before long, he left.

Although Keenan tried to act normal, everyone could feel the shift in his mood—as if a dark cloud were hanging over him and wouldn't go away. And it didn't go away for the rest of the afternoon.

———

After driving Keenan, his mother, and his brother home, Wanda lingered. She and Keenan sat on the front veranda under the pergola. Mandevilla vines laden with white blossoms formed a roof over their heads. Next to them were two glasses of water, still untouched.

"Your dad doesn't approve of you painting, does he?" asked Wanda, breaking the silence.

Keenan shook his head. "It's all I've wanted to do, ever since I was little. But Dad seems to be allergic to anything related to art. I don't know why. Mom used to be a painter, too. But when she got married, she stopped. Dad didn't want me to continue living in Amsterdam because he was afraid I'd become an artist. He thought that if I got a degree in economics, my interest in painting would go away. But instead—"

"You met me," finished Wanda.

Keenan let out a bitter sigh. "And when he found out my work was good enough for a gallery like yours, he must have been shocked. He probably feels threatened."

"Does he run his own business?"

"Yeah, a trading company. Imports and exports. He built it all up from nothing. How did you know?"

"My dad's the same. And I'm an only child. I know the pressure." Wanda smiled. "Luckily, I like Dad's line of work. And I'm very serious about working in the art business. But still, I have to work hard to show Dad and Auntie Rani that I'm capable of helping run Warsita." Gently, Wanda placed her hand on Keenan's. "We're very alike, you know," she said, almost whispering. "Can I ask you something? What is it you want most?"

Keenan turned and gazed deep into Wanda's eyes. "To be myself," he said firmly. "I know I have a comfortable life. And I'm lucky to be at such a good university. But I'm not afraid to leave all this behind—if the right opportunity came along. The only reason I put up with it all is because I'm still financially dependent on Dad. I can't support myself yet."

"If you keep painting, you will be able to support yourself. I have faith in your abilities. It's only a matter of time."

Keenan smiled briefly. "Yeah. Meaning I have to wait for someone to buy my paintings, right?"

"Absolutely," said Wanda, nodding. Then she fell silent and gazed off into the distance. But the wheels in her head were turning at full speed.

After she returned from Keenan's house, Wanda lay in bed all night staring at the ceiling. She thought and thought, until finally, she came up with a plan, which she would carry out as quickly as possible. She couldn't wait for morning to come.

———

By 9:30, Wanda was already at the gallery, scanning the long list of their collectors and patrons and marking off certain names. Then she set her slender fingers dancing on the telephone buttons, dialing the names one by one.

"Mr. Halim? Hi, it's Wanda. Have you received our newest catalog? If you look at the section in the back, you'll see some work by a new painter. His name is Keenan. Have you taken a look? Well, yes, of course he's still new, but he has excellent prospects . . ."

"How are you, Mrs. Lien? This is Wanda from Warsita. Have you found anything that suits you from our new catalog? Personally, I'd recommend one of our new artists, Keenan. You'll find him in the back. No, he hasn't held any exhibitions yet, but . . ."

Wanda kept at it the whole day, calling every person on her list until, finally, she gave up. Not a single one was interested in investing in Keenan's paintings. They all gave the same reason: Keenan was still too young and unknown.

Wanda studied her list again. All the people she had called were longtime players in the art game, and were used to collecting work by well-known painters. Only now did Wanda realize what challenges her father had been talking about. He was right. The Warsita Gallery wasn't a good fit for Keenan's paintings, at least not at this stage. Wanda bit her lip, and the wheels in her head began turning once more. She had to change her strategy.

Once more her fingers danced across the buttons on the phone, but this time she didn't look at her list. She was calling her friends.

"Pasha, it's me, Wanda. Could you do me a favor? I just need your name and info for my customer list. No, you don't need to buy the painting, you just need to say that you've bought it. Is that okay, hon? Thanks . . ."

"Virna, dear? Could I ask you for a favor? I want to buy a painting, but I can't buy it under my name. Could I use yours? I just need your info, that's all . . ."

In a matter of minutes, all four of Keenan's paintings had been sold. They'd been bought by four different people. But all of them had been paid for by one person: Wanda.

CHAPTER 14

THE BOOK OF HIDDEN TREASURE

June 2000

Keenan and Bimo pulled the CJ-8 Jeep into the one parking space next to the small health clinic.

"Talk about the middle of nowhere," said Bimo as he looked around. "I come here a lot with my off-road riding club." His eyes came to rest on a narrow, steep clearing off the main road, partially obscured by bamboo. "Ical said to follow this path for about half an hour until we come to a mosque. He'll be waiting for us there." He parted the thick curtain of bamboo leaves.

Keenan imagined little Kugy walking down this path every day to teach. Suddenly, he felt moved.

Ical was already waiting for them at the mosque, and they all set off toward the chili pepper field and the thatched shelters where classes were held. Before long, they arrived at a shelter made of bamboo, where Ami greeted them.

"That's where I teach," said Ical, pointing to another smaller shelter among some hills. "Kugy teaches over there." He pointed to a large banyan tree where several children were seated on a mat.

Even at a distance, Keenan could make out Kugy's silhouette. Her back was to him, and her little hands moved to and fro, as if she were demonstrating something.

"We don't have any constraints on what we do here," explained Ami. "Since you're joining us as a guest teacher, just come by whenever you want. There are no specific times."

"The children are really excited about learning how to draw," Ical added. "Just show up every once in a while and they'll be happy."

"Whose class should I teach first?" asked Keenan, slinging his backpack of art supplies over his shoulder.

Ical and Ami exchanged glances. "Any class you want. It's up to you," answered Ami.

"I'll teach that class first, okay?" Keenan pointed to the banyan tree, where he'd been wanting to go since he had arrived.

———

Keenan approached right when Kugy was pretending to be Dombrut the Sheep. Dombrut was about to go on a rampage and—so the story went—be defeated by General Pilik and the Alit Brigade. Head down, butt in the air, holding her hands on either side of her head to mimic horns, Kugy froze when a familiar maroon backpack with a *K* suddenly came into view. And a familiar-looking pair of shoes. And a familiar-looking pair of legs. Hastily, Kugy straightened up to find Keenan standing in front of her, a smirk on his face and two fingers on either side of his head extended like antennae.

"Agent Keenan Klappertaartmania reporting for duty," said Keenan, adopting a soldier's stance.

"*Klappertaart*?" Kugy's eyes brightened at the mention of the Dutch-influenced dessert. But she tried to look serious. "What's the password?"

"Banana."

Kugy looked thoughtful. "Hmm. All right. Permission to join." Her face assumed its usual cheerful expression. "Students! We have a guest teacher joining us today. Say hello to . . . *Kang* Keenan!"

Keenan had an amused frown on his face. He'd never been addressed as *Kang* before. It was a Sundanese term of respect for an older-brother-type figure.

"What did you say? *Rangginang*?" shouted one of the children. The transformation of *Kang* Keenan's name into a type of rice cracker was greeted by shrieks of laughter.

"Pilik, you don't even know what *Kang* Keenan can do yet!" Kugy said. "He can draw anything you want—in one minute or less!"

Keenan frowned again.

"How long is one minute?" asked Pilik.

"One minute is sixty seconds," Kugy answered. "So all of you have to count out loud from one to sixty together. If you can't, just repeat after me. But everybody has to join in. Ready?"

"Ready!" the children chorused.

"Okay, let's go!" Keenan exclaimed, marker in hand. "What do you want me to draw?" He stood next to the large sketchpad he had propped up on his wooden easel.

"Draw Hogi!" one of the children shouted.

Keenan frowned for the third time. "What's a Hogi?" he asked Kugy under his breath.

"He's a rooster. Large. Black. Make him handsome—that's the main thing. Got it?" Kugy turned again to her students. "Okay, *barudak*! Get ready to count! One . . . two . . . three . . . four . . . five . . ."

They counted to sixty with enthusiasm. And by the time they reached forty, Keenan was already sitting down relaxing, legs stretched

111

out in front of him. The drawing of the rooster they had asked for was complete.

The children were amazed. It had come to life so quickly, before their very eyes. They cheered. And then they proceeded to bombard Keenan with requests.

"Draw a robot!"

"Draw a plane!"

"Draw Mr. Somad!"

Keenan spent the rest of the day fulfilling their requests. Every drawing was greeted by shouts of astonishment and cheers. Keenan's presence among them that day was like that of a superstar among fans. They demanded he distribute the drawings among them to take home. And they accepted them from him with pride, as if they were autographs from a famous movie star.

"You'll come often, won't you, *Kang* Keenan?" pleaded Pilik. He rolled up his drawing and put it into his bag, which was made from an old flour sack. "Next time, draw a picture of me and the Alit Brigade."

Keenan didn't quite understand what Pilik meant, but he nodded anyway, unable to refuse.

"Oh, by the way. I'm General Pilik." Pilik puffed out his chest and gave Keenan a firm handshake. "*Tong hilap!* Don't forget!" Then he scurried away after his friends. "Hey, troops! *Dagoan euy!* Wait for me!"

Keenan turned to Kugy. "I don't get how you always manage to turn everyone around you into weirdos as well. Or maybe you're just fated to be among other weirdos."

Kugy chuckled. "That kid. Talk about miracles. He used to be my sworn enemy, but once I succeeded in taming him, he became my ally. And because the whole class follows Pilik's lead, they all became my allies, too."

"What's your secret, Agent Karmachameleon?" Keenan asked with a serious expression.

With equal seriousness, Kugy drew something out of her bag as if she were unsheathing a sword. "This is my secret, Agent Poffertjesmania!" In her hand was a worn-looking notebook.

"*Klappertaart, poffertjes*—my mother's Dutch, not a pastry chef. What is that, anyway? *The Weirdo's Handbook*?"

Kugy plunked down next to Keenan. Her eyes were aglow with excitement. "Take a look. It's an adventure series I've been writing since I started teaching here. The characters are my own students. They didn't want to learn how to read at first, so I promised them that I'd write fairy tales about their adventures. But they would have to learn how to read in order to understand them. And that's how General Pilik and the Alit Brigade came about. All the characters in the series are drawn from their lives. See, here's Hogi the Saintly Rooster . . . Palmo the Stubborn Goat . . . Gogog the Amazing Swimming Dog . . . and Somad the Stealthy . . ." Enthusiastically, Kugy showed him one page after another.

"These kids don't know about teddy bears or Barney or Elmo. And when I told them about Snow White, Peter Pan, and Little Red Riding Hood, all I got were blank stares. But once I created something based on their own world—something they recognized—it was like something inside them suddenly came to life. Like self-confidence, or hope, or excitement . . ." Kugy stopped to catch her breath. "Like . . . a miracle."

Keenan took a deep breath as well. He realized he had also forgotten to breathe—he was so carried away by what Kugy was saying. "You're amazing," he said, his tone filled with wonder. "You're the real miracle. I can feel it—how comfortable the kids are just being themselves."

Kugy shook her head. "They're the ones who are amazing. I'm just someone passing through who's been lucky enough to witness it all. I don't know how long the Sakola Alit will last. But I'm grateful for the opportunity."

Keenan gazed into Kugy's shining eyes. And boldly, Kugy returned his clear gaze. For a long time they were silent. There was nothing but the wind rustling through the leaves. There was nothing but the insects in the trees calling out to each other. The two of them just kept gazing at each other without saying a word.

"I miss you," said Keenan finally, almost whispering.

A wave of emotion hit Kugy with such force that she felt like her chest was about to burst. She genuinely didn't know how to respond. It was as if Keenan's gaze had swept every word from her mind. At last, Kugy simply bowed her head.

"We fellow agents have to support each other," she finally managed to say. "You're going to be a professional painter soon. I heard what Wanda said at the gallery. That if you're really serious, you'll have to make time for producing more work. Then, you'll have to hold exhibitions. You'll have to go on tour. You won't have time to stand under a tree drawing pictures like you did today." Kugy tried to make her voice sound as steady as possible. "I still have a long way to go compared to you. You've already found someone who can help you achieve your dreams." The words were difficult to say, but Kugy felt compelled to speak them. "Your dreams are more important than anything else. We each have a mission. And soon, you'll have accomplished yours. We can't let our whims get in the way or we'll break down in the middle of the road." Kugy swallowed. "Remember those signs on the back of buses: if two buses belong to the same company, they shouldn't interfere with each other's routes."

Suddenly, Kugy felt her chin being tilted upward. There, again, was that heart-piercing gaze.

"I have no idea what you're talking about," Keenan said gently. "I'm grateful you're so mindful of my hopes and dreams and the chance I've been given to fulfill them. But all that aside, I miss you. You've disappeared recently."

Slowly, Kugy turned her face away, until her chin was beyond his fingers' reach. "I don't know what you're talking about. I haven't gone anywhere." She spoke softly and tried to smile. "Now you know where my headquarters are. All you have to do is look for me under this tree."

They heard footsteps approaching. It was Ami. "Hey, let's head home. It turns out Bimo's still waiting in front. The five of us can pack into his car like sardines." Ami chuckled.

"Yeah, let's go!" Kugy rose to her feet.

Keenan held her back. "Kugy and I will catch an *angkot*. You guys go ahead. That way we won't have to be sardines."

"Are you sure?" asked Ami, noticing the contrast between Keenan's certainty and Kugy's hesitation. Kugy was about to protest, but Keenan was clutching her wrist so tightly that she felt she shouldn't say anything.

"Positive," Kugy said, finally. "We'll take an *angkot*. See you, Ami!"

Once Ami was far away, Keenan loosened his grip. "To pay you back for disappearing for so long, I'm booking you for the whole day."

"Contact my manager first. Her name is Madam Noni. You're lucky it's the low season at the moment, so you'll be able to get a cheaper rate." Kugy grinned and gave Keenan's shoulder a nudge.

They spent the rest of the day hanging out. They walked to a bookstore, killed time at the zoo in Taman Sari, and had an afternoon coffee on Jalan Dago. Finally, Keenan brought Kugy back to her boarding house.

They stood in front of the white wrought-iron gate. The sky was beginning to grow dark and the lights on the front lawn turned on. They could hear the sound of the nighttime insects calling faintly to each other.

"Okay, Little One," said Keenan. "I'm heading home. Today was a lot of fun. Thanks for everything." His voice felt heavy in his ears. His feet felt heavy, too.

"As a bonus for booking me the whole day, I want to give you something to remember it by." Kugy handed him the worn-looking notebook containing the adventures of Pilik.

Keenan looked surprised. "But—"

"I've reached the end of the notebook, anyway. I have to get a new one."

"You're really giving this book to me?"

"It's the only thing I have to give you," she said.

Suddenly, she found herself in his arms. Her entire body became stiff as a board. Her eyes were wide open. *What's happening?* she thought. Then, slowly, she felt the warmth spread from Keenan's body into hers, melting her muscles, causing her eyelids to droop. The fact that she was being embraced began to seep in and she surrendered to it with all her heart.

Seconds passed. The embrace loosened. Then he let her go. Keenan smiled a little and gave Kugy's hair an awkward ruffle. "Take care of yourself, okay, Little One?" he murmured. Quickly, he turned around and left.

"You, too," Kugy murmured back. She wasn't sure if Keenan heard her or not. But she was sure he must have heard the beating of her heart when he had pulled her close to him—just as she had heard the beating of his.

———

Under the glow of his desk lamp, Keenan opened the notebook Kugy had given him. The rows of small, neat handwriting were so straight they looked like they had been typed. He read story after story and laughed. Kugy's writing made him feel as if he were sitting in a movie theater, watching the plot unfold and seeing the characters brought to life, taking on a reality of their own. Keenan couldn't stop reading.

His gaze drifted to a doodle on one of the pages. Keenan wouldn't have been able to guess what kind of creature she had tried drawing if she hadn't written "Hogi" under it. A few pages later, it seemed that Kugy had tried to draw something again—this time, a man of distorted proportions with a *peci* on his head. "Somad the Stealthy," read the caption. Keenan could imagine how much effort Kugy had put into these scribbles. He could imagine her serious expression, as if she were in the process of creating a masterpiece. He felt very moved.

Closing the book, he dragged his chair over to the blank canvas next to his desk. He had been keeping it on standby for a while, but it had remained blank. Keenan hadn't felt compelled to paint anything new since he'd come back from Amsterdam, but that night the old impulse returned—as if something was waiting for him to come and get it. What that something was, Keenan wasn't sure. He just let his hands move, allowing them to dance and sweep over the blank canvas until, gradually, something took shape.

Keenan painted and painted until morning.

CHAPTER 15

SEARCHING FOR SINCERITY

It was two in the afternoon. The boarding houses were usually quiet at this time, filling up again only later, when the students returned from campus. So Eko wasn't surprised at how desolate this one was—especially since it only had five occupants. He was more surprised that one occupant *hadn't* left the boarding house, or been seen on campus for several days.

Eko knocked and the door to Keenan's room opened. Keenan stood before him, his hair disheveled and his eyes half-closed.

"Whoa. Did you just wake up?"

"Mmph," Keenan mumbled as he went back inside and threw himself onto the bed.

"Bimo says it's been days since you've gone to class. What's up, man?"

Keenan pointed at the canvas.

"Wow. New painting?" He shook his head in amazement. "It's crazy cool."

"It's not finished yet . . ."

"This unfinished painting is crazy cool," Eko amended with a laugh. "Anyway, I'm actually here to deliver a message from Wanda. She's been trying to find you for days. She says she has some super important information for you, but she hasn't been able to reach you. She also says that it's high time you got a cell phone, and that she's coming to Bandung this afternoon for the express purpose of seeing you."

"What for?"

Eko shrugged. "It sounds like something really important. So I'll take you to buy a phone this afternoon, okay?"

"Eh," Keenan answered in a muffled voice. He'd buried his face in his pillow.

"Technophobe. A true artist to the core. This is the new millennium. It's absurd that you *don't* have a cell phone."

"Can't be bothered. Don't need one."

"Anyway, second order of business: Are you and Wanda a couple yet? Be honest."

At this, Keenan lifted his head and slowly straightened himself into a sitting position.

"Okay, okay, I'll rephrase my question: Are you interested in her? Be honest."

"Honestly, I'm more interested in . . . Wait, why are you asking me this all of a sudden?"

"Well, you've been hanging out with each other for almost five months. It's obvious you two are a good match. It's obvious she's always making an effort to spend time with you, and you couldn't ask for anyone more helpful for your career. And it's obvious that she's . . . well, Wanda! That girl's got it all! What healthy red-blooded male wouldn't drool and paw at the ground at the very sight of her?" Eko spoke with great zeal. "So?"

"So—what?" Keenan looked at him blankly.

Eko frowned. "It's time you were honest with me. Are you straight?"

Keenan chuckled. "The last time I checked, yes."

"If you're not attracted to Wanda, something's not right."

"It's not that I'm not attracted to her. I don't have a problem with Wanda at all. She's kind, she's smart, she's mature, and you're right—when it comes to art, we're a great match. And she's helped me out a lot. I'm aware of that. Is she beautiful? No doubt about it. Even a blind person would agree. But, do I want her as my girlfriend?" Keenan took a breath. "I don't know. I'm still not sure."

Eko stared at him in disbelief. "*Man!* If you're really not gay, you're a straight guy who doesn't know what's what! How many weekends has she spent in Bandung just so she can be with you? And here you are, shutting yourself up in your bear cave while she makes the effort to track you down! What are you not sure about?"

Keenan shook his head. "Dunno. It's just that there's something that doesn't feel . . . right."

Eko flung his arms above his head. "I give up. I give up! The fact is, if you really don't have any feelings for Wanda, don't leave her hanging—and don't get her hopes up. You're not being fair to her."

In the end the cousins went out to eat and didn't talk about the matter again. But when Eko went home, Keenan sat in his room, lost in thought. For the first time, he was forced to confront how he really felt about Wanda.

———

That night, Wanda worked up the courage to drive to Keenan's place alone, without Eko or Noni to guide her. She hoped the whole way that she wouldn't get lost. Finally, she arrived, smiling when she reached the front gate. She couldn't wait to share the good news.

Before she went to Keenan's room, Wanda remembered to check herself in a mirror. Tonight she was dressed all in red, with a denim miniskirt that showed off her long legs. Her makeup was still immaculate. Everything was perfect.

She knocked on the door cautiously. "Keenan? It's me, Wanda," she called out sweetly.

Seconds passed. The door opened. It was Keenan. He had just bathed and was wearing a white collared shirt. He greeted her with a wide smile. Suddenly, Wanda couldn't breathe.

"Hi, Wanda. You look beautiful," he said.

Wanda blushed. She couldn't help but smile. "You look very handsome as well."

"Red and white. Together, we're the national flag! Someone should hoist us up a flagpole." Keenan laughed. "Come in. I have a surprise for you."

Wanda giggled. "A surprise? For me?"

Instead of answering, Keenan covered Wanda's eyes and steered her toward the canvas. Only then did he take his hands away.

For a long time, Wanda didn't move. She stared at the painting, barely blinking.

"Do you like it? I just finished it."

"Keenan . . . this is it," whispered Wanda. "This is the real *you*."

"What do you mean?"

Wanda pressed her hand to her chest. Her heart was filled with awe. "Oh, gosh. Dad is going to change his tune when he sees this painting."

"Why? What did your dad say about my paintings before?"

"Oh, no. Dad likes your paintings. But he said you still have a lot of digging to do in order to unlock your potential and find your"—Wanda looked uneasy—"your signature style. Your X factor. Your true defining quality. And in my opinion, you've finally found it."

"Wait. Why didn't you tell me this before?"

Quickly, Wanda smiled and took Keenan's hand. "I have more important news for you. Ready?"

Keenan nodded.

Standing on tiptoe, she whispered in Keenan's ear, "Your paintings—the ones in our gallery—they sold out. All four of them." Wanda slipped a check into his hand, made out to him from the Warsita Gallery.

This time, Keenan was rendered speechless. He tried to comprehend what Wanda had just said, but he couldn't. Keenan repeated the words in his head. *Your paintings . . . all four of them . . . sold out.* He knew exactly what this meant. It was impossible to describe how happy he felt. The final step in realizing his dreams was now complete.

Slowly, Keenan extricated his fingers from Wanda's and gave her a heartfelt hug. "Thanks for giving me this chance," he whispered. "I don't know what to say."

Wanda leaned in, burying herself deeper in Keenan's arms. "This is more than enough," she whispered softly.

———

Keenan and Wanda decided to eat dinner at a restaurant overlooking Bandung. It was situated among the mountains and had a view of the city lights. Even though they were sitting inside the restaurant, they could still feel gusts of piercing cold wind blowing against their skin.

"You're freezing, aren't you?" Keenan asked. He had noticed Wanda rubbing her bare knees.

Wanda nodded. "Pretty much. Could I sit closer to you?"

Before he could say another word, Wanda was at his side, wrapping her arms around his waist. His body tensed. Wanda was now pressed to him like a joey in a kangaroo pouch.

"Ehm." He cleared his throat. "I was going to say, if you really are freezing, you can have my jacket."

"Never mind. This is warmer," Wanda answered as she tightened her embrace.

Keenan couldn't argue with this. But the stiffness of his posture signaled his discomfort.

Wanda was beginning to get the message. She loosened her hold. "Are you okay? Do you feel uncomfortable being seen as a couple in public?"

Keenan immediately removed Wanda's arms. "Wanda, I'm so sorry," he said, choosing his words carefully. "I don't want you to misunderstand. But I don't think we ever said we were a couple."

Wanda's expression changed and she shifted away from him. "Well, don't all romantic relationships begin with talking things out? I thought that the two of us were really . . ." Wanda faltered midsentence and her eyes filled with tears. "Have I been embarrassing myself? So you aren't attracted to me?"

"It's not that!" Keenan exclaimed. "How can I not be attracted to you? You're kind, you're thoughtful, and you've helped me so much. But do we really want to go straight into a serious relationship?"

Wanda's lips suddenly clamped shut. Her jaw clenched. "I've worked so hard for you and your paintings. Every word you're saying is breaking my heart."

Keenan moved toward her and Wanda jumped in surprise. Gazing deep into her eyes, he asked, "Have you been helping me all this time because of my paintings—or because of *me*?"

Wanda swallowed, trying hard to stop herself from trembling. "Keenan, I'm a professional," she whispered. "Your paintings are fantastic, your prospects are extraordinary—even more than you know. But all of that has nothing to do with how I feel."

Keenan's piercing gaze didn't waver. "So, how do you feel?"

Wanda summoned the courage to look him in the eyes. There was no turning back now. "I'm in love with you," she declared.

Keenan felt something stir in his heart. His gaze softened. He had been trying to plumb the depths of those eyes for a long time, looking past the colored contacts in search of something he hadn't yet found. He was looking for sincerity, and though he couldn't be absolutely certain, he felt there was something new about Wanda. Something that wasn't there before.

"So, how do *you* feel?" Wanda asked.

It was Keenan's turn to swallow.

The flickering candles bathed Kugy's face in a golden glow. The night sky, the dim lighting under the canopy in the restaurant, and the candlelight all made her look very beautiful to Josh, who had been staring at her for some time now. But her face also looked mournful. She was gazing off into the distance.

"What are you thinking about?"

Kugy was startled. But when she saw Josh's scowl, she tried to smile. "What's wrong? I daydream too much, don't I? Sorry, Josh. I've been a bit out of it."

"Is something wrong?"

"No." Kugy shook her head. "Or to be honest, I don't know. It's just that I've been feeling weird recently."

"Does it have something to do with me?"

Kugy regarded Josh for a long time before answering. "No."

"I feel like we haven't been spending enough quality time together. I really want for us to go somewhere. Maybe a vacation."

"You mean to Singapore?" Kugy looked puzzled. "I told you I don't want to go."

"No. We don't have to go all the way to Singapore. But what about Bali?"

"Just the two of us?"

"We can go with friends. The Jakarta crowd would love to come along. One thing's for sure: we can really relax over there, have fun—"

"I don't have the money," Kugy said. "I have my savings, but I can't spend it on a vacation. I'm saving up to buy a laptop."

Suddenly, Josh placed something on the table. Kugy squinted. Two plane tickets.

"You bought me a ticket?"

"Now you have no excuse," declared Josh, before breaking into a smile.

"When are we leaving?"

"At the beginning of next month. We'll take off on Friday, come home on Sunday. I'll drive you back from Jakarta. The point is, everything's taken care of. All you have to do is bring a bag and yourself."

Kugy took a deep breath. She saw Josh's hopeful expression.

Not giving up, Josh picked up the tickets and held them to his forehead. He looked at her pitifully, like a puppy dog who'd lost its mother. "Please? Woof, woof . . ."

Kugy laughed—and nodded.

———

It was almost midnight by the time the black sedan pulled into the hotel parking lot in Ciumbuleuit, where Wanda was staying. Keenan accompanied her into the lobby. The flames in the fireplace were beginning to burn low. No one else was there and the sofas were empty. The grand piano, whose tinkling music had been playing all night, was now locked shut.

"You can go up to your room," said Keenan. "I'll wait here. My taxi will arrive soon."

Wanda shook her head. "I'd rather freeze here than lose a moment with you."

"Next time, remember this is Bandung. It's colder in the mountains than it is in Jakarta. The only people who should be wearing a miniskirt on a night like this are the ladyboys on Jalan Veteran—they're tough and know how to stand the cold."

"Oh, you. You're so unromantic," Wanda complained with a playful pout.

Keenan chuckled. "I'm just reminding you. Next time you should wear long pants. And bring a jacket or a sweater."

"When will next time be?" Wanda asked flirtatiously.

Keenan pretended to think. His expression was mischievous. "Hmm. Next Saturday night?"

Wanda beamed. She moved closer and draped her arms around Keenan's neck. "So, we're a couple?"

Keenan gave her a small smile. Gently, he pulled her arms away and gave her fingers a slow kiss. "We'll take it slow, okay?"

Though the fireplace was several yards away, Wanda's eyes shone brightly. The coldness of the night vanished as happiness spread through her whole body, filling her with warmth.

Keenan's taxi pulled up in front of the lobby. He was just about to turn and leave when Wanda grabbed his hand.

"You know what?" Wanda said softly. "You don't have to go back to your boarding house tonight. You can stay here with me."

Keenan smiled, then kissed her forehead gently. "Slowly, Wanda."

Soon afterward, the taxi pulled away from the hotel. Wanda was still standing in the same place, motionless. She was so happy she felt as if she were going to shoot through the roof. Suddenly she remembered something. Noni. She had to call Noni. Right away.

CHAPTER 16
FALSE HOPES

Kugy reached into her pocket, drew out a small key, and unlocked the boarding house gate. She had anticipated how late she would return and had offered to lock the gate for the night so no one would have to wait up.

The rooms down the length of the corridor were already dark, and the blinds in the windows, which looked out into the hallway, were already drawn. But she saw the light on in Noni's room. And she heard Noni's distinctive high-pitched voice speaking to someone and shrieking excitedly.

She was just about to open the door to her room when Noni emerged. Her friend's eyes were wide and alert, as if she'd just eaten some spicy *rujak*. "Kugy! Guess what just happened? This very night? Oh gosh, I shouldn't make so much noise, should I? But I can't help myself!"

"Do you need to pee or something?" asked Kugy, watching Noni bob up and down.

"No, silly. I just got off the phone with Wanda. Oh, I'm so happy." Noni laughed. "Wanda and Keenan are officially going out. I don't know the details, but Wanda finally asked Keenan where they stood. I know, right? Guys these days. They make everything so hard. Tell me, why didn't Keenan take the lead? He really is a strange creature—like you. Can't guess what he's thinking." At this point, Noni took a much-needed breath.

Kugy felt a bitter taste in her mouth. Her heart raced as she waited for Noni to continue.

"So, Wanda asks Keenan what's going on, right? And then, get this. Keenan says, 'It's impossible for me not to be attracted to you.' I know, right? Keenan is so cute! I got goosebumps just hearing about it. And *then* they go back to the lobby of Wanda's hotel. Can you believe it? How romantic!" Noni pressed her hands to her cheeks. "A fireplace! With nobody else around! Just the two of them! Oh boy, Eko's in trouble! He's never taken me anywhere like that. The only place we go is the Hunger No Longer."

"Then what?" Kugy demanded.

"They're a couple," said Noni happily. "Ta-da! The project was a success! I was born to matchmake!" She did a little dance.

Kugy felt a small part of her evaporate into nothingness. "Then what?"

"Aren't you going to congratulate me or something?" Noni asked.

"Congrats. You're the Matchmaker of the Millennium. But what happened next?"

"Use your imagination. In a romantic place like that, complete with fireplace, the two of them alone and in love. What more is there to ask?" Noni looked irritated. The coldness of Kugy's response surprised her. "You're not excited? This was our project after all."

Kugy shook her head. "This was yours and Eko's project, remember? But yeah, I'm happy for you, I guess." She spoke curtly. "I'm going to bed. I'm beat. Nite-nite." Without waiting for any further reaction from Noni, Kugy went into her room and closed the door.

She didn't even have the energy to turn on the light. She stood in the dark, motionless. The afternoon at the Warsita Gallery passed through her mind—when she and Keenan had been watching Wanda from afar. *If I were a guy, I'd be stupid not to like Wanda,* she'd murmured. *There are stupid guys,* he'd murmured back.

Kugy shook her head. She must have misheard him. That, or she'd been mistaken. The afternoon beneath the banyan tree near the chili field passed through her mind—when Keenan had told her he missed her. She remembered how he had looked at her. Then Kugy shook her head. Her eyes must have deceived her. Or again, she'd been mistaken. Then that evening outside the gate passed through her mind—when he had embraced her, their hearts beating together as one. Kugy shook her head. She must have been wrong. All this time she'd been wrong.

Finally her memory came to rest on the words Keenan had whispered, which she had treasured and thought about almost every night. The words, which refreshed her heart without fail: *This moon. This journey. Us.* Kugy shook her head again. That same moon was in the night sky now, but how different she felt. Just thinking about it made her eyes burn. Kugy wiped the wetness from her eyes. Once. Twice. But however many times she wiped them away, the tears wouldn't stop flowing.

July 2000

The color screen on Wanda's cell phone lit up. Her face brightened, like the sun at high noon. The door to her room had been ajar, but she closed it hastily. She wanted to enjoy this call without being disturbed.

"Hey, babe. Whatcha doing? I miss you already. I'm in my room, daydreaming. Why don't you come over?" Wanda laughed lightly. "Just kidding, sweetie. Stay in Bandung and work hard on your paintings. I want to arrange an exhibition for you soon."

Keenan laughed as well. "That's exactly why I called!"

Wanda's laughter faded. "So, you're only calling me on business?"

Keenan laughed again. "Don't be so sensitive. Just think of it as me being professional."

"Fine," she snapped. "What do you want to talk about?"

"I've been thinking about what you said—about my latest painting having a different quality to it. I feel the same way. I just want to get your opinion. What if I made a series of paintings around the same theme?"

"Good idea." Her tone was curt.

"I have a completely new perspective on things since knowing my work has sold so well. I feel confident that this is the right path to take."

Wanda sat up straight. "What path are you talking about?"

"I just want to paint. I think it's time to consider becoming completely financially independent. Once this semester is over, I'm going to talk to Dad about discontinuing my studies."

"Keenan, do you know what that means?" asked Wanda. Now her tone was serious. "You'll have to depend entirely on proceeds from selling your paintings. You can't just fool around."

"I'm not fooling around," Keenan insisted.

"And I'm not fooling around about your exhibition," continued Wanda. "You have to produce around twenty paintings, thirty if possible."

The very thought of an exhibition sent adrenaline pumping through Keenan's veins. His excitement mounted. "All right. I can do that," he answered decisively.

"I'll give you six months. And for your sake, I'll extend the break I'm taking from my own studies for another semester."

She could hear Keenan let out a long breath.

"Wanda, you've already done so much to help me. Sometimes, I feel guilty—"

"This is how I am," Wanda said. "When I love someone and believe in them, I won't do things by halves. I'm not asking for anything. Just . . . love me. Okay?"

There was silence on the other end.

"Keenan?" Wanda asked. "Don't you have anything to say?"

"Sorry," he answered finally. "I'm at a loss for words, that's all."

"It's okay. I've grown used to it. You probably only know how to express yourself when you're standing in front of a canvas. Not when you're talking to me." Wanda said this with some sarcasm.

More silence on the other end.

Wanda sighed. "All right, it seems I'm making you uncomfortable. We'll just talk about something else."

Before long, their conversation was flowing as smoothly as before. And although the call ended on a sweet note, Wanda felt irritated. Keenan's attitude was beginning to bother her, especially when their conversation touched on the matter of feelings. It was as if Keenan considered the words "love" and "sweetie" taboo. From the moment they began spending time together to when they officially became a couple, Keenan had never openly expressed his feelings to her—not even once.

Wanda's cell phone rang again. "What's up, Virna? Oh, sorry, I'm just in a bad mood. What? Come on, now you're just making my mood even worse."

"I'm so sorry," said Virna. "But I really don't have any place to put your painting. Pasha has the same problem, actually. He just feels bad about telling you. Neither of us can store them for you, hon."

Wanda sighed. "You really can't keep it? Just put it in your bedroom. Or just hang it in the bathroom."

"What do you think it is, a poster? It's too big. Plus, my mother controls what goes on our walls. She's not hot on modern art. You know her taste: oil paintings of horses and carp, portraits of my grandparents." Virna sounded defensive. "There's really no space at your place? Your house is humungous."

"It's not that. The problem is—" Wanda stopped. It was best to keep this matter to herself. "Fine. It's okay. I'll send someone over to pick it up—the one at Pasha's place, too."

After she hung up, Wanda roamed her house looking for a safe hiding place. Her search ended in her own room, underneath the bed.

———

The trio gathered in the shelter where Ami usually taught. Ami looked as if she was about to cry. She had been waiting all day to tell them the news.

"Kugy, Ical, I have an announcement to make." She took a deep breath. "The Sakola Alit has been permitted to participate in the elementary school competition for the district."

Kugy and Ical jumped for joy. Ical even ran around the shelter, screaming. Not one to lose out, Kugy followed behind him.

"I know we've been permitted to join because they want to be nice, or they feel sorry for us, or because they don't think we stand a chance of winning." Ami chuckled. "But that doesn't bother me. It's not about winning or losing. If our kids get to participate and meet contestants from other schools, it'll inspire them and help them take school seriously. They've never done anything like this. We'll be entering the contests for poetry reading, Sundanese poetry singing, and writing. Today I'll finalize which students will be representing us."

"We're ready to rumble!" Kugy yelled. "When's the competition? And where is it?"

"Next Saturday. In Lalu Lintas Park."

Kugy clapped her hands. "Fantastic! They can play in the park at the same time. They'll be so happy." A few seconds later, her expression changed. She had just remembered something. "Wait, did you say next Saturday?"

"Yeah, why?"

"I-I promised to go out of town with someone."

Ami bit her lip. "Oh dear. It'll be hard for the two of us to manage without you. It's not just about chaperoning. If the kids know you're not going, they won't be excited. You're their role model."

Kugy thought hard. "Give me until Monday. I'll try my best to come."

"Please try, okay? We have to start preparing the kids." Ami sounded hopeful.

Kugy glanced at her watch. Josh was already on his way to Bandung. If she told him to cancel their trip to Bali, who knew what would happen tonight.

———

Keenan surveyed his work. The subjects of the painting were eleven small children. Ten of them were marching in a crooked line and one child was in front leading them, a rice paddy hat on his head. On the back of the canvas, Keenan had written its title: *General Pilik and the Alit Brigade*.

Keenan examined his handiwork. *It's not just a matter of technique,* he thought. There was something about the painting's content that made it stand out from all his other ones. It gave him goosebumps. It set something ablaze in his soul.

He stepped back, surveying it again. *Life,* he finally concluded in his heart. The painting possessed such energy. It radiated life with such strength and poignancy.

Then his gaze fell upon something on his desk—the battered-looking notebook Kugy had given him a month ago. Keenan remembered what he had said—that the notebook was a treasure that Kugy should keep. He would never have guessed that he was the one who would discover the treasure hidden within. Kugy had bequeathed him something of great value—greater than anything either of them could have anticipated.

CHAPTER 17

JUST THREE WORDS

Even the comedy they had just watched couldn't lift Kugy's spirits. That entire night—from the moment they set out, all through dinner, to the rolling of the film credits—Kugy had remained in a state of apprehension, constantly on the lookout for the right moment to tell Josh about her dilemma.

Suddenly she heard someone calling her name. "Kugy!"

Kugy turned. It was Eko's ticket agent, Mr. Itok. He waved and laughed. Kugy waved back.

"Where have you been? You don't come to the midnight showings with the rest of the crew anymore? It's mostly just Eko and Noni these days."

"We've taken up a new hobby," said Kugy uncomfortably, just for the sake of saying something. "Now we play dominoes together."

"You should invite me!" Mr. Itok guffawed. "I thought it was because you and Keenan broke it off. Is this your new boyfriend?"

Josh and Kugy stiffened. "Oh no. He's an old edition. See you later!" Hastily ending the conversation, Kugy took Josh's hand and left.

The whole way back, Josh looked sullen. He didn't utter a word until he pulled the car up in front of Kugy's boarding house. "Is there something you haven't told me that I should know?" he asked.

"About what?" Kugy asked cautiously.

"That Mr. Itok may be the world's biggest gossip, but I'm sure he had a reason for saying what he did. There's really nothing going on between you and Keenan?"

Kugy was quiet for a moment. "No, nothing," she stated simply.

"I may be the world's most jealous boyfriend, but my radar is never wrong. Enough already. You like him, don't you? And he likes you?"

Kugy felt as if her heart were shriveling. Whenever Josh spoke to her in this tone, it meant he was really mad. "Josh, Keenan already has a girlfriend, and I already have you. We're just friends. No more, no less."

"Liking someone is still liking someone," Josh stated. "It doesn't have anything to do with having boyfriends or girlfriends."

"I can't go with you to Bali," Kugy blurted. Even she was surprised at the words that tumbled out of her mouth.

"*What?*" Josh exclaimed.

"The Sakola Alit is participating in a district-wide competition next Saturday for poetry and writing. It won't happen if I'm not there. I know you already bought the tickets and organized everything, but I really can't go. We can take a vacation some other time—"

"I'm not sure if there will be some other time," he said, raising his voice.

Kugy fell silent. There were so many thoughts swirling around in her head, but her tongue felt too dry to speak.

Josh took a deep breath. "I'm tired of always coming last in your life. Ever since you moved to Bandung, I've felt more and more neglected. It's like you're in your own world. Like I'm the only one making an effort."

Kugy's eyes began to feel hot, and her chest tightened.

"I've been trying to keep up with you ever since we started dating. I've tried to be a part of your world, but you don't just run away, you fly. And you forget—I live on Earth, Kugy. My feet are still on the ground. How can we go on together if we don't even share the same reality?"

One by one, tears began to run down Kugy's cheeks. She still couldn't speak.

"Do you like Keenan? Are you in love with him?"

The tears began to fall faster. She shook her head slowly. "How I feel about Keenan doesn't matter. I love you so much . . ."

"This isn't just about Keenan. It's about where I stand as a priority in your life. Now let's just make everything simple. Leave next Friday with me or stay in Bandung. What do you choose?" Josh spoke matter-of-factly. Even so, she heard the note of hurt in his tone, the tremor in his voice.

"But I really can't go. That Saturday I have to . . . Can't we go another day—"

"See how simple that was?" Josh's tone was bitter.

Kugy said nothing, only sobbed.

"Go with me on Friday or everything ends right here," Josh declared.

"Why do you have to give ultimatums like this?" she shouted help-lessly. "Why can't we just postpone it? You're not giving me a choice, Josh. You're cornering me!"

Josh gazed deep into his girlfriend's eyes, then said slowly, "If you really loved me, we wouldn't need to have this conversation. You would know your answer already."

They were silent again, but the air was filled with so much emotion, so many feelings.

Josh leaned over and opened Kugy's door. He said in a low voice, "I'll be waiting for you at the airport on Friday afternoon. Our flight takes off at three. If you're not there, it means everything is over."

Before getting out of the car, Kugy gave Josh one last look through her tears. All the memories they had shared over the past three years flashed before her. Kugy ran inside and burst into her room. Unable to stand the tightness in her chest any longer, she cried her heart out. She had made her decision. And she mourned the loss to come.

———

The two couples decided to spend their Saturday night at Keenan's boarding house. Two boxes of *martabak* pancake—one savory and eggy, one sweet and buttery, both nearly demolished—sat in the center of the group. Noni and Wanda were deep in discussion. Noni was celebrating her twentieth birthday at Wanda's house in Jakarta in September. The house, situated in Kebayoran Baru, had a large lawn, and was perfect for the garden party theme Noni had in mind. Because it was going to be a fairly big event, Noni was preparing far in advance, assisted by Wanda, who had a reputation as an experienced party planner.

Wanda busily jotted down notes, then handed them to Noni.

"Damn, you're such a pro!" Noni read Wanda's notes in amazement.

"Planning events like this is just par for the course for me. I coordinate almost all the events for Warsita. No need to hire an event planner." Wanda beamed. "If there's anything else you want to add, just let me know and I'll arrange everything."

Eko was sitting with his legs stretched out in front of him, strumming his guitar. "Who knew?" he chimed in. "Wanda's a regular foreman! Talk about taking charge. She's even starting to look the part."

"*Excuse me?*" Wanda's eyes almost popped out of her head. "And what do you mean by that?"

Eko's guitar playing slowed. He realized he had just struck Wanda's most sensitive chord—her appearance. But before he could check his mischievous tongue, he continued, "Well, I've noticed you've gotten more relaxed about your appearance. You used to be the Queen of

Coordination." Eko snickered. "Now you never wear nail polish, and all your clothes are too big. They used to be too small." He chuckled. "Where'd you get that huge shirt?"

"It's Keenan's."

"And the jacket you were wearing just now?"

"Keenan's."

Noni couldn't help giggling. "Eko's right. To be honest, I've wanted to say something for a while. You're dressing more and more like Kugy. And no wonder. You've adopted the same strategy—you're borrowing other people's clothes."

Wanda's expression underwent a dramatic change—especially when Eko burst into laughter at what Noni had said.

"Actually," said Keenan, quickly trying to neutralize the situation, "I told Wanda that she should wear more practical clothing when she's in Bandung. It gets cold here."

"Ha! There's a big difference between dressing practically and dressing à la Kugy. If you ask me, it looks like a case of the latter." Eko resumed laughing.

Wanda's face reddened. Though she tried to join in the laughter, her mood was already ruined beyond repair. Then Eko and Noni departed, leaving Keenan to deal with the sticky situation by himself.

"Eko is so annoying!" ranted Wanda. "As if he understands anything about fashion! As if he's the only who knows how to wear clothes! Noni, too—comparing me to Kugy! Do I really look that bad?"

Keenan offered no comment and allowed Wanda to vent. He decided to open his sketchbook and absorb himself in doodling. This would enable him to be both a good listener and a good dumping ground for her feelings. But as Wanda continued, it became clear she didn't want to stop.

"I only wear your clothes every once in a while, and even then, only when I have to. Kugy on the other hand has made bad fashion her trademark!" She pouted angrily. "Do you remember when Kugy came to the gallery? Would I ever wear something like that? Ugh. As if."

"Why are you getting so worked up about this?" Keenan finally asked, raising his head. Wanda had been complaining for nearly an hour now.

Wanda paused. "It's just irritating, that's all. How dare they compare me to Kugy. Kugy's such a disaster—"

"If you ask me, she looks just fine," Keenan said firmly. "If you ask me, you look fine, too. If you want to be the Queen of Coordination, go ahead. If not, that's okay, too. It doesn't matter to me."

"But Kugy—"

"What is it with you and Kugy?" Keenan asked, raising his voice.

"What is it with *you* and Kugy?" Wanda shot back.

Keenan's brow furrowed.

"I saw the title of your new painting. Alit is the name of the school where Kugy teaches, isn't it? Is she your inspiration now? That girl must really be something else for you to make a whole painting for her."

Keenan took a deep breath. "Yes, it's true. I based the painting on stories Kugy wrote for the kids at the school. So what?"

"I may be spoiled, Keenan, but I'm not stupid. I'm not blind. I've seen the way you look at her. The clothes you tell me to wear, and now that painting. You have feelings for her, don't you?"

Keenan was quiet.

"Don't you?" Wanda pressed.

"Wanda, this is pointless. You're just jealous—"

"You're damn right I am!" she declared. "And I should be jealous. Do you really think I don't know you're trying to turn me into her? Well, it's never going to happen! Because I'm not her, and I don't ever want to be her!" Her chest was heaving with emotion.

Keenan studied Wanda for a long time. "Wanda, you're free to believe whatever you want," he said evenly. "If that's what you think, so be it. I can't change what you think. I can't make you trust me. Only you can change those things."

"Bullshit," hissed Wanda.

Keenan rose to his feet. "Do you want me to take you home?"

He tried to touch her shoulder, but Wanda brushed it away. "There is something you can do to make me trust you." Wanda gazed straight at him. "Look at me and say you love me."

Keenan was startled at Wanda's demand, but it was too late—they had already locked eyes.

"It's so simple," Wanda whispered. "I just want to hear you say those three words." They were only a few inches apart. Her searching gaze penetrated to the innermost depths of his heart.

She saw Keenan's mouth open, the muscles of his face tensing as if he were about speak, but seconds passed and not one word came out—just the sound of his ragged breath.

Wanda bit her trembling lip as she tried not to cry. Then she grabbed her purse and ran for the door.

As quick as lightning, Keenan caught her hand. "Wanda, don't go. I'm begging you. I'm sorry."

Wanda was sobbing. "'Sorry'?" she shrieked. "Damn it, Keenan! I don't need you to say sorry. I just want you to love me. Why can't you just love me?"

All Keenan could do was pull Wanda toward him, hold her as she struggled, and submit to her flurry of weak punches—until at last she gave up and fell into his arms, weeping uncontrollably.

It was the first time Keenan had ever felt so moved. His guilt was so overpowering he felt as if it were filling every nook and cranny in his body, penetrating even his bones, and he felt like he was about to burst. But even more heartrending was that, despite his overpowering guilt, Keenan still could not force his lips to speak. He tightened his embrace and stroked her hair—and in this way, he tried to stop her sobbing. He kept hoping to himself that this would be enough.

CHAPTER 18

DEPARTURE AND LOSS

August 2000

Kugy could hear footsteps in the corridor. They got closer and closer, until they finally came to a stop in front of her room. Someone rapped on her door.

"Come in," said Kugy, her eyes still fixed on her computer screen.

Noni burst in with a panicked expression. "You broke up with Josh?"

Kugy looked at Noni without saying a word, then gave a small nod.

"Why? How? I just got off the phone with him. He's so upset. Why didn't you tell me? What happened? What's wrong?" Noni fired off her questions in quick succession.

Kugy had no idea how to respond. She just shrugged. "Maybe it was just time," she said simply.

"What kind of an answer is that? Why aren't you being open with me? I love you both. You know that. I'm upset, too, you know." Noni sounded disappointed. "You're a phenomenal pair. Everyone is so jealous of you. You're such a good match."

Kugy smiled bitterly. "Oh please. Josh and I were worlds apart. Our relationship was a time bomb waiting to explode."

Noni's expression grew serious. "You're my friend. You'll always have my support. But to be frank, I've seen a big change in you. It's like you're pulling away on purpose. Josh felt it, too, and he spoke to me about it a long time ago. He thought something wasn't right." Noni paused. "I didn't want to say anything, but to be honest, we all miss the old Kugy."

Kugy thought hard, trying to piece together an explanation, but all she could come up with was a tangled ball of yarn. She didn't know where to start. Everything was muddled. "Thanks for your concern," Kugy said finally, "but really, I'm fine. I don't know what 'old Kugy' you're talking about, but this is me. If I really have changed, well then, take me as I am—the same way I take you, Eko, Josh, and Keenan as you are. That's what friends do."

The look of protest on Noni's face was plain, but Kugy's words seemed to silence her. "Whatever you say," she said coldly, and closed the door behind her.

Kugy sat in front of her computer lost in thought. She caught a glimpse of her reflection in the mirror. She understood what Noni had meant when she said they missed her. She felt the loss as keenly as her friends did. But Kugy didn't know where she should look to find herself. It was all too bewildering.

———

The atmosphere in the room was unbearable. Keenan and his father sat facing each other at the dining table, but there was no food in front of them. Between them sat Keenan's mother, watching the fight intently, like a referee at a boxing match. Meanwhile, Jeroen had shut himself in his room. He hated hearing people argue.

"This is why I never approved of sending him to Amsterdam!" Keenan's father shouted. "This is why! Lena, look at your son. Who does he think he is? He dares to ask if he can withdraw from school just because he's sold a few paintings. He doesn't consider how I, his father, have nearly worked myself to the bone to pay for his education." He turned to Keenan again. "Bring me a calculator! Let's work out how much money has been spent on you. Can you pay back all your school fees with the check you got from the gallery? Come on! Let's work it out!"

Keenan looked like he was about to explode. But he controlled himself, clenching his jaw. "This isn't about money, Dad," he said with restraint. "I'll never be able to repay you for everything you've given me. But I really can't bear to pretend that I like being at university any longer. I can't bear to continue doing what I don't like when my heart lies elsewhere."

"What is wrong with you? You managed to get the highest GPA in your class without even trying! Why is it so hard for you to continue your studies?"

Keenan spoke slowly. "I don't belong in that world, Dad. That's not the path I want my life to take."

Adri snorted and shook his head. "What do you know about life? You're not even twenty years old. You don't know anything!"

Keenan answered bitterly, "I know that the life I've been leading is the life you want for me, not what I want for myself. I'm withdrawing from university. Starting next semester, I won't burden you any longer. I'll find a way to make money and support myself."

"Keenan!" Lena exclaimed. "*Let op je woorden! Ga niet te ver.* Watch what you're saying."

Adri stood up. He stared at his son in disbelief. "Don't think I'm impressed by your efforts to be financially independent. You don't know what you're up against out there—"

"I'm sorry," Keenan said firmly. "I don't want to hurt you or Mom with my decision, but I can't go on like this any longer."

Lena was about to speak, but her husband held up his hand to stop her. "Okay. If that's what you really want, go ahead." Adri's voice was fierce, decisive. "From this moment on, I withdraw my financial support. By all means, experience what life is really like. Manage your own affairs. But I don't want to know anything about them."

Lena couldn't control herself any longer. "Adri! Don't you do anything rash, either. We can discuss this later—"

Keenan also stood up. "Enough, Mom," he said calmly. "*Het is goed zo*—if that's how it is, then fine. This *is* what I want. I'll pack up now and head back to Bandung."

"Yes. Let him go," Adri answered.

"You two!" Lena protested. "You're exactly the same—hard-headed and full of pride! Come, let's sit back down. This isn't the way to resolve this problem. There must be a better solution."

But neither Keenan nor his father sat back down. They continued standing where they were, glaring at each other.

"*Laat maar gaan*, Lena. We'll see who returns to our doorstep, begging for forgiveness and swallowing his words." Adri's tone was frigid.

Keenan smiled darkly. "Yes. We'll see."

———

When he returned to Bandung, Keenan didn't delay in carrying out his plans. He was aware he was turning his life upside down, and his emotions were a mixture of excitement and fear. But he knew there was no going back.

For the entire semester break, Keenan bustled about, seeing to the paperwork necessary for his withdrawal. Then with Bimo's help, Keenan moved to a much smaller boarding house in an alley in Sekeloa, where rent was several times cheaper.

Keenan didn't touch the check from the Warsita Gallery. He was determined to cash it only if his circumstances became dire, and was relying entirely on what he had left of his personal savings. As a result, he knew that he couldn't live as he did before.

Bimo set the last box down on the floor. The small room felt too cramped to hold even the two of them. Bimo hastily opened the door to let in some fresh air.

"You're the craziest person I know," he said, shaking his head. "I'm not sure whether you're stubborn or stupid. But I salute your courage."

Keenan grinned and wiped the sweat from his forehead. "I don't know whether I'm crazy or not myself. But what I do know is I feel like this is the best thing I've ever done."

"You're definitely out of your mind. The highest GPA two semesters in a row, and you drop out! Pass on your knowledge, man! Take pity on a guy like me. My GPA's in the 1.0s."

"Relax. As long as I'm in Bandung, I'll always be able to help you out. You know where to find me." Keenan smiled.

"Does anyone else know you're living here?"

"Only you."

"Eko?"

Keenan shook his head.

Bimo took this as a sign that he shouldn't tell anyone else Keenan had moved. A lot of questions came to mind, but he felt it was better to ask them some other time. "Our class has lost its specter," Bimo sighed as he clapped Keenan on the shoulder.

"Who knows? Now that I don't have to be a university student, maybe I'll roam the campus in some other form. A tiger, maybe."

"Please don't. The freshman girls will be here soon, and I don't want to have to compete with you." Bimo laughed again before heading out.

Once Bimo was gone, Keenan sat in his new room lost in thought. It was located in the attic. Clotheslines hung with laundry crisscrossed in front of his window. This would be his view every day. Cats sunning themselves on the neighboring roofs would be his constant companions. And he would have to breathe this warm, stuffy air for who knew how long. He didn't have many belongings, but their presence made the small room feel even more cramped. Still, for the first time since he had returned to Indonesia, Keenan felt free.

———

Kugy had decided to enroll in courses over the semester break. At times she admitted to herself that the decision had not been for purely academic reasons. Rather it was an attempt to run away from the circumstances she found so uncomfortable and oppressive. Better to immerse herself in her studies and a growing pile of tasks than deal with Noni, who was now keeping her distance; Eko, who'd felt obliged to stick with his girlfriend; and Keenan, who had vanished without a trace—not to mention the lingering guilt she felt about Josh.

After returning from classes and teaching at the Sakola Alit in the afternoon, Kugy couldn't wait to collapse onto her bed. But her quick pace changed into a slow tiptoe when she saw Fuad parked outside her boarding house. As carefully as possible, Kugy slipped in and headed to her room.

Just as Kugy was about to turn the handle and enter her room, Eko popped out from behind Noni's door. "Hey, you. You've been gone for ages."

Kugy felt obliged to be pleasant. "You're the one who's been gone," she said with a wide grin. "I've been here this whole time."

"Oh really? So why is it that every time I come over, you're never around? Every time I invite you out, you never want to come? Word on the street is you're taking courses over the break. In a hurry to graduate so you can abandon us, huh?" Eko stepped out of Noni's room and shook his head. "Liar. Where've you been? We miss you, you know."

"I miss you, too. But I've been really busy lately." It was true. Never mind hanging out with Eko or any of her other friends—she rarely even had time for a nap.

"I get that you're busy. But make the time to come next week, okay?"

"Come where?" Kugy asked.

"Noni's birthday. You didn't know?" Eko looked at her in dismay. "She wants to throw a party in Jakarta. It's going to be huge. Actually, we're driving there later this afternoon. She wants to get everything ready."

Noni poked her head out. Her expression changed when she realized who Eko was talking to. "Hey," she said reluctantly. "Did you just get home?"

"Hi," Kugy responded, half-mumbling.

Eko looked at Noni, then at Kugy. "I think you two need to talk. I'll just wait out front, okay?" Then, ignoring the stares they were giving him, he strolled away.

"I heard you're having a party next week," Kugy said stiffly. "Cool."

"Yeah, hopefully. All my friends know about it. A bunch of people in Jakarta already said they'll come. Some people here in Bandung said they'll come as well." Noni spoke deliberately—pointing out that Kugy, ironically, was the last to know.

Kugy was well aware of the deeper meaning behind Noni's tone. "I'm sorry. I know our last conversation didn't go well. I hate how we've been acting so cold to each other. I'm so sorry, Noni. Really I am. I've been insensitive and inconsiderate to you and Eko."

Noni lifted her head and looked at Kugy, and she knew she loved the strange creature standing before her too much to stay angry for long.

"It's okay," said Noni. "I'm sorry, too, for interfering with you and Josh. I'm sure you had your reasons, and I didn't have the right to meddle. Whatever the case, you're still my friend." A hint of a smile appeared on her face. "But can I make one request?"

"Anything," Kugy answered, smiling.

"Come to my birthday party next week, okay? You're my oldest friend. We've known each other since we were kids, and now we're approaching our twenties. It'll mean so much to me if you could come. Please?"

"I'll be there," declared Kugy.

Noni gave her a hug. "You monkey. Don't disappear on me again," she whispered.

"I won't. Except when I go looking for bananas," Kugy whispered back.

Noni laughed. "I'm off to Jakarta. I'll see you next week at Wanda's house, okay?"

Kugy swallowed. Her heart shrunk a few inches. "Wanda's house?"

"I'm having a garden party and borrowing Wanda's backyard," said Noni cheerfully. "It's huge as hell. Everything's going to be awesome. Wanda's organizing it. All you have to do is show up and have fun, okay? Gotta go! See you next week!"

Kugy watched as Noni happily scurried away, following her friend's retreating figure until it disappeared behind the front gate. Now that she knew where the party was being held, she felt a new weight pressing down on her shoulders. She imagined what the party would be like and envisioned a variety of painful scenarios. Dragging her feet, Kugy returned to her room more exhausted than before.

CHAPTER 19

THE DISASTROUS PARTY

Wanda almost fainted when she entered Keenan's new boarding house. Luckily, she summoned the strength to make it to Keenan's room. She sat down on the thin mattress.

"What are you doing in a place like this? I admire your courage in withdrawing from school for the sake of your art. But this? This is extreme! Why don't you just come to Jakarta? I can find you a place." Wanda wiped her face with a tissue. Bandung may have been cooler than Jakarta, but Keenan's room was on the top floor—the roasting it received from the midday sun made it hot and stuffy.

"I'm better off in Bandung. The cost of living is cheaper here. And I can concentrate on painting without too many distractions." As Keenan spoke, he opened the door and window to let in some air.

"How can you paint anything in a crummy place like this?" protested Wanda, fanning her face. "My family has a mountain villa in Puncak. If you want to stay there and paint I could ask Dad. I'm sure he'd let you. It's closer to Jakarta, too. How about it?"

"Nah. It's nice enough here at night. You can see the open sky from out there." Keenan gestured to the window and smiled. "Want to see?"

Wanda turned away. "How long are you going to stay here?"

Keenan shrugged. "Dunno. But one thing's for sure—once I make enough money from selling my artwork, I'll definitely find a better place to live. But I can't think about that now. What's important is preparing for the exhibition and painting as much as possible."

"So, just because you paint poor kids, you feel you have to live like them, too?" Wanda snapped. "Is that it?" She crossed her arms.

Keenan clenched his jaw and summoned all his patience. "I can take you back to the hotel if you're uncomfortable here. Tomorrow, we'll meet up and leave for Jakarta together, okay?"

"Where will you stay in Jakarta, since you can't go back home? I'll book a hotel room, okay? I can keep you company."

"You don't have to. I'll stay with Bimo."

Wanda rose to her feet. "Fine. Up to you," she said curtly. "Don't get up. I can go back to the hotel myself. I'll see you tomorrow."

Keenan knew Wanda was sulking, but he decided not to say anything. He let her go.

Just as she was about to leave the room, Wanda turned around. Her face was flushed—partly because she was too hot and partly because she was annoyed. "You know what? I can't count how many guys would kill to be this close to me, to get 10 percent of the attention I give you. Maybe Eko and Noni are right. You're so . . . weird!" Then she spun around and stalked away.

"Wanda, be careful . . ."

He heard the sound of someone's head hitting wood.

Keenan winced. "The ceiling above the stairs is very low. You have to duck—"

But Wanda didn't want to hear any more. He could hear her heels clicking swiftly away down the stairs. Her disgust at his new home was now complete.

At long last, Kugy could take a break. Although it was only for one day, she tried to make the most of her free time. After spending the whole day at an Internet café, Kugy went to the supermarket. She had almost run out of food. Singing softly to herself, she carried her shopping basket to the drink section to stock up on her favorite fruit juice.

To her surprise, she saw Wanda there reaching for the same juice. Kugy hurried away, but she sensed Wanda walking in the same direction right behind her. She prayed Wanda wouldn't recognize her.

Kugy reached the housewares section and found herself cornered. There was no avoiding it—Wanda was headed straight for her. Kugy snatched a broom and hid her face behind the black bristles. She could hear the steps coming closer. This couldn't be happening. It was all a bad dream.

She heard a voice. "Kugy?" It was both a greeting and a question.

Kugy had no choice but to lower the broom. She mustered up the heartiest laugh she could manage. "Wanda! Are you looking for a broom, too?"

"No. I was just passing through." Wanda smiled sweetly. "That's a big broom. Planning to sweep the streets with it?"

"No, planning to fly with it," Kugy answered with an even sweeter smile. "When did you arrive in Bandung?"

"I'm heading home to Jakarta in a little while with Keenan. I'm just shopping for him. Poor thing, he works so late, and never has any food." Wanda pointed to her basket, which was almost overflowing.

"If you're getting that much food for him, he'll definitely need a hand. I'd be happy to help him finish it." Kugy chuckled.

Wanda frowned in surprise. "So you know where he lives now?"

"He's no longer at his boarding house?" It was Kugy's turn to be surprised.

The sweet smile returned to Wanda's face. "Don't you know? Keenan's withdrawn from university. He wants to devote himself to painting. And he's moved."

Kugy's jaw dropped. "Keenan's withdrawn? Why didn't he tell me?"

"I guess he only told his close friends," said Wanda, shrugging. "Anyway, he's busy preparing for the exhibition. After that, we're moving to Jakarta. Because after *that*, we're traveling together to promote his paintings." She spoke nonchalantly. "His family's mad at him because of his decision to quit school. So"—Wanda let out a long sigh, a look of concern on her face—"except for me, he doesn't have anyone now."

Kugy was silent as she tried to digest Wanda's words. At last she said, slowly, "Tell him congrats for me. For his upcoming exhibition, I mean."

Wanda nodded. "You're coming to Noni's party, right? It's going to be fun. Noni, Eko, me, and Keenan are all hosting it."

"I'll try," Kugy answered curtly. Then she and Wanda said good-bye.

To steady her wildly beating heart, Kugy decided to walk home. She couldn't articulate her feelings. The tangled ball of yarn felt even more tangled. Kugy was shocked at Keenan's decision, and also disappointed because she hadn't heard about it from him. And she felt heartbroken knowing Wanda and Keenan were so close. Suddenly, she felt stupid. All this time she had thought she occupied a special place in Keenan's life. It turned out she was wrong. She was nothing more than an insignificant extra.

September 2000

The vast lawn and area around the swimming pool were beginning to fill with guests. Torches were being staked in the garden, and tables laid with food. Wanda was the busiest one there, hurrying to and fro.

Noni witnessed the preparations with an anxious expression. Among their wider set of friends, Wanda had been dubbed the Queen of Coordination and Kugy the Mother Alien, but Noni had her own title as well: Ms. Perfectionist. To Noni, everything had to be error-free. She felt Eko touch her elbow.

"Just relax, darling," he said. "Don't worry so much. There are lot of people helping. There's me, Wanda, Keenan . . ."

"What if no one ends up coming? Some people still haven't called. What if the guests from Bandung suddenly cancel?" Noni was babbling nervously.

"Then we'll just celebrate on our own and stuff ourselves silly." Eko laughed.

"Don't make me more nervous than I already am!" Noni pouted.

"I know how you are. If I take you seriously, you'll be stressed out. If I make jokes, you'll be stressed out, too. So I might as well make jokes. At least one of us will be happy."

"Kugy's coming, right?" asked Noni, biting her nails.

"Definitely. She'd be crazy not to."

"You have the medal, right?"

"All taken care of!"

———

Kugy had been staring at her enormous backpack for more than half an hour. It was lying on the floor, empty. She should have been packed and at the station a long time ago. But Kugy had sat quietly instead, imagining what would happen if she didn't show up at the party, and what would happen if she did.

If she didn't show up, there was no doubt Noni would be disappointed. And the conclusion her friend had reached about her would be proven correct: she had indeed changed, she was avoiding them, and she was distancing herself. If Kugy did show up, she would be the one with the broken heart.

Kugy took off her jacket and tossed it on the floor, then threw herself onto the bed. Half of her was annoyed at herself, aware of how much one person had disrupted her life—had made her lose her ability to act with confidence and not care what others thought. Keenan had left her paralyzed.

The other half of her was shocked and amazed. Only now did she realize how deep her feelings for Keenan were and how much she had fallen for him. Kugy knew what her final decision was. She wasn't going. "Forgive me, Noni," she whispered.

———

The lawn was packed. There were lit candles and torches everywhere. Music blasted over the speakers. Everyone was enjoying themselves. But Noni's face was creased with worry, like an unironed shirt.

Noni approached Eko for the umpteenth time. "Did you call her house? Has she arrived yet?"

"Yeah, I called," answered Eko. "They said she's probably not coming after all. If she does, though, she would come straight here." He tried to sound as relaxed as possible.

"She's not coming?" Noni's eyes widened.

"*Probably* not coming. No one knows for sure, okay?" Eko tried to calm his girlfriend's nerves. "Her cell phone's been off for a while. No one's answering the telephone at her boarding house, either."

"Kugy, this is too much," Noni murmured. She couldn't hide the disappointment on her face.

They heard Wanda calling them. "Noni! Eko! Come over here! We'll be blowing out the candles soon!"

Noni dragged herself over to the table where the cake was to be placed. Wanda stood there, all smiles. "Hey, guys. I have a special treat for you." She presented them with two glasses of champagne. "Dom Pérignon. I got a bottle from Dad's cellar. *Sssh*. Don't tell anyone, okay? This is just for us." Wanda giggled, though no one else did.

Eko took a glass, but Noni shook her head. "You have it, Wanda."

"Oh, come on, girl! Have fun! Why the long face?" As Wanda spoke, she gulped down the contents of the glass Noni had refused.

"Why don't we just blow out the candles?" Noni suggested.

"Okay. Everything's ready, right?" Wanda put down the glass. She had emptied it in the blink of an eye. "Do you have the medal Noni wants to give Kugy?"

Eko reached into his back pocket to make sure it was there. Noni had been planning her twentieth birthday party for a long time, and she had come up with the idea of bestowing Kugy with a medal as a token of their friendship. She and Eko had ordered one from a sporting goods store. *For my best and oldest friend,* it read. Eko swallowed. The medal was ready and waiting, but he doubted there would be any need for it tonight.

"Just use it as a doorstop or something," mumbled Noni. She left without another word.

CHAPTER 20
A GIGANTIC LIE

The party had flopped, though Noni's other friends didn't realize it. Many of the guests who were expected from out of town never showed up—and Kugy's absence had been the most fatal of all. Eko, Keenan, and Wanda tried to put on a good show so it would feel like everything was going well—except Noni disappeared, causing the party to finish earlier than expected. By ten, only a handful of people remained, and most of them were Wanda's servants.

Keenan approached Eko, who was putting away the chairs. "Where's Noni?"

"Migraine." Eko averted his eyes. "Ms. Perfectionist always gets them. Can't handle stress. Luckily, she just ran away to sleep, not to bash her head against a wall."

"You sure she's all right?"

Eko nodded. "She's out like a light. And her older sister is looking after her. But if anyone should be looking after someone, it's you."

"What?"

In answer, Eko pulled out the bottle of Dom Pérignon, which was already three-quarters empty. "If I hadn't confiscated it, she would have drained it to the last drop. We could have used it as a flower vase."

"Wanda?" Keenan was startled. "Where is she?"

Eko shrugged. "You'd better find her and take her to her room right away. If Wanda's dad sees his daughter drunk on stolen champagne"— he whistled—"we're all in big trouble."

Keenan looked around. "Okay, I'll find her."

———

Two people were dancing in a shadowy corner near the pool. Keenan recognized them immediately: Wanda and Ivan, the DJ.

"Hey, babe. Where've you been?" Wanda said brightly. Her movements seemed unsteady.

Ivan looked startled. Hastily, he withdrew his hand from Wanda's waist. "Keenan, whassup?" he said, trying to look relaxed.

Keenan didn't answer. "Wanda, you're drunk. I'm taking you to your room. Now."

Tottering, Wanda took Keenan's hand, then leaned into his arms with her full weight. "I can't walk . . . ," she whispered in Keenan's ear.

"If you can still dance, you can still walk. Come on." Keenan spoke in a firm voice. He removed Wanda's arms from around him, took her by the hand, and guided her away.

With great difficulty, Wanda tried to keep up. "Don't go so fast," she whined. But Keenan ignored her and kept walking at the same pace, stopping only when they reached the door to her room. "You shouldn't have drunk so much," he said. "Why can't you have some self-control?"

Wanda looked straight into Keenan's eyes and, to his surprise, smiled. "Are you mad because I was drinking or because of Ivan?" Her smile grew wider. "Are you jealous?"

"From the look of things, Ivan is just a side effect," said Keenan sternly. "The main problem is you've had too much to drink. You're lucky your father's not home yet."

Wanda laughed. "Oh, he wouldn't know the difference. Dad's an expert at understanding art, not his own daughter."

"You should rest, Wanda. Drink a lot of water. Take a hot bath first if you need to." Keenan turned to leave. "I'm going home."

"What?" Wanda pulled Keenan into her room and closed the door. "You can't go home!"

Keenan glanced at the closed door behind him. Following his eyes, Wanda quickly slipped around him and leaned against the door, blocking it.

Keenan sighed. "Wanda, please. Don't be childish. I have to go."

"Why do you have to go? You're supposed to be my boyfriend. I want you to stay."

"Because you aren't sober, that's why," Keenan answered. "And I don't want us to do something stupid because you're drunk."

In one swift motion, Wanda's arms were around Keenan's neck. "Can you imagine what a guy like Ivan would do if he were in your shoes?" she whispered, pressing her lips against Keenan's. "In this room, together with me?"

Keenan pulled away. "Wanda, please listen. It's not that I don't want to, and it's not that I don't understand what kind of opportunity I have. But you're drunk. This isn't right."

"Damn it! You're such a hypocrite!" Wanda screamed. "You never want to do anything, even when I'm not drunk! Don't use that as an excuse. You never wanted me. You never loved me. You never did—even though I'm bending over backward doing everything for you! I'm willing to do anything for you!"

Keenan was quiet. He knew Wanda wasn't fully aware of what she was saying, but her words pricked his conscience nonetheless. He tried to pull her into his arms, but she slapped his hand away.

"I don't need you to humor me!" Wanda shrieked. "I don't need your pity! I'm sick of begging for your attention! You think I don't have any self-respect? Get out!" She jabbed her finger toward the door. "Just go back to Bandung! Back to that rotten hole-in-the-wall you call a home! Go!"

Keenan tried to remind himself that Wanda was under the influence, that she didn't really mean what she was saying. "Fine," he said, trying to remain calm. "Get some rest tonight, okay? I'll come over tomorrow."

"What's the difference—tonight or tomorrow?" Wanda snapped, her voice rising higher in pitch. "Like you'll suddenly want to be with me tomorrow? Forget it, Keenan! There will be no tomorrow!"

Unsteadily, Wanda stooped down, lifted the hem of the bedcover, and pulled out several large tubes wrapped in brown paper. "And take these with you!" She hurled them at him.

Keenan felt his throat close up. He had a bad feeling about this. He picked up one of the tubes and peeled away some of the covering to reveal rolled-up canvas—and his knees went weak. His heart was pounding. He realized how many rolls there were. Four—the same number of paintings on display at the Warsita Gallery that had reportedly been sold.

Trembling, Keenan dropped the tube and stepped toward Wanda. "How did my paintings get here?"

"Because *I* bought them! Satisfied?"

Keenan froze, trying to comprehend what was going on. Everything fell into place. His intuition had been trying to tell him something all along—something he could never explain. He connected the dots, and it was as if he were witnessing a lie swelling, growing larger and larger. Now here it was, staring him in the face. Keenan turned away. He couldn't bring himself to look at her.

As Wanda witnessed the change in Keenan's expression, panic welled up inside her. "Keenan, I meant well," she stammered. "I just wanted to help you."

Keenan felt the lie was too gigantic to comprehend. His head spun. His heart churned. The Warsita Gallery, the check, his confidence, his determination to paint . . . One by one, in a matter of seconds, his dreams were shattered.

As Wanda's mask fell away, her eyes grew wet with tears. Her anger, so explosive just seconds before, was now replaced by the other extreme—she was sobbing. "Keenan, I'm sorry. I know it was wrong. Please understand, I love you so much. Don't leave. Please . . ." Wanda fell to her knees, hugging Keenan's legs.

Keenan looked down as Wanda clutched his thighs, her sobs growing louder and louder. He felt his pants become wet with tears. But he couldn't bring himself to do or say anything. The turmoil he felt exceeded anger, exceeded any emotion he knew.

He stood there for a long time, letting Wanda sob until, slowly, he removed her arms from his legs and pulled her to her feet.

"Keenan, please say something, anything. You can be as angry as you want, I understand. I can take it. Just don't go."

Keenan picked up the paintings, his heart broken beyond all repair. "I'm giving back your money. All of it. And I'm taking these back," he said softly.

Wanda looked at him, devastated. "Don't go."

"You may be able to buy these paintings, Wanda," Keenan hissed as he opened the door, "but you'll never be able to buy me." He hoisted the tubes over his shoulder. And without looking back, he left.

———

Once Keenan was back in Bandung, he went to the post office. With him were five cardboard cylinders—the four paintings he'd gotten from Wanda, and one more for *General Pilik and the Alit Brigade*.

"Are you done with the form?" the post office employee asked, glancing at the paper he had given Keenan. It was still blank.

"Almost," Keenan answered. He looked again at the five cylinders, rolled up and tied neatly with string. At last, with a heavy heart, he filled out his details.

The man looked it over. "Ubud, Bali, huh?" he mumbled. "It'll arrive in three to four days. Anything else I can help you with?"

Keenan shook his head.

Another employee came to take the packages.

"Please be careful," Keenan blurted anxiously. "Can you label them 'fragile'? And please don't let them get wet."

With an understanding smile, the man got out the stickers Keenan had requested.

Keenan watched the five packages until they were taken away to the storeroom. In a little while, they would set sail for the Island of the Gods. Keenan felt like he was sending them off to heaven. Who knew when he would see them again?

In his heart, he bid farewell to his dreams. Whether he was prepared to do this, he couldn't say. He didn't have the courage to consider it further. But he knew his paintings would be in good hands. Right now, that was the most important thing.

CHAPTER 21

A PAINFUL EMPTINESS

Half an hour ago, the room had been dark. But now, the light was on and the colorful letters on the sign hanging on the door read "Noni Is In." Kugy stood before it, her heart trembling.

It had been three days since the party, and Noni had just returned from Jakarta. They hadn't spoken yet. Or more precisely, Kugy hadn't had the courage to contact Noni. Even now her tongue felt too dry to speak.

The door opened to reveal Noni holding a bag of garbage she was going to throw away. Kugy was startled, but it was too late to flee.

Noni quickly averted her eyes.

"Hi," Kugy said with a slight tremor in her voice.

Noni didn't answer, much less glance in her direction. As if Kugy were invisible, she walked away.

Kugy knew she should chase after Noni, to try to talk to her, but her feet felt like lead. She didn't have the nerve. In the end, Kugy went back to her room. A cold war had officially begun, and there was no way of knowing when it would end.

———

It was ten o'clock at night. Keenan's belly was rumbling as if there were a soccer match going on inside. The last time he had eaten was noon, and it looked like his stomach wasn't going to get anything else to eat until the same time the following day.

Keenan patted his stomach slowly and whispered, "Be patient. Don't cramp up on me yet. I still have to go out and look at the sky."

He sat down near the clotheslines, just outside his window. From there he could see the rooftops and glowing lights spread out before him in the dense wilderness of alleyways.

He looked up. From where he sat, it looked as if the sky had been bedecked with crisscrossing lines of laundry, a few pairs of damp under-wear and jeans still hanging out to dry. But he didn't mind. Watching the night sky was a simple pleasure that always made him feel a little better.

Keenan didn't mind being hungry, either. It was simply a conse-quence of being frugal. He only had a few rupiah left. But nothing could alleviate the emptiness of his soul, and this feeling was more painful to him than anything else. *Rice can be bought. But conviction? Confidence? All the money in the world can't buy those,* he thought bitterly. Money could never be the measure of things. Conviction and money—they existed on completely different planes. He knew that now.

There was a sour taste in his mouth. Only now did he feel sorry for himself. He would have sent himself flowers to express his condolences if he could. *No conviction . . . no dignity . . . nothing—emptiness.* How could emptiness be so painful? Shouldn't emptiness mean that there was nothing there? Shouldn't "nothing there" mean that there were no problems? No pain?

Something stole into the emptiness. Sadness. A shining moment had come and gone in the blink of an eye and had been nothing more than a farce. Keenan felt like an unlucky actor whose scene was over, but who had been left onstage to dream on.

The face of his grandmother in Amsterdam passed through his mind. Keenan remembered their last day together, when Oma had made *bruinebonensoep*, which they had enjoyed in silence. He remembered the sadness they had felt but never fully expressed. Keenan wished he could return there tonight and leave everything behind. But the roof was the farthest his legs would carry him. His memories of Oma and the night sky mingled. Everything seemed to melt and grow blurry as his eyes welled up with tears.

October 2000

Kugy would never forget this morning. The villagers had built a new shelter for her class to move into and she was teaching in it for the first time. The Sakola Alit's presence, along with the consistent efforts of Ami and her friends, had finally attracted the sympathies of the area's inhabitants. The locals had pulled together, and this new shelter was the result. The monsoon season had arrived, and they were worried that school would be disrupted since one of the classes was being conducted underneath a tree.

Even though all the children were excited about their new classroom, they couldn't help but look glum—today they were learning multiplication and division. Kugy surveyed her students. They looked dejected and she felt ready to give up hope. She still hadn't come up with a creative way to teach the subject.

Suddenly she saw one of her students, Dadi, sprinting toward the shelter, his face beaming and his finger pointing somewhere behind him. He broke into a laugh, revealing a missing front tooth. "Ms. Ugy! Mr. Rangginang is here!" he yelled.

Rangginang? Kugy thought. She craned her neck in the direction Dadi was pointing and realized whom the child meant. She couldn't have been more surprised. "Keenan," she whispered.

For a split second, Kugy bowed her head and shut her eyes in an attempt to gather her energy and strength. In the blink of an eye, there was a merry laugh on her lips, and she called out to him. "Hello, Teacher! Welcome to our new classroom!"

Keenan smiled. Seeing Kugy laugh in that distinctive way of hers filled his heart with warmth. He called it "the laugh of grace"—it was like the sun, continually bathing the earth in its rays, harboring no ill will. That was the effect the laugh had on him, bringing him warmth without requiring pretense or effort. Pure grace.

Only after Keenan had come closer did Kugy realize how changed he was. He had lost weight. She could see from his eyes he was tired. Kugy was also aware the same thing had happened to her.

"What's up, Little One?" said Keenan. "You've gotten even littler."

"The Hunger No Longer raised their prices, so I haven't been as well nourished." Kugy chuckled. "You've gotten skinny, too. Is everything all right?"

Keenan shrugged and grinned. "It's fine," he said simply.

His presence was like a breath of fresh air. The children saw in him a savior who would liberate them from the morning lesson. Pilik began dancing for joy, shouting, "Draw something! Draw something! Draw something!"

Kugy shook her head. "No, no! You all have to learn math."

Her words were greeted by sounds of protest.

Keenan picked up a piece of chalk and began to draw. Quickly, he drew six kites. "Come on, let's count. How many kites are there?"

The children counted to six.

"Now let's say Pilik has to divide these kites between him and Dadi." Keenan drew a line. "How many do each of them get?"

"Three!" they answered in chorus.

Kugy smiled. Today she would have to let her class take its cues from Keenan.

———

Kugy's class finished later than usual. The children acted like they had when Keenan had last visited—like fans meeting their favorite star—and they used various ploys to keep him around.

When the children had dispersed, Kugy and Keenan set to work cleaning up the shelter.

"Sometimes I wish you could be one of the regular teachers here," said Kugy.

"Why?"

"So the children could have someone to teach them how to draw. Plus, there are so many creative ways to teach something when you're here—ways I can't teach when I'm on my own."

"Oh. And I thought it was because you wanted to see me every day," said Keenan mischievously.

Kugy laughed. "Yeah, I guess that would be a bonus, too. I wouldn't mind."

"Me, neither."

Both of them were quiet for a moment. Kugy picked up her backpack and was about to sling it over her shoulder when she put it back down. "Where have you been?"

"Around," mumbled Keenan.

"Why didn't you say you'd moved?"

"It's a long story."

"Then you should start telling it now," Kugy said firmly as she sat cross-legged on the floor.

"I stopped going to classes this semester," blurted Keenan. "I've withdrawn from the university."

"Yeah, I know," said Kugy softly. "Wanda told me. What about your family? What did they say?"

"I'm not talking to them anymore. My father doesn't approve."

Kugy thought about this for a long time. Then she burst into a smile. "You're really brave. I salute you. It's a big decision to make for the sake of your art."

"I've given up painting."

Kugy jumped to her feet. "Wha—? Why?" she stammered.

"I thought painting was my life path. It turns out I was wrong." Keenan kept his tone even.

"But didn't you want to hold an exhibition? I ran into Wanda, and she told me you were concentrating on painting. That you were going on tour, moving to Jakarta . . ."

Keenan smiled darkly. "She was just joking. The exhibition, the gallery, going on tour . . . it was all just one big joke."

"I don't understand." Kugy shook her head. "You mean there were never any plans to have an exhibition?"

"It turned out Wanda's dad was never on board with accepting my paintings from the start. According to him, my work was still too immature. But he took them because Wanda asked."

"But your paintings sold out in the end. All four of them! Doesn't that prove people like your work?"

"One person, to be exact," said Keenan bitterly. "Wanda. It turns out she bought all my paintings, and hid them in her house. She let it slip when she got drunk at Noni's birthday party."

Kugy stared at him in disbelief. "So all this time . . ."

"All this time, it's been nothing more than a story about a rich girl falling in love with a dreamer. But it's nobody's fault." Keenan smiled darkly again. "I don't blame Wanda, or even her father. I'm the stupid one."

"It doesn't mean you should just give up on your dreams, though. You're really going to stop painting? Just because someone like Wanda—"

"It's not because of Wanda!" shouted Keenan. "Don't you get it? I've already withdrawn from school and left home. I was so naïve—so sure I could prove to my family, to everyone, that I could make a living as a painter—"

"Exactly! So why don't you prove it?" Kugy said. She stared at him in confusion. "Keenan, you're the most amazing painter I know. Whatever Wanda's dad says, whatever ulterior motives Wanda had, whatever those collectors think . . . to me, you paint with your soul, and that's what counts!"

"If I were really as amazing a painter as you think, Wanda's dad would have accepted my paintings right away. She wouldn't have had to coax him. And, if I were really as good a painter as you think, people would have bought my paintings. Wanda wouldn't have had to secretly buy them."

"So based on one gallery and a bunch of people you don't even know, you're giving up all your dreams. Is that it?" Kugy's voice rose in pitch.

"Wake up, Kugy." Keenan turned away. "The Warsita isn't just any gallery, and those aren't just any people—they're experienced art collectors. You and Eko can say my paintings are good because you're my friends. But those people know better."

Kugy shook her head again. "No. *You* wake up! Who cares what the gallery says? Who cares what those people say? You have to be sure of yourself."

"You're right," Keenan answered firmly. "I should wake up and face the facts. The reality is Wanda used my paintings to get close to me, and it was my stupidity that allowed it to happen."

"You said this wasn't because of Wanda, but you keep bringing her and the gallery up. If you ask me, I'm the one who doesn't see what Wanda or the Warsita have to do with it. This is about you believing in yourself." Kugy almost sounded reproachful. "All this time, you're the one who's been inspiring me to hold on to my dreams. Thanks to you I've started writing again. I'm not going to let you give up like this—"

"I never asked to be anyone's role model!" yelled Keenan. "Don't put pressure on me like that!"

Kugy fell silent. Her hands trembled as they put away the rest of the things scattered around the shelter. Then she slung her bag over her shoulder. "I guess I've thought too much of you this whole time," she whispered, not looking at Keenan. Before long, her brisk strides took her away behind a clump of bamboo. She walked hurriedly, without so much as a backward glance.

Keenan didn't move. All he could do was watch. He regretted what he had said, but now it was too late. He didn't even have enough confidence to stop Kugy.

A gust of cold wind pierced his skin and penetrated his veins, leaving a sense of loss that spread throughout his body. Keenan shuddered. It wasn't just loss he was feeling—it was abandonment.

CHAPTER 22
COME BACK TO UBUD

Alone in her room, Kugy began writing as if she were possessed. That night, she was determined to pour everything out onto paper. Her handwriting filled the white blankness—sheets and sheets of it. As she wrote, the occasional tear slipped out, leaving an inky stain on the paper where it fell. Kugy didn't know if they were tears of sadness or anger, and she didn't care.

On page three, the pace of her writing began to slow. Her feelings, which had started out so muddled, began to show their true colors. She should have been happy when she found out Keenan and Wanda's relationship had ended. She should have been relieved when she found out Keenan wasn't going to move to Jakarta after all, or leave her to promote his paintings. But she wasn't. And Kugy realized that this was true heartbreak. It had broken her heart when she had thought Keenan was meant for someone else. But now that she knew Keenan wasn't the same person she had fallen in love with—now her heart was really and truly broken.

Kugy began to weep. She didn't write much beyond this—only a few more lines of disappointment. Kugy realized that all this time she had created an illusion of who Keenan was, and had loved that illusion instead. The reality was that Keenan was broken and weak.

She heard a door open, then Noni's footsteps in the corridor. Kugy swallowed. There was a bitter taste in her mouth. Not only had she lost her true love, she had lost Noni and Josh because of it.

She folded the sheets of paper into three paper boats.

———

Beside the university was a shantytown, and next to the shantytown, a stream. It was the closest body of flowing water Kugy could find.

That morning, before going to class, Kugy stopped by the stream. A few children were catching tadpoles. She kept going, lest the children abandon their play and decide the object she was about to set afloat was more interesting. She had an important mission and she didn't want it to fail.

Only after she felt she was at a safe distance did Kugy stop and approach the water. She pulled out three paper boats from her backpack. There were no other channels of communication, no other friends she could talk to. *No one but Neptune,* she thought. One by one, she set the paper boats afloat on the stream.

As the boats sailed away, it was as if something lifted from her heart. She felt like she could breathe again. How long had she kept this habit buried away! And how much had it taken for her to resurrect it! Kugy had forgotten how relieved she felt whenever the stories and woes her heart had to tell were sent floating out to sea, even if she didn't know how long their journey would take.

November 2000

It was the first of November. Keenan was surprised to find Bimo at his boarding house so early in the morning.

"Hey, Keenan. How are—" Bimo stopped midsentence. "Wow. You're so skinny."

Keenan stood in the doorway and smiled. It was the standard comment he'd been getting from his old classmates whenever he saw them.

"Hi, Bimo. Come on in," Keenan said. He opened the door wider.

"I have something to give you." Bimo handed him a white envelope.

Keenan recognized the handwriting instantly. The return address on the back confirmed his suspicions. It was a letter from Uncle Wayan in Ubud, addressed to his old boarding house.

"When did this arrive?" asked Keenan.

"A long time ago—almost two weeks. But I only got ahold of it last week, and this is the first chance I've had to come over. Sorry."

"It's okay. Thanks. I should have come to you."

Bimo laughed. "How were you supposed to know the letter was there? Telepathy? You don't have a cell phone, and this place doesn't have a landline! You're so skinny I think your brain must have shrunk, too."

Keenan grinned.

"How about breakfast?" Bimo asked. "My treat. When was the last time you ate a good meal?"

Keenan thought for a while, then shook his head. "I can't recall. My brain's shrunk, remember?"

Bimo chuckled. "Okay then! A good meal it is!"

———

Breakfast with Bimo ended up stretching into the afternoon. Keenan visited the campus and spent the day hanging out with his old friends. He realized how much he had missed such companionship. Ever since the incident with Wanda, he had kept to himself, shutting himself away like a hermit. After he'd spent so long in the stuffiness of his soul, Bimo's visit was a breath of fresh air.

Back in his room, Keenan pushed the window wide open. The place needed some fresh air, too. He picked up the envelope and fingered it, wondering whether the letter would provide another refreshing breeze. Keenan shook his head. He was tired of hoping.

Without further thought, Keenan opened the envelope. Inside was a handwritten letter, two pages long, along with another slip of paper. Keenan had to sit down when he realized what the slip of paper was. Hurriedly, he read the letter. Even when he was done, Keenan didn't move. He sat for a long time.

He stared at the papers in his lap. Uncle Wayan's letter had given rise to such a sudden surge of emotions that his mind and heart were still trying to digest what he had just read. Keenan reread the letter, this time more slowly.

Uncle Wayan wrote how surprised he was to receive Keenan's paintings—they had come without warning, as if they had fallen from the sky. Although Keenan had explained that he was sending them as something to remember him by and as a token of appreciation, Uncle Wayan felt that something must have happened. However, he hadn't been able to reach him.

The painting Uncle Wayan liked the most had been mounted onto a wooden frame and displayed in his studio. A few weeks later, the painting had caught the attention of an art collector, who expressed interest in buying it. Uncle Wayan had already said the painting wasn't for sale, but the person was determined to buy it. He had fallen head over heels for Keenan's painting.

Uncle Wayan then apologized—he didn't mean to overstep. But he said his heart had told him to let the person have it:

> *As love may bind two hearts together without warning or explanation, so I felt the painting had found its soulmate. I know the person who bought your painting*

*well. So I am certain it is in the right hands. He bought
it not as an investment, but out of love.*

Keenan continued reading:

*The painting is truly very beautiful, and its spirit
is strong. Although I very much wanted to keep it for
myself, I also didn't want to stand in the way of your good
fortune. Hopefully this money will come in handy. When
will you come back to your home in Ubud? The rest of
the family and I hope continually for your return. When
you receive this letter, please send us news.*

Keenan stared again at the slip of paper. It was a check for three million rupiah. On it was written, *For* General Pilik and the Alit Brigade.

Keenan spent the rest of the day lost in thought. It was a lot of money—enough to buy a motorcycle if he wanted. Late afternoon turned into night. The orange of the sky gave way to blackness. And he remained lost in thought. His mind was in so much turmoil. He didn't dismiss the matters that had been raised, but he didn't take steps to address them, either. He felt doubtful, traumatized, shaken. But still he heard that question buzzing in his ears: *When will you come back to your home in Ubud?*

———

Lena couldn't stop the tears from flowing. They had agreed to meet at a time when she would be alone and everyone else was out of the house. Her heart was cut to the quick to see her own son acting so furtively, like an escaped convict terrified of being caught.

Keenan waited as his mother spent the first fifteen minutes of their reunion crying.

"But you're doing all right?" Lena asked.

"I'm all right, Mom," answered Keenan with forced nonchalance. "I may be skinny, but I haven't gotten sick."

"You can come home anytime you want. Trust me. Your father's heart will soften. He's hard on the outside, but in reality he misses you very much."

Keenan gave her a thin smile. "I didn't want to meet you today to discuss coming home. Actually, I want to say good-bye."

Lena was shocked. "Good-bye? Where are you going?"

He took out the envelope containing Uncle Wayan's letter and handed it to his mother. "Read this, Mom."

Lena began to read. When she got to the end, she let out a long sigh. She knew a second parting was about to take place, but this time she felt somewhat relieved, for she knew her son would be well taken care of.

"I'm going to live with Uncle Wayan," Keenan said. "I'm leaving the day after tomorrow."

Lena gazed at her oldest child through a film of tears. She realized her little boy had become a man who had chosen his own life path. Soon, he would spread his wings and fly, and neither she nor anyone else could stop him.

Lena's voice trembled. "Behave yourself over there, okay? Don't give your Uncle Wayan any trouble."

Keenan swallowed. It was obvious that his mother was trying to act composed for his sake. His eyes grew hot and his vision blurred. He steadied his breathing before continuing. "I have one more request, Mom."

"What is it?"

"Please don't tell anyone I'm in Ubud. Not Jeroen. Especially not Dad."

Lena felt her chest tighten.

"I really want to turn over a new leaf. Start from scratch. This is the path my life has to take, Mom. My old life was a prison, and I'm not going back."

Finally, heavily, Lena nodded.

Keenan rose to his feet. He kissed his mother's forehead and held her close. Every second that rolled by mattered. There was only silence—and the tears that fell from their eyes.

CHAPTER 23

CATCHING STARS

Keenan sat on the bus for twenty hours as it carried him from Bandung to the Ubung Terminal in Denpasar, Bali. And for all twenty hours, his eyes remained wide open. Something about this journey made him both nervous and excited. This was the biggest decision he had ever made. He felt it in his heart, too—something big was waiting for him in Ubud.

From the bus window, he saw Uncle Wayan and his nephew Agung waiting at the terminal, pacing back and forth. Keenan immediately recognized them. They were similar in height and build, and each was dressed in a sarong and collared shirt and wore an *udeng* on his head. They looked as if they had just come from a ceremony.

"Poyan! Agung!" Keenan waved as he stepped off the bus.

At once Uncle Wayan's face broke into a bright smile, and Agung sprinted over to help Keenan with his bag.

"Looks like we're going to have to get food into someone fast, Agung—before all the dogs in Bali start eyeing him. He looks like a walking collection of bones." Uncle Wayan chuckled.

Keenan chuckled, too. "Sounds good to me, Poyan. I won't refuse a meal. Especially if we eat soon."

Uncle Wayan gave Keenan a big hug. "I'm happy you've decided to come home to us. The whole family is waiting for you."

Something in Keenan's heart stirred. He was moved. He then realized how much he had missed the idea of coming home . . . of family.

———

The car arrived at a high wooden gate surrounded by leafy trees and wild brush growing tall and dense. Rising up beyond the wooden gate were the spires of a temple, so high they were visible even from the road. There, on twelve acres of land, lived Uncle Wayan's enormous family, spread out among several houses. There were also three large studios for all the different activities and materials the family needed for their artistic endeavors.

The sight of that familiar wooden gate took his breath away. This was his new home. He couldn't suppress the smile spreading across his lips.

Uncle Wayan hadn't exaggerated when he said the whole family was waiting. Keenan felt moved again when their car pulled up in front of the complex and he saw everyone gathered on the terrace.

"Keenan! Brother! What's up?" It was Banyu. Of all Uncle Wayan's nephews, he was the closest to Keenan. He went right up to Keenan and enfolded him in a warm embrace. He was followed by Uncle Putu, then the others.

"Your room is all ready for you," said Auntie Ayu, Agung's mother and Uncle Wayan's sister-in-law. She sounded cheerful. "We've added an armoire. You'll be living with us from now on, right?"

"Yes, that's the plan," Keenan answered with a broad laugh. "Here, I've brought a few treats from Bandung. They're for everyone." He handed her a large bag of sweets and snacks he'd purchased before boarding the bus yesterday.

"You must be tired," said Uncle Nyoman, Uncle Wayan's younger brother and also a painter. "You have bags under your eyes."

"I had trouble sleeping on the bus," answered Keenan. "I haven't slept since yesterday. But I feel okay."

"If that's the case, you'd better get some rest straight away!" Ayu exclaimed. "Take a nap. We'll wake you later when dinner's ready, all right?"

"Thank you so much," Keenan answered with a nod. This sounded just fine by him. Stepping foot inside the house again, he felt as if his entire system had shed all the burdens he'd been carrying, and now he could feel how tired his body was.

"Luhde!" Auntie Ayu called. "Could you please take Keenan to his room? And don't forget to give him something to drink."

Keenan frowned. The name was unfamiliar. And sure enough, an unfamiliar woman who had been standing in the corner behind everybody else made her way shyly to the front. She looked at him and ducked her head slightly.

"Keenan, this is Luhde Laksmi, my niece from Kintamani," Uncle Wayan explained. "Luhde will be living here as well. Her father, Made Suwitna, sent her. He came to visit around New Year's, when you were here last. Do you remember him?"

Keenan nodded. The man was a very famous Balinese dance choreographer. Keenan glanced at Luhde. She looked like a typical teenage girl. Her frame was petite, and her bashful expression made her look even more delicate. What stood out was her long hair, which she wore loose over her shoulders so that it looked like a black shawl hanging down to her waist. And yet, for all her apparent fragility and bashfulness, her large eyes shone with curiosity. Keenan was transfixed. There was something familiar about her, though they were meeting for the first time. He didn't know what it was.

"She looks shy, but she knows a lot," Uncle Wayan continued, chuckling.

Luhde's face reddened. "Come, *Beli*. I'll take you to your room." Hastily, she began walking. She had spoken softly, but her voice was clear, like dew.

"Just call me Keenan," he said. *Beli* was the Balinese term of respect for an older brother.

Meekly, Luhde nodded.

Uncle Wayan patted Keenan on the back. "Get some rest. You're home now. We'll talk again later tonight."

Keenan looked around once more, to reassure himself he wasn't dreaming. He was too tired to dream anymore.

——

Eko watched as Noni straightened up her closet. Their social life had undergone many changes recently. He and Noni spent more time by themselves. There were still several friends they went out with, but things just weren't the same anymore.

"How long before you two start talking to each other again?" Eko asked.

Noni was startled, but hastily resumed folding her clothes. "You mean me and Kugy?"

"Yeah," answered Eko as he turned away. "Are you really okay with things the way they are, even though you two are living in the same boarding house? I don't know what to do—I feel bad taking anyone's side. You're my girlfriend. Kugy's my friend. But you're not speaking to each other."

Noni shrugged. "What can we do? Haven't you seen what she's like now? She can't even be bothered to say hello." She motioned with her chin in the direction of the corridor.

Eko poked his head out and saw that Kugy had just returned. Her face had become hard, to the point of looking cruel. Her sunken eyes emanated exhaustion. She was more ghost than person—silent, gloomy, as if she were carrying the weight of the world on her shoulders.

"Could you be bothered to say hello if you saw her looking like that every day?" Noni quipped. "Enough already. What's the point, anyway? We'll never be able to go back to how we were before."

"What's wrong with her?"

"She's changed ever since she started teaching at Alit and broke up with Josh. I don't get it, either. And she clearly doesn't want to be open with me. So, fine."

Eko looked into Noni's eyes. "You really don't miss her? You could try approaching her, or make a bit of conversation . . ."

Noni glared back at him. "She's the one who should approach me and make a bit of conversation, and apologize for not attending my party! Not the other way around!"

Eko was quiet. He let Noni go back to what she was doing. Her face was set in a sullen expression.

"Noni," he murmured after they had been silent for a long time. "An antelope can run as fast as lightning, but when it sees a lion, it'll stand as still as a statue."

"What are you talking about?"

"What I mean is, even though an antelope is scared of a lion, it won't be able to run away. It won't be able to move at all."

"So? What does that have to do with me?"

"Have you ever considered that Kugy feels guilty about what she did to you? And because of that, she's like that antelope? But she can't do anything about it. She's become stiff, quiet, aloof. It's not because she wants to be that way. But she can't help herself because she feels bad about what she did. And she's too scared to approach you."

Now it was Noni who was quiet for a long time. Then, as she folded her last item of clothing, she mumbled, "Oh please. Don't psychoanalyze me. You've been defending her this whole time. In your eyes, Kugy can do no wrong." Noni left the room, leaving him wondering what he had done to make her so upset.

———

Under the shelter of the open-air *bale*, Keenan sat perfectly still. This was his third week in Lodtunduh. He was beginning to feel there was no difference between him and the free-range chickens Uncle Wayan kept in the backyard. Raised neither for their meat nor their eggs, they were simply allowed to roam free into their old age. Perhaps all Uncle Wayan required of them was their presence, their sounds, their movements, to liven things up. Sometimes Keenan even felt that the chickens were more useful than he was. He tried to help out every day with household chores, but he still felt useless. He was beginning to feel tired and frustrated about it all, and the kindness and sincerity of Uncle Wayan and his whole family only made him feel even worse. For three weeks, all he had done was sleep and eat. And that wasn't why he was here. He was here to paint.

Before him was an empty canvas, and strewn next to him were all the tools he needed. Every morning, he set up the same equipment in the same place. But he didn't feel even the slightest urge to paint.

He heard something behind him scrape against the wooden floor, and he turned around to find Luhde on the *bale* stairs, sitting with her legs to one side. She was surprised as well. She turned pale, as if she were a thief caught red-handed.

Keenan greeted her with a laugh. "Hello, Your Highness. You've been parked there the whole time? When did you come in?"

"A-a while now," Luhde answered, stammering. "I wanted to watch you work."

Keenan laughed again. "Don't you value your time? If you've been there for a while, it means all you've seen me do is daydream."

Luhde smiled. "A good painter can give expression to anything, even emptiness," she said in her low, gentle voice.

Keenan was astonished. "You're a quiet one, but when you speak, you say some really smart things."

Luhde came over and sat beside him. "It's common for painters around here to draw their inspiration from a single source, and to rely on that one source for as long as they paint. In that way, it becomes possible for them to attain the highest levels of spiritual transcendence. Perhaps you should search for something similar."

Once again, Luhde's words astounded him. He would never have guessed such wisdom could spring from the lips of a seventeen-year-old girl.

"Take Poyan's younger brother for instance. He draws his inspiration from the *sesajen* we offer to the spirits, so all his paintings are depictions of them. Or Poyan—he draws his inspiration from our traditional rituals. Banyu's paintings are abstract, but he draws his inspiration from the patterns in Balinese textiles. Just look at their work. It's true, isn't it?" Luhde was happily prattling away. "Once you find your soulmate, your brush will follow."

"My soulmate?"

"Every artist has a soulmate," Luhde continued. "As long as they persevere and remain open, they'll find it. So don't lose hope so quickly. A canvas with nothing on it can speak volumes. And without nothingness, how would you start something new?"

Keenan couldn't bear it any longer. Something tightened in his chest. He had yearned for so long to talk to someone about the pressures he faced, and today, Luhde had appeared like an angel of mercy, knocking on the door of his heart, allowing him to let down his defenses. "Luhde, to be honest, I don't know where to start. I'm not even sure I can ever paint again . . ." Keenan spoke with great difficulty.

Luhde didn't respond right away. Instead she approached the blank canvas. "Think of this as the sky," she said as she placed her finger on it.

"It looks like this sky is empty. But we know the sky is never empty—for there are many stars. An infinite number of them, in fact. You have to believe this, Keenan. This sky is full of clouds, that's all. If you can part these clouds, you will find many stars. And one of them is fated to be with you. I will pray that you find your star." Luhde bowed her head and pressed her palms together in front of her chest. Then, she glided slowly toward the stairs, leaving Keenan by himself once again.

Keenan stayed there until dusk. He lay on his back staring at the sky, trying to see into the distance, beyond the clouds, hoping to find something there.

CHAPTER 24

THE FIRST BUYER

December 2000

Kugy set out early in the morning shouldering a big backpack bulging with books. Her pace was brisk as she left the boarding house, which was quiet these days since all the residents had left for vacation. She was determined not to waste time. Vacations weren't part of her agenda anymore. Once again, she was taking as many extra courses as possible during the semester break. Now she only had one goal: to graduate quickly.

There was almost nothing left to keep her in Bandung, apart from her courses and the Sakola Alit. For the most part, the dreams she'd had and the happy times she had shared with her friends were now gone. Her relationship with Noni hadn't improved. The friend she had known since childhood had become a stranger.

Kugy also felt that being in her boarding house had become uncomfortable, living just one room away from Noni, who never spoke to her anymore. She couldn't possibly continue to act as if Noni wasn't there. She was too tired for that. Quietly, Kugy began looking for a new boarding house to move to before the new semester began.

Kugy had also stopped writing almost entirely. She had abandoned her ambition of being a fairy tale writer. Her imaginative powers were replaced by a logical chain of thought, which worked mechanically, robotlike, at studying, and nothing but studying.

The only writing she did anymore was for the paper boats she set afloat on the stream. Kugy felt those letters were what enabled her to preserve her sanity and strength—letters where she poured out her heart to Neptune, regardless of whether he existed or not. It didn't matter. Whenever she watched her paper boats drift away on the stream's current, Kugy felt as if she could breathe again. Her heart was at ease once more.

She told Neptune about her troubles, her inner restlessness, and how much she missed the way everything used to be, how beautiful it had been—and also, how much she missed Keenan.

A paper boat lay folded in her pocket. She would set it afloat before going to campus. If the boat were unfolded, its reader would find only a couple of lines:

> *Neptune, all fishermen trying to find their way use*
> *the stars as their guide. May he find his star. May he find*
> *his way home.*

———

Every morning, in that same *bale*, Keenan painted, filling canvas after canvas. His fingers and brushes danced in sweeps of strokes and color.

The clouds had parted at last. At his side, he kept a worn-looking notebook. Once, Kugy's tiny hand had danced across its pages, filling it with the adventures of General Pilik and the Alit Brigade.

From the terrace of the main house, Luhde gazed at the *bale* in silence.

"Poyan . . . ," she whispered to Uncle Wayan.

"He's extraordinarily talented, isn't he?" Uncle Wayan commented. "His wounds are beginning to heal as well. He's becoming more like the Keenan he was before." He spoke as if he were reading Luhde's mind.

Luhde smiled at her uncle. Her expression was bright. "Keenan has found his star."

———

The end of December was here, and Bali was filling up with tourists. There was a celebratory feeling in the air, and even Keenan was affected by it. He felt he needed time away from the whir of creative activity that had so occupied him for the past month. Recently, he had been falling asleep in the *bale* instead of painting. However, that afternoon, his nap was disrupted.

"Keenan, wake up!" Luhde said, shaking him. "There's a visitor in the gallery who wants to meet you. Come on, wake up!"

With great effort, Keenan opened his eyes. He felt Luhde pulling him by the hand, and then Banyu appeared, ready to take him to the gallery on his motorbike.

"You go first. I'll follow!" yelled Luhde as Banyu and Keenan sped off to the gallery with Keenan perched on the backseat.

The ride only took three minutes. Keenan didn't even have time to gather himself. Still unsteady on his feet, he entered the gallery and saw Uncle Wayan. "Who's the visitor, Poyan?" he asked, rubbing his eyes.

"Ah, here's our painter. He's just woken up!" Uncle Wayan laughed.

A handsome young man stood next to him, smiling as well. He looked neat and clean even though he was dressed only in a plain T-shirt and jeans. His body was toned and healthy and his skin was clear. Keenan could tell the man wasn't from Bali. He was from a big city—probably Jakarta.

"Keenan, meet your number one fan—the person who bought that first painting of yours. He's come all the way from Jakarta to ask about your latest work. I told him you've come to stay."

"Your style has matured," the man said. "I'm very impressed. Extraordinary."

"Thank you," Keenan answered with a broad smile. For the first time, someone genuinely appreciated his work. Joy filled his heart. "Which ones do you like?"

The man cast his eyes around the room, surveying all of Keenan's paintings.

"I can't decide, to be honest. May I ask you something? These paintings make up a series of stories, don't they?"

Keenan nodded energetically. "Yes, the characters are the same— only their adventures differ. I was inspired by a series of children's adventure stories, written by a friend of mine. Each painting's theme corresponds to a story. So, they're more like illustrations, but in the form of paintings."

"So that's the problem," said the man with a light laugh. "That's why I can't decide. If I may, I'd like to buy all of them. That way, I'll have the complete collection."

"If you buy in bulk, then you'll get a good discount," Keenan joked, chuckling. "But may I ask: What is it exactly about my paintings that interests you?"

The man looked excited, as if he had been anticipating this question. "The theme of your paintings is unique. Unusual, genuine, unpretentious. Also, I think the way you paint is fresh. Original. Clean. Illustrative—and yet they don't feel like illustrations. They feel more like monuments in and of themselves rather than complements to another work. And most importantly, your paintings have a strong spirit about them. I've been collecting paintings for a long time. And to me, a good painting causes the viewer to reflect. But your paintings don't just do that—they invite the viewer into your world. To appreciate a painting in that way is an extraordinary experience. Very rarely does a painting possess all three of these elements."

Keenan swallowed. He didn't know how to respond.

"It's very unfortunate, but I can only take two paintings today," the man continued. "But rest assured, I'll be adding many more to my collection in the future." He walked over to the paintings he had chosen. "How much?"

Keenan swallowed again. He glanced sideways at Uncle Wayan, his eyes pleading for help.

———

A check for ten million rupiah lay on the table.

"It's not so hard, is it, setting a price on your own work? You'll have to get used to it, but you'll get smarter over time." Uncle Wayan chuckled.

Keenan shook his head. "I still can't believe it. This is the first time I've actually witnessed someone buy one of my paintings." Suddenly he took Uncle Wayan's hand. He gripped it firmly and bowed his head. "Poyan, thank you so much for everything. I don't know what to say or what I should do. But if it's all right with you, I want to split half of the proceeds from this sale with the gallery."

Uncle Wayan shook his head. "No. None of that now. You're a new painter, and you're like my own son. You need that money for yourself. Don't think about making money for the gallery just yet. I can earn a living from selling my own work. If I really do need your help, I'll let you know. But not now. Okay?" His tone was firm.

Keenan had no choice but to nod.

"Luhde, get over here. What are you doing, spying on us from there?" Uncle Wayan called out to his niece. She had been standing behind a partition watching them for some time now.

Slowly, Luhde emerged, a sheepish smile on her face. She came over to them.

"Why spy on us like that?" Keenan asked. "It's that art collector— you like him, don't you?" he teased.

"What? No!" Luhde protested in a panicked voice.

"Keenan's right, you know," Uncle Wayan chimed in. "If you're looking for a mate, you should look for someone like him. Handsome, successful, still in his prime. And an art lover, too!" He was beside himself with laughter. "Avoid people like us. Our pockets have asthma. They're gasping for breath!"

Luhde's face turned even pinker. She didn't agree with her uncle at all.

New Year's Eve 2000

At everyone's urging, Keenan finally agreed to buy a cell phone. Sitting on the shore at Jimbaran beach, he contemplated the small object in his hands. He still felt strange holding it. There weren't many numbers stored in it. Only those of Uncle Wayan's family in Bali and a few names he'd transferred from his address book.

Keenan glanced at the time on the screen. Five minutes till the New Year. The voices behind him were growing more raucous, competing with the sound of the waves before him. He pressed some buttons, looking for that one name. And then, when it appeared on the screen, he froze. The words he would say popped into his mind: *How are you doing, Little One?*

Suddenly, Keenan felt nervous. Maybe she had changed numbers. But for whatever reason, he felt an overpowering desire to . . . He pressed the green button. *Connecting.* Keenan stared at that one word, glowing on the screen. Would he be able to speak? Could he—*No.* Keenan shut his eyes. His thumb pressed the red button. *Disconnecting.*

———

Most of Kugy's family was gathered in front of the TV. The rest had made plans to ring in the New Year elsewhere. Kugy hadn't received any invitations, but she couldn't be bothered to go out, anyway. She was perfectly happy sitting on the sofa with her feet up, eating snacks and providing commentary on what was on the screen as she chuckled to herself.

Suddenly Kugy sat up. "Did my cell phone ring?"

"No. It's just the TV," said Kevin.

"Where *is* my cell phone?" Kugy began rummaging around under the sofa cushions. "Kev, stand up for a bit." Kugy gave her older brother a shove. "I think you're sitting on it."

"No way!" Kevin exclaimed, eyes still glued to the screen. "My butt is very sensitive. I'd be able to tell if there was something wedged underneath it."

But Kugy didn't give up. She kept shoving at Kevin, searching the nooks and crannies of the sofa.

"Kugy, come on!" Kevin complained. "Stop poking around like that. You're such a pain!"

"Ha! What's this?" Kugy said holding up her phone. "So much for sensitivity! You should go on a diet. Maybe your butt will be able to feel something then!" Immediately, Kugy checked to see who had called.

She frowned. She didn't recognize the number. And yet, she continued to stare at it. There was something about that number. Kugy sent a text message: *Who is this?*

An hour passed. There was no reply.

———

Lena opened the door and looked out into the family room to see her husband still sitting in front of the TV.

"Adri, aren't you coming to bed? It's already two in the morning," she said, yawning.

The man glanced up and saw his wife in her dressing gown, a sleepy expression on her face. "In a little while. There's something good on TV. I'll come in once it's over." He spoke in an expressionless tone.

Lena peered at the screen. Though doubtful about her husband's definition of "good," she decided not to press the matter and went back into the bedroom.

After his wife left, Adri returned to gazing blankly at the TV, as he had been doing for the past few hours. He was watching another show in his head—memories, questions, thoughts—all centered around one person: Keenan.

Keenan, where are you? Where are you spending the New Year? Are you lonely? Hungry? Cold? Only in his heart could he address his son and ask him those questions. Only when he was alone. Only in Keenan's absence.

With all his might, Adri tried to contain himself—to the point where it became unbearable. And a single tear rolled down his cheek.

CHAPTER 25

A GIFT FROM THE HEART

January 2001

It was less than a week since Kugy had moved into her new boarding house. She was still adjusting to the look and feel of her new surroundings, but because it was closer to campus, she didn't have to spend as much time traveling to and fro. It fit in perfectly with her plan to graduate as quickly as possible.

She still hadn't finished organizing all her things, and she spent her late afternoons by herself, tidying up. She was beginning to enjoy this solitude. Today was no different.

"*Yoo-hoo!*" called someone in an earsplitting screech. "Anyone home? Can I come in?"

Kugy put down her books and hurried to the door. *Eko?*

She was right. There he was in the doorway, wearing that distinctive grin of his. "Hey, Mother Alien!"

"Eko! How did you know I was here?"

"I asked around," he answered lightly. "I was thinking about you and wanted to see you. I miss you."

Kugy let out a sigh even as a bright smile spread across her face. "I miss you, too."

"Come here, you!" In one swift motion, Eko put his arm around Kugy's neck and ruffled her hair. They both laughed. "Do you need help with anything? You must have some unpacking to do."

"Yeah! Help me put away my books! And buy me dinner, too!"

Eko pursed his lips. "You monkey. This is why everyone's fed up with you."

Kugy doubled over in laughter. "Too late! You're trapped!"

Before long, they were squatting on the floor among Kugy's scattered possessions.

"Does Noni know you're here?" Kugy asked suddenly.

"No. But I'll tell her later," Eko answered. "Why?"

"Oh, nothing . . ." Kugy stopped what she was doing, trying to decide whether she should finish her sentence.

"Yes?" Eko asked.

"All this time I thought you were keeping your distance, too. I really do want us to be able to talk about things and be as close as we were before. But I understand you're between a rock and a hard place. You're Noni's boyfriend after all, and like it or not, you have to take her feelings into account." Kugy spoke softly. "But, honestly, I miss you two so much."

"You know what?" said Eko. He looked her in the eye. "I'm happy you moved—not to mention relieved. Now that you're living farther away, I don't have to choose sides anymore and you and I can be close again. I can visit you from time to time without getting dragged into your conflict with Noni. I miss you a lot, too."

Eko continued. "Right now, Noni's heart is still in the process of healing. I don't know how long it'll take. And though she's my girl-friend, and though I've been hanging out with you since we were teen-agers, I don't want to get mixed up in what's going on between you two. I believe you'll find your own way to resolve your problems. The most important thing for me is to remain close to both of you—like how it's always been. Noni's my girl, and you're my friend. Whatever happens between you doesn't change how much you both mean to me." Eko spoke decisively.

Kugy was moved. "Thanks, Eko," she said, almost whispering. "In all my life I never would have thought I'd get so mushy in front of you. But you coming here today and saying what you just said—it's the most beautiful thing that's happened to me this whole year."

Eko smiled, but it vanished quickly. "Hey, the year's only ten days old! Of course this is the most beautiful thing that's happened to you this year, you moron! What's more, I've even helped you tidy up, and you have the nerve to order me to buy you dinner? You heathen, you!"

They both burst into laughter.

"The year's only ten days old and I've already succeeded in tricking you twice!" Kugy clutched at her sides. "This doesn't bode well for you."

"Yup. And once again, the nightmare begins." Eko stood up. "I'm hungry. Let's go eat!"

"Hey, my room isn't clean yet," Kugy protested.

"Why don't you and your mushy feelings clean it up then?" Eko chuckled. "Hey, do you have enough cash for us to hail an *angkot*?"

"Didn't you drive Fuad?"

"Yeah. But right when we pulled up in front of the boarding house, he stalled. So I'll leave him out front, if that's okay with you. Then when I'm ready to head home later, you can help by giving him a little push. Sound good?"

Kugy glared at Eko. "Hey, why am I beginning to feel like the unlucky one here?"

February 2001

Keenan had officially turned over a new leaf. There was a different rhythm to his life in Bali now. All day long, everything he did revolved around creating art and attending rituals at the temple. If he wasn't busy painting, he was helping Uncle Wayan's family with the accoutrements, music, and performances required for all sorts of rites, from the *ngagah* rituals to the *ngaben* ceremonies.

Keenan felt comfortable donning a Balinese *udeng* and sarong wherever he went nowadays. He had made friends with the locals his age, and occasionally went with them to watch traditional Balinese cockfights, mingling without the nervousness he once felt.

But it was Uncle Wayan who was the happiest to have this new family member among them. He looked upon Keenan as his own son— the child he had always wanted and whom he could take pride in. As it turned out, Keenan was gifted not only in painting—he could sculpt as well. He quickly learned the basic forms of traditional Balinese carving, like the *patra kuta mesir*, the *taluh kakul*, and the *pungelan*. His abilities even surpassed those of other young artists in the area who received their training in Uncle Wayan's studios.

Whenever people praised Keenan's paintings, Uncle Wayan felt the proudest of all. He always introduced Keenan in Balinese by saying, *"Niki putran titiange ane lanang, I Wayan Keenan"*—"This is my eldest son, Keenan"—adding a title reserved for an oldest son. Keenan was always at a loss for words.

If he wasn't out, he spent all his time in the *bale*, painting or just chatting with Luhde, who faithfully kept him company.

"You need to start learning Balinese," Luhde told him gravely.

"Sure. Teach me something," Keenan said.

"Repeat after me." Luhde cleared her throat. *"Cang bojok . . ."*

"Cang bojok . . ."

"Care bojog."

Keenan repeated after her. *"Cang bojok care bojog."*

"Very good." Luhde nodded, suppressing a smile.

"What does it mean?" asked Keenan.

"It means 'I'm as ugly as a monkey!'" she exclaimed before collapsing into fits of laughter.

It was Keenan's turn to nod. "I see," he said in mock-seriousness.

But Luhde immediately stopped laughing.

"You're terrible at making fun of people." Keenan chuckled. "That's why you should stick to writing. I heard you want to be a famous writer."

Luhde smiled. "Yes. It'll be like you and your friend. I'll write the stories and you can make the paintings."

Everything seemed to freeze. Keenan was speechless.

Unaware of this change, Luhde prattled on, "Everyone in my family has their own specialty. Banyu is good at sculpting. Agung is good at painting. All my older siblings are fantastic dancers. It's just me who's the odd one out. But according to Poyan, words actually can be painted—and sculpted, and even danced. So I *can* paint—I can paint words as beautiful as any painting. And I can sculpt words as lovely as any sculpture. And I can make words dance as gracefully as any dancer."

"I agree with Poyan. You do have that ability. It comes effortlessly to you. I'm often amazed by what you have to say. And . . . you often remind me of someone."

"Memories are nothing but ghosts in the corners of our minds. They will always remain ghosts if we don't deal with them. They will never become reality."

Keenan was startled by Luhde's words. And Luhde was, too—for the words seemed to leap from her lips before she could stop them.

"Sorry. I didn't mean to be so forward," Luhde said hastily, "but . . . if I may ask, who wrote that book?" She spoke with great caution. "The thing is, I've noticed that you can't paint if you don't have the book nearby."

"A friend of mine from university."

"Your friend must be clever, and gentle in spirit," Luhde commented.

Keenan didn't respond.

"So your friend. Is she a girl?"

"Yes."

"You must be very close."

"We were, yes."

"Could you introduce me to her sometime?"

Keenan looked up, and his gaze met Luhde's. "I can't make any promises."

"Why not?"

"Because I'm not sure if I'll ever see her again."

There were still many questions tucked away inside Luhde's mind—questions she had been accumulating and storing for some time now. But Keenan's bitter tone prevented her from asking them. Maybe she didn't need to know—just understand. Because, without saying anything, Keenan had told her a lot—with his paintings, with his movements, with his silence. He had told her more than he knew.

———

As they left the doctor's office, Lena read over the test results once again. The doctor had just given his analysis and her husband had been presented with a long list of prescriptions, as well as all sorts of advice.

"How could it come to this? We always bring home-cooked meals to your office. You're as physically active as ever. I don't understand it." Lena shook her head. "Is there something I don't know about?"

Adri started the engine. "What do you mean?"

"The doctor said it might be because of stress. Do you feel stressed about something that you haven't told me about?"

"Oh, stress schmess. Nowadays they say everything is caused by stress." Her husband turned away as he spoke. "It's nothing."

For the entire ride, in the back of his mind, Adri was aware of something. Although he could choose not to be open with his doctor, and even his wife, he couldn't lie to himself. There was one matter that was always on his mind, that was slowly gnawing away at him from the inside. *Keenan.*

March 2001

Luhde was brewing cinnamon coffee for the whole family. This was part of her regular routine, and she did it every afternoon. But she almost spilled the thermos of hot water when Keenan came up from behind her and grabbed her by the shoulders.

"Hey, it's your birthday next week, isn't it?" Keenan exclaimed.

Luhde turned around. Her face brightened. "How did you know? Who told you?"

"Banyu." Keenan smiled playfully. "You're going to be eighteen, huh? You won't be a kid anymore. What do you want? Lipstick? Perfume?"

"No. Nothing like that," she said as she pressed her hands to her cheeks in embarrassment.

"Why not? I mean, girls your age are usually starting to wear makeup. Or do you want something to wear? We can go to Kuta to find something."

Luhde shook her head even more vigorously. "No, not that!" Her hands were now covering her face.

"Okay, okay. So what do you want? How about a book?"

Luhde was quiet. She was thinking. Slowly, she lowered her hands. "I know," she said as a hint of a smile appeared on her face—a smile that transformed her. She looked beautiful. And grown up. "There *is* something—something you've put all your heart into making." Luhde's voice rang pure and clear.

Keenan was taken aback. First, by Luhde's beauty. And second, by her request, which he felt unable to fulfill, even though he understood what she meant by it. Keenan swallowed. "I put all my heart into every painting I make. You can choose whichever one you want. Or if you like, I can paint one especially for you."

Luhde shook her head. "You created those paintings out of your love of art. But that other thing . . . When I saw it, I wept. It was so beautiful. And it was beautiful because you created it out of an even deeper love."

Keenan was at a loss for how to respond.

In the blink of an eye, Luhde changed back into a shy teenage girl. "But I understand if you can't give it to me," she said, sounding embarrassed. "I'm sorry I'm always so forward with you." Hastily, she picked up the tray of coffee cups and left.

Keenan didn't move. A great dilemma was raging in his heart, one he had never experienced before.

CHAPTER 26

A NEW LEAF

In the middle of the night, as everyone lay sound asleep in their rooms, one person was still to be found outside. He was looking up at the clear night sky and the innumerable stars scattered across it.

Keenan sat alone. He remembered other nights like these, spent on the roof above his room in Bandung, enjoying the heavens so clear and vast, thinking about the same person he was thinking about now.

In his hand he clutched a wooden heart the size of his fist. It was something he had made more than a year ago—something he had meant to give to someone, something he still polished every day, though he kept it to himself. Its surface was covered with an abstract relief resembling ocean waves. Such precision and detail. Making it had caused his neck to ache for a week. He smiled at the memory.

Once again he studied the relief and rubbed it. Hidden among the waves were two initials: *K & K.*

Suddenly, he heard the wind whistling. It shook the hollow bamboo *kentungan* hanging from the eaves and they reverberated with a sweet, melodious sound. Keenan shivered as the wind blew against his skin, but he still refused to stir.

The sound of the *kentungan* reminded him of Kugy for some reason. He remembered Luhde's words. *Memories are nothing but ghosts in the corners of our minds.* And all this time he had been clinging to his love for a memory, an apparition who was nothing more than a shadow—even if Kugy was the most beautiful shadow ever to haunt his heart.

Keenan closed his eyes, immersing himself in the sharp pain filling every cell in his body. But he also knew it was time to let that shadow go. He gave the carving a slow kiss. "Little One, maybe this really isn't meant for you after all," he whispered. And with this gesture came the sharp pain of separation.

———

The sun was beginning to rise, its rays slowly wiping away all traces of the night sky and stars, and the roosters crowed.

Keenan knew the room was unlocked. He also didn't want to wake the room's occupant. Carefully, he opened the door and stepped inside.

Luhde was sound asleep, a peaceful expression on her face. The covers were pulled up to her neck and her long hair lay strewn across the pillow.

Slowing down every movement to avoid making a sound, Keenan placed the wooden carving beside her. "Happy birthday," he whispered.

May 2001

Eko met Kugy again at the Hunger No Longer. They ate lunch together, as they had been doing recently at least twice a week. This new habit was a saving grace for Kugy. It had been so long. Eko was her closest friend now.

That afternoon, Kugy discussed her plan to graduate in the next two semesters.

"Well, I'll be a dead gecko!" Eko exclaimed. "So you're going to start the process of submitting your thesis?" His eyes looked like they were going to pop out of his head.

Kugy nodded and gave a small smile.

"Whoa." Eko shook his head. "It's too much! You've gone too far! This isn't you at all!"

Kugy's grin broadened. "What do you mean by that?"

"Look. I know once you're obsessed with something you'll work at it nonstop," Eko protested. "It's like you're possessed by the djinns who built Prambanan in one night. But *this*? This is official academic-type stuff! When were you ever this crazy when it came to school? Are you really so desperate to get it over and done with?"

Kugy laughed. "I'm not desperate to graduate early because I love studying. I want to get out of here! That's why I've been working like crazy."

"Oh, I see," Eko murmured. His eyes grew wide and he gave Kugy a knowing look. "It sounds like someone's trying to run away from something."

Kugy frowned. "Run away from what?"

Eko's expression grew serious. "Kugy, there's a lot I haven't wanted to ask you because I respect your privacy. I know you're not the kind of person who talks a lot about her problems. So I've left the ball in your court this whole time. If you want to tell me, great! If not, I'm not going to force you. But, please, I just want to know one thing: What's been going on with you for the past year? You've completely changed, you've pulled away from us, and we don't know why."

Kugy looked at Eko for a long time. There were so many things she wanted to tell him all jumbled together on the tip of her tongue, waiting to come tumbling out. But once again, she felt paralyzed. Kugy shook her head and gave him a thin smile. "Sorry, I'm still not ready to tell you."

Eko let out a long sigh. "You don't miss the old times with the midnight movie gang?"

"Of course I do," Kugy answered softly. "But I also don't mind how things are now. Sometimes, it even feels better. I have more space."

"If you say so," answered Eko.

The two of them were silent.

"I miss Keenan," said Eko all of a sudden. "Do you know where he is?"

At the sound of Keenan's name, Kugy jumped. She tried her best to look calm and unfazed. "He's your cousin. Can't you ask his family?"

"His family doesn't know where he is, either."

"Oh," mumbled Kugy. Her expression didn't change, but she couldn't help but feel uneasy.

"It's like the kid's been abducted by a UFO. Vanished without a trace. Crazy, huh?" Eko looked up at Kugy. "The two of you really are weirdos! One of you has run away, the other is trying to run away—what's with you guys?"

Kugy couldn't help but smile. "You know, the fact that you're angry is a sign of your affection."

"Affection? Yeah, it does affect me—how annoying you are." Eko made a face. "But I guess I'm still willing to be your friend a little while longer. It must be out of affection. Or maybe it's because, deep down, I like to collect rare and ugly specimens like you."

Kugy laughed. "I love you, too," she said.

"Shut up!"

October 2001

It hadn't even been a year yet, but Keenan's paintings were generating a lot of talk. His name was circulating among the gallery and art-collecting set. But he was still unwilling to show his work in Jakarta, and remained with Uncle Wayan's gallery in Ubud. He had developed a following and a number of collectors inquired frequently about his newest paintings, but there was no collector as eager as that first one—his first buyer. It was as if he could predict the patterns in Keenan's creativity. Rarely did other buyers beat him to it. He seemed obsessed with collecting the complete series of Keenan's *Alit* paintings, which were beginning to be the talk of the town.

Keenan meanwhile felt funny knowing that his work was an object of discussion and rivalry. Lying before him was his savings account statement. After those difficult times in Bandung—the most difficult in his life—he had never dreamed he would have so much money. And suddenly, Keenan felt compelled to ask Uncle Wayan a question.

"Poyan, what will happen if I hit a wall? Or burn out? Or what if people get bored with my work?"

Uncle Wayan chuckled softly. He pulled up a chair and sat beside Keenan. "It's true that we can't predict what collectors will like. We can't control what curators will think, either. Like fruit, they have their seasons." There was a broad smile on his face. "You're right to be worried. When it comes down to it, the most difficult people to predict are ourselves. There will come a time when you'll ask yourself: Where has all my inspiration gone? Suddenly, you'll feel abandoned. All you'll be able to do is sit there, not producing anything. You'll feel like you've run dry. But it won't necessarily mean you'll have to find a new subject or source of inspiration. It's like finding your soulmate. If you're having problems with your girlfriend, it doesn't mean you should get a new one, does it? Still, love does have to be renewed. Love can spring up by itself, but that's no guarantee it will last forever, especially if it isn't tended to. Do you understand what I'm saying?"

Keenan shook his head.

"General Pilik's stories have inspired you. But in order for General Pilik to truly come alive and not just be a character in that book, he has to become a part of you. He has to live on in your heart. Do you understand?"

This time Keenan nodded. Nonetheless, the depths hidden in that afternoon's conversation still escaped him.

New Year's Eve 2001

Kugy sat alone on the front terrace, a mosquito-repellent coil keeping her company and Snoozy, their basset hound, dozing at her feet. Everyone else was inside fast asleep.

She had gone two years without making any resolutions. It was a change from her usual practice of writing down her goals, and then hiding them to be read again the following New Year's Eve. In this sense she had been like Snoozy, who loved hiding bones so he could one day return to dig them up.

Yet, before her lay a sheet of paper and a ballpoint pen—not for writing down resolutions, though. After much reflection, Kugy began to write:

> *Neptune, I really hope this letter reaches the ocean this time. Why? Because to be honest, I miss him. I miss him so much. And I feel that tonight he is near the ocean. Give him my regards, okay? And if you don't, watch out—this agent is going on strike.*

Kugy folded the sheet of paper into a boat. She'd have to wait until tomorrow to set it afloat on the stream. Tonight, she would have to find another way. Kugy held the letter to her chest, closed her eyes, and imagined the wide open sea and the sound of the waves. She had once told Keenan that the sound of waves was nature's sweetest song. She could almost hear them now.

Wherever you are, may this message reach you. Even without a boat. I miss you very much.

———

As Keenan watched the waves, lost in thought, he realized there would always be times when he had to stop and think about her.

Oh, Little One, if only you were here. You would be so happy. Didn't you tell me once that the sound of waves was nature's sweetest song? Keenan let out a long sigh. *I wonder what you're doing these days.*

"Keenan!" a man's voice called out. It was joined by a woman's, also calling his name. Keenan returned to the present. He was in the middle of a New Year's Eve party at the house of one of Uncle Wayan's good friends. The backyard, which looked out directly onto the beach, made it possible for him to enjoy the openness of his surroundings without being disturbed by the crowds.

"Keenan, come inside for a bit," said the man. "Mr. Wayan is looking for you."

Meanwhile, Luhde appeared at Keenan's side and took his arm. How radiant and happy she looked tonight. This was the first time Luhde had ever attended a party. But what made her the happiest was being able to share the experience with Keenan.

"Sorry, I have to leave you for a minute. But I'll be back soon. You'll be all right, won't you?" Keenan gently stroked Luhde's hand.

"I'll be fine. I have someone to keep me company." Luhde glanced at the man next to her.

Keenan laughed. "Thanks for taking care of Luhde for me. Hopefully she won't wear you out."

"No problem," the man answered with a smile. "I enjoy talking with her. She's smart and full of surprises."

Luhde ducked her head, like the involuntary response of a touch-me-not plant, closing upon contact. But in her heart she was overjoyed.

Luhde knew this man wasn't just anybody. He was the first buyer of Keenan's paintings, and now he and Keenan were friends. Every time he visited Bali, he stopped by the gallery, taking time to walk around and talk with Keenan and her family. And tonight, the man had even decided to spend New Year's Eve in Bali with them.

Keenan returned to the house. As he walked, he looked out at the sea one last time. In the distance, he could hear people still blowing on their party horns. The New Year had now begun. The turning over of a new leaf.

He felt dizzy. Looking straight ahead, he left the beach behind him.

CHAPTER 27

A PROMISE IS A PROMISE

January 2002

Kugy had received an A on her thesis proposal and was celebrating by returning home to Jakarta for the first time in months. Now she was enjoying her days relaxing. On Sunday afternoon, her family gathered in the TV room. The noise was a hallmark of all K Family gatherings.

"So, once the semester begins, all you have to do is write your thesis?" asked her older sister, Karin.

"Yup!"

"Kevin, you're so slow!" Karin exclaimed, slapping her younger brother on the forehead. "You've been going to community college for four years now and still no signs of graduating. Kugy's beating you and she's getting a bachelor's degree!"

"It's the end result that's important!" Kevin shot back. "Now look. I'm social. And I've done a lot. Kugy's a nerd. Of course she's going to graduate quickly."

"You have done a lot," Kugy said with a smirk. "We can tell from all the free T-shirts you get from organizing 'important' events."

Karin chuckled. "Yeah, Kev. Are you going to be busy with extra-curricular activities forever?"

"Soon you'll be asking permission to drop out so you can make extracurricular activities your life: hiking events, chess competitions, car shows, badminton championships, fashion shows . . . It'll never end." This comment came from their father as he walked by.

Kugy laughed. "'Kevin: The One-Man Organizing Committee. A Million Events and Counting.' Put that on a T-shirt and you'll never have to take it off!"

"*You're* the weird one!" Kevin protested. "You should try being human—it's fun! Three years of university and you're already writing your undergrad thesis? What's up with that? Not living life—that's what I call it."

Kugy's older brother, Karel, spoke up. "Seriously, though, Kugy. What are you going to do after you graduate?"

"Get a job, of course!"

"Kugy, Kugy . . ." It was Kevin's turn to shake his head. "Do you really want to get a job so soon? Jobs are tiring, you know. It's good to be a student. Otherwise you'll end up like Karin: nothing but skin and bones."

"I'm not skinny! You're obese!" Karin said, glaring at Kevin.

"I'm not fat, my darling sister. I'm just not that tall."

"What kind of job do you want to get, Kugy?" Karel asked.

"It has to involve writing somehow. But I don't want to be a reporter. I'm not that talented when it comes to journalism."

"So you don't want to be a—what was it again? It began with *t*." Kevin tried to remember.

"A tire repairman?" Keshia suggested.

"A teller! That's it! A *story*teller!" Kevin snorted in derision.

"A teller of tales," Kugy corrected him, annoyed. "Maybe someday, when I'm old and retired. How will I earn any money if I do that?"

Karel raised his eyebrows. "Suddenly you're thinking about money?"

"I'm much more of a realist now," said Kugy with a tight smile. There was a bitter taste in her mouth as she spoke.

"Okay, how about I help you look?" said Karel. "My friend recently set up his own advertising firm. Maybe he needs a copywriter. You could probably start out as an intern first, before you officially graduate."

"Ask him! Ask him!" said Kugy. "I can work without pay first! That's fine!"

"One minute you're proclaiming yourself a realist, the next you're saying you don't need to get paid." Kevin laughed. "You're terrible at thinking about money! How are you going to get rich?"

"Look who's talking," said Karin, laughing even harder. "As if there's any money to be made serving on organizing committees all the time! If you had a hundred rupiah for every time you've helped organize an event, you'd already have your own house."

But Kugy's mind was already soaring far away, to graduation, to her first day of work. Whatever it was, wherever it was, the important thing was she would be able to leave and turn over a new leaf.

March 2002

Wayan watched his niece as she sat in the *bale* writing furiously. She happily scribbled away on the pages of the thick notebook she carried everywhere. Even though she'd been given a computer, Luhde still preferred writing by hand.

"What kind of story are you writing?" Wayan asked gently as he sat down in front of her.

"A children's story," said Luhde. She kept writing.

"You're still serious about becoming a writer?"

"Yes, Poyan. I want to write children's stories. Later, Keenan will provide the illustrations."

This startled Wayan. He looked again at Luhde. Her eyes were shining with excitement, though her tone was serious, as if she were in the middle of pouring her whole life and soul onto paper.

"Luhde. Poyan ka ngomong kejep," he said in Balinese. "I want to talk with you for a moment."

Luhde put down her pen and shut her notebook. Whenever her uncle started speaking in Balinese, it meant he wanted to discuss something serious.

"I understand. You're growing up. Your heart wants to go somewhere, to put down anchor and rest. But that journey has its risks."

Luhde's face turned red. "What do you mean, Poyan?"

"Of all the people in this house, I'm closest to you both. I can feel the change between the two of you."

Luhde's brow furrowed. "Who—"

"You and Keenan," said Wayan matter-of-factly.

Luhde fell silent. All she could do was blink nervously.

"Be careful. Take your time. Fall bit by bit, not all at once. Learn from my experience." Wayan spoke gently, but there was a bitterness in his faint smile.

Slowly, Luhde nodded. She knew what her uncle was referring to.

"It isn't easy being someone else's shadow," Wayan continued. "It's better to wait until the heart heals and makes its decisions with more clarity, free of shadows entirely." He patted Luhde's shoulder. Then he left.

Luhde stayed there for a while, perfectly still, reflecting. Finally, her eyes came to rest on her notebook. She realized what she had been putting all her heart into trying to achieve. She realized what shadows her uncle was talking about. Her eyes grew hot.

May 2002

Eko was late again. He should have picked up Noni from her boarding house ten minutes ago. For the past six months, Noni had been giving private English lessons to a group of middle school students. She conducted lessons at one of the students' houses once a week. With an irritable expression and her arms folded, Noni was sitting in a chair on the front terrace. Several bags containing papers and books were at her feet.

Eko knew what lay in store for him.

"Noni . . ."

Noni gathered up her things and approached Fuad briskly, her lips clamped tight.

"Here, let me help—"

"I've got it," she snapped. "Enough already. Let's just go. I'm so late."

"I'm really sorry . . ."

"If you can't pick me up, just say so! I could have taken an *angkot*, or called a taxi, or gotten a lift with someone else. But now my whole schedule is thrown off. And my poor students are waiting for me. Where were you?"

"There was an emergency. I'm so sorry."

"What emergency?"

"Kugy's computer crashed and her thesis defense is in two weeks. So she panicked and I helped bring her computer to a repair shop. Luckily, they managed to retrieve all the data. Crazy, man. I don't know what would've happened if the whole thing had to be typed up again."

For the past few weeks Eko had been at Kugy's boarding house all the time helping her with her thesis. Eko had even canceled a date with Noni to help Kugy type it up.

For the whole ride, Noni didn't say a word.

Fuad pulled up by the gate in front of the house. Eko turned off the engine and looked at Noni with despair. "Please say something. Swear, complain—do what you usually do. But don't be silent like this. I'd rather you got mad at me than give me the silent treatment."

With great difficulty, Noni picked up all her bags and got out of the car.

"Wait! Let me help!" Eko scrambled out of the car and trailed after her. She was walking so fast that it looked like she was running away.

"Why don't you wait till after Kugy defends her thesis before you see me again?" huffed Noni as she kept walking.

June 2002

Doing a little *joget* dance to Duran Duran, Kugy double-checked to make sure all the documents for her presentation tomorrow were complete, including the notes she had prepared in anticipation of questions the committee might ask. Reassuring herself that everything was ready, she let out a deep breath. Now she really felt ready. And this song never sounded so good.

"Is the situation under control?" asked Eko, dancing a *joget* as well.

"Roger that, Commander," said Kugy as she gave him a thumbs-up. "Hey, we should choreograph this. Could be a military-style *joget* or something."

"I'm all in," said Eko. "Know why I'm dancing? I'll tell you why—I'm in awe. Who'd have thought a friend of mine would be one of the few to get their diploma in less than four years? Damn you all."

Kugy stopped in her tracks. "Thanks, Eko. From the bottom of my heart. I don't know whether I would have finished this if it weren't for you."

"I told you already, don't get all mushy in front of me or I'll poke you in the eye." Eko chuckled.

"I'm serious," Kugy said. "If there's anything I can help you with, please let me know, okay? I owe you one."

Eko stopped dancing and thought for a minute. "Actually, there is something I need your help with."

"Anything."

"I want you to speak to Noni after you defend your thesis. Make things right. I can't guarantee you'll be able to reconcile right away. But at least, you'll have tried. Okay?" His voice was gentle. "For me? Please?"

Of all the requests Eko could have made, Kugy had dreaded this one the most. But a promise was a promise. She nodded.

———

The door opened and Noni greeted Eko in a flat voice. "Yeah. What is it?"

"Are you still mad?" asked Eko.

"It doesn't matter," Noni answered. "As long as Kugy still has to defend her thesis, nothing matters—"

"She's defending it tomorrow," Eko interrupted. "You could come to show your support. She'd be so happy if you came."

"Will she be happy or will you be happy?"

"Noni, come on! You two have been friends for how many years? Are you really going to give it all up over a little problem like this? You don't even know what the problem is! All of a sudden you just stopped talking to each other. And on top of it all, you're both equally stubborn! I don't get it."

"The problem has always been out in the open," Noni declared. "Namely that she's not! She's never open with us! *That's* the problem. And what makes it even more annoying is you're always taking her side!"

"Noni, that's not true. I'm not taking sides, I just want you two—"

"Are you really so naïve, or are you just playing innocent? Just admit it already."

Eko frowned. "Admit what?"

"You've had a crush on her since middle school, long before we started dating. And the part of you that's crazy for Kugy still hasn't changed. You're always praising her. She can never do wrong in your eyes. You love her and she'll always have a special place in your heart.

Isn't that right?" Noni was trying not to cry. Her voice quivered. Everything she had been holding in was finally coming out.

Eko's jaw dropped. "Noni! She's my friend! Of course I love that lunatic! But it's not the kind of love you think. Geez, what's with you?"

"Why don't you ask yourself that question?" Noni yelled. "What's with *you*?"

She slammed the door in Eko's face. He knocked and called her name, but it was no use.

CHAPTER 28

ADVOCADO

Kugy's thesis defense was attended by her closest friends. Ami, Ical, Eko, and Bimo were there, among others. Only Eko waited with her as the committee made its decision. He and Kugy sat on a bench outside the room. They didn't say much—just gazed blankly ahead.

Suddenly, Mr. Danar, the administrative assistant who was on friendly terms with Kugy, poked his head out. "The decision is in!"

"From the look on Mr. Danar's face, I think you got an A," Eko whispered as he followed Kugy down the hall.

"Really? I saw a C written on his face . . . or that I didn't pass. Oh, I'm so nervous."

"Here," said Mr. Danar. "You can see for yourself." He posted the sheet announcing the results of the three thesis-defense sessions held that morning.

"An A plus?" cried Eko.

Kugy clapped her hands over her mouth. Her eyes looked like they were going to fall out of her head. "I don't believe it."

"You got the highest score, you moron!" Eko shouted, shaking Kugy by the shoulders. "Damn it! You're so amazing!"

Kugy turned around to face him and hugged him tightly. "Thank you, Eko," she whispered, teary eyed. "I would never have been able to do it if it weren't for you."

Eko was caught off guard by her reaction, but slowly, the tension in his body melted away, and he returned Kugy's embrace. "No problem. I'm so happy for you." Then he gave Kugy's forehead a playful slap. "Hey, be careful. I've already been your errand boy for the past two months. Don't get all sentimental on me now. And stop crying all the time."

Kugy loosened her embrace. "From now on, I will forever be your errand girl."

Eko reached into his pocket and handed over his car keys. "You can start by being my driver."

"Sure thing, boss," Kugy answered, standing at attention. "Please, let me drive. I'll also get you something to eat. And something to drink. But as usual, you'll have to pay."

"You're the worst employee ever!" Eko sputtered, laughing.

Someone was watching them from a distance as they walked away, their arms around each other. It was Noni. That morning, she had begun to regret the accusations she had hurled at Eko, and she had felt compelled to come to campus to show Kugy her support. With fear and reluctance still weighing on her heart, Noni had managed to overcome these emotions and had gone to the rooms where the thesis-defense sessions were held. But after what she'd just witnessed, she and Kugy were finished.

Part of her was devastated. What she feared most had in fact become reality. Eko really did love Kugy. And from what she had just seen, it wasn't unrequited, either.

Noni tried to stay strong and hold her head up high as she walked away. Her chest rose and fell with the effort it took to hold back her tears. She wished she could just fly away and be gone. Then her strength failed her.

Kugy hadn't been to the boarding house in ages. She had lived there for two years. It was her first home in Bandung. Yet soon she would be leaving the city entirely. She looked around, every corner stirring up a whole series of memories. Kugy shook her head, as if she were trying to shake something off. She continued walking toward the room, then glanced at the sign: "Noni Is In."

Kugy took a deep breath and knocked. The door opened and there was Noni, caught by surprise. She hadn't been expecting Kugy at all.

Kugy contorted her lips into the widest smile she could manage. "Hi, Noni! How are you?"

Noni didn't say a word. She gave Kugy a look that made it clear she didn't want to be disturbed.

"I passed my thesis defense this morning, and Karel is already trying to find work for me in Jakarta. I'm going to try interning before getting a paid job. So I want to say good-bye. And I'd love to chat for a bit." Kugy tried to keep her tone as bright as possible. "Can I come in?" she asked hesitantly.

Noni didn't budge. "Congratulations on graduating," she said. "But I have a lot of work to do. Sorry."

"Maybe I can help?" Kugy offered.

Noni shook her head.

"Actually, there's something I really want to speak to you about," Kugy said with a slight stammer. "I-I want us to be friends again, like before. I'm sorry about everything. But even now, I don't know where to start—"

"I appreciate the effort," Noni interrupted. "But that's all history now. It's better if we keep things the way they are. It's a lot easier—for me, for you, and probably for Eko, too."

Kugy felt a sharp jab in her heart. She dreaded what would come next, but she couldn't help herself. "Why?" she asked.

Noni clenched her jaw. How she longed to spew out all her frustrations, like a barrage of bullets. But she didn't know where to begin. "All my life, for as long as we've been friends, I've always had to accept that you're prettier, smarter, and better than me at everything. Still, I was never jealous—because I loved you so much. But this time, you've hurt me too much, using all your strengths to your advantage . . ." Noni tried to control her voice as she spoke.

Kugy tried to digest her friend's words, but she couldn't grasp what she was saying.

"I know Eko sympathizes with your situation. He loves you. We both did once. But just because he's the only one left who'll talk to you doesn't mean you have the right to overstep your boundaries. If you really had a heart, you would know your place. If it's a choice between acting all buddy-buddy but stabbing your friend in the back, or becoming a stranger and not backstabbing, I suggest you do the latter. Either way, I don't have room for you in my life anymore."

"Noni, you've got it all wrong! Completely!" Kugy was so stunned she could barely breathe. "I didn't mean anything like that. There's never been anything between Eko and me. We're just friends—"

"Okay." Noni cut her off sharply. "I have a confession to make. I came to campus earlier to attend your thesis defense and show my support. Now I have something to ask you." Her expression hardened. "Was Josh ever my constant companion for weeks on end? Did I ever go around hugging him in public?"

Kugy tried to understand what was going on, what Noni had seen, what she was thinking. "You're talking about what happened on campus this afternoon? I was just . . . Geez, Noni. I've been friends with Eko for ten years. We're like brother and sister. How can you compare my relationship with Eko to your relationship with Josh?"

"If you cared about my feelings, you wouldn't make excuses like this. You should know your place. Don't play innocent, Kugy. Eko's always had a soft spot for you. Now it's up to you: Are you going to acknowledge I'm his girlfriend, or are you going to act like I don't exist?"

Kugy bowed her head, recalling all she'd been through these past two years. Suddenly she felt exhausted. "That is the stupidest thing I've ever heard you say," she said slowly.

Those words pierced Noni's heart, but she kept her composure. "See?" she said coldly. "Now you get it, don't you? Why I said we shouldn't change anything? It's better this way."

Kugy nodded. "Yes, it's better this way."

Noni closed the door.

When Kugy reached her boarding house, she didn't waste any time packing. She was going home to Jakarta as quickly as possible. There was nothing keeping her in Bandung. Nothing at all.

That night, Kugy also decided to get rid of all the memories and problems weighing on her heart and cast them far, far away. Noni included.

August 2002

Kugy stared at herself in the mirror—something she'd been doing on and off for the past half hour. This was probably the longest she'd ever looked at her reflection. In fact, she'd hardly ever used the mirror before this because she didn't really care about what she saw there. Yet today, she felt that something was definitely not right.

There was something wrong with the knee-length skirt she was wearing, with the high heels on her feet, with the clutch purse she was carrying, with the sudden fullness of her hair due to the curlers she'd worn all morning.

"Why do I look so awful?" she moaned, turning to Karin—the person responsible for the way she looked.

"I'll tell you what's awful, Kugy—your eyesight and your fashion sense. If you want to work in an office, if you want to look interesting, attractive, and professional, then this is how you dress!"

Karel, who had just finished breakfast, poked his head in. "Kugy, let's go—" He stopped midsentence and stared in amazement at his younger sister. "Did you get your information right? You know, you're going to be a co-py-wri-ter." He enunciated each syllable. "Not a fashion editor. Not a receptionist. And not a sales promotion girl!"

Karin glared at him. "Karel, this is what you call 'style,' okay? Something you wouldn't know anything about, either. So leave it to the expert, please?"

"Karin, I've been to this office several times. Even the boss wears jeans to work. And Kugy is going to be in the creative department. In this matter, I'm the expert. So please, don't use our little sister as a guinea pig for your fashion experiments, okay?"

"Fine, fine." Karin turned away. "Obviously the problem here is that we have different tastes."

This was Kugy's cue to shout for joy. "Hooray! So I can just wear my own clothes, right?" She ran to her room to change.

Before long she was standing in the dining room, inviting her siblings to comment. "What do you think of this?"

She wore the long black skirt she'd bought for her thesis defense and the white collared shirt she'd been required to wear to Founding National Principles class. Karel's denim jacket was draped over her shoulders, and on her wrist was her Teenage Mutant Ninja Turtles watch, painful as always to behold.

Karel swallowed. He glanced at Karin, his eyes pleading for help.

———

Before entering the office building, Kugy stopped and surveyed it from the front. Printed in large leaf-green letters on the stone wall was the company's name: AdVocaDo. Everything still looked new. Located in a residential area in South Jakarta, the small two-story building looked very artistic and almost gallery-like. Its design was minimalist but with bold red accents on the door and window frames, and the statues were overlaid in bright metal. That wasn't all—the office was surrounded by a tropical Balinese-style garden, lush and beautiful.

The interior was equally as impressive. From the lighting to the furniture, Kugy could tell at once that the person in charge had above-average taste. And from the works of art she saw everywhere, Kugy quickly deduced that the owner of the firm was a dedicated art lover.

As she sat with Karel on the sofa in the waiting area, Kugy's eyes roamed her potential new workplace.

Before long, a man emerged and walked toward them. "Karel! How are you?"

Karel rose and the two men embraced. Kugy stood up as well. She felt awkward. She rarely gave people's appearances a second thought, but this man had changed the atmosphere of the room just by his presence. Kugy had imagined Remigius Aditya would be much older, but the owner of AdVocaDo was still very young. He looked approachable in his short-sleeved collared shirt and black jeans, and his face was handsome and fresh, as if he'd just come from a spa.

"Let me introduce you. This is my little sister, Kugy." Karel pushed her forward.

"I'm Remigius," he said in a friendly tone as he shook her hand. "You can call me Remi."

Karel shook his head. "No, no. That's too informal."

Remi gave a low laugh. "Just Remi," he insisted. "Please."

Kugy smiled. "I'm Kugy."

"Thank you so much for this opportunity," said Karel. "Hopefully she won't be too much of an embarrassment."

"She's one of the K Family, isn't she?" Remi laughed. "I have faith in her." He turned to Kugy. "Your resume looks very good, and you've come at just the right time."

"Really?" she said.

"We have a lot to do—new projects, media campaigns, the works. One thing's for sure, you'll be busy right off the bat." Remi spoke breezily. "Come on. You can start right away. I'll introduce you to the different teams."

Kugy's palms were sweating. The university campus, her boarding house, the Sakola Alit—she could see them so clearly, as if everything had happened only yesterday. Now she was embarking on something entirely new. Just then, Kugy wished she could fly back to Bandung.

CHAPTER 29

THE WORLD STILL TURNS

September 2002

Kugy couldn't believe she had made it through her first month at AdVocaDo. Because she had graduated so recently, she was dubbed "the new kid." Her team was headed by a creative director who was also supervising several other projects, and an art director named Siska and a senior copywriter named Iman made up the rest of its members.

While the lower level of the building belonged to accounting, the creative department occupied the second floor. And while the ambience of the first floor was more orderly and the people there more neatly dressed, the second floor was lively, rowdy, and more chaotic. Kugy worked on the second floor, occupying a corner cubicle with a computer and a desk.

Remi was right. She was incredibly busy right off the bat. Every few moments, someone new appeared from behind the cubicle partition. "Can you scan these?" they would ask, handing her a pile of drawings. "Can you photocopy these?" they would ask, handing her a pile of documents. "Can you cut out all the marked drawings for a storyboard?"

they would ask, handing her a pile of magazines and a small pair of scissors. Kugy felt the only job she hadn't been given yet was to make coffee or tea, and that was only because those were the duties of the office boy and office girl. Sometimes, Kugy felt more like a senior office girl than a junior copywriter.

The hours were unpredictable. The office boy and office girl left at six, but Kugy sometimes had to stay until eleven—longer if there was a client presentation coming up, though when it came time to give the presentation, she was never asked to join.

Whenever she returned home, Kugy faced a barrage of questions from her family, who were excited about her new job. "How's work going? Do you like it?" "Hey, what ads have you come up with?" "I heard your boss is good-looking. Is it true?" Kugy was frank and told them that since she had started working at AdVocaDo she had become skilled at cutting and photocopying, and that it all would come in handy if she ever opened her own photocopy service kiosk. Occasionally, she answered these questions with a snore as she lay sprawled on the living room sofa, where she remained fast asleep till morning.

———

It was Friday. Kugy had been looking forward to it all week because she was planning to spend the entire weekend vegging out. She would be task-free. Her thoughts were already at day's end, in bed, playing with Snoozy and devouring a pile of new Japanese manga comics.

But today, she was trapped in a staff meeting, discussing an upcoming candy bar ad campaign. She knew any involvement on her part would consist only of cutting and scanning. Stirring her coffee, she tried to look like she was paying attention, even though she wanted to die of boredom.

Iman was working hard to convince Remi about his proposed concept. "But this text is catchy. I know we'll have to cut a lot of it to make room for visuals, but the message will still be clear."

"Yeah, I know. But how do I say this?" Remi thought for a while. "I don't feel like it hits the mark. So many ads have taken the same approach."

Fani, from another team, spoke up. "Narration is central to the concept. Tammies: Swiss chocolate, real caramel, crispy wafers, hazelnut cream, etcetera, etcetera. Those are the details we need to push."

Remi shook his head. "It's stale. And I feel like it's not a good fit for the demographic we're targeting."

"But it's what the client wants," Iman protested. "They want to highlight the quality of the ingredients, the taste, what the wrapper looks like. If not through narration or text, how?"

Gina, the account director, cleared her throat. "Friends, I don't mean to make the situation more stressful, but I want to remind you that the client has given us a difficult product on purpose. If we score a goal with this one, they'll put us in charge of everything. The company is launching four products in Indonesia this year alone. The Tammies bar is just a trial run, but it's crucial we get it right."

"So which concept are we going with?" asked Tasya. "My team's, Iman's, or Fani's?" Her team had been the last to present and Remi had shot them down as well.

Remi took a deep breath. "Sorry, guys. I'm still not satisfied."

Everyone looked disgruntled. All those days of hard work had been for nothing. Not only that, but they would have to start again from scratch. Remi looked around. Everyone was watching him anxiously, awaiting his final decision. Almost everyone. Remi's eyes came to rest on Kugy, who was stirring her coffee at the far end of the table. Her chin was propped up on one swaying hand. It was clear from her drooping eyelids that she was about to pass out.

"I want an opinion from someone who hasn't spoken. Kugy, what do you think?"

At the sound of her name, her sleepiness vanished and she sat up. "Wha— Opinion? About what?"

The others snickered at the scene: Kugy, the student who had been caught sleeping in class, and Remi, the fierce teacher ready to dole out punishment.

"The Tammies bar ad," Remi repeated, his voice growing sharper. "What's your opinion?"

"We're still discussing that?" Kugy asked innocently.

The snickering continued.

Remi began speaking slowly, as if talking to a child. "In your opinion, which of these three concepts best hits the mark?"

Kugy was quiet as she racked her brain, trying to play back everything that had happened in this meeting so far. They'd been there for an hour now. She hoped the memory was still somewhere in her head. "Um. I don't like any of them," she said finally.

The titters subsided. In the blink of an eye, smirks were replaced with serious expressions.

Remi was curious. "Okay. Why not?"

"They're all too ordinary, if you ask me."

The atmosphere in the room, already still, now froze. Kugy was besieged by glares, left and right.

Now her sleepiness was really gone, and what she had just said, as well as its consequences, began to dawn on her. But there was no turning back now. She had to continue.

"The three concepts contain a lot of information, but they're too chatty. Visually speaking, all three fulfill the client's requirements. But they don't have any kick. There's nothing special about them. They don't make me drool. I wouldn't want to buy a Tammies bar if I were a viewer. We have to make people intrigued about the Tammies bar—make them want to try it."

"Simple in theory," Iman blurted in a high-pitched voice. "What does it mean in terms of concept?"

Kugy fell silent. *How should I know,* she thought. But everyone in the room was waiting for her answer. They looked like a pack of hungry lions, too fierce and terrible for her to admit she had no idea. So, instead, Kugy decided to say whatever came to mind.

"Picture this: a black background. And silence. No music, no voice—like the TV's gone dead. But it hasn't. Then there appears . . . a single wafer. Then a stream of hazelnut cream. Then another wafer. And a drizzle of caramel. After this, a layer of chocolate, melting, coating it all, and a shower of crisped rice. Then the chocolate hardens. All with dramatic sound effects. Like the time Mr. Freeze wanted to freeze all of Gotham City. Finally, the bar is slipped into a wrapper: Tammies. And the following words: *More taste, less talk.*"

The room was silent. But it was a different kind of silence than before. Kugy had set everyone adrift, visualizing her idea.

"The tagline's not bad," murmured Fani. Despite her reluctant expression, she liked it very much.

"It's unusual," Tasya acknowledged. "I like the idea of the TV suddenly going dead. And the idea for that sound effect—Mr. Freeze? I don't know who that is, but it's memorable."

"I'd certainly want to buy it," Siska chimed in. "My mouth is watering just thinking about it. The visuals will be a lot of work, but I'm optimistic we'll manage."

Gina chuckled. "It's economical, too. We don't need a jingle, or overdubbing, or anything."

Iman glanced at Remi. So did everyone else. He was the only one who hadn't said anything yet.

Remi slammed his hand down on the table. "Great. It's a done deal. Tammies: *More taste, less talk.* Sound effects and visuals just as Kugy described. We're good to go, then. I want Kugy to be the project leader for this pitch. Get the presentation ready, okay, Kugy? Good luck." Then Remi stood up. Gazing warmly at Kugy, he patted her on the shoulder. "And . . . good job."

Kugy felt her blood grow warm. Gradually the tension that had gripped her melted away, and she smiled. Kugy knew this was the end of her career as AdVocaDo's designated arts-and-crafts employee and her first real day on the job.

———

When Lena heard the news from her husband's office, she went straight to the hospital. Half running, she hurried down the corridor, looking for Adri's room. Jeroen followed, still wearing his school uniform.

She found her husband lying in bed. His face was pale, but he was obviously trying to look as if nothing was wrong.

"Hi, Lena. Jeroen." He greeted them with a forced smile.

"Dad, what's wrong? What happened?" Jeroen asked, panicked.

"Oh, it's nothing," Adri answered, trying to calm his son. "It was just a little stroke. I couldn't move my hand. See? But it'll go back to normal soon. There. I can move the fingers a little already."

"What causes a stroke, Mom?" Jeroen asked.

"All sorts of things, dear. They can happen if you're too tired, or stressed, or . . ." Lena was still too dazed and breathless to finish her sentence. Though she too was trying to appear calm, she couldn't conceal her deepening worry. It was written all over her face.

"I'm fine. Really. A few weeks of physiotherapy and I'll be back to normal." Adri stroked his wife's arm. "Everything will be back to normal," he repeated as if trying to assure himself.

Lena was lost in thought. This was more than just a matter of physiotherapy. She was worried about what hadn't been said, what was hidden away, and what would continue casting a shadow over their family from here on out.

———

Keenan had been holding the block brush for some time now. The white canvas was before him, ready and waiting. But there wasn't a single stroke of color on it. It was as if his hand were paralyzed. This was the first time in the two years since taking up painting again that he had experienced such a creative block. The feeling was strange. Worse—it was terrifying.

Keenan felt a nervous energy spread throughout his body, slowly and steadily engulfing him. He felt restless. Even the clear late-afternoon sky held no meaning for him. Something was wrong. But he couldn't figure out what.

Keenan saw Banyu passing by the *bale* and called out to him. "Banyu! Where's Luhde?"

"She went to the temple at Puri Saren Agung," Banyu said, continuing on his way. "She'll be home in a bit."

Maybe it's because Luhde's not here, thought Keenan. *Usually when she's here, everything is fine.* Finally he decided to lie down and wait. But he kept turning from side to side, almost feverishly. The restlessness was becoming unbearable. There was nothing he could do.

"Keenan, were you looking for me?" Luhde asked from behind him.

Quickly, he sat up, feeling incredibly relieved. "Why were you away for so long?" he asked, tugging at her hand.

The unusually warm greeting startled her. She sat down beside him. "I'm sorry. Did we have plans?"

Keenan laughed. "No, but I feel strange today. I guess I missed you. It felt strange not to have you here with me."

Luhde swallowed. She had never thought she would hear those words from Keenan. As if that wasn't surprising enough, he suddenly rested his head in her lap.

"It feels so peaceful like this," Keenan murmured. He closed his eyes.

Luhde's body tensed. But she let Keenan rest, his body leaning against her legs. He looked so relaxed. She tried to get used to this position, this view.

"Why can't I paint today, Luhde?" Keenan asked. "My heart is empty, my mind is blank. Nothing's flowing like it usually does."

"It's understandable if you're tired of painting. You've been working almost nonstop for months now."

"But what if it's not just because I'm tired? What if it's because I—" Keenan couldn't finish what he was going to say.

"Sometimes the sky looks like a blank sheet of black paper," Luhde continued gently, "even though it's not. The stars are still there. It's just that the world is turning."

Keenan let out a long sigh and hoped Luhde's words were true. He grabbed her hand and placed it on his chest. "I don't know what I would do without you," he whispered.

They were silent once again. But a sliver of that whisper reverberated in Luhde's soul, filling every corner of it. She had never heard Keenan express his feelings so explicitly, so clearly. Luhde had never felt this happy. Slowly, her hand smoothed the strands of his hair. Each stroke was filled with emotion. And with every movement of her fingers, Luhde hoped Keenan would feel what she was feeling now.

CHAPTER 30
THE NONAQUARIAN AGENT

The minute Kugy stepped foot inside the lobby, she was told to report to Remi's office. She glanced at her watch. Due to all the work she had been doing for the Tammies presentation, she had been arriving at the office after eleven for the past four days. She had been working late every night, and couldn't bring herself to open her eyes any earlier than eight in the morning. Jakarta's rush-hour traffic meant further delay. She wouldn't be surprised if she was in for a reprimand.

"Morning, Kugy," said Remi, greeting her cheerfully. "Please, come in." Gina was there as well.

"Sorry I'm late," said Kugy. "I was exhausted after the presentation yesterday, so I tried to get plenty of sleep. I don't want to get sick."

"Yes, you should definitely look after yourself," Gina said. "You really can't get sick. Because . . ." Smiling mysteriously, she glanced at Remi.

"We scored the Tammies account," Remi finished. "The client loved your concept. They want to launch a huge campaign."

"They also want to go with us for all their new products. The thing is"—Gina cleared her throat—"they want ideas as brilliant as the one you came up with for the Tammies bar. Concepts that are fresh, that are outside the box."

Remi swooped in. "We want you to be the project leader for all their products."

Kugy's jaw dropped. "Me? But how? Why me?"

"Because I think you've got what it takes," he said matter-of-factly. "You have fresh ideas. You think outside the box. And because you're a new kid on the block, you don't have any preconceived notions. Your personality suits the client's outlook well. Very rarely do we have clients who choose not to play it safe. So synergy-wise, I think you two are a perfect match."

"But I don't have any experience. I've only done one presentation."

"What about your team, honey?" Gina asked with a light laugh. "I'm sure they'll help you."

Kugy tried to digest what she had just heard. She—the peon in charge of photocopying—now had her own team? She wanted to burst out laughing. Though she knew Remi and Gina weren't kidding, it all felt like a big joke. She tried her best to put on a serious face.

"Okay." Kugy took a deep breath. "So . . ." She was at a loss for what to say.

"So at our next meeting," Remi said, "you'll have something else to do besides daydream and try to stay awake." He gave her a small smile.

"Congrats!" Gina added.

Soon afterward, Kugy left the room and returned to her little corner. There she chuckled to herself to her heart's content.

———

Kugy had been waiting for her taxi for half an hour. This was the downside of leaving during rush hour—the competition for public transportation was fierce. But Kugy was too tired to try an alternative means of getting home. All she wanted to do was sit quietly in the backseat and maybe even doze off before arriving at her front door.

"You said you were going straight home."

Kugy looked to her left to find Remi standing beside her. He was dressed more smartly than usual.

"My taxi hasn't come yet," she answered. "What about you? Going clubbing?" She chuckled.

"Actually, I had an appointment, but it got canceled. I can give you a lift home if you like."

Before Kugy could open her mouth, Remi was telling Anita, the receptionist, to cancel Kugy's cab, and before Kugy could respond to Remi's offer, he said, "Wait here," and vanished. Moments later his car was out front, waiting for her to step inside.

Kugy felt a bit uneasy as she climbed in. Although Remi was always relaxed when it came to dealing with his employees, Kugy was still intimidated by the fact that her boss was driving her home. But Remi seemed calm and unaware that anything unusual was happening. Finally Kugy decided she was the one who should get over her own uneasiness.

The car was extremely clean, and the fragrance of the seat leather mingled with the scent of air freshener. Music thumped softly in the background. "Is this Dead or Alive?" she asked, then began singing along.

"You know this band?" Remi asked. "Were you even born when this song came out?"

"Yeah, yeah, I know." Kugy laughed. "But as people say, I'm something else. This is the music I've been listening to forever. It's like I'm stuck in the 1980s."

"Yeah, that's pretty unusual," said Remi, nodding. "But I'm not surprised. Karel told me how 'unique' you are."

"'Unique' is just a polite way of saying I'm weird."

"Life is too short to be ordinary," said Remi. "I appreciate all things unique, weird, and extraordinary. Maybe that's why I hired you. I have a sixth sense for sniffing out weirdness. And it looks like I made the right choice."

Kugy couldn't help but grin. "Thanks for giving me a chance to be a project leader. I know all I have going for me is luck."

Remi shook his head. "Winning the lottery—that's luck. This is different. You have natural talent. All you have to do is be yourself in the role you have now. All someone like you needs is a chance."

Kugy nodded slowly. It felt too awkward to say anything. She looked out the window and watched the traffic, which was nearly at a standstill.

"Are you in a hurry to get home?" Remi asked.

"Why?"

"This traffic is terrible. It might be better to wait until it's less busy before getting back on the road. It's not a problem, is it?"

Kugy shook her head. "Not at all."

Remi pointed to a café up ahead. "We'll stop there first, okay? Their coffee's pretty good."

"Sure," she said with a slight shrug, though deep down she was marveling at it all. *What a strange day,* she thought. Not only had she suddenly gotten a huge promotion—the owner of the company was having a conversation with her in his car. She couldn't wait to tell Neptune about this.

———

After two cappuccinos, two servings of ice cream, and an enormous plate of fries, they might as well have been two old friends talking and laughing, equal in age and status. Kugy forgot about the eight-year age gap between them. And she also forgot that their respective ranks were as removed from each other as heaven and earth—one of them was an intern who had just graduated, and the other the owner of his own company.

Kugy told him she had wound up at AdVocaDo because of her love, starting in childhood, of anything to do with words. She related her life story in her usual storyteller manner, full of energy and fire. Remi's response was to listen earnestly, gawk, smile, and at points, double over with laughter.

"You're beginning to regret it, aren't you? Hiring me as one of your employees?" Kugy was shaking and clutching her sides as she asked this. She felt very comfortable being herself in front of Remi now.

"As an employee, you're an asset—the most promising I've ever come across. But as a friend, yeah, I'm beginning to have my doubts." Remi chuckled. "Still, I want to be one of Neptune's secret agents, too."

"What's your sign?"

"Libra."

Kugy shook her head, her expression serious. "That may be difficult. A basic requirement for becoming one of Neptune's agents is that you have to be an Aquarius. So Libra, huh? With its scales of justice? Hmm. Whose agent could you be?"

"How about an agent for the National Bureau of Logistics? They're in charge of food distribution. I could weigh rice."

"That could work. And agents who work for Neptune need to eat rice, too, don't they? Me especially. So when it comes down to it, we need each other."

"I feel like there's an imbalance here. If I give you rice, what'll you give me? Seawater?"

"Seafood," Kugy answered. "It goes well with rice. How about it? Good deal, eh?"

"Sure. How about tomorrow night after work? Sixish? We'll eat dinner at a seafood restaurant. There's a really good place in Radio Dalam."

Kugy felt that what happened earlier in the lobby was repeating itself. She thought of boxing for some reason: Remi was an agile and formidable opponent, slipping in several blows before she'd even had the chance to adopt a fighter's stance. Unprepared, and unable to put up any opposition, she nodded slowly and accepted Remi's invitation.

———

"Excuse me, Noni?"

Noni, who had been busy sweeping her room, propped the broom against the wall and went to answer the door. It was Ellen, the freshman now occupying the room next to hers.

"Yes, Ellen? What is it?"

"I was just cleaning my cupboards, and I found this." Ellen handed her something wrapped in plain blue paper. "I almost threw it away by accident."

Noni took it with a frown. It was large and heavy, and judging by its shape, it was a book or a photo album.

"The person who used to live in my room—she was a friend of yours, right? It must be hers."

"I've never seen it before," Noni said with a shrug. "But I'll ask her about it if I see her. Thanks, Ellen."

When her new neighbor had left, Noni sat down and placed the object in her lap. She was annoyed because now she had no choice but to hold on to it for safekeeping.

She felt a passing urge to open the package, but hesitated. In the end, she placed the object inside her desk drawer. *Don't bother thinking about it.* Then Noni picked up the broom and resumed sweeping.

———

Kugy counted the empty shrimp shells on both their plates. "You lose by two," she said.

"But in the steamed-clams category, you lose by three," answered Remi.

"That's not my fault," Kugy protested. "The portions weren't even. If there'd been an extra ten clams on my plate, I would have eaten them all, too, you know."

"That's the way it goes." Remi grinned. "So, have I eaten enough to become one of Neptune's agents?"

"Now hold on, hold on." Kugy thought for a moment. "According to the protocol in the astrological agent's guide, if non-Aquariuses want to join, they must meet certain requirements. First, they must be good at eating seafood."

"I've obviously passed," said Remi.

Kugy looked again at the empty plates. "True. You've met the first requirement. Second, you must know how to make a paper boat."

"Here, let me demonstrate," said Remi. He snatched up one of the printed menus on the table, which doubled as disposable placemats. Deftly, he folded it, and before long, he produced a boat.

"Amazing!" Kugy clapped her hands. "You've met the second requirement!"

Remi's eyes gleamed as he rubbed his hands together. "I'm beginning to feel optimistic. What's the next one?"

Kugy thought and thought. Then she grinned. "There is no third requirement yet." She laughed. "Hold on, it's coming."

"What kind of HR department do you guys have?" Remi complained. "Here I am, ready and waiting!"

"I'll bring this matter to the attention of the official association for the HR Departments of the Underwater Kingdom, and I'll let you know, sir. Thank you for your patience." Kugy spoke in a serious tone.

Suddenly, the room grew dim. Several lights had been turned off. The restaurant was about to close. The waiters were standing and watching them, forced smiles on their faces. They looked polite, and also like they wanted to kick them out. Stifling their laughter, Kugy and Remi left.

Remi dropped off Kugy at her house shortly after eleven.

"Say hi to Karel for me," he said before Kugy got out of the car.

Kugy nodded. "Thanks for dinner." She opened the door and had one foot on the curb when Remi stopped her.

"Kugy, wait a minute. Can you do something for me?" He handed her the paper boat he had made back in the restaurant.

"What's this for?" Kugy asked.

"It's for you to set out to sea tomorrow," said Remi smoothly, warmth creeping into his gaze. "I want to send a message to Neptune."

"A message? Well, that means you'll have to write something on it." She spoke quickly. She was beginning to feel nervous.

"No problem," Remi said calmly. He turned on the car light and took a pen from his bag. He unfolded the paper and wrote on it, using the dashboard as a writing surface. Then he folded it into a boat again and gave it to Kugy. "And because you're the courier, you're allowed to read my message," he added. His gaze made Kugy even more nervous.

"Actually, it's forbidden to send or receive letters until you receive confirmation that you have the job. But I'll see what I can do. I can't make any promises, though." Laughing, she got out of the car.

"It's okay." Remi shrugged. "No harm in trying. See you tomorrow."

"Bye!" Kugy waved. She watched the car until it disappeared around a bend. Without delay, she unfolded the paper boat and, with the aid of the street lamp, read what Remi had written:

> *Thank you for sending Agent Kugy to my office and making this night such an enjoyable one. It's okay if I can't be one of your agents. But I'd really like to have dinner with her again. Hopefully your agent does, too.*

Kugy stood motionless, clutching the sheet of paper in her hand. She felt confused, anxious . . . and happy. She couldn't tell which emotion was most dominant—all three had mingled and become one. She didn't know what to call it. But she felt there was only one surefire antidote: sleep.

CHAPTER 31
THE TOILET SORORITY

October 2002

This was the first time Kugy had attended a gathering for employees of different ad agencies. She was new to this game, and this was her first night interacting with other people in the advertising world, seeing people whom she had only known by name, and meeting people from various firms, ranging from senior executives to newcomers like herself.

There were almost a hundred people at the event, which was being held at a wine bar. Glasses of red and white wine along with light snacks were being circulated on trays. Kugy hadn't eaten dinner yet, and her stomach was showing signs of dissent.

"Iman," she whispered, "do you think they serve food here? Rice, maybe?"

Iman burst into laughter. "This is a *wine* bar, girl. Plus I don't think they'd serve anything substantial at this hour. You could leave and get some fried rice from a warung by the roadside."

"Great. Thanks for the info," Kugy answered sourly. She looked around. No one seemed to be hungry like she was. Maybe they had more experience and had anticipated the matter by eating dinner beforehand. Or maybe conversation and wine could fill one's stomach—though obviously, that wasn't the case with her.

Then her eyes came to rest on Remi. Women swarmed around him like bees around honey, doing whatever they had to just so Remi would glance at them and offer up a sentence or two. Some took the opportunity to steal in for a moment and exchange kisses on the cheek with him in greeting, slipping their arms around his waist. But once this ticket had been used, they had to get back in line and wait their turn.

What made Remi look in her direction, she didn't know, but their eyes suddenly met. Hastily, she looked away. Her heart shrank in panic. *How embarrassing,* she thought. And Kugy's panic only grew when she realized Remi had left his circle of bees and was walking straight toward her.

"All alone?" he asked. "Don't you want to mingle?"

"Looking for something to eat," Kugy answered with a grin.

"Over there." Remi pointed at a tray of tiny bread rolls and potato chips which were being served in pinch-sized paper cupcake holders.

"I'm looking for more robust portions," answered Kugy as she patted her stomach. "My pet anaconda is starting to kick up a ruckus. I don't think it'll be content with small-talk food anymore. I'm heading off, if that's okay."

"I'll go with you. Give me five minutes. Meet you out front." Remi hurried away.

Kugy tried to say something, but he had already vanished into the throng of people. *Huh. I didn't even say yes.* She shook her head in amazement at how quick Remi was.

While she waited, Kugy went to the bathroom. A group of women were lined up in front of the mirror reapplying their makeup. She didn't know any of them, but she immediately caught the gist of the conversation they were carrying on.

"Damn. The man gets better looking every day!"

"I'd like to be locked up in a room with him for a week."

"Me, too—for a month. Who else wants to join?"

"You know Sandy, the account executive at ViaAd? She went on a date with him."

Several jaws dropped. "Whaaa? Sandy?"

"Damn! Lucky girl!"

"It's because of . . . you know . . . her front bumper . . ."

They all laughed.

"You always think about the physical!"

"But she only got as far as one date. They're not going out."

"A girl like that can't go far, no matter how big her boobs are. In the end, it's the brain that counts."

"*Please*. The walls have ears," said someone in a half whisper. "So are you saying Sandy doesn't have a brain? Oops! Did I say that?" She followed this with a sprinkle of laughter. Her friends followed suit.

"Well, anyone who's relying on her body to do the work isn't going to stick around long. These days, it's what's inside that counts."

"Yeah. What's inside your blouse!"

They laughed again.

"So Remi isn't interested in anyone? He's still eligible?"

"Looks like it. My spies in Avocado haven't had anything to report."

"There's no one from Avocado here, right?" someone exclaimed suddenly.

Kugy quickly turned toward the wall. "Avocado" was the advertising world's nickname for AdVocaDo. Kugy thanked her lucky stars she was new. Nobody there knew who she was.

"It wouldn't matter even if he did have a girlfriend. Before the wedding vows are said, anything is fair game!"

"Who cares about wedding vows these days? Before the death rites are read, anything is fair game!" The woman who said this laughed.

"Dirty girl!"

Just as it was her turn to enter a stall, Kugy decided to slip away. The competition for Remigius Aditya's attentions was fierce, and things were heating up too much for her liking. She never would have guessed the man was so popular. After seeing how sought after Remi was, Kugy didn't know whether to feel lucky or cursed. If those women knew she was going out to eat with Remi in the next five minutes, she wasn't sure she would have made it out of there in one piece.

———

Kugy had just polished off a plate of fried rice, and her mouth was now watering at the slice of toast Remi had ordered for himself. "I want some, too," she said as she looked around for a waiter.

"You're one hell of an eater. But where does it all go? How can all that food fit inside that tiny body?" Remi shook his head.

"Intestines. Everywhere," Kugy joked. "If you sliced open my hand, you'd find intestines there, too." Before long, she had placed an order for toast and a mug of hot chocolate.

"Other women must be jealous," Remi commented.

Kugy burst into laughter. "Tonight I can say with all certainty that you're right. But it has nothing to do with my eating. It's"—she tried to suppress her laughter—"my eating companion they're jealous about."

Remi frowned. "What do you mean?"

"I've just learned I'm eating with the most eligible bachelor in town! Almost every woman at that event was showering you with adoration and fighting over you!" Kugy chuckled. "There was even a sorority gathering in the ladies' room discussing you!"

Remi smiled and looked away. "Oh, whatever. It's nothing," he said with a wave of his hand.

"Well, of course," Kugy answered. "It's just funny, that's all. It seems like I'm the only one who doesn't realize what"—she hesitated, wondering whether she should continue—"what a valuable opportunity I have here." She took a deep breath. "At least, in their eyes," she added quickly.

Remi gave Kugy a look—the same look he had given her a couple of weeks ago in his car, when he had given her the paper boat. And once again she felt nervous.

"I'm happy you don't," said Remi softly. "This way, you can just be yourself. So can I. And I think that's been the most enjoyable thing about us spending time together."

Kugy swallowed. "I agree. It's best when you can be yourself," she answered, not knowing what else to say.

Remi sipped his hot tea and said lightly, "What they don't know is that I'm the one who has the valuable opportunity."

Just then, Kugy's toast arrived. She began eating with gusto, partly because she was still hungry and partly because she was trying to compensate for how awkward she felt. She was beginning to feel something wasn't quite right about all this. Not about Remi. And not about herself.

November 2002

Keenan sat in the *bale*, leaning against a wooden pillar. How many months had he spent in that exact spot? But nothing was the same anymore. Bali wasn't the same anymore.

The bomb that had exploded in Kuta a month ago had done more than just physical damage. It was as if a smoky haze still lingered in the air, casting a spell over this happy island and turning it into an island of fear. Everyone was talking about what lay in store—the dark times ahead.

Even though no one in the family had been hurt—no one lived in Kuta—a sense of mournfulness was present in that big house nonetheless. Nobody was safe from its spell, including Keenan. The only difference was that Keenan had been experiencing a darkness in his soul even before the bomb had gone off.

For the umpteenth time, Keenan flipped restlessly through the pages of the notebook, back and forth. He had read all the pages—so many times that he knew them by heart. He had turned every single story into a painting. All that remained of the book was the last page, which was blank. And he'd been tackling that, too, for the past several months. The result? A blank canvas.

Almost everyone had been saying the same thing: "Your subject matter has always come from within. How can you not know what to paint?" And he could only keep silent. How could he explain that everything he'd been painting was what Kugy had written down in an old notebook, and now that there were no more stories left, he had no inspiration?

It wasn't that Keenan hadn't tried to imagine things outside Kugy's book. He'd tried hundreds of times, but to no avail. He wasn't the one to take part in those adventures. He hadn't written those stories. And now it felt like all the praise that had been showered upon his paintings had forced him into a corner, bringing him to one conclusion—he was nothing without that book. It was a terrifying truth.

It had been two years since he had come to Lodtunduh, two years since it had all started, right here in this *bale*. His heart trembled at the thought that everything might end here as well.

———

"What's wrong, son? You've taken a turn for the worse. You're no better than when you first came." Wayan chose his words as carefully as possible. Keenan looked like a glass figurine ready to shatter at the slightest touch.

A cool breeze rushed past them and shook the bamboo *kentungan*. Now their sound cut him to the heart. All Keenan could do was bow his head and look down at the wooden floor beneath his feet.

"You know you can tell me anything," said Wayan. "But it's all right if you don't feel ready. I won't force you to."

"Actually . . ." With great difficulty, Keenan tried to explain. "Poyan, there is something I want to talk to you about. But I don't know where to start. I . . ." He blinked in confusion.

"Not knowing is a good start. Everything begins with not knowing. Just go with the flow." Gently, Wayan patted Keenan's shoulder.

"Everything's gone, Poyan. Everything! Just like that! I can't paint."

"You're not alone. Everyone else on the island is grieving, too."

Keenan shook his head. "It's not just that, Poyan. I haven't been able to paint for a long time. It's all over. It's like something has died—in here!" Keenan pointed to his chest. "If I can't paint anything, I'm useless to you all." He was almost sobbing as he spoke.

"Son, we think of you as family. Your presence here means something to us, whether you paint or not. Don't burden yourself with such matters. Not once have I ever set any conditions on your living here. This is your home. And remember, all painters experience what you're experiencing now, including me—for many years. But it doesn't mean we should give up. Painting is the path I've chosen. It's my soulmate. And isn't it the path you've chosen, too?"

Keenan's head hung even lower. He felt even more crestfallen than before.

Wayan spoke firmly. "Be patient, son. Your home is here. You don't need to run anymore."

Keenan raised his head. He looked desperately at the man whom he had come to regard as his father, pleading for help. "I've finished the book, Poyan," he whispered.

Wayan was startled. *Was he that dependent on it?* After a few moments of silence, Wayan said, slowly, "Son, whether you like it or not, you have to pick up where the book left off. That, or you have to find a new star. It's not easy, I know. For now you'll just have to accept that you can't paint anymore. The path will clear by itself."

Wayan understood Keenan's pain all too well. He had experienced a similar wound decades ago. With great difficulty, he'd risen, staggering, to search for something to replace his heart's star, his inspiration. And now he was standing firm once more, though he knew the star would never return.

———

Adri had been feeling there was something wrong with his body since that morning. He had woken up feeling exhausted, and the exhaustion had persisted, even after eating breakfast and doing some light exercise to reinvigorate himself. Adri decided to go to the office, anyway. He didn't want Lena to get suspicious and ask him about his health.

He heard his secretary's voice over the telephone intercom. "Mr. Adri. Mr. Ong from Malaysia is on the line."

Adri picked up the phone. Two minutes into the conversation, his right hand, which was holding the receiver, began to tremble. In a matter of seconds, the trembling turned to shaking. Adri was stunned. He pressed a button and put the call on speaker. He could no longer hold the phone.

"Sorry, Mr. Ong, it looks like I'm going to have to call you back. I—" Something swept through his entire body, sapping him of strength. In the blink of an eye, Adri collapsed. His body lay stretched out on the floor, stiff. He didn't move.

CHAPTER 32

THE NINJA OF LOVE

December 2002

Keenan tried this time. He really, really tried. He had decided he would not succumb to artist's block. He put the notebook away in his room and reminded himself that an artist's soul was free—able to come and go as it pleased, dependent on nothing and no one. He wanted to free himself of that book. The time had come.

Keenan painted and painted.

Luhde faithfully remained at his side. "I'll clean your brushes," she said, taking away the ones whose bristles had become stiff with paint. It was a task she was accustomed to doing. She had been helping the painters in the family since she was little.

"Thanks, Luhde," Keenan answered and paused to watch her. "You're an angel." The sentence sprang from his mouth before he could stop it. It was a pure expression of what he felt in his heart.

Luhde looked up. "I'm happy to see you're painting again," she said earnestly.

Keenan smiled. "I'm painting for you."

Luhde ducked her head and her cheeks turned red. "Yes, but you're also painting for yourself," she said almost whispering. Still, she couldn't help but smile.

Keenan put down the brush. Something compelled him to approach her, to sit down and gaze into her face. "*Titiang tresne teken Luhde*. I love you, Luhde." He spoke deliberately and with great respect.

Luhde had been cleaning the brushes, but now she stopped. She felt as if her heart had stopped beating as well. Two years she had waited. Two years she had hoped. Two years she had drawn near to him, pouring out everything she could give him. Now for the first time, Keenan was telling her, directly and plainly, how he felt.

Luhde gazed into Keenan's eyes. She felt happy, moved, and embarrassed all at once.

The sight of such beauty before him took his breath away, and something urged him to come closer still and bestow a tender kiss on Luhde's lips.

———

There was a new hot topic of conversation at AdVocaDo. It was being discussed everywhere, by everyone, all the time: Kugy. Not only did people see her as a prodigy—she also had a nickname: the Ninja of Love. Who would have guessed a girl like her, fresh out of university and sporting a Teenage Mutant Ninja Turtles watch, could leave so many women heartbroken—all the women who had set their sights on Remi?

The intimacy that had grown between Remi and Kugy over the past two months had become too obvious to dismiss. Remi gave her a ride home almost every day. They went out to dinner together at least two or three times a week. The whole office had grown used to seeing Kugy in the passenger seat of Remi's car.

Meanwhile, the Ninja of Love didn't seem too concerned about it. She wasn't even aware she was attracting attention. Kugy's pile of tasks kept her busy, and she didn't have time to think about how unexpectedly her career had taken off. To her, Remi was such an enjoyable traveling companion that she didn't feel she was in any sort of competition. Getting close to Remi hadn't been on her agenda. It had all come naturally—just like that. And she was too used to not caring what other people thought to worry about what they were saying.

Her coworkers had made plans to go clubbing. She'd been reluctant, but they had convinced her to come along. So there she was, in a crowd, in the dark, heart-pounding music blasting away. There were a lot of familiar faces, many she had met at the gathering two months ago. There was also a group of women she recognized: she'd dubbed them the Toilet Sorority.

Kugy was able to hold out for longer this time because she had eaten dinner before coming. But two hours had passed and she began to feel uneasy. Just because she had a full stomach didn't mean she felt comfortable. Almost everyone had found something to occupy their attention, and Kugy found herself the odd one out, unable to connect with anyone. Slowly she began to inch away, intending, in stages, to make herself scarce.

Suddenly, she bumped into someone's shoulder. "Sorry," Kugy said. She took a step in another direction, but someone else blocked her path. Kugy tried to back away, and again bumped into someone else. At last she realized she was being surrounded.

"You're the one they call Kugy, aren't you?" one of them asked.

Kugy looked at the woman's face and recognized her as a member of the Toilet Sorority. "Yes, I'm Kugy," she said with a wary nod.

"The one who's interning at AdVocaDo, right?" someone else asked.

Kugy nodded.

"Where's Remi? How come he's not here with you?" asked a third woman.

"I—I don't know," Kugy answered. Where was this interrogation going?

"Have you been going out with Remi long?" The voice that asked this was sharp and shrill.

"We're not going out," said Kugy, shaking her head.

"If you are, that's okay. You shouldn't feel shy about it. Congrats!" The words were accompanied by a smile. A very unpleasant one.

"Yeah, how'd you pull it off? Who's your witch doctor, missy? What special charm did he give you?" The woman laughed at her own joke.

"Hey, girls," someone else chimed in. "Look at her watch! That's her charm! You should all go buy one. They probably sell them at some stall in Pasar Baru. You get a Spiderman one, you a Superman one, and you a Barbie one. Any one will do, as long as it's tacky and made out of plastic!"

"*Vogue* tells me they're all the rage, you know!" They all cackled.

Kugy didn't find this funny. Not at all. She wanted to get out of there as quickly as possible, but they blocked her steps left and right, and she found herself unable to move.

Suddenly an arm penetrated the circle, grabbed Kugy's hand, and pulled her out.

It was Remi with his usual charismatic smile. He looked at the group politely.

"Sorry, can I borrow Kugy for a minute?" Then as if he'd done it hundreds of times, Remi put his arm around her waist in one smooth motion and pressed her body close to his. "Let's go home," he said lightly. He brushed back her bangs.

The women gaped—Kugy included. She was dumbfounded. But she didn't let them see how surprised she was. She smiled sweetly at Remi and squeezed the hand encircling her waist. "Let's go," she said with a small nod. Then she looked in the direction of the Toilet Sorority. "See you," she said in the friendliest tone she could manage.

Once they were outside, they burst into laughter.

"That girl who was standing next to me—did you see her face? She looked like a house gecko that lost its tail!" Kugy clutched at her stomach, her body shaking with laughter. "What a show we put on! Brilliant, just brilliant!"

Remi looked at his watch. "It's one a.m. How about some late-night rice porridge?"

"Sure," Kugy said cheerfully. And they walked toward the parking lot. It was only when they reached his car that Kugy realized Remi's arm was still around her waist.

———

The bowl of porridge, practically overflowing at first, was now empty. All that remained was a thin film at the bottom, and Kugy was even scraping that into her mouth with gusto.

"If I sold porridge," Remi told Kugy after watching her for a while, "I'd make you my brand ambassador. You'd receive a 10 percent commission of all sales and eat as much as you wanted, anytime, for free. All you would need to do is eat exactly like you're doing now in front of customers. You'd make their mouths water like nobody's business. And they'd order seconds, even if they were full."

"Spoken like a true ad man," said Kugy. Suddenly curious, she asked, "When did you get interested in advertising?"

"Since graduating from university. I started out as an intern like you before becoming a junior art director. Then I was made project leader for a really big client, and they loved my idea. The ad was a success, too. I got an award that year, and I've been winning prizes ever since. Then I resigned from that company and struck out on my own. Luckily all my old clients followed me. And that's how AdVocaDo came to be what it is today."

Kugy nodded. She'd seen the row of plaques on Remi's office wall. Everyone had told her that Remi had once had a reputation in the ad world for being a prodigy.

"But do you really want to be in this line of work forever?" Kugy asked. "Don't you have any other passions?"

Remi shook his head. "This is my world. I've always been good at helping people sell things, ever since I was young. My parents, my siblings—whenever they tried their hands at something business related, they'd ask my opinion, and I'd give them ideas. They always worked. It was the same at school and university—whenever I helped out with events, they did well. And I got a lot of satisfaction from it."

"Wow." Kugy shook her head in amazement. "You are very, very lucky. You love your job and you're good at it. A lot of people must envy you."

"Maybe." Remi shrugged. "All I know is there's only one kind of person I envy."

"Who?"

"Painters."

Kugy was startled. "Painters? Why?"

"I love paintings. They make me so happy." Remi's eyes were shining. "A painter's soul can bring a whole new world into existence. They speak through images, color, composition." He let out a long sigh. "If I could be born again, that's what I'd want to be."

Kugy was quiet. *A painter . . .*

"How about you? If you could be born again, what would you be?"

Kugy answered without hesitation. "A whale."

———

Luhde woke up earlier than usual. She didn't know why. Suddenly she had found herself sitting up in bed feeling uneasy.

Slowly, she got up and left her room. There was no one in sight. But she heard a sound coming from the direction of the *bale*.

She stopped when she saw what was going on. Keenan was tearing up a painting—the same one he had finished just a few days ago.

"Keenan!" Luhde exclaimed, running toward him. "What are you doing?"

Keenan froze, still clutching the halves in his hands.

"Why are you tearing up the painting?" she asked.

"Because it's no good," he answered flatly.

"But that's the first painting you've finished in a long time," Luhde wailed in confusion. "You said it was good at the time. What was wrong with it?"

"I can't paint like I used to," he said softly.

"Says who?" she protested, crying. "You shouldn't talk like that! You have to give yourself a chance! Why did you have to ruin it?" She yanked the torn canvas from his hands. "Why did you have to ruin it?" she sobbed again.

"Because this painting—" Keenan faltered. He couldn't explain. How could he say it without breaking Luhde's heart? That this painting didn't have the same soul or strength? That this painting couldn't stir or give voice to his inner being the way his previous paintings had?

And Luhde couldn't speak, either. She didn't understand, and part of her refused to accept it. This was the first time Keenan had painted *for her*. And that same painting had now been torn in two.

"It's still too early. You'll catch a cold. Go back to your room." That's all Keenan could say. Then he turned away from her and gazed at the empty courtyard. It was far easier to look at that than Luhde's tearful face.

"I want to stay here," Luhde whispered. Carefully, she approached the man she so loved. Embracing him gently from behind, she buried her face in his back, and wept.

———

Lena sat beside the hospital bed, lost in thought. Adri had just spent the last two days in critical condition and today he was beginning to regain consciousness. Every now and then he would open his eyes, even though his body was still stiff as a board. This stroke was much more severe than the first one. Moreover, the doctors were doubtful he would fully recover. It would take a miracle, they said. Even months of physiotherapy would only be able to restore 70 to 80 percent of his abilities. The fact Adri was still alive was already amazing. Hopefully, they told her, there was another miracle to come.

At times like this, Lena realized just how lonely she was. Jeroen was still in school. The only people in the room were her and her husband, who lay unconscious without making a sound.

Lena rose to her feet and stroked her husband's hair. She whispered in his ear, asking him the burning questions that had remained unanswered: "What is really the matter? What have you been hiding? How can I help?"

Lena stood like that for a long time, stroking his hair gently and whispering, until at last she caught something out of the corner of her eye. Adri's eyelids opened.

Lena gazed into his eyes and smiled. She squeezed his hand. It felt cold and hard. "Hi," she said gently.

His eyes blinked. Saying something. Pleading.

Lena stroked her husband's face. "I'm here. You'll get better. You're going to be okay."

His eyes blinked faster. More urgently. Trying to convey a message. But not a single sound came out of his mouth.

Lena tried to read his restless gaze. "What do you want me to do, Adri?"

Summoning all his strength, Adri's facial muscles began to move. Bit by bit. His mouth trembled, forcing a sound from his throat.

"Kk . . . kk . . . kee . . ."

Lena pressed the button to call the nurse. "Yes, what is it, Adri? What do you want to say?" She leaned closer to Adri's lips to hear him more clearly.

In a strangled voice, Adri tried with all his might to utter that one word. "Kk . . . Kee . . . nan . . ."

Upon uttering the name, Adri's eyes shut once more.

Lena was in shock. *Keenan?* He was the cause of all this? This whole time, Adri hadn't given any indication he cared about Keenan's whereabouts. He had even warned her several times not to look for him, that their son would have to contact them first. Since Keenan had left, not once had Adri discussed him, or even uttered his name. It was as if Adri had rounded up all memories of him and put them away in anticipation of some day in the future when Keenan would return home and apologize, like he wanted him to.

Lena was beset by a deep sense of guilt. She was the only one who knew where Keenan had gone. She was the only one who knew their child was, in fact, safe. Meanwhile, her husband had persisted in a state of ignorance, refusing to find out and refusing to care. Yet all this time Adri must have been asking himself over and over that one question which had finally gnawed away at him from the inside: Where was Keenan?

Lena bit her lip. She had no choice.

CHAPTER 33

THE POWER OF LOVE

Lena hadn't stepped foot in Bali since marrying Adri twenty-one years ago. As the plane neared the ocean, preparing to land, a strange feeling came over her. Then there she was in Ngurah Rai International Airport, being greeted by the lilting sounds of Balinese music reverberating softly through the speakers. Lena didn't know if she was ready to come back here. She felt like returning to Jakarta. She felt regret that she had come. And yet she also realized just how much she had missed this place.

Lena couldn't imagine how she would feel on the road later, seeing so many things that would resurrect old memories—ones she had succeeded in burying—of when she was still living on this island, when she was still painting, when she was still with Wayan.

Before she left the airport, she sat down, trying to calm herself. She reminded herself not to be influenced by unreliable emotions. They would only trap her in the past. She reminded herself she was only here to get her son. That was what she needed to keep in mind. She would be back home that night. Away from this place. Away from the memories.

———

The journey passed, minute after minute, mile after mile, tearing her heart to pieces until it reached its climax. The car pulled into the compound. She had arrived. As she waited for the door to open, Lena wondered how she had found the strength to return, or even stand upright.

The servant who greeted her asked Lena to wait on the front terrace. Before long, she heard footsteps approaching. And from the sound of them, she knew who it was.

"Hello, Wayan," she said, greeting him with a smile.

Wayan was stunned.

"I want to see Keenan."

"What's wrong?" asked Wayan, trying to control his voice.

"Adri's in the hospital. He had a stroke."

"Wait here," he finally whispered. "I'll call Keenan." With each step he felt as if he were going to sink right through the floor. For a moment, he even thought he was dreaming. In that woman's presence, everything had fallen away—his strength, his defenses. He was changed now that Lena was there. He felt lost in his own house. Unsteadily, Wayan walked to the back of the house, calling for Keenan.

———

It had never crossed Keenan's mind that he would one day sit with his mother in the *bale*, the breeze blowing and the sounds of the bamboo *kentungan* in their ears. Longing and sadness mingled and became one.

"I know you said that coming home would be like returning to prison," said Lena. "I also understand that this is your home now. But I won't go back to Jakarta without you."

Keenan nodded heavily. "Of course I'll come home," he said. "I'm not going to leave you, Dad, and Jeroen like this. It's just that I don't know what kind of work I would do in Jakarta. I dropped out of university. I'm even having trouble painting here. I won't be able to do anything to help."

"The only thing I need from you is you," Lena said firmly. "And that's all your dad needs, too. The only thing he can say is your name, Keenan. His entire body is paralyzed, but he can still say your name. You're the only thing he wants."

Hearing this broke Keenan's heart. "Anything, Mom. Anything Dad wants, anything Dad needs from me—I'll do."

"Then we'll leave tonight, on the last flight. I can't stay any longer than that." Lena gripped her son's hand.

Keenan rose and gave his mother a hug. "I'll start packing," he whispered.

———

Their parting, so sudden and unexpected, brought about a transformation in Luhde. Calmly and coolly, she helped Keenan get ready. She didn't whine or sulk. She didn't even ask questions. It was as if she had always known this day would come. Luhde acted like a true woman that day, though she was just nineteen.

She handed Keenan a pile of neatly folded shirts. "This is the last of what's in your closet. If there's anything you've left behind, I'll send it to you in Jakarta."

Keenan took the shirts, feeling deeply moved. The way Luhde was handling the situation only broke his heart even more.

"Agung has already packed your things from the studio. If they're not too heavy, you can bring them with you tonight. Otherwise, we can send them later." Luhde looked around the room again, making sure nothing had been forgotten. "That's everything," she said with a firm nod. "Come. I'll help you carry these."

Keenan couldn't bear it any longer. He took the bag Luhde had picked up and set it back down.

"I'll come back. Luhde. I promise. When my father recovers and everything is all right with my family again, I'll return. I want to come back . . . for you." Keenan paused. "I'm sorry I have nothing to give you. Nothing compares to everything you've given me while I've been here—"

"Your being here has been enough."

"I'll come back," Keenan repeated.

Luhde's eyes filled with tears. "Just follow your heart," she said softly, her voice trembling. "Wherever it takes you. The heart never lies. If you don't come back, I'll understand."

"Luhde, please, don't speak like that. *Titiang me janji*," he said earnestly. "I've made my promise."

A sad smile appeared on her face. "Just hearing you say that is more than enough for me. I mean it. You don't have to prove anything. It's only been two years and you've brought such meaning to my life."

Keenan embraced her—gently, but also as if he would never let her go. "Wait for me, okay?" he whispered.

Slowly, Luhde extricated herself from Keenan's embrace. She pulled something from the cloth bundle she was holding. "Here, take this back." Luhde placed it in his palm.

Keenan was startled. "Why are you giving it back to me? It's for you."

Luhde lowered her head. It hurt so much to be truthful. "I know. Even though you gave it to me a long time ago, I've always felt that it's not mine. I don't know why."

"Luhde Laksmi. Watch closely." Keenan lifted her chin with his finger and looked into her eyes. He then unwrapped the cloth bundle, opened Luhde's hand, and placed the wooden heart in her palm. "Here. This is the second time I'm giving this to you. And there won't be a third." He smiled.

Luhde smiled, too. A single tear rolled down her cheek.

"I have to go," said Keenan, stroking her hair. He kissed her lips and pressed her to him once more.

As Keenan held her, Luhde held the carving to her chest, tightly, as if she never wanted to part with it, because she knew the heart never lied.

———

Wayan knew he didn't have much time. In a few hours, she would disappear again from his life. Every cell in his body was trembling with fear, but Wayan knew he would never have another chance like this again.

Keenan was still packing, and Lena was waiting on the veranda of the main house, alone. Wayan approached her. Hearing the sound of footsteps, Lena turned around. She was even more startled when he walked up to her, pulled up a chair, and sat down.

"You don't have to say anything, Lena," he said hastily. "I only ask that you listen. And I don't have much to say." Wayan summoned the courage to look into Lena's eyes, trying to ignore the fact that his heart had stopped beating. Oh, how he had loved her.

"I've spent twenty years trying to forget you," he said. "But I never had any regrets, not one. The love I have for Keenan is the most beautiful thing I've experienced—second only to my love for you. I love him like a son. I'm grateful to you and Adri for giving him the chance to be part of my life. Thanks to Keenan, I've learned to forgive myself, and you, and Adri, for everything that happened." As the words, pent up for decades, flowed from him, Wayan's heart felt more at ease. "Don't ever tell Keenan how much I love his mother. Just let him think of me as an old friend of yours. Nothing more." He stood. "I wish Adri a speedy recovery."

"Wayan," Lena whispered. "I'm sorry."

"You don't need to apologize for anything, Lena. I've let it all go. For your sake." Wayan gave her a thin smile.

Lena felt a fluttering in her chest, as if something inside her were trying to escape. She could barely stand or speak, but she knew she would never have this chance again, either. She had to tell him. "I had to leave you. I was pregnant with Keenan and wasn't willing to sacrifice him. I didn't make my decision because of Adri—he never had my heart. I made my decision because I was going to have his child—"

"Lena, enough. I know. I understand. And I'm so happy you decided to keep Keenan."

"Adri and I shouldn't have done that to you. We weren't thinking. Things spun out of control. What happened between us—"

"What happened between you two doesn't concern me anymore. You and Adri have proven yourselves by staying together for so long. I'm happy he was able to love you and provide well for you." Wayan tried to steady his breath. "Your heart would have been mine once. I know that. Just as my heart has always been yours. But the heart is able to grow and survive in the face of other choices, too. Sometimes that's enough. I've come to feel it's enough."

Lena felt her eyes grow hot, but no tears came.

"We will be praying for you all," said Wayan. Lena's hand was on the table and he stroked it for a moment. Then he turned and left.

Lena was by herself on the veranda once again. Still no tears came, though her heart resumed the unceasing sobs that had haunted her for decades. The sobs she would always have to keep locked away in silence. The sobs she would have to bury deep inside her once again.

———

Something in the house had changed. There was something missing. Everyone felt it.

After Keenan and Lena left, Luhde and her uncle sat in the *bale*, each shrouded in a thick fog of emotions.

"So that was Keenan's mother," said Luhde. "She's beautiful. As beautiful as the portrait you painted of her." She recalled the face in her uncle's painting. It was Lena, many years ago, and the one portrait of her that he'd kept.

"Has Keenan's mother seen your painting, Poyan? Why didn't you show it to her? What if she never returns—"

"Enough," he said, interrupting her. "There's no point." He stood up and walked away.

Luhde watched him with a sense of remorse. She hadn't meant to make him even sadder. Lena's coming must have unsettled his heart and reopened old wounds from decades ago. She regretted adding to his sorrows unnecessarily, all because she hadn't been able to stop herself from asking about the painting.

Since Lena had left him, her uncle had never fallen in love with anyone else. He had chosen to live unmarried and alone. To him, Lena was his last love and no one could ever take her place. It was better to live alone than to live in a lie—that's what her uncle always said.

Poyan was famous for his paintings of Balinese ceremonies, but those closest to him knew that his current subject matter was nothing but a refuge from what he was fleeing. Poyan's paintings were far better once, people said. Before, Poyan had only painted women. More specifically, one woman. Who knew where those paintings were now? Scattered among collectors or stored away who knew where. One thing was clear: her uncle would never paint like he did before. For several years, he had even stopped painting altogether. And of all the paintings from that period, he had kept only one. And it was from that one remaining painting that Luhde recognized her. Lena. The woman whom Poyan had so loved and whom he would never be able to have.

A falling star had slipped from his hands and he would never be able to hold it again—that was how Poyan described the story of their love. And Poyan continued to dwell in his solitude and his memories. His love for Lena would remain with him always, and that was enough, he'd once said. Furthermore, it was enough for him to have Keenan to love as his own son, though Keenan's arrival was why he and Lena had had to part.

Luhde's gaze remained fixed on her uncle's back as he retreated into the darkness of the forest, merging into its shadows. The man had taught her how strong the heart was—how strong love was. And today, her heart had undergone its own trial.

———

It was another late night for Kugy at the office. She was so exhausted she almost fell asleep on the lobby sofa waiting for her taxi to arrive. Suddenly the door opened and four people entered, making a lot of noise, carrying a large painting wrapped in brown paper.

A security guard appeared and instructed them to unwrap the painting and hang it on the wall behind the receptionist's desk. The commotion continued, with the security guard barking commands. "That's it. Move it to the left a bit. Too much. Yeah, right there. A bit lower and to the right. Stop! That's enough! Perfect!"

The security guard nodded admiringly and whistled. "This new one sure looks great."

Kugy had to take a look for herself. Her jaw dropped. "This painting," she stammered. "Where did it come from?"

"From Mr. Remi's house," the guard explained. "He said to bring it here at night so we wouldn't bother anyone during working hours." Before long, the guard and the movers left.

Kugy was grateful they had gone so quickly so she could be alone. She gazed at the painting, illuminated by a single spotlight from above. It was as if the painting had seized her by the heart and pulled her into the magic of another life.

Something about the painting felt familiar—the children and the animals playing together. A simple scene, but so full of life and sound.

She felt as though she were there herself, playing with them, experiencing the happiness and brightness of their world.

"Oh gosh, don't cry," she muttered, wiping her eyes. Suddenly, her heart was overwhelmed by an intense longing. She remembered the Sakola Alit. Her students. Pilik.

Kugy's eyes swept over the big beautiful canvas. All she could find were two small initials in the bottom right corner: *K. K.*

CHAPTER 34

THE LAST NIGHT OF THE YEAR

When Keenan arrived in Jakarta, he headed straight to the hospital, and stayed there around the clock. That was only a day ago and everyone could see his father's condition had undergone an immediate improvement. Although Adri couldn't speak or move much yet, having Keenan with him had rekindled an enthusiasm for life. There was a freshness about his face, and new progress was being made almost every few hours.

Lena was filling out the necessary paperwork to take her husband home. There was no doubt about it—the miracle the doctors were hoping for had happened. She was bringing him home. Once again, her family was complete.

Keenan stayed at his father's side, watching and waiting. He never imagined he would one day see his father—so big and strong, so energetic and industrious—reduced to this. Every time his father opened his eyes, calling out in a weak voice that sounded more like a moan, Keenan assured him he was there. But his father kept calling out, anyway.

Slowly, the door opened and Lena entered cautiously. "We can take Dad home tomorrow," she said with a smile.

Keenan let out a sigh of relief.

"I have a recommendation for a nurse who'll be able to help take care of him at home. He can start slowly with the physiotherapy."

"Mom." Keenan hesitated. "Who's running Dad's business?" It was the one question he dreaded learning the answer to, but sooner or later, he had to ask. Keenan knew just how much his father's business relied on him. The trading company his father operated was his and his alone. He had been the head of the entire company and everything depended on him. Who knew how long it would be able to survive in his absence.

The expression on Lena's face underwent a dramatic change. Like Keenan, she had tried to avoid discussing the matter, though she knew they would have to talk about it eventually. Lena pulled up a chair beside him and held his hand.

"Keenan, I know we don't have many options, but we should focus on your father's health for now. Don't think too much about business matters—"

"Dad has already been here for more than a week, Mom. Time marches on whether we like it or not. Someone has to fill his shoes. If not, the company will be ruined. And so will we."

Lena bowed her head. She had hoped she wouldn't have to ask. She'd tried to ignore it, but the matter wasn't going to go away on its own. Still, she couldn't bear to make the request.

"I'll take over for Dad," he said softly.

Lena was stunned.

"I don't know where to start. But I'll do the best I can."

Lena tightened her grip on her son's hand. "Of all the people in the world your father would trust to take his place, you're the best one. I'm sure you can do it." But even as she uttered the words, Lena's heart was cut to the quick. She knew how costly a sacrifice her son was making. Once again, Keenan was being forced to cast away his dreams and ambitions—to set aside his paintbrush, his canvas, and what he loved.

New Year's Eve 2002

A gentle breeze blew in from the beach. It felt warm against her skin, even though it was well past midnight. Kugy sat on the swing barefoot, letting her feet drag on the ground, playing with the sand between her toes.

"You look like a little kid sitting on that swing," said Remi from behind her.

Kugy turned around. "Hey, why aren't you inside?" She motioned toward the cottage and their coworkers carousing inside. Thanks to the initiative of a few, and the assent of more than a few others who happened not to have any special plans for the night, a group of them were spending New Year's Eve together on Ancol Beach. They'd rented a large cottage and were having a party.

"Too crowded," said Remi. Then he approached Kugy and gave the swing a gentle push.

"It's nice here," said Kugy. "You can hear the ocean. Nature's sweetest song."

"I agree. I spent last New Year's Eve on the beach, too. The waves there sounded much sweeter than the ones here."

"Oh yeah? Where?"

"Sanur."

"Bali, huh? Lucky you. I dreamed about spending New Year's Eve on a beach last year. I was on the terrace in front of my house." Kugy chuckled.

"And this year you made it. You got to the beach after all."

Kugy nodded. "Yup! First stop, Ancol. Hopefully next year, I'll be able to upgrade to Sanur."

"You don't have to wait till next year to go to Sanur," Remi said with a smile. "When do you want to go? I'll come with you."

"Next week?"

"Sure."

"Hmm. Next month?"

"Sure."

"How about sometime midyear?"

"Sure."

"Is that all you can say? 'Sure'? Can't you put up some opposition?" Kugy laughed. And suddenly Remi spun the swing around so they were facing each other.

Remi stooped down and put his face close to hers. "Anywhere you want to go—be it a warung for fried rice or the beach at Sanur—and anytime you want to go—be it today or who knows when—I'll go, too. As long as I can be with you."

Kugy's mind tried to process what Remi had just said, but her heart already knew. Had known for a long time. "Remi . . . you're my boss," she stammered.

Remi nodded. "Yes, I know. This violates all the rules of ethical workplace conduct. I'm putting you in a difficult position. And I'm putting myself in a difficult position as well. But it would make even less sense if I let those things stand in the way of being true to my heart."

Kugy swallowed. "But, you're Karel's friend."

"Do you have a problem with your boyfriend being older? With dating a friend of your big brother's?" Remi smiled.

At the word "boyfriend," Kugy's heart raced and her body tensed. She tried to calm her heart and to steady her breathing, to keep her gaze cool and her voice from trembling. "I do have a problem having someone for a boyfriend if I don't know what his true feelings are."

Remi's expression changed. He was always so relaxed, so smooth. But now he looked anxious. He opened his mouth but no words came out. He looked away for a moment, nervously, as if summoning up the strength to speak.

"You . . ." Now his voice was trembling. "You've given me a new reason to go to work every day. You give me energy. You make me laugh.

You make me want to do so many things. You put me at ease . . ." Remi paused, trying to calm his own wildly beating heart. "I . . . I'm not just amazed by you. I'm in love."

Now Kugy lost her ability to play it cool. A tremendous conflict raged in her heart. She was facing a dilemma she had never had before. Up to this point, she had known exactly whom she desired, whom she dreamed of, whom she yearned for. But nothing was clear anymore. What she did know was that Remi was so close, so real, so within her reach. Remi was there every day, not just in her dreams.

"Don't you get it?" Remi whispered gently. "I'm crazy about you."

Kugy didn't trust herself to speak. But for the first time, she saw the person in front of her in a different light. She only hoped that Remi could see it, could read it in her eyes. The dilemma in her heart had been resolved. Her heart had made its choice.

As if hearing what she had left unspoken, Remi smiled tenderly. He moved closer, bringing his face to hers, and planted his lips on hers, kissing her with all the passion he had been suppressing.

The waves swept across the sand behind them, enveloping them in their sweet, never-ending cadence. But the same sound reminded Kugy of something else. In her heart, she bid farewell to the person whose name she had clung fast to for so long. She released the name into the wind and the waves and cast it adrift on the sea. She let it go, along with the last night of the year.

———

Keenan sat alone on the terrace, contemplating the cell phone in his hand. He was looking at the phone number on the screen. He had been looking at it for a while, but he hadn't dialed it. He didn't know whether the number was still active, but he had kept it, anyway, looking at it every now and then. Like he was doing tonight.

Though the distance between them had lessened, Keenan felt as if they were somehow farther apart. He didn't know why.

Little One, it feels like you're so far away. I hope you still remember me.

January 2003

It was the first day of classes after the break—the first day of Noni's and Eko's last semester.

Noni was sorting through the textbooks from her first year that she didn't need anymore. Her room looked like a warehouse, filled with stuff she hadn't used for years but that she'd kept because she hadn't wanted to throw anything away. Eko always complained about this problem of hers and had bestowed on her the title "Scavenger."

She was almost halfway through when her eyes fell on something she had hurled into a drawer months ago and hadn't looked at since—the package wrapped in blue that Kugy had left behind, and that Noni was keeping for her.

Noni took the package and placed it in her lap. *It must have been a present from Josh,* she guessed. Her hands were itching to open it, but Noni suppressed the urge. *I should just leave it. This is Kugy's business, not mine. Besides, she probably left it on purpose. But do I really want to keep it here forever?* Finally, she opened it.

It was a scrapbook, untitled, with cutouts of drawings pasted on the pages. Next to each drawing was a handwritten story. Noni recognized the handwriting immediately. It was Kugy's. Noni also recognized the stories. They were from a collection that Kugy had written over a period of several years, but never published. She had only showed it to a few people. Noni was one of them.

On the first page was a photocopy of Kugy's handwriting from when she was little. Noni knew what it said by heart. Kugy wrote it inside the covers of fairy tales she owned—especially her favorites. It was a quote by W. B. Yeats:

Let us go forth, the tellers of tales, and seize whatever prey the
heart long for, and have no fear. Everything exists, everything
is true, and the earth is only a little dust under our feet.

Noni remembered how proud little Kugy was of that quote when
she had announced, "Noni, I want to be a teller of tales." Noni still
didn't understand what the quote meant. But Kugy had.

On the inside of the back cover was a sleeve. Noni wouldn't have
looked inside it if she hadn't seen a piece of paper poking out. It was a
white envelope containing a card. "'Happy birthday'?" Noni mumbled.
Whose birthday was it?

Noni opened the card and read Kugy's words:

> *I dream.*
> *I dream about writing my first book of fairy tales.*
> *Ever since you drew these for me, I feel like I'm one*
> *step closer to attaining that dream.*
> *I have never been this close.*
> *I dream about something else, too.*
> *I dream about writing fairy tales for the rest of my life.*
> *I dream about sharing the world in those tales with you.*
> *With you by my side, I'm not afraid to be a dreamer*
> *anymore.*
> *With you by my side, I want to give this book a title.*
> *For it is only with you by my side that everything is*
> *within reach, that everything exists, that everything is*
> *true. And the earth is only a little dust under our feet.*
>
> *Happy birthday.*

Keenan! There was no doubt about it. Noni looked at the date
printed in the upper right-hand corner: *January 31, 2000.*

She felt weak. Noni knew Kugy well enough to understand the significance of what she had written, how intense the feelings behind them were. Slowly, she put it all together.

She realized why Kugy had started avoiding them, why Kugy hadn't come to her party, why Kugy had decided to break up with Josh, why Kugy had always seemed under great pressure. Why they had drifted so far apart these three years. Slowly, she understood. Everything.

She slipped the card back in the sleeve. She was so distressed, she nearly cried. Three years was a long time to keep something like this hidden away, to stay silent.

———

Eko raced to Noni's room after parking Fuad out front. "Noni!" he called as he ran.

Noni rushed out of her room. "What is it?"

"Mom just told me that Keenan's in Jakarta!"

Her eyes widened. "He came home?"

"Yeah, because Uncle Adri's so sick," Eko explained. "Mom says he's been in Bali this whole time. I have to see him! I mean it! I can't wait! Oh, that kid!" Eko was so happy he was practically screaming. "Just in time, too! He'll be able to come to our—"

"I'm coming to Jakarta with you," said Noni softly.

"You want to see Keenan, too?"

"I want to see Kugy."

It was Eko's turn to be shocked. "Are you sure? Are you ready?"

Noni nodded. "There's something I need to tell her."

———

Keenan was in his room looking at himself in the mirror. He'd been going through the same routine for an entire week. He stared at his reflection in its unfamiliar garb: dress pants, a smart collared shirt, loafers. In his pocket, he even carried a necktie, which he occasionally had to wear. He felt like he was wearing a costume.

Every morning, he woke up and went to work in his father's office, making the commute along with millions of other Jakartans. Frequently, he only came home after dinner was over. He beat the traffic this way, but also, there was so much he had to learn.

How quickly time passed here. It sprinted, it surged—so different from his days in Ubud, where minutes ambled, where seconds dripped. His assumption of his father's responsibilities was consuming all his energy and attention. He felt he didn't even have sufficient time for life at home with his parents and his brother.

There was only one thing that diverted him and cheered his heart: seeing his father as he got better with each passing day. Every morning, in his wheelchair, he sent Keenan off with a smile. And when Keenan came home, Jeroen was always waiting for him so they could chat for a while before going to bed. And his mother was there, too, always making sure everything was all right and that he had all he needed.

Except for his immediate family, he hadn't had the chance to see anyone—not friends, not cousins. He hadn't even contacted anybody. He'd been gone for so long that he didn't know where to start. Suddenly he took a deep breath. *Eko.* He remembered his cousin and how much he missed him.

And Kugy. Keenan sat down on the bed. Now that he wasn't in Bali anymore, he was confronted by all the memories he had of her—in the sky, in the clouds, in the street—as if all his thoughts and feelings were racing to the surface. Though the chances of running into Kugy were much higher now, he still didn't want to—as much as it was possible for him not to want to.

Keenan buried his face in his hands. He wished there were some way—a giant eraser, perhaps—that would clear his mind of such memories, of the emotions that welled up and niggled at him from time to time, causing him to feel guilty about his behavior toward Luhde. Suddenly, Keenan was angry at himself. *Why can't you just forget her?*

Then he rose to his feet, checked his reflection once more, and left for work, stepping into the swiftly spinning whirl of Jakarta time, hoping to drive Kugy's shadow far, far away.

CHAPTER 35

A TRUE PRINCE

It was Sunday, Kugy's weekly Independence Day, meaning she was free to sleep as much as she wanted. Except someone was shaking her by the shoulder. And judging by how heavy her eyelids were, it was still far too early to wake up.

"Kugy, wake up! Yoo-hoo! Wake up!"

For a moment, Kugy thought she was dreaming. She knew those barbaric shrieks all too well, but . . . *Impossible!* Kugy pulled the covers over her head.

"Kugy!" The voice was rising in pitch. "Come on, wake up! You're so mean! I've come all this way!"

Kugy forced herself to open her eyes. "Noni?" she muttered in disbelief. She sat up and Noni immediately gave her a hug. *As if this dream wasn't bizarre enough,* Kugy thought. She was still in a daze.

Noni whispered in her ear, "Forgive me. I'm so sorry about everything." And then Noni began to sob.

Kugy was confused. "Noni, what's wrong?"

"Now I understand. Three years, and only now do I understand. I'm sorry." Noni's words were interspersed with sobs.

"Three years? Wha—" Kugy was even more confused.

Slowly, Noni pulled away. She reached inside her bag and handed Kugy a package. "Sorry, but I opened and rewrapped it. You left it in your old room at the boarding house."

Kugy was startled to see it again. For an instant, she felt a surge of panic. She shook her head slowly. "You don't need to give this back to me," she said bitterly. "Just take it. Keep it. Do whatever you want with it. It's up to you."

Noni shook her head, on the verge of bursting into tears again. "Kugy, why didn't you say something? If I'd known how you felt, it wouldn't have come to this."

"I wanted to tell you. Really, I did. But I didn't know what to do. You and Eko wanted to set Keenan up with Wanda. Then you pulled it off and I was still with Josh, anyway. I was confused about what to say, how to act . . . I thought it was better to just keep my distance." Kugy's eyes began to fill with tears. "And about Eko . . ."

Noni sobbed. "I was wrong. Please forgive me. I've always felt I was living in your shadow, but I never wanted to admit it. So when Eko still seemed to care about you, when he tried to stay close to you, I overreacted—though I know he didn't mean anything by it. I was jealous that you two were still close, even though you and I had grown apart." The tears streamed down her face.

All Kugy could do was hug Noni and rub her back.

"You forgive me, don't you?"

"Only if you forgive me," said Kugy softly.

They held each other for a long time, thawing what had been frozen between them all those years.

"I have something else to tell you," whispered Noni.

"Let me guess. You're Batman!"

Noni almost choked on the laugh that caught her midsob. "You moron! This is serious!"

"Okay, okay. What is it?" Kugy folded her hands in front of her.

"It has to do with my parents. They've been bothering me about, well, you know what. So . . ." Noni cleared her throat. "On Valentine's Day, Eko and I are getting married."

Kugy's jaw dropped. "I . . . How . . . And here I was waiting for you to tell me you're really Batman!"

Noni burst into laughter as she wiped away her tears. "You crazy girl! I've missed you so much!"

Kugy smiled. She couldn't help but hug Noni again. "Congratulations," she said, laughing, then added, "It's about time you two set to work destroying each other's lives. But seriously, you two are the most compatible couple I know. I'm happy to have two friends who have come this far together. You guys deserve it."

"Thanks," Noni answered. "But you know something? We've always felt that you and Keenan were the ones who belonged together. You're both weird. You're both a mess. You're both incorrigible."

Kugy feigned indignation. "Are these compliments or insults?"

Noni grinned. "So if the opportunity arose, you'd give the book to Keenan?"

Kugy's expression turned somber. Then she shook her head. "I can only give that book to someone I will always love. And it looks like it's not him."

Noni was silent. She wanted to tell Kugy that Keenan had come home—that they were both in the same city now. But instead she kept quiet and let it pass. Kugy would find out for herself.

"Now it's my turn to tell you something." Kugy smiled brightly.

Noni noticed the change in her friend's expression. "Are you in love? No way!"

Kugy nodded. "I have . . . a boyfriend!" Kugy bobbed up and down with excitement.

Noni screamed. "Who?"

"My boss!" Kugy laughed.

Noni froze, then frowned. "How'd you wind up dating your own boss? It's like something out of that bad soap opera—*Inem the Sexy Waitress*." But seeing Kugy's shining eyes, Noni shook off her reservations and before long was laughing along. "I'm happy for you, too. I want to meet him!"

"Of course. I'll bring him to the wedding."

"Awesome!" Noni clapped. Then, quick as a flash, she slipped something over Kugy's head.

"Huh? What is this?" Kugy looked down at the thing hanging from her neck.

"Congratulations. You're number one. No one can ever take your place." Noni smiled.

Kugy read the gold medal. *For my best and oldest friend.* She took a deep breath and tried to contain her emotions. "Seriously, though," she whispered. "I'm still waiting for you to tell me that you're really Batman."

———

Upon reaching the front gate of the house, Eko saw his aunt watering the potted plants around the gazebo.

"Auntie Lena!"

Immediately, Lena put down the hose and went over to him, arms wide open. "Eko! My goodness! How are you?"

"I'm well, Auntie." Eko hugged her back. "Mom told me that Keenan—"

"YOU GODLESS DEVIL, YOU!" someone yelled from the house.

"YOU SCREWED-UP TURD!" Eko responded, then saw his aunt's expression. "I'm sorry, Auntie. I'm just expressing my affection—" Before Eko could finish, his cousin pounced on him and gathered him into an embrace.

Keenan and Eko hugged each other, laughing and cursing at each other. Lena winced to hear them swearing, but before long, they went into the house and up to Keenan's room, where they spent the rest of the day swapping stories, each one astonished at what the other had to say.

"So you're writing your thesis this semester and graduating this year? Great! Welcome to the real world!" Keenan clapped Eko on the shoulder.

"Eh, it's nothing special," said Eko. "I mean, I'm graduating on time, but that's not unusual. You know who's really crazy? Your fellow alien. Kugy graduated last year. Got a job. Successful and everything."

Keenan felt something tug at his heart. "Kugy? Where is she working?"

"In an advertising agency as a copywriter. It suits her major perfectly."

Keenan raised his eyebrows. "I thought she wanted to write fairy tales."

"Hello? Earth to Keenan. Who writes fairy tales these days? Where do you think we live? Fairyland? And you! Who would've ever guessed Keenan would become a big-city businessman?"

Keenan felt a second tug. "Well, I'm hoping it's only for a little while," he said heavily. "One thing's for certain—right now, I don't have a choice. Or rather, my family doesn't have a choice."

It was Eko's turn to put his hand on his cousin's shoulder. "I understand, man. If I can do anything, let me know, okay?"

Keenan smiled. "You don't need to. Just seeing you makes me feel like life is back to normal."

"That's crazy talk." Eko made a face. "Since when has your life been normal?"

"Good point," Keenan said, nodding in agreement. "So when can I meet up with you and Noni?"

"Anytime! And guess what? Noni and Kugy made up. Perfect timing, huh?"

"Made up?" asked Keenan, surprised. "What happened?"

"You didn't know? They stopped speaking to each other after Noni's birthday party. Almost three years ago! Imagine that. Now that's what you call a miracle."

The third tug. The memory of that night still affected him. "How did it come to that?" he murmured.

Eko only shrugged. He wanted to tell Keenan what Noni had told him about the birthday present Kugy never gave him, the feelings she had kept bottled up for so many years, and how those feelings were the main cause of her withdrawal. But Eko was also apprehensive. What was the use? Keenan now had a girlfriend in Ubud. Kugy had her own life. If there was only one thing he could ask for, it would be for the four of them to be friends again. That would be enough. *If Keenan has to find out, let him find out for himself,* Eko thought.

"Anyway, good luck for February," said Keenan, giving his shoulder a squeeze. "I'll definitely be there."

"'Be there'? After disappearing for so long, you think I'm going to let you just 'be there'?" Eko turned away in mock disgust.

"So what do you want me to do?"

"You're going to be my best man. You know, the ring bear."

Keenan burst into laughter. "I'm honored. But just so you know, the best man and the ring bear*er* aren't the same thing."

Eko thought for a moment. "So what should I call you? The ringman?"

———

After weeks of working overtime, Kugy's body finally conceded defeat and she had to spend her birthday in bed with the flu. Secretly, she was grateful. She'd heard rumors the whole office was planning to go all out with the practical jokes today, and it wasn't so much because it was her birthday as the fact that she was officially the Big Boss's girlfriend.

Her birthday merely provided a convenient excuse for her colleagues to express how they felt about her new relationship with Remi—whether that meant wishing her the best, pelting her with eggs, dousing her with water, or whatever else they could think of.

She remained in bed the entire day, surrounded by a heap of pillows, enjoying her rest very much indeed. Suddenly there came a knock on the door. Kugy glanced at her watch. It wasn't even seven in the evening yet.

"I'm not hungry! I'll eat dinner later!" she called.

But the door opened, anyway. And there was Remi, his face shining, illuminated by a small candle. Kugy sat up a little. *Remi? A cake?*

Sure enough, Remi entered, bearing a small chocolate cake with a candle in one hand and a bunch of fresh daisies in the other. He sang "Happy Birthday" in a low voice.

Kugy sat up fully, startled but also on the verge of laughter. She forced herself to wait until Remi finished singing, then blew out the candle. "You! What are you doing, parading into my room with all this?"

"Why? Is there a problem?"

Kugy shook her head. Her cheeks were red. "I'm just embarrassed," she said softly. "Being treated like this makes me feel awkward."

"Strange," said Remi, amused. "Imagination is your trade, but you're thrown off by a little something like this. Been single for too long, huh? Happy birthday, my Kugy." He kissed Kugy's forehead. "You still feel a little warm."

Kugy pressed her palm to her forehead. "I guess. But I feel better. Especially since you've come here bearing cake and flowers."

"I have something that'll cool you down." Remi took a slim black box from his pocket. He opened it and Kugy stared in amazement at what was inside—a bracelet made of small glittering blue stones.

"It won't go with your Ninja Turtles watch. But wear it anyway, okay?" Remi fastened the bracelet around Kugy's left wrist. "They're sapphire," he explained. "Their blue is like the blue of the ocean. So whenever you find yourself longing for the sea, just look at this bracelet."

Kugy was speechless. She swallowed.

"What is it now?" Remi smiled as he stroked Kugy's cheek.

"I don't know what kind of trick you're pulling," Kugy whispered, "but this is the most beautiful present I've ever received." Her body still felt weak, but she leaned in and embraced Remi as tightly as she could. "Thank you. I'll wear it every day."

"This isn't a trick," Remi whispered. "I love you. It's as easy as that."

As Remi held her, Kugy realized something: Keenan was the prince she'd dreamed for herself when she was eighteen. Someone out of a beautiful fairy tale. But now reality—plain and simple—had woken her from her long slumber. Remi was her true prince. He was real. He was here. And he loved her.

CHAPTER 36

A REUNION OF FARMERS

February 2003

It was Friday evening and Noni's and Eko's wedding ceremony was starting in two hours.

Because she wouldn't have time to go home and change, Kugy had brought everything she needed to the office. She emerged from the restroom, where she had changed her clothes and done the best she could with her makeup, and did a final check in the mirror. She was wearing a dark-blue velvet dress that came down to her knees. It was the first dress she'd bought in a long time, and she'd fallen in love with it because of its cut. It was simple enough so that she wouldn't feel embarrassed leaving the office in it. But it was also elegant enough so that she wouldn't feel underdressed at the reception. Last of all, she put on the sapphire bracelet. She smiled with satisfaction. It was the perfect finishing touch.

Kugy found Remi in his office. "Remi, it's five o'clock already. The traffic's going to be terrible and the wedding starts at six thirty."

Remi quickly concluded his phone conversation and gave Kugy a panicked look.

"Shall we go?" asked Kugy with a broad smile. "Why do you look so surprised?"

Remi took a deep breath and bit his lip. "Because of two things. First, you're absolutely gorgeous."

Kugy's smile grew even brighter. "And the second?"

"I can't come."

"*What?* But you promised!"

Remi gave her shoulders a squeeze. "I know, I'm sorry. But remember the project we're doing with Vector Point? Their top guy leaves town tomorrow, so he and I have to give the final presentation to our client tonight. I can't do it any other time."

Kugy felt like she was going to cry. "But these are my childhood friends. I wanted to introduce you to them. And it's such an important event."

"If there were any way I could go, I would. But I really can't. I'll make it up to you. I promise."

There was no point whining or complaining. Remi couldn't come and she had to try and be realistic. Slowly, she nodded.

Remi took Kugy's hand and kissed it. "Tonight this little blue fellow will just have to go in my place," he said, stroking the bracelet around her wrist.

———

Keenan hurried out of the car and sprinted into Eko's house. Auntie Erni, Eko's mother, was already waiting for him at the back door.

"My goodness, Keenan!" she exclaimed "Did you run into traffic? Lucky for you, everything's still a mess. Come this way. We're just starting. Here's the ring. Hold on to it." Auntie Erni pressed a small box into his hands.

Keenan squeezed his way through the crowd and took his place beside Eko and Noni.

At the sight of him, Eko's face relaxed. But there was no time to chat. They gestured and smiled at each other from afar.

Meanwhile at the front door, Kugy had just arrived and was fighting her way through the throng. The line of relatives in front were the most difficult to break through, but Kugy didn't want to miss out. She wanted to get a good view of Eko and Noni exchanging rings.

It was Noni's turn to relax when she saw Kugy suddenly emerge, pushing through the crowd with a little wave of her hand. *She made it after all,* Noni thought, relieved. She didn't know what she would have done if Kugy had disappeared again and missed her wedding.

Kugy sighed. Noni looked so beautiful in her pink *kebaya* and Eko looked very handsome in his suit. The exchanging of rings was about to commence. Everyone watched, waiting for the little box to appear and for Eko to open it. And then . . . her heart stopped. Kugy blinked, trying to make sure her eyes weren't playing tricks on her. There was no doubt about it. Kugy knew the person standing beside Eko—the person handing him the box containing the rings. She knew the sound of his laugh, the warmth of his gaze. Kugy shook her head. *It can't be.*

At that very moment, something made Keenan look in Kugy's direction. He froze, unsure what he was seeing. A warm sensation spread throughout his entire body. He felt whole and at peace. Only one person was able to make him feel like that, and all she needed to do was be present, to *be.* Yet Keenan still couldn't quite believe his eyes. It was too good to be true.

Only when their eyes finally met did they both know: this was no mirage.

Even then, Kugy felt like running as fast and as far away as her legs would take her. But at the same time, her feet seemed rooted to the floor. Kugy remained in this state of paralysis until the ceremony was over and Keenan made his way toward her.

It was as if he were walking through the sea during a storm. But his feet kept moving, as if he were hypnotized. "Kugy?" he called out. "How are you?" That was all he could manage to say.

"Good," Kugy answered, simply. For that was all she could manage in reply.

Suddenly, the crowd began jostling them. All the guests were coming up to congratulate Eko and Noni. People were passing between them, and their view of each other was obscured.

Kugy's sudden disappearance startled Keenan. In his panic, he grabbed for Kugy's hand, and she screamed in surprise as she was jerked forward.

"Sorry. Did I scare you?" He was bewildered by his reaction. He had felt a sense of loss that he wasn't willing to experience ever again.

"I'm okay." Kugy tried to smile.

Keenan smiled, too. It was the first time they had smiled at each other in a very long time. "Let's go congratulate them," he said, keeping her hand in his.

At the sight of Kugy and Keenan coming toward them, Eko and Noni waved. They were grinning madly.

"Hey!" exclaimed Eko. "My ringman! And you!" he said, hugging Kugy. "My ringworm."

"Wow, this is great!" Noni exclaimed. "The four of us are back together!"

Kugy looked at Eko and Noni and laughed, even as her eyes revealed her bewilderment. "Yeah, huh? Who'd have thought? The four of us together again, without any warning."

"You're right," said Keenan, staring in Eko's and Noni's direction. "Whoever orchestrated this reunion was awfully clever."

Hastily, Eko gave Noni a nudge. "Okay, we have to make the rounds and mingle. You two get something to eat. Catch up. When things are quieter, the four of us can hang out, okay?" And in a flash they were gone, leaving Keenan and Kugy alone in all their awkwardness.

"Hungry?" asked Keenan, trying to make conversation, though seeing Kugy had made his appetite vanish.

Kugy shook her head. Her mind was in such turmoil she couldn't even think about food. "Maybe later. How about you?"

"I don't feel like eating, either," Keenan confessed.

In the end they wound up sitting on the veranda in Eko's backyard, supplied with two glasses of fruit cocktail, which neither of them touched.

Kugy was the first to speak. "I never would have guessed I'd run into you like this," she said, trying to dispel the almost crippling awkwardness between them. She smiled and gave Keenan a sideways glance. He was wearing a black jacket and a dark-colored tie. His hair, which he had always worn long, was now short and neat.

"Doesn't suit me, huh?" said Keenan with a low laugh.

Kugy didn't reply, unwilling to give him an honest answer about how different he looked and how he never ceased to amaze her.

"You're not the only one. I never would have guessed that I'd run into you in a . . . dress." *You're even more beautiful than before,* he added, in his heart. "You've convinced me: Charles Darwin was right. Evolution really can happen."

"You monkey!" Kugy sputtered, laughing.

"Yes, that's it exactly," said Keenan. "From an unkempt monkey to a beautiful human being in a velvet gown." He burst into laughter.

Soon, they lapsed into silence again. There were so many words buzzing around inside their heads. But how difficult they were to utter!

"Where did you go?" Kugy asked finally. The question had been on her mind for a long time.

"Bali," Keenan answered simply. Too much had happened. He didn't know where to begin.

Kugy smiled bitterly. "That's it? You disappear without telling anyone—just like that—and all you can say is that you were in Bali, like you just came back from vacation?" She spoke evenly, but there was a sharp, accusatory tone in her voice.

Keenan looked annoyed. "No, it wasn't 'just like that.' I didn't leave just for the heck of it. And I didn't 'disappear' and take a 'vacation.' I left to make a fresh start. I wanted to go where my heart chose to go. However I chose to leave, it was the right decision at the time. I don't regret anything," he finished firmly.

Kugy didn't feel like she could ask him anything else. He had decided to leave them all behind, leave himself behind, without saying a word. But that was his choice. He hadn't done anything wrong. *No, it wasn't his fault,* thought Kugy. *I shouldn't have hoped for so much.*

"So why did you come back?" murmured Kugy. "Did you follow your heart again?"

"No," said Keenan matter-of-factly.

"Then why are you here? Why stop following your heart now?" Kugy's voice betrayed her hurt feelings. She looked away.

"I came back for my family," said Keenan. "My dad was unwell, paralyzed because of a stroke. Honestly, if it wasn't for that I probably would have never returned. I'm working in my dad's office now. He spends all his time in therapy. His condition has improved a lot. Even though I'm taking his place now, hopefully it won't be for long." He sounded bitter.

Kugy was genuinely shocked. "I'm so sorry, Keenan. I hope he recovers. I had no idea he was unwell." She turned to him. "But once he gets better, will you leave again to follow your heart?"

Keenan was quiet. As she gazed at him, he realized there were two places his heart wanted to be. He had been diligent in keeping his heart faithful to *her*—that certain someone, waiting for him in Bali. But his brief encounter with Kugy had taken everything he had built up with such care and effort and turned it upside down.

At Keenan's silence, Kugy took a deep breath. Inside she was screaming. *Why did he come back? Why appear, only to disappear the very next moment?* In the space of a few minutes, Keenan had plunged her heart into chaos. Kugy's fingers moved to the chain of small jewels encircling her left wrist and clutched it, as if it would give her the strength she needed.

"Nice bracelet. Are those sapphires?"

She merely nodded, and found herself powerless to resist as Keenan took her wrist and examined the bracelet more closely.

"A perfect accessory for one of Neptune's secret agents," he said. He glanced at Kugy and gave her a small smile. "Neptune didn't give it to you, did he?"

Kugy shook her head. "It's from my boyfriend," she said. *The sooner he knows, the better.*

"Oh," said Keenan, trying to hide the tremor in his voice. "He must know you well. Someone from work?"

"Yes."

"Is he a copywriter, too?"

"My boss."

"Oh," Keenan said again. "He's older then?"

"Yes."

"Is he serious about you?"

Kugy shrugged. "One thing's for sure. I never play around."

Keenan didn't even attempt to respond.

Kugy took a deep breath. She considered how best to phrase her question. "Balinese girls are pretty. Did anyone catch your eye?" She tried to keep her tone light.

Keenan nodded. "Yes, my girlfriend is Balinese. Uncle Wayan's niece. She's still young, but she's very mature."

"I see. Is she a painter, too?"

Keenan looked at her. "No. She likes to write. Like you."

There was suddenly a bitter taste in Kugy's mouth. "Oh yeah? What does she like to write?"

"She . . ." Keenan considered this. "She's naturally gifted with words, written and spoken. Talking to her is like reading a book of proverbs. She could write anything she wanted to. But at the moment, she wants to write children's stories."

Kugy wanted to say something, to speak her mind, but she couldn't. Her heart had been wounded—and it stung. Almost unconsciously, she moved her hand again to clutch her blue bracelet. "I'm happy you're back," she blurted, in a cheerful voice. "I've had a hell of a time finding a new partner. Life as a secret agent isn't nearly as fun without you."

"Now think for a minute," said Keenan. "How can I continue being one of Neptune's secret agents if the only person who knows I'm an agent is you? I can't be a secret agent when you're not around." Playfully, he poked the tip of Kugy's nose.

Kugy grinned. So everything was finally back to normal. As long as they didn't touch on what was really going on in their hearts, everything was fine. And now they were free to talk about anything, about Keenan's time away and his life in Lodtunduh, about Kugy's job. And they could have talked forever. Before they knew it, half the guests had already left. Things were beginning to quiet down.

Suddenly, Eko clapped them both on the back. "Hey, Weirdos United! How many plates of rice have you polished off?" Noni appeared behind him, smiling, and they sat together on the tiled floor.

"It's so hot in these clothes!" Eko complained as he took off his jacket. "I think I'm going to change into a T-shirt and sarong."

"What are you, a farmer?" joked Keenan. "While you're at it, why not brew up a pot of coffee—boiled with sugar, the old-fashioned way? We can fry up some cassava, listen to some AM radio, talk about the harvest and the price of vegetables . . ."

"Genius!" exclaimed Kugy. "Why don't we give this reunion an agrarian theme? How about 'Back on the Farm'? In the spirit of those agricultural programs that aired on national TV back in the day."

Eko looked at them. "More like 'Alien Resurrection' if you ask me."

"'Back on the Farm' sounds good to me!" said Noni. "I'll get some costumes from your mother, Eko." She ran into the house and came back with four T-shirts and four sarongs.

Soon they had all changed and were sitting with four steaming mugs and a plate of snacks. Before they knew it, a rooster was crowing in the distance, affirming that night had rolled by, all too fast.

CHAPTER 37

A BARRIER THAT CAN NEVER BE BROKEN

March 2003

As Noni's and Eko's campus commitments began winding down, the four friends were able to get together more often. They met up at least every two weeks, and this week, Keenan was hosting.

Lena was happy to see them. It had been a long time since she had seen Keenan socialize with his old friends, and to her this was a sign he was beginning to settle into life in Jakarta. She was so happy that she offered to make them food—so much of it that it could barely fit on the dining table.

At the sight of it all, the group was astonished.

"Mom, it's just the four of us," said Keenan. "There's enough food here for an entire party!"

"But Keenan's forgetting to take our pets into account, Auntie," Eko chimed in. "Kugy has a pet anaconda, I have a pet dragon, Noni has a family of lions, and Keenan has adopted a band of vagrants—"

"Eko!" Jeroen came out of his room.

"Jeroen?" Eko hardly recognized him. The little kid in his middle school uniform was in high school now. He had shot up and was almost as tall as Eko. "And you! What pet do you have and how did it make you so big?"

Jeroen chuckled. "A troupe of dancing girls."

Lena's eyes widened. "I wouldn't put it past him, this kid. He has so many girlfriends. What a headache. I have to play both mother and receptionist. The telephone rings nonstop with girls looking for him. And it's a different one each time."

"It's okay, Auntie," said Eko. "Since Keenan suffers from the opposite problem, it all balances out."

Keenan's father glided out of his room in his wheelchair, maneuvering the contraption with ease. He gave them all a friendly smile and though his speech was slow, his articulation was clear and sounded close to normal. When he reached the table, he asked to be helped to his feet. Carefully, he walked over to his chair.

"Keenan's father is already walking," Lena explained with pride. "He can do almost everything he could do before, just more slowly."

Kugy took it all in. *So this is the sacrifice Keenan has made. Hopefully it won't be permanent,* she thought, though she knew it meant Keenan would probably leave again. Suddenly she felt it again—the wound in her heart. But Kugy ignored it. A night like tonight was too precious to pass in pain.

———

"You two should go first," said Keenan as the group stood on the front veranda. "You have to drive back to Bandung in the morning. I can send Kugy home."

"You sure?" asked Noni and Eko in unison.

"It's not too much trouble?" Kugy asked.

Keenan shook his head firmly and bid Noni and Eko farewell. Then they were left alone—him, Kugy, and a chorus of night insects.

"Kugy, I have something I really want to speak to you about. It's a very personal matter, and it involves you and me. That's why I didn't want to bring it up in front of Noni and Eko."

Kugy looked calm, but she felt uneasy. Her heart was pounding.

Keenan gazed deep into her eyes. "I want to thank you."

"For what?" And then she saw him produce something from behind his back—something he'd been carrying since coming out to the porch.

"You lent me something. It's very precious to me. But I have to return it to its rightful owner." He handed her a worn-looking notebook.

Kugy was startled. She never thought she would see the book again. "General Pilik?" she said, her voice trembling.

"This book has played such an important role in my life," said Keenan gently, "and you'll find out why. But I want to tell you in a special way."

Kugy was even more confused. She took the notebook, her emotions in turmoil. "So, you've had the book with you all this time? Even when you were in Bali?"

"And I read it almost every day." Keenan smiled. "You do realize, don't you, that you're going to be an amazing fairy tale writer?"

Kugy's throat closed up. It had been so long since anyone—herself included—had mentioned, or even touched on, that other life of hers.

"Now I want to ask you for something else," Keenan said, almost whispering. "Give me just one day. I want to take you somewhere. Just let me know when you're free. Then you'll understand why this book has been so important to me."

Kugy didn't understand what Keenan was talking about, but she nodded, anyway.

———

It was Saturday morning. Keenan was already in Kugy's living room at five minutes to seven. Before long, Kugy emerged. Her hair was still wet and she was struggling to keep her eyes open.

"You really are crazy after all," said Kugy, wobbling as she walked. "Did we really have to meet at seven o'clock?"

"The only rules in effect today," said Keenan with mock sternness, "are my rules."

"So I'm about to be enslaved?" asked Kugy, weakly.

"Just remember, you only have one task for the day: trust me. Okay, first rule: we have to bring extra clothes. You've done that, right?"

"Right."

"Good. Second rule: your cell phone must be off, from now in this living room until when we return."

"Got it."

A few minutes later, they left. Kugy was enjoying their conversation so much that before she realized it, their car had merged onto the Cikampek highway.

"Wait a minute," she murmured suspiciously. "Where are we going?"

Keenan grinned. "Our first stop of the day: Bandung. We're going to see Pilik."

"Bandung? Pilik? Hooray!" she exclaimed, bouncing in her seat.

———

It had been three hours since they'd started out. They had gone right through Bandung and were heading north.

"I don't get it," said Kugy. "Why were you thinking about Pilik? You only saw the students twice. I should have thought of the idea. I was their teacher. I saw them almost every day for two years."

"Enough already," Keenan answered with a smile. "No more questions. It's just one of today's surprises."

They arrived in Pilik's village. They could see the footpath leading to the Sakola Alit. "I should park here, right?" asked Keenan, seeing the sign for the health clinic, which had been his landmark on previous visits. It looked empty and run-down—as if it had been shut for months. "Everything seems different," he murmured as he looked around.

Kugy looked around, too. Keenan was right—everything was different. The footpath to the school was wider, and it wasn't grassy anymore—as if large vehicles were using it now. The dense clump of bamboo trees that usually sheltered the parking space was no longer there. The sun beat down, making everything look desolate and dry.

They started down the path. What greeted them was stranger still. They passed several workers carrying sand, cement, and rocks in the opposite direction. And when they arrived, they were horrified to find half the village razed to the ground. Flat red earth stretched out before them. No houses. No fields. Only big trucks, backhoes, cement mixers, and workers coming and going across the large clearing.

Kugy and Keenan were stunned. The Sakola Alit was gone without a trace.

Without wasting any time, they asked around, looking for the remaining inhabitants.

"They're going to make it into a housing development," a man told Kugy in Sundanese. He was carrying firewood.

"There used to be houses here, sir. Where did they go?" asked Keenan.

"*Atos ngaralih. Sadayana atos digusur,*" the man answered, motioning with his hand. "They've moved. All of it's been cleared."

"Where did they go?" Kugy exclaimed.

He shrugged. "*Duka atuh, Neng. Da paburencay.* Don't know, miss. But they've been kicked out."

Haltingly, Kugy tried to communicate in Sundanese. "*Upami Bapa terang teu Pak Usep ayeuna di mana?* Would you happen to know where Mr. Usep lives now?"

"Oh, *Pak Usep anu gaduh kebon sampeu?* The one who owns the cassava plantation?"

Kugy nodded. "*Muhun, muhun. Anu putrana namina Pilik.* That's right. The one who has a son named Pilik."

The man chose his words carefully. "*Pak Usep mah kagusur ka caket susukan, Neng.* Mr. Usep had to go live down by the creek, miss."

Kugy knew the creek he was talking about—a narrow filthy stream near a garbage dump.

"Do you know where it is?" Keenan asked Kugy.

She nodded. "Let's go find them," she murmured. She could already imagine the condition they would find Pilik and his family in. They thanked the man and hurried away.

In fact, it was worse than Kugy imagined. There were several broken-down huts by the side of the stream, unfit to be called homes. They saw several people moving about.

"It's Mr. Usep!" Kugy exclaimed.

"Ms. Ugy!" Mr. Usep was equally surprised. He poked his head into his hut and called to his wife. "*Kadieu, enggal! Ieu, aya guru-guruna Pilik!* Come out, quickly! It's Pilik's teachers!"

A woman in a faded housedress emerged. She looked as if she had seen an angel. She ran over to Kugy and hugged her tightly. "Ms. Ugy," she greeted Kugy. "Pilik . . ." She burst into tears. Her body shook. Mr. Usep could only hang his head in silence.

That was when Kugy and Keenan knew something was very wrong.

———

It was just the two of them again, along with the blowing wind and the creaking bamboo. The roar of construction could only be heard faintly from where they stood. In the meantime, a bird circled overhead, cawing. It perched on top of the wooden grave marker before them.

It was Pilik's resting place. All that remained were the memories of his boisterous voice and the way he used to run around, his shaved head and his bright, clever eyes. And how all the kids had looked up to him. Kugy saw it all in her mind, like a film, while sorrow filled Keenan a thousand times over.

Keenan clutched a checkbook. He had planned to present it to Pilik and the Sakola Alit. It showed all the money he had been setting aside from the sale of his paintings. With bitterness, he gazed at the grave marker, thinking about how ironic reality was compared to the world of fairy tales. The world of General Pilik and the Alit Brigade was beautiful, and Keenan had tried to realize that beauty through all his works. And then there was the real life of Pilik bin Usep, a kid whose family was kicked off their land because they didn't have any proof they owned it. Who had to live in a hut next to a garbage dump, and who came down with typhus three months back but couldn't get any medical help, because the clinic had been shut down long ago. Mr. Usep told them that in less than a week, Pilik's condition took a turn for the worse, and his little body had surrendered. Pilik departed, taking with him his unrealized dreams of going to middle school someday.

"Oh Keenan, if only I could have seen him. I had no idea. I lost contact with Ami, too. Pilik should have had a chance. He was such a smart kid . . ." Kugy's voice wavered as she spoke.

Pilik should have had a chance. Overcome with grief, Keenan knelt beside Kugy, who was weeping, and held her.

"I thought of Pilik so many times," Kugy wailed, "and the other kids, too. But now, I'll never have the chance to see them again. I still have a whole notebook of the adventures of the Alit Brigade. They haven't even read it yet . . ." She buried her head in Keenan's shoulder and wept until she could weep no more.

"They'll read it someday," said Keenan gently. "I'm sure of it. Don't stop writing."

It felt as if he had been hurled back into the past. To a time when he and Kugy had shared a dream. When all they had needed was the world and each other. When that one simple moment he had shared with Kugy had crystallized forever in his heart. But time had passed and the world had turned, and now they could never go back. Reality and fairy tales were separated by a barrier that could never be broken.

CHAPTER 38
A MOST WONDERFUL KIDNAPPING

Kugy gazed at Keenan's checkbook, overwhelmed. She was surprised, moved, and angry all at once. Kugy would never have thought her stories would play such a large role in Keenan's life. She was touched by Keenan's genuine desire to thank her, the Sakola Alit, and the Alit Brigade. But she was also angry that for all their good intentions, they had been unable to help General Pilik.

"You're giving them this money?" asked Kugy.

"Yes," Keenan answered. "It's for Mr. Usep, Mr. Somad, and all the members of the Alit Brigade whose families were evicted. To me, this money is rightfully theirs."

"So what do we do now?" Kugy rubbed her eyes. She was exhausted.

"There's somewhere else I want to take you. Today's rules are still in effect." Keenan smiled and stroked her hand.

Kugy didn't have the energy to protest, or the inclination. It didn't matter what Keenan's plans were. All she wanted to do was sit in the car and go wherever fate took her.

Before long, their SUV had left Bojong Koneng district. Then it left Bandung altogether.

———

Kugy slept through the second half of the trip. She was dimly aware they were heading toward the city of Garut, then south toward Pameungpeuk. For the remainder of the journey, she was fast asleep with the seat reclined.

When she opened her eyes, Keenan's car had come to a stop. The first thing she saw through the windshield was the open sky, spreading out before her. It was reddish—ablaze, as if it were on fire. She watched as several processions of clouds, blushing orange, were swallowed up by the western horizon. She became aware of something else—the roar of crashing waves, coming from somewhere below. Then another thing hit her—Keenan was gone.

Quickly, she sat up. She saw they were parked on top of a grassy green cliff. Stretched out beneath her was the vast ocean, where she could see waves churning and whirling, breaking and falling, sweeping across an expanse of coral and white foam. Kugy scrambled out of the car.

As if that weren't enough, she was awestruck anew at the emergence of hundreds of bats from beneath where she stood. They flew in a swarm, forming a cluster of black clouds that quickly filled the sky. Astonished by all this beauty, which had appeared so suddenly before her eyes, Kugy lowered herself onto the grass.

She heard Keenan's voice. "Little One!"

Kugy turned her head. There he was, standing near a small grass-thatched shelter, waving. She ran over.

"Where are we?" Kugy had to shout over the roar of the waves.

"Welcome to Ranca Buaya." Keenan grinned. "Another one of today's rules: your kidnapper gets to take you anywhere he wants. I came across this beach by accident once, when I was with Bimo and some other friends. It was love at first sight. I've wanted to come here again for years, but I've never had the chance. And now I'm here, with you. So, enjoy!" He held out a cold drink from the cooler he'd brought.

Kugy took it. Gradually, the look of protest on her face disappeared. "Well, Agent Nowheretoturnia, I have to admit. As far as kidnappings go, this is very agreeable." She chuckled. "Cheers."

"Cheers."

They sat on the edge of the cliff. With the grass beneath them and two cans of soda beside them, they watched the sun set until it vanished, engulfed by night. Then they gazed in wonder at the Indian Ocean spread out before them.

They drove down to a sloping part of the beach where several food vendors had set up stalls. The night was still young, and clear. A scattering of stars appeared in the cloudless sky, and the moon glowed majestically in all its fullness.

"This is the best instant ramen I've ever had in my life," Kugy declared as she slurped up her noodles. She was already on her second bowl.

Keenan glanced at the empty package on the table. "Are you sure?" he asked doubtfully.

"Of course," Kugy affirmed. "First, I haven't eaten anything since lunch. And second, this place has the most beautiful view I've ever seen. Nothing compares—not even the most expensive restaurants in Jakarta. Am I right?"

Keenan laughed and moved on to his second bowl as well. "So you don't regret being kidnapped?"

Kugy stopped chewing. "Can I ask you something? What's the real reason behind all this?"

Keenan also stopped chewing and looked at her for a moment. "Finish eating first. I'll tell you later. But not here. Not now."

Kugy's eyes widened. "We're going somewhere else?"

Keenan nodded. "Just twenty yards over."

Ranca Buaya beach was hemmed in by coral reef, except for a cove where fishermen kept their boats, right where the food stalls were. Nearby was a small, empty stretch of sand.

There on that stretch, Kugy and Keenan finally had the opportunity to wade in the ocean. The sand beneath their feet was made up of broken clamshells, creamy yellow in hue. Hundreds of tiny waves sparkled silver in the moonlight. They could see little mounds of coral peeking out of the water, shimmering, gilded by sea foam.

After she had her fill of playing in the waves, Kugy threw herself down on the sand. "I'm so full," she said. "I'll sleep soundly tonight."

"Want me to make you a bed?" asked Keenan.

"How?"

Keenan ran to the car and came back with a small pail and shovel.

Kugy laughed. "Were you planning on planting something? You brought a shovel and everything!"

"Don't ask too many questions," Keenan reminded her. "That's one of today's rules." He got down to work.

"What are you doing?" Kugy was still lying on her back, gazing up at the night sky.

Then she felt herself being lifted up.

"What are you doing?" she shrieked.

A few seconds later, she was set back onto the sand, into a shallow pit.

"You won't find this kind of bed anywhere, not even in the most expensive hotels. It's a sand bed. All natural—and therapeutic, too. It works like reflexology." He rattled this off in the easy manner of a medicine-seller hawking his wares. He continued to pile sand on top of her as he spoke, using his bucket as a scoop.

Kugy offered no resistance. She even giggled. The grains of sand tickled as they flowed over her skin.

"How's your bed, Little One? Comfy, huh?" Keenan's smile was triumphant.

"Better than a five-star hotel." She sighed, closing her eyes. Once her body was completely covered with sand, Keenan lay down beside her.

"Of course it's better," he said. "This is a million-star hotel. You can order instant noodles and hot tea, the rooms are enormous, and there's a massage bed and live music playing nonstop. The waves. Nature's sweetest song."

Kugy turned to him. "You mean you—"

"Think of this as a belated birthday present. Think of this as a small token to celebrate our reunion. Think of this however you want." Keenan inched toward her, keeping his eyes on her. "This is my way of thanking you for all the valuable inspiration you've given me."

Kugy froze, and the pile of sand on top of her made her feel weaker still. She couldn't move. She couldn't even speak. All she could do was gaze into his face hovering above her, so very close.

"Little One," Keenan continued, "I've always remembered what you said. How much you love the sound of the waves. I hope coming here has made you happy."

Kugy could barely speak. "I've never been happier. Thank you."

Keenan shook his head. "I'm the one who's thankful. And I have one more present to give you. The same rules still apply: you have to do whatever I tell you. Okay? Now, close your eyes."

Kugy obeyed, though she was incredibly nervous. Her eyes were closed, but she could feel Keenan coming closer. His breath felt warm on her face. Her heart was beating so fast it felt like it was going to burst right out of her sand bed. But Kugy couldn't have moved if she tried.

"Open your mouth," he said gently.

Apprehensively, Kugy did as she was told. She felt something on her lips, in her mouth. She knew that scent. She had been holding her breath. Now she released it. But she didn't say anything because her mouth was full.

"It's a banana. Your favorite." Keenan chuckled. "I brought a bunch with me."

"Very clever," she said between bites. "You thought of everything, didn't you?"

Keenan placed his index fingers against his temples, like antennae. "Neptune radar," he said lightly.

"All right, fellow agent. We've finished the main course. Now we're eating dessert. What next?"

Keenan's expression became serious. "It took four hours to get here from Bandung. It'll take three hours to get back to Jakarta. If we try to drive home tonight, we'll be exhausted. What about going back tomorrow morning before sunrise?"

"But where are we going to sleep? We're not really going to spend the night here, are we?"

"Don't worry. I'm a very responsible kidnapper." Keenan went back to the car again and returned with two sleeping bags. "We can sleep in the shelter back over there, or on the beach. Up to you, Little One."

Kugy thought for a while. "I think I'd prefer to stay here. But is it safe?"

"It's safe," Keenan answered confidently. "Your kidnapper has security under control."

"Oh yeah? How?"

"Prayer."

———

Noni frowned when she saw the unfamiliar number on her cell phone screen. "Hello?"

"Hi. Is this Noni?"

The man's voice was unfamiliar. "Yes, it is," said Noni. "Who is this?"

"This is Remi." There was a pause. "I'm Kugy's boyfriend."

"Oh!" Noni exclaimed. The name wasn't new to her, but she hadn't anticipated Remi calling her out of the blue. It was eleven o'clock at night.

"Sorry I'm calling so late. I got your number from Kugy's little sister. I was wondering if you know where Kugy might be? Her cell phone has been off all day, and her family doesn't know where she's gone."

"Wow," Noni said, genuinely surprised. "I don't know, either."

"Her sister said Kugy often meets up with old classmates. Maybe you know something?"

"Actually, I'm one of the classmates Keshia's referring to," Noni said with a grin. "There were four of us who used to hang out together, and we've been hanging out a lot again recently. But as far as I know, we didn't have any plans to meet up today."

"I wonder where she is," said Remi, sounding worried. "How could she just disappear and not tell anyone?"

"I'm sure she's fine." Noni chuckled. "She does a lot of weird things. She'll turn up tomorrow at the very latest."

Noni's words failed to put Remi at ease. On the contrary, he felt even more anxious.

———

Kugy opened her eyes and found the sky already reddish in hue. Keenan hadn't woken her up. She scrambled to her feet and saw that his sleeping bag was neatly rolled up next to her, its owner having gone who knew where. She had been left in the shelter, all alone.

Kugy began walking toward the beach. The sky looked like it had been divided in two, reddish on the eastern horizon, with the rest of it still dark blue, preserving the traces of night and its flock of stars. The moon was still glowing, silver and round like a single pearl perched on the edge of the sky, ready to fall into the waiting mouth of the dawn. She spied Keenan not too far away, standing and staring out at the beach.

Sensing Kugy was close, Keenan turned. He saw Kugy's smiling face backlit by the sun's rays against the sky. Her fine hair fluttered in the breeze. He had been enjoying the morning's beauty. But now it seemed the morning had a rival.

"Good morning, Little One."

"Morning, Mr. Kidnapper." She walked over to him.

"Come over here." Keenan tugged gently at her hand. "One final rule—no protesting," he whispered. "Just for a little while, you have to let me do this." Slowly, Keenan moved behind Kugy and put his arms around her, hugging her from behind. He spoke into her ear. "Wherever life ends up taking us, I can honestly say your work has been my greatest inspiration. If you'll let me, I want to continue working with you. Kugy—Little One—do you want to write fairy tales again?"

Kugy gulped. "I do. As long as you want to paint again."

"I do. For Pilik," whispered Keenan. *For you.*

"For Pilik," Kugy whispered back. *And for you.*

They were silent. It was as if the silence had a pulse. They could feel it beating, each beat conveying what remained unsaid. Then there was a whisper. For a moment it hung in the air. Then, as if it were an ocean wave, it flowed into their hearts, and stayed.

Unconsciously, Keenan tightened his embrace, savoring this silent heartbeat. Because only when they were together could he taste eternity. If only for a moment.

CHAPTER 39

WORKING TOGETHER

When Kugy returned home, the first thing she did was call Remi. The first thing he did was yell at her.

"Do you have any idea how worried I've been?" he shouted. "It was like torture, I was so distressed! And I couldn't do anything about it, except call everyone I could think of, asking about you! Except wait up all night till dawn for you to call, which you didn't! I was just about to call the police!"

"I'm so sorry."

"Just one minute on the phone with you! Not even that—just thirty seconds! And it would have been completely different!"

"Yes, I know, but—"

"Kugy, you're too much." Remi spoke coldly. His words pierced her.

"It was all unexpected. I went to Bandung, and I found out a former student of mine died, so I—"

"Look, I don't care why you went. That's not the issue. Why didn't you tell me anything? Why was your cell phone off all day and all night?"

"The thing is . . ." Kugy squeezed her eyes shut. *I can't tell him.* "The thing is, I left my cell phone in my room, and it was switched off. I'm sorry. It was really irresponsible."

There was silence on the other end, followed by a deep breath. "If you ever disappear like that again, and if anything happens to you, I'm not sure I could ever forgive myself."

"But Remi, I'm fine—"

"And how was I supposed to know that if I couldn't contact you? How?"

Kugy was speechless.

"Someday you'll know. You're too precious to me. I can't lose you. You can't imagine how I felt yesterday. It was excruciating. Please, don't ever disappear like that again."

Before Kugy could stop herself, tears were streaming down her cheeks. Remi's words had made her realize something.

"It's all right. The important thing is you're home. Nothing's more important than that." Remi spoke as if it were himself he was trying to reassure. "Are you feeling all right, darling? Are you tired? You're not upset at me, are you?"

"I'm fine," Kugy said emphatically, trying to hide all traces of her crying.

"I'll come over later, okay?"

"Yes. I'll be waiting," answered Kugy. And when the conversation ended, she sat for a long time, wiping away the tears that fell in a seemingly endless stream. She realized now that, for one night, she had been able to return to the land of fairy tales. It was a perfect world, where love was eternal. But this was the real world. This was the life she was leading. It wasn't as beautiful as that other land, but she had made her choice.

Bitterly, Kugy reminded herself that Keenan was nothing more than a fairy-tale prince. The tale that ended with them living happily ever after would never come to pass. Remi was her reality—right there, within reach, and madly in love with her. She wasn't sure she could ever forgive herself, either, if she hurt Remi. She had deceived him this once—and that was already one time too many.

———

It was Monday, and Keenan was returning from the office. He couldn't stand it any longer. He had spent hours resisting the urge to call her, and he felt as if his entire body was suffering from an overwhelming thirst. He just wanted to hear her voice, her laugh, her snicker. He dialed her number.

"Hey, Little One. Whatcha doing?"

"Mr. Kidnapper!" Her voice sounded cheerful. "I'm still at the office, and I was just thinking of you. I was about to text you."

"Oh yeah?" It was Keenan's turn to sound happy. "What's up?"

"Are you ready for this?" Kugy cleared her throat. "Today I started writing again! The General Pilik series is back!"

Keenan's eyes brightened. Kugy's words had kindled something within him. "I have an idea. Listen carefully, okay? Then give me your honest opinion." Keenan's tone was serious. "Every time you finish a story, I'll make a painting for it. I don't know exactly what final form it will take—maybe a book, or an exhibition, or both. This whole time, people have gotten to know General Pilik through my paintings. But they don't know what started it all. If you ask me, it's time for you to come out as the creator of General Pilik and the Alit Brigade."

Kugy was stunned. "So, we'll be working together?"

"Little One, you haven't known it, but to me, we've always been working together. The only difference is that now we'll be walking side by side as well. That's if you're willing. It would be a great honor for me."

For a long time, Kugy said nothing. She needed time to process. Her dreams were so close, so possible. Something she had once thought out of reach had suddenly fallen to earth, right in front of her. And all she needed was the courage to step forward.

When Kugy finally spoke, it was with determination. "Right. When do we start?"

April 2003

It took seven days for Kugy to finish each new installment of General Pilik and the Alit Brigade, which meant that Keenan received a new manuscript every week. Kugy wrote in a notebook, just as she had done at the Sakola Alit. Once Keenan had the manuscript, he had his secretary type it out on a computer.

Kugy spent much of her time in the office thinking about and writing the series. Nasty gossip began to circulate and snide comments were the new norm.

"Well, what do you expect? Kids these days. They do everything halfheartedly."

"What's the use of a brilliant mind if you don't have the professionalism to back it up?

"Turns out prodigies have their expiration dates, too, huh?"

At these comments, Remi's ears were reddest of all. He knew what Kugy was capable of. If the kid put even a little bit of effort into it, she could finish all her work in the blink of an eye. The problem was Kugy's attention was being siphoned by something else, and he didn't know what. In the office she could always be found hard at work at her desk. Yet none of her tasks were being completed.

Remi was forced to confront her.

"Kugy, I can't ask the client for any more time. They have to shoot in a week. It's nonnegotiable. But there's still no storyboard and the main concept hasn't been pinned down, either. You're supposed to be the project leader. The decisions have to come from you. When you can't focus, you leave your team in chaos."

Kugy looked at Remi with panic on her face. How could she tell him that she still hadn't done anything at all? How could she say it was time for him to stop relying on her so much, to stop making her a project leader, because she was powerless to keep her energy and attention from being sucked into that whirlpool, that other dimension, the world of General Pilik? When she was in the office, she felt like a zombie. Her body was there, but it was an empty shell. Meanwhile, its contents were elsewhere, doing other things.

"What's the problem?" asked Remi.

"I've been working on a new project," she said hesitantly.

"A project?" Remi's brow furrowed.

"I'm writing a fairy tale series."

Remi let out a heavy sigh and rubbed his face. "Kugy, I don't need to remind you of your priorities. You're old enough to know what they should be. What worries me is your inability to separate your professional life and your . . . hobbies." His tone was sharp. "I don't want to have this conversation. But you're being paid to create ad concepts, not write fairy tales. It's up to you if you want to spend all night at home writing them. But not here. Your job here is to meet your deadlines."

Kugy had nothing to say. She knew the weakness of her position. It was no use defending herself. Whatever way she looked at it, it was clear she was at fault for neglecting her work.

"So when will the storyboard be ready?"

"As soon as possible."

"This afternoon, then. Before six." And with that, the conversation was over.

———

At five-thirty, Kugy submitted her work to Remi. He flipped through the sketches, looking pleased.

"So, you could do it after all, once you put your mind to it."

Kugy gave him a watery smile in return.

"How about dinner tonight? Seafood?"

Kugy nodded.

That night, at their favorite seafood restaurant, Remi decided to urge Kugy to be as open as possible. He took her hands and held them tightly. "This time, you have to be honest," he said. "What's really going on with you?"

Kugy looked at Remi with that same panicked expression from earlier in the day. There was so much she wanted to say but didn't know how to express. She wasn't sure Remi would understand.

"Nothing's going on. I just really enjoy writing fairy tales. But you're right. I guess I have trouble separating my hobbies from my professional life."

"Are you sure you don't have a problem with us being in a relationship?"

Kugy shook her head. "It's true that being coworkers makes things more challenging, but I don't think it's a problem."

"And you're not having issues with anyone else in the office?"

"No, not at all," Kugy answered.

"You don't like the work anymore?"

Remi's question hit the mark. At last, she made an attempt to explain the truth—which, until now, she had found so difficult to share. "Ever since I was little, the only thing I've ever wanted to be was a fairy tale writer. I know it must sound silly, stupid, infantile even. What kind of an aspiration is that for someone my age? And I know I sound ungrateful. I have such a good job, and I'm just throwing it away. The problem is, I've realized something recently. I can't force myself to like something I'm not passionate about, even if I am good at it. And I can't just pretend to forget about all my hopes and dreams. Let everyone laugh at me. This is what I really want. I want to be a fairy tale writer. It's what I wanted then and it's what I want now. Nothing's changed."

"So you're willing to give up your career?" Remi asked.

"If that's what it takes, then yes, that's what I want." Kugy gave a decisive nod. "If there's even a sliver of a chance for me to realize my dreams, then I'll pursue them. And I'm willing to quit the job I have now."

She stopped for a moment before continuing. "Remi, that sliver . . . it's finally here." She was almost whispering. "I really can't tell you too much about it. But one thing's for certain: I don't want to throw that chance away."

"Are you sure?" Remi pressed.

"Of one thing at least." Kugy took a deep breath. "That someday, what you call my hobby will be my profession. It's unlikely I'll make much money, but I don't care. You probably don't understand—"

"I do," said Remi, then more slowly, "I really, truly do." He sighed. "Are you saying you want to resign?"

Kugy's expression changed to one of confusion. In the blink of an eye, her year working at AdVocaDo flashed through her mind. Her first meeting with Remi, all the concepts that she'd come up with, all the projects she'd led, the late nights, the lack of sleep, the Toilet Sorority, the paper boat that Remi had given her that night, that momentous night on Ancol Beach. Now here she was, face-to-face with Remi again, about to make an important decision. She was going to leave AdVocaDo—the very place she had taken refuge when she was trying to leave her old life in Bandung behind.

Solemnly, Kugy nodded. "I think it's better not to hang on. It feels better for you, for the rest of the team, and . . . it's definitely better for me."

"Then I won't stand in your way."

At that moment, she felt an enormous burden lift from her heart. She hadn't fully anticipated what her decision would mean. Suddenly, her face broke into a bright smile. She squeezed Remi's hand and kissed it. "Remi, thank you for understanding. I don't know what to say."

"You don't need to say anything. As your boss, I'm sad to lose you. You're one of my best employees. But as someone who loves you, I'm happy you've chosen what's best for you." Remi smiled gently.

"I'll finish all the projects I'm currently working on, and after that, I'll hand in my official resignation. How does that sound?" Kugy gave him a mischievous look.

Remi shook his head. "If those are the only conditions, you'll be done within a week." A glimmer of a smile appeared on his face. "But I'll keep you until after the company retreat in Bali in May."

"Oh ho-ho! Well, if it means I get to go on the retreat, then it's a deal!" Kugy cackled gleefully. "I'm shameless, I know. You'd think I was a civil servant."

The rest of the night was wonderful. And Remi came to a realization of his own. Kugy's decision to leave AdVocaDo had set him unexpectedly at ease. For the first time, Remi felt completely free to love her. For the first time, he felt free from the professional restrictions that, up to this point, had cast a shadow over their relationship. And that night, he was even more resolved in his determination to support her and make her happy, whatever the steps his beloved wanted to take to pursue her dreams. It had been a month since they had officially started going out. But never had Remi felt so happy or walked with such a spring in his step.

———

Luhde approached her uncle. "Poyan?" she asked hesitantly.

"Yes?"

Luhde paused, wondering how to continue. She was used to seeing Keenan almost every day and now she hadn't seen him for months. She was in torment. She couldn't begin to express how much she missed him. And she was all too aware of the limitations of her family's financial situation. But she felt she couldn't take it any longer. She had to see him.

"How far is Jakarta from here, Poyan?"

"It's only an hour and a half by plane," said her uncle, still absorbed in his painting.

Luhde thought about the small amount of money she had saved up. "What about by bus and ferry?"

"A day and a night," said Wayan. Suddenly, he gave his niece a sideways glance. "You want to go to Jakarta? What for?" Then he realized. "There's no point. You should stay here and wait for Keenan to come."

Luhde was taken aback by the unexpectedness of her uncle's response. Quickly, she ran out of the studio.

CHAPTER 40

AN OASIS

May 2003

Luhde's mind was made up. Using all her savings, she bought a bus ticket and left for Jakarta. Her uncle was away in Lombok for a week and this was her chance. She was determined to make the trip.

It was early. The ferry was crossing the Bali Straits to the island of Java. Luhde sat alone on deck, curled up on a wooden seat and gazing out at the ocean. She was wearing sandals, and she covered her feet with her jacket to keep them warm. Luhde had never left Bali. She didn't have the faintest idea what Jakarta would be like—apart from what she had seen of the city on TV. A scrap of paper with Keenan's address written on it was her only guide. All she could do was pray for protection along the way.

She squeezed her eyes shut and tried to think only of being at Keenan's house by evening.

———

Luhde didn't have much money left. She didn't know what she would do if this wasn't Keenan's house. Fatigued by the long journey, her heart beating anxiously, she stood in front of the white house and pressed the doorbell.

A woman opened the door. Luhde knew the face well.

"Good evening, ma'am," she said. In one hand she carried her bag of clothes, in the other a plastic bag full of gifts.

Lena looked at the girl. She could hardly believe it. "You—you're Wayan's niece, aren't you? Luhde?"

"Yes," answered Luhde. She was immensely relieved. She was safe at last.

———

When Keenan found Luhde standing on the front terrace of his house, he looked like he had seen a ghost. There she stood, calmly awaiting his arrival. Keenan on the other hand was so surprised he almost drove the car into the garage wall. He scrambled out.

"Luhde?" whispered Keenan.

At the sight of him, Luhde was so overwhelmed that she froze. All she could move were her eyes, which grew brighter and brighter, following him as he approached her.

"How did you get here?" he asked in amazement. He stroked Luhde's cheek, slowly, as if trying to assure himself she was really there.

Smiling, she took the laptop bag from Keenan's shoulder. "Let me carry this for you."

Keenan took her in his arms.

———

It was Sunday night—time for Keenan to pick up the new manuscript. It was a ritual that Kugy looked forward to. Keenan would appear at the front door, and her little sister, Keshia, would immediately try to attract his attention in a million different ways. Keshia had a crush on him, and this gave Kugy a million different things to tease her about, though she herself got a charge from seeing him. Sunday night could never come soon enough.

But this week, Kugy felt something strange was going on. She had been waiting to hear from Keenan all day, and she still hadn't received any word. Finally, she called him.

"Hello, fellow agent! Are you ready to complete today's task?"

"Hi, Kugy," he replied stiffly.

"What time are you coming over?" she asked.

Keenan hemmed and hawed before letting out a heavy sigh. "I can't tonight. Maybe next week. Sorry."

Kugy felt her chest tighten. Keenan's voice sounded so far away, as if he were speaking from behind a wall. "Sure. Next week is fine. But just wondering—why can't you come tonight?"

"I . . . I have a visitor from Bali."

"Oh," murmured Kugy. She hadn't anticipated this at all. She shut her eyes for a moment and tried to collect herself. "No problemo!" She was proud of how natural she sounded. "But that means we'll experience some delays. I'll be gone next week."

"Oh yeah? Where to?"

"It's a company retreat. We're going to Bali."

Bali? Keenan swallowed. "No problem," he said, trying to sound as relaxed as possible. "Maybe I'll have some good news for you after you get back."

Kugy's muscles tensed. *Did he say "good news"?* Kugy screamed silently. *It better not be . . .*

Keenan explained. "I managed to contact someone who collects my paintings and owns a publishing company. He was extremely interested when I told him about our project. He's been a huge fan of General

Pilik for a long time. If he really is interested, it means we'll be even closer to achieving our dream of creating something together."

Kugy's face broke into a grin. "Keenan, if I were a firecracker, I would explode."

"Good thing you aren't." Keenan chuckled. "If you blew up, the project couldn't continue."

Kugy laughed, too. "All right then. So see you in two weeks. Give my regards to . . ."

"Luhde."

"Yes. My regards to Luhde," she repeated.

"Okay. Bye, Little One."

"Bye." Slowly, Kugy lowered the phone. She had been so happy when Keenan had told her the series might be published. But at the same time, the conversation had made her sad. Once again, reality had slapped her in the face. It was as if life were continually trying to remind her that an impenetrable barrier existed between her and Keenan, and all she could do was accept it, willingly and gracefully.

They each had made their choice.

———

Keenan and Luhde sat in the gazebo behind Keenan's house, enjoying the warm night breeze.

"You're hot," Keenan said as he wiped the beads of sweat from Luhde's brow. "The weather here is different than in Ubud."

"It really is. It feels better"—she glanced shyly at Keenan—"because I'm with you."

"I'm sorry."

"Why?" asked Luhde.

"Because I'm always working. Even on Saturdays. It's not like Ubud, where we could be together all the time. You've already been in

Jakarta for almost three days, and I haven't even had time to take you out once. All you do is wait for me to come home from the office."

"I don't mind," said Luhde. "I'm happy here. I can help your mother. Jeroen's nice, too. They've shown me around the neighborhood. And even if I only see you for three or four hours a day, I'm content. You shouldn't feel bad. I was the one who came without warning on a workday. It's my own fault."

"Luhde, Luhde . . ." Keenan shook his head as he ran his fingers through her long hair. "I can't stop thinking about how brave you are for coming to Jakarta by yourself. What if Poyan finds out?"

"I'll get back before Poyan returns from Lombok," Luhde answered.

"When is he coming back?"

"In three days. I'll go home the day after tomorrow by bus."

"Not by bus," he said firmly.

Luhde gave him an anxious look. How else would she get back? She hardly had any money left.

"I'll take you," Keenan continued. "We'll go to Bali by plane."

Luhde's eyes grew round. "You're coming to Bali with me?"

Keenan gave a small laugh and shrugged. "I might as well. It's better than being in Jakarta and hardly seeing each other. Even though I can't stay long, we'll have all day together. I promise I won't tell Poyan about your coming here—as long as you allow me to accompany you to Lodtunduh."

"I feel like a firecracker!" exclaimed Luhde, blushing. "I'm so happy I could explode!"

Keenan was startled. Kugy had said almost the same thing earlier that night. What it meant exactly, he wasn't sure.

———

The sun beat down on Kugy's cheeks, making them look like ripe tomatoes. She had been outdoors all day, but she didn't mind. She scurried to and fro, engaging in various beach activities. She had soared through the air on a parasail; she had ridden a banana boat which had capsized twice; she had tried jetskiing; she had tried it all. And she was still going strong.

"Attention, friends!" It was Dani, the retreat organizer, on her megaphone. "After this is over, there will be a shopping excursion in Kuta, followed by dinner in Jimbaran."

The announcement was greeted with a buzz of excitement.

"Ugh. Shopping," Kugy whispered to Remi.

"What do you want to do then?"

"I want to take photos. I've been lugging around that camera I borrowed from Karel, but I haven't had time to use it. What would I take photos of in Kuta? There's nothing but stores."

Remi's eyes gleamed. "Let's get out of here," he whispered back.

"Awesome! But how?"

"Easy. We'll hail a car and join them in Jimbaran later. How about it?"

"Let's do it!" she exclaimed. "Where to?"

Remi just smiled.

———

A great change had come over Wayan in the past few days. He looked happy, cheerful, full of life—and everyone knew why. Keenan.

Now that Keenan had returned to Lodtunduh, their days of relaxing and chatting in the *bale* were back. Luhde wasn't the only one happy about his return. In Keenan, Wayan found the peace he had been longing for, an oasis in the midst of a desert, though he knew it would end in a matter of days.

That morning, Keenan and Banyu left for Denpasar to take care of Keenan's return flight to Jakarta, which had been delayed. Then,

Luhde went to temple, leaving Wayan alone to enjoy his afternoon in the gallery.

An unfamiliar minivan pulled up in front. Wayan went out to take a look, and was surprised to see who emerged from the front passenger seat.

"Remi? How are you? When did you arrive in Bali? Why didn't you tell me you were coming?" Wayan pelted his visitor with questions.

Remi laughed. "I wanted it to be a surprise." The two men embraced.

"Where have you been? It's been a while," said Wayan.

"Work has been very busy this year. By sheer coincidence, my company is on a retreat in Bali. So I took off for a bit to come to Ubud and drop by."

"Please, come in, come in!" said Wayan. "You came alone?"

"No," Remi said as he entered the gallery. "But the person I came with wanted to walk around by herself and take photos. The rest of the group is in Kuta."

They strolled around the gallery together. Wayan told him about the paintings on display. "There are no paintings by Keenan?" Remi asked, after he had seen all of them.

Wayan took a deep breath. *So Remi hasn't given up,* he thought. "Not yet," he said.

"Mr. Wayan, please tell me. Where has he disappeared to?"

"Keenan . . . Well, he . . ." Wayan hesitated. "There's a very urgent family matter that came up at the end of last year, and he had to return home. Before he left he told me not to tell anyone about his departure. I'm sorry, Remi. I made a promise."

Remi fixed his eyes on Wayan's face. "I respect the promise you made. But to me, Keenan isn't just some artist whose paintings I've bought. I think of him as a younger brother. I'm surprised he could just disappear and stop painting like this. It's been so long since the sale of his last work. He hasn't produced anything for almost a year."

"That's just how it is," said Wayan, finally. He was stirred by Remi's genuine concern. "I'll ask him whether I can give you his number. If he agrees, I'll let you know as soon as possible."

"Thank you, Mr. Wayan. I look forward to hearing how he is."

For months Wayan had kept Keenan's situation a secret from everyone who had asked about him. But Remigius was different. Wayan felt deeply uncomfortable about it all, and knowing Keenan was in Bali at that very moment only added to his discomfort. He hoped Remi and Keenan would meet again somehow.

CHAPTER 41

A BOOK AND EXHIBITION

Kugy felt drawn to this temple for some reason. She had seen it from the car along the way. It was small and quiet, and right beside the road. There was nothing special about it at first glance. Yet Kugy felt she just had to go in. Remi could visit his favorite gallery by himself. With Karel's camera hanging around her neck, Kugy began to look around for interesting shots and angles. Her manner was that of a professional photographer. Painfully aware of her deficiencies when it came to drawing, Kugy had recently begun to think about finding other ways to compensate—hence, photography.

Her lens fixed itself on something—something so beautiful that, for a moment, all she could do was stare. It was a young Balinese woman, kneeling to arrange a *sesajen* offering that she had brought with her. She lit some incense, picked up one of the flowers, and waved it around slowly and with great feeling—like a dancer. Her eyes were closed. Her lips were murmuring something. She was praying. Kugy was overcome with feeling at the sight of her. There was such truth on that lovely face. It seemed to symbolize sacrifice, devotion. Kugy had never seen anything so stirring.

The girl opened her eyes. Kugy took aim and snapped several shots to avoid losing a single moment.

As if sensing something, the girl turned around, and caught sight of Kugy kneeling nearby. Hastily she stood up to leave.

"Hey! Don't go!" Kugy ran after her. The girl's footsteps slowed. "Sorry, I should have asked permission first. I was just playing around. I'm learning how to take photos. I'm really sorry." Kugy extended her hand and gave the girl a friendly smile. "I'm Kugy. I'm from Jakarta."

The girl smiled back as she took Kugy's hand. "My name is Luhde," she said.

Kugy's heart leapt on hearing the name. "Luhde? What a coincidence. My friend's girlfriend is named Luhde." She chuckled.

"It's a common Balinese name," Luhde answered, giggling. "I'm not the only one."

"Do you live here?"

Luhde nodded. "I live with my uncle's family. I'm from Kintamani originally. Are you staying in Ubud, miss, or just stopping by?"

"I'm staying in Sanur with a bunch of coworkers," Kugy explained. "I'm only visiting Ubud for a little while. Later tonight there's something going on in Jimbaran. And please, don't call me miss. Kugy is fine."

"Kugy?" Luhde sounded awkward as she said it.

Kugy laughed. "Exactly." And Luhde joined in.

Before long, they were sitting together in the temple courtyard, chatting like two old friends. Luhde was impressed by Kugy's cheerfulness, cleverness, pleasant demeanor, and independence. They were all qualities she aspired to. Kugy in turn was taken by Luhde's gentleness, brightness, and maturity. She would never have thought that such a simple, innocent-looking girl would have a mind so wise and profound, or feelings so gentle yet perceptive. Not only that—Luhde was very eager to learn and grow. The two of them were even more excited when they found out they shared the same hobby: writing.

"You're writing a storybook? Wow. That's amazing." Luhde's eyes shone. "When will it be published?"

"I don't know yet, but hopefully I'll find out next week! I really hope it makes it. I've been dreaming about this since I was little."

"I've been dreaming about the same thing since I was little, too," said Luhde softly. "But I don't know what to do with my work, or where to send it. I'll probably just keep it to myself."

"What do you write? Do you write fiction, too?"

"I also write children's stories," said Luhde. "I want to take ancient Balinese *hikayat* and make them into tales for children. Balinese culture has lots of good material to offer. It's not just about catering to tourists. But it seems like people aren't interested in finding out more about it."

Kugy shook her head. "You'll never know if you don't try. Don't stop writing." Then she reached into her backpack and pulled out a pen and a scrap of paper. She wrote down her address, telephone number, and e-mail address. "Luhde, if you ever want to send me something—your stories or anything else—don't be shy. Write to me. And if you ever plan to visit Jakarta, let me know. Here. I'll write down directions as well, just so you don't get lost."

Luhde watched Kugy's hand as it danced across the paper. At the sight of Kugy's writing, she held her breath. "This is so detailed. You're very kind. Thank you so much." Her voice trembled.

"If my book really does get published, I'll send you a copy."

"Please do!" said Luhde eagerly. "I mean that. Please don't forget." She wrote down her address for Kugy.

"Luhde Laksmi," Kugy murmured, reading the piece of paper. "You have a very beautiful name. It fits you."

"Well, you're the most beautiful woman I've ever seen," Luhde answered.

"Uh, thanks." Kugy chuckled. "By the way, there's nothing wrong with your eyesight, right?"

Luhde only laughed and shook her head. Carefully, she pressed the piece of paper to her chest.

Suddenly a car appeared and came to a stop on the other side of the road. It gave a short honk. Kugy rose to her feet and picked up her backpack and camera. "That's my ride. Till we meet again, okay? Don't forget to contact me if anything comes up. I'm very happy to have met you today." She hugged Luhde.

"I'm very happy, too. Till we meet again," said Luhde. Kugy didn't notice the slight strain in her voice. "And . . . thank you."

Kugy chuckled. "Thank you? For what? And really, I should be thanking you for letting me take a photo of you."

Luhde couldn't bring herself to say anything more. All she could do was tighten her grip on the piece of paper. As if in a trance, she watched as Kugy waved, crossed the road, and climbed into the car, which sped away.

Luhde walked to the front of the temple, following the car with her eyes until it disappeared from sight. And she remained there, staring into the distance, even though all she could see on the road now were clouds of dust. Luhde wanted to run away—where to, she didn't know.

Upon seeing the handwriting, she had known at once who was before her. There was no doubt. How could she not recognize the writing she had been reading for more than two years? The pages and pages of it she had absorbed from that worn-looking notebook of stories written in that very same hand. How could she not know it by heart? Keenan brought that book everywhere he went. He had made it his guiding star, his inspiration, for the whole of his glittering career as a painter when he was in Ubud. Keenan had painted with such love—with all his heart and soul.

Kugy would never know the depth with which Luhde had thanked her. Luhde was grateful they had met, grateful for the opportunity to see the woman face-to-face. Luhde gave thanks, because now she knew why Keenan's heart was so firmly anchored there. And though it was very difficult, Luhde tried to give thanks for the pain that, at that very moment, was slicing into her heart.

Luhde turned and went back inside the temple—back to her acts of devotion. And this time, she let herself go. Her strength vanished. Helpless to prevent the tears from falling, Luhde let them flow, every last one.

———

It was Keenan's last day in Ubud. He was flying back to Jakarta later that afternoon. Once he had finished packing, he went looking for Luhde, but she was nowhere to be seen.

Keenan sensed that Luhde had been avoiding him since yesterday. She seemed more withdrawn, as if she were holding something back. After searching everywhere for her, he found her holed up in her room. He had to knock on the door for a while before it finally opened.

"Luhde, what's wrong? Are you sick?"

Luhde shook her head.

"So what is it then?"

She was silent.

"I have to leave for the airport in a few hours. If you have something to say, tell me now. Don't keep quiet like this. It makes me feel nervous about leaving. You are coming to the airport to see me off, aren't you?"

Luhde shook her head again. "It's better if I don't," she murmured.

"What's wrong? Are you angry? Have I done something wrong? Just tell me." Keenan's tone was pleading, but Luhde only smiled at him. It was a strange smile—so distant. Keenan had never seen that expression on her face.

"I can't go on like this," said Luhde, almost whispering. "Not knowing when you'll come back, or if you'll ever want to come back . . ."

"What are you talking about?"

"You don't have to come back if you don't really want to. Don't feel burdened by your promise to me."

"Luhde, listen. We've managed to stay together this long because we have faith in each other. What will happen if you begin having doubts like this? Don't you believe in me anymore?" Keenan sounded agitated.

"I believe that you will always try to keep your promises. But how long can you go on like this, Keenan?"

"It's like you don't know me," said Keenan, exasperated. "Having faith in me means having faith that I *can* keep my promises. Please help me. I'm not strong enough to do this on my own."

Luhde trembled. She could barely contain herself. *Of course I want to help you.*

"Luhde, don't cry," Keenan whispered gently.

Suddenly she ran over and hugged him tightly. "I'm so selfish," she sobbed. "I don't want to lose you. I don't want to . . ."

Keenan still didn't understand why she was so upset, but he didn't want to press the matter. All he wanted to do was distract her, cheer her up. In the meantime, he heard Luhde utter the same words again and again, filling the space between them: "I don't want to lose you."

———

It was Sunday night. After some delay, it was time for Keenan to pick up the latest installments of General Pilik. But tonight, he was also picking up Kugy. They were going out for dinner.

"The way you're dressed is making me suspicious. Where are we going?" Kugy eyed Keenan. He had shown up in a black turtleneck sweater. His hair, which had grown out a little, was still wet. He looked so fresh, so handsome. In the background she could hear Keshia screaming in excitement. That kid. She'd been hanging around for some time now so she could spy on Keenan when he arrived.

"Obviously, not for instant noodles at a warung," he said with a smile.

Kugy looked down at her T-shirt and jeans. "Let me change. I'll find an appropriate costume."

"Long live Darwin!" exclaimed Keenan, amused. "Once again we have proof evolution really does happen! Suddenly, Kugy Karmachameleon grasps the concept of dressing appropriately."

Kugy made a face. "It's a shame Karel moved out," she said as she walked away. "I can't wear his jacket anymore. Tell Darwin that it's put a crimp in my evolutionary process."

———

Keenan had made reservations at a well-known Japanese restaurant in the Mulia Hotel. Upon arrival, Kugy turned pale. "You've got to be kidding!"

"Come on, you!" Keenan teased. "You've been to a million-star hotel, and you still feel embarrassed at a place like this?"

"I hope you brought enough money," she murmured.

"Spoken like a true Hunger No Longer patron."

They were seated by the window. Keenan peered at Kugy from behind his menu. "Do you know what you want? Or do you want me to—" He stopped talking. He stared at Kugy reading the menu, her head inclined, the lighting striking her face just so. Her lips were red, even though she wasn't wearing lipstick. Her eyebrows were as black as charcoal. Her eyes sparkled, and her complexion was so fair and clear. She played with the ends of her fine hair.

Kugy never changed. Not even since they had first met, when she had come along to pick him up at the train station nearly four years ago. Keenan had never forgotten that day. And now, after all this time, he realized he had liked Kugy from the very start. She was so unique. She seemed to stand out from the crowd wherever she went.

"I'm going to get . . . um . . . How about this? Whatever you order, make it a double."

"Good strategy." Keenan grinned.

After he had ordered, he placed a cup of hot green tea into Kugy's hands. "I wanted to bring you here because I felt we had something to celebrate."

Kugy rubbed her hands together in anticipation. "And what would that be?"

"We're going to have a book *and* an exhibition."

Kugy practically fell out of her seat. "*What?* You're not pulling my leg, are you?"

Keenan looked around. "You think I'd bring you to a place like this just to pull your leg? Come on."

Kugy covered her mouth and screamed. "I can't believe it! This is a dream come true!"

"It is! Our dreams have become a reality." Keenan smiled and let out a sigh. "I met a man named Mr. Ginanjar. He was one of the first to buy my paintings. In addition to having a publishing house, he's an art collector and has financial interests in several art galleries. Mr. Ginanjar was very interested when he found out I was painting more of the General Pilik series. But what really won him over was when he found out that you, the creator and writer of General Pilik and the Alit Brigade, were collaborating with me on the project. I showed him some photos of the new General Pilik paintings, along with part of your manuscript. He came up with the idea of making two books. One would be a regular book, with simple, more accessible illustrations—I'll probably use watercolor. But the other would be an art book—a coffee-table book—with all your stories and all my paintings, including the ones I'm working on. Then there would be a series of exhibitions to promote the book. Do you know what this means? This would be the first exhibition dedicated entirely to my work . . ."

"And the launch of my first book," said Kugy, choking up with emotion.

"No." Keenan shook his head. "Books, plural. There'll be two of them, remember?"

It was Kugy's turn to let out a long sigh. It felt so hard to believe— too beautiful to believe.

"Mr. Ginanjar wants to meet you next week. We'll go together, okay?" Then Keenan raised his cup of green tea. "A toast. To Pilik."

"To Pilik." Kugy smiled warmly. "And to us."

CHAPTER 42

THE CASTLE STILL STANDS FIRM

Remi glanced at his watch. He was five minutes late. He was usually on time for his appointments. And this was Sunday, too, so he didn't have a good excuse. But he had encountered a lot of traffic on the way to the hotel. There was a big exhibition nearby and cars were backed up looking for parking.

He checked the messages on his cell phone to make sure he had gotten the location of the meeting correct. "Okay . . . the café . . . ," he mumbled. The elevator doors opened. Remi rushed out and collided with someone coming in.

"Sorry," he said hastily. The man whom he had run into apologized at almost the same time.

"Remi?"

Remi, who had ducked his head in apology, looked up at the sound of his name. "Keenan?" he exclaimed in disbelief.

Keenan shook Remi's hand warmly. "How are you? I never would have thought we'd run into each other here."

Remi recovered and gave Keenan a hug. "I'm more surprised than you are. I've been looking for you for almost a year. How . . . Why are you here?"

"I live in Jakarta now. I moved at the end of last year."

"Still painting?"

"Just started again," Keenan answered brightly.

Remi clapped him on the shoulder. "Good! Good! That's what I've been waiting for. Let me have a look."

"Sure. In fact, I'm in the middle of preparing for an exhibition. Mr. Ginanjar is helping me."

"You traitor!" joked Remi. "You contacted Mr. Ginanjar but not me? Forgotten your first client, have you?"

Keenan laughed. "I would never forget you. But I was trying to find the right time to meet with you. I heard you stopped by the gallery in Ubud. I've been wanting to contact you since last week, but I've had a lot of work to do since I got back to Jakarta."

"What kind of work?"

"I'm helping my father. He's not well, and now I'm running his trading company."

Remi's jaw dropped for the second time. "You? Running a trading company?"

"Not a good fit, huh?" Keenan grinned. "Hopefully it'll only be for a little while longer. My father is getting better every day."

"Let's arrange a time to meet," Remi said. "I won't take no for an answer. I've been waiting to hear from you for months. We should get coffee. You owe me that at the very least."

"Of course," said Keenan. "Sorry, I don't have a business card on me. I left my wallet in the car. I was just going to get it."

"No problem. I'm out of business cards, too." They exchanged numbers instead.

"Are you here for something?" Keenan asked.

"I have a meeting at the café. You?"

"I'm having dinner with a friend."

"I'll wait to hear from you then," Remi said. "This week?"

"Sure. Sometime this week." Keenan gave an enthusiastic nod.

The elevator doors closed. Inside, Keenan shook his head in amazement. Who would have guessed he would run into Remi like this.

Meanwhile, on his way to the café, Remi was still thinking about his chance encounter with Keenan. It was hard to believe. He'd been searching high and low for him for so long, and today, life had unexpectedly brought them face-to-face. *There are no coincidences,* thought Remi, unable to comprehend just how significant their meeting had been.

———

When Remi was determined, he didn't play around. It was he who called Keenan, eager to arrange a meeting.

"It just so happens I'll be near your office this afternoon. If you have time, maybe I can stop by for an hour or so?"

"Sure," answered Keenan. "Give me a call when you're close. I'm not going anywhere."

Remi arrived right on time and entered Keenan's office, mouth agape. "So you really are the director!"

"What did you think I was? The security guard?" Keenan chuckled.

"I just can't get over it. I thought you said you didn't like business—that it wasn't your thing."

"Well, that's still true." Keenan gave him a tight smile. "But never mind. It's a long story."

"I still have an hour to spare," said Remi. "Let's hear it."

Keenan relented and told him everything, starting with what happened at the Warsita Gallery and ending with his father's stroke. Remi was even more dumbfounded.

"How extraordinary. I never would've thought . . ." Remi shook his head. "When you were in Bali, you didn't seem to have any problems.

But I'll be honest, I always felt there was something special about your life, even when you suddenly dropped off the radar. I was sure something big must have happened."

Again, Keenan gave him that same tight smile. "Enough of this," he said with a wave of his hand. "Let's talk about something else. How have you been doing?"

Remi shrugged. "There's not much to tell."

"About work maybe? Or how about your love life?" Keenan grinned.

Remi's face lit up. "As a matter of fact, I do have news on that front. Or to be more exact, plans. And I haven't told anyone about them, including the person involved."

"Oh, this is exciting." Keenan chuckled.

"I've been thinking about proposing to my girlfriend."

Keenan raised his eyebrows. "Wow! Congratulations! I don't know who she is, but she's a very lucky woman. I'd like to meet her sometime."

"She came with me to Ubud when I was in Bali, but unfortunately, she didn't visit the gallery because she was at a temple taking photos. You two would definitely get along. She's fun, she's smart, and in short"—Remi paused to take a breath—"she's very special to me."

Keenan grinned. "I believe you. You must be so in love."

"I am. I've never felt like this before. Never."

"And I'll never forget how you helped me, Remi. If you hadn't been interested in my first General Pilik painting, I probably would have given up art long ago. So if you ever need me for anything—your big plans or anything else—just let me know. Who knows? I might be able to help."

"Keenan, you don't owe me anything. It's truly an honor to be the owner of your first work." Remi clapped Keenan on the shoulder. Before long, the two men parted, unaware of how much they had in common.

———

Luhde leaned her head against the wall, watching her uncle, who was sitting with his back to her. He had been doing a lot of painting these past few days, most likely because Keenan's recent visit had re-energized him. And these past few days, Luhde had been unable to sleep. She felt anxious. As with her uncle, it was because of Keenan's visit.

"Poyan?"

"What is it, Luhde?"

"How does one know when to give up and when to hang on?"

Wayan turned around to look at her. "I don't know," he answered.

"Before, when you decided to give up and let Keenan's mother choose someone else—when did you feel that was the right decision?"

"To be honest, I've never known whether that was me giving up or hanging on—even now. Have I given up? Sometimes it seems like I'm still hanging on." He sighed. "To get back to your question, I don't know. But life does."

Luhde bit her lip. She had something she wanted to tell him, but was nervous about his reaction. Still, she felt she had to say it. "Poyan, don't be mad at me for saying this, but I don't want to be like you, or Keenan's mother. Ten, twenty years from now, I don't want to be thinking about the same person, hovering in confusion between acceptance and regret . . ."

Wayan fell silent. He felt as if someone had crammed a fistful of bitter pills down his throat. They tasted terrible. And they hurt. But he felt the truth of Luhde's words. "You're right," he said softly. "Don't end up like me."

"But do I have a choice?" she cried.

"Luhde," Wayan said gently. "I believe everything happens for a reason. All we can do is keep going, as confusing or painful as it seems. And all you can do is rely on your feelings. You'll know the answer. That's how it is with him, too. These things can't be forced—whether or not Keenan really belongs to you . . . or to someone else."

Luhde's heart stopped. *Poyan knows.*

"At the end of the day, you can't force something to happen. Not with promises. Not with loyalty. Even if he decides to stay with you, it won't be due to force. The heart can't be forced."

Luhde bowed her head, trying to hide her tears. She understood what her uncle was saying. What she didn't understand was why it had to hurt so much.

———

Remi stepped onto the terrace—which is what he did most Saturday nights. But this night felt different. He stopped to look at the ceiling, the chairs, the table, the tiles, and everything else—because tonight would be a night to remember, and this terrace would be there to witness it. A shiver ran through his body. When Kugy emerged, laughing happily, Remi's stomach began to churn.

"Hi, darling," said Kugy. She was holding a stack of photos. "Where are we going tonight?"

"Don't know yet," said Remi after swallowing a few times. "I feel a bit too tired to go anywhere. But let's see how it goes. You don't mind if we stay here, do you?"

"Not at all," said Kugy. "I want to show you the photos I took in Bali. They're pretty darn good," she added, jokingly.

Kugy spoke about each photo with great energy and Remi responded with comments. "Oh yeah. Nice. Hmm. This one's nice, too . . ." But his mind wasn't on Kugy's photos at all. *Is now the right time?* Remi thought. *Yes. It has to be now. Or next week? No, no. But who knows, maybe next week would be better. But not here. Somewhere else. Where? When? Tonight?*

"Aha!" exclaimed Kugy, holding up a batch of photos. "Now these next ones—these are my masterpieces!"

Remi was startled out of his reverie. Kugy laid the photos in a row one after another.

"Wow. Yeah, yeah. These are really . . . Wait!" Remi frowned. He studied the photos more closely. "I know this woman," he murmured.

"Luhde?" said Kugy, puzzled. "You know her?"

"Yes! Luhde! Mr. Wayan is her uncle. He owns the gallery I visited when we were in Ubud." Remi laughed. "So, I know her uncle and you know his niece. How funny."

"How do you know them?" Kugy still couldn't believe it.

"I've known the family for a long time. I even spent New Year's Eve with Luhde and her family once. In"—Remi tried to remember—"2000. She was still a teenager back then. She's dating my favorite artist—the one whose painting I hung up in the office foyer."

Suddenly, Kugy felt shaken to the core. *The painting.* "Remi, please tell me—what's the painter's name?" Her voice sounded strained. "As I recall, he only signed his initials, K. K."

"His name is Keenan. He paints children. He's incredibly talented. I'm a huge fan." Remi spoke smoothly, lightly. "He disappeared from my radar. I don't know where he went—I used to see him often. Then I ran into him last week, completely unplanned. It turns out he's moved to Jakarta. I stopped by his office for a while. He said he just started painting again and he's having an exhibition."

Kugy's gaze became unfocused. *Keenan. Luhde. Keenan and Luhde. All this time . . .* Her heart trembled.

Remi saw how tense Kugy looked and was confused.

"Actually, I have something I want to say to you tonight."

Kugy's face still looked rigid. She stared at him.

"Kugy?" asked Remi gently. "Are you all right?"

Kugy looked at Remi anxiously. She wanted to say, "It's nothing," as casually as she could. She wanted this night to go back to normal. But it couldn't. Kugy remembered this feeling. It was the same one she'd had when she found out about Wanda. The difference was, she really liked Luhde. She really did. And though she had been sure all this time that her heart had changed, once again, she was being brought to the bitter realization that it hadn't. Keenan was still the prince of her heart, enthroned in a castle of dreams.

But Luhde's involvement sent everything tumbling down. Her castle had been razed to the ground. She had no choice. *They must love each other so much. They'll be so happy together. Luhde is like an angel.*

"Darling, what's wrong?" Remi's voice brought her to her senses.

With a heavy heart, Kugy said, "Sorry, Remi. I want to be alone tonight. I'm not mad at you or anything. But I really need some time to myself. I'm really sorry."

Remi gazed at her. "Okay, if that's really what you need," he answered gently. They said good night.

Back on the terrace, he tried to reassure himself. *The right time will come. It might be next week, or the week after. But the right time will come.*

CHAPTER 43

A RING IN A SILVER BOX

June 2003

Keenan had arrived early and was standing in Kugy's living room. As usual, Keshia made sure she was the one who opened the door. That evening, he was wearing a short-sleeved white linen collared shirt and blue jeans. This was enough to make Keshia turn bright red, run to her room, and swoon.

Keenan looked relaxed but also excited. Today he had promised to bring Kugy to meet Mr. Ginanjar, who was impatient to meet her. If everything went according to plan, they would be able to sign a publication contract for the General Pilik and the Alit Brigade series sometime this week.

Before long, Kugy came out, her face paler than usual.

"Hey," she said. "Why are you here so early? Aren't we meeting Mr. Ginanjar at seven?"

"I wanted to take you out for ice cream first," he said brightly.

Kugy gave him a faint smile, then nodded.

"Is everything all right?"

Again, Kugy gave him a weak smile and a nod. *Bring the situation under control,* she reminded herself.

On the way, Kugy didn't say much. Keenan made several attempts to start a conversation, but her answers were perfunctory. By the time they pulled into the parking lot of their favorite ice cream parlor in Kemang, her heart felt even more weighed down than it had before. And when they got out of the car, she felt like her feet were getting heavier as well.

The two of them entered the restaurant and sat by the window. It was drizzling outside. Kugy stared at the rain. Keenan watched her. Her eyes looked as if they were trying to avoid something. The strangeness of it all, from when they had left the house until now, began to fully dawn on him. "Kugy, are you sure you're all right?"

"Positive." Kugy tried to look happy. Luckily, she was saved by the waiter handing them the menu.

"The usual?" asked Keenan. She nodded, and he ordered a platter of waffles, four scoops of ice cream, and chocolate sauce. Ten minutes later, their order arrived along with two small spoons and two glasses of water.

Kugy picked up her spoon but the hunger in her stomach had vanished.

They sat in silence. "Kugy, what's wrong?" Keenan finally asked.

"You're what's wrong," said Kugy, trying to sound lighthearted. "You've been asking me that nonstop."

Keenan looked into Kugy's eyes. "Little One. You've always been a terrible liar."

Slowly she put down her spoon. She kept her eyes downcast, trying to translate the storm raging in her heart into words. "Would you mind if I took a break from writing for a while?" Kugy said finally.

"You mean the General Pilik series?" asked Keenan. "Not at all. This is your project, too. You should do whatever you feel comfortable with. I'll talk with Mr. Ginanjar. How much time do you think you'll need? A week?"

Kugy looked at Keenan nervously. "A month?"

Keenan immediately frowned. "A month? Are you sure?"

Kugy shook her head. "Maybe more," she answered softly. "I'm not sure."

Keenan put down his spoon, too. "Kugy Karmachameleon, tell me the truth. What's wrong?"

Kugy felt her throat seize up, as if there were an entire durian stuck in her windpipe. "I . . ." Kugy continued with great difficulty. "I . . . don't think we should see each other for a while. There are some things I need to take care of . . ." She held her breath. "With myself. When it's time, we can meet again."

"May I ask what you have to take care of?" Keenan asked gently.

Kugy shook her head. "Not right now. Right now I just want to go home."

Keenan remembered their appointment with Mr. Ginanjar in two hours, then let out a heavy sigh. "Okay. I'll take you home."

Kugy shook her head. "It's okay. I want to go by myself. I'll take a taxi. Sorry for all the trouble. I didn't mean to confuse you. But—"

"Kugy, I'm taking you home. We'll leave now."

Kugy shook her head more vigorously and stood up. "No. I want to go home by myself. It's okay if you're mad at me. But I really have to go. I'm sorry." Then she practically ran through the doors of the restaurant, hurried to the side of the road, and hailed down a cab. Keenan didn't even have a chance to chase after her.

Once she was in the cab, the tightness in her chest lessened. Kugy was able to breathe again. She pulled her cell phone from her bag and turned it off. She wanted to be alone. She wanted silence.

I don't have the strength after all, Kugy sobbed inwardly. *I don't have the strength.*

———

The sky was growing dark when the taxi entered Kugy's housing development. "Miss. . . Miss. . ." The taxi driver tried to wake her up. "We're here. Which house is yours?"

Kugy woke with a start. "Oh! Sorry! First street on the right, second house on the left."

"The one with the black sedan in front, miss?" he asked.

A black sedan? Kugy felt her entire body go weak. *Remi?*

"Yes. Stop here." Reluctantly, Kugy got out of the cab. She felt like jumping back in and taking off—somewhere, anywhere. She didn't want to see anybody right now. But it was too late. Remi, who had been waiting on the terrace, had seen her arrive.

"Darling, why is your cell phone off?" he asked as she approached him. "I ended up following my instincts and came straight here. Good thing you came home so quickly." Remi hugged her and felt how tense she was. "Are you okay?"

Kugy felt like she was going to explode if she heard that question again. "I'm fine," she said curtly.

"Do you want to change into more comfortable clothes first?" he asked.

"No, it's okay." Kugy smiled and sat down in a chair. "What is it, Remi?"

Remi was surprised by this response. He studied Kugy's expression, trying to see if he could detect any change. But he couldn't find anything. Remi took a moment to steady his breath. *Do it now. If you want to surprise her, do it now.*

"I have something to ask you," Remi said carefully. "I don't know if tonight is the best time or not, but regardless, I have to talk to you eventually. Sooner or later, today or next week, next month, next year— it doesn't matter. So please, listen to what I have to say . . ." Remi knelt in front of her.

Kugy's throat closed up. The same panic she'd felt at the ice cream parlor was back. Unconsciously, she retreated into her seat, pressing into the back of her chair.

Remi took out a silver box from his pocket. "Kugy Alisa Nugroho, I don't know if this ring will fit your finger perfectly or not. I didn't have the chance to measure it, so I made an estimate. But what I do know is this: the love we have for each other is a perfect fit for me. I offer you this in the hope you'll wear it. But what I'm really offering is my heart. My life. If you're willing to share those with me, then please—accept this ring."

Remi was holding the box close to her hand. But Kugy offered no response. Remi looked up and found Kugy looking bewildered. *She's really surprised,* he thought. Carefully, Remi took Kugy's left hand. He slid the rose-cut diamond ring onto her finger.

"It fits," Remi whispered, trying to control his emotions. Gently, he kissed her hand.

Kugy's chest tightened. It became hard to breathe. Every word Remi uttered was like a concrete block hitting her in the chest. Together they formed a barrage of concrete blocks. And the glittering ring on her finger was like a sledgehammer, delivering the final blow. Kugy shut her eyes. Everything that she was experiencing and hearing today was too much for her. She wasn't ready. She didn't have the strength. She pressed her lips shut. She continued to retreat from him, pressing even farther into the seat.

Remi sensed something was wrong and he began to panic. "I'm sorry," he stammered. "I didn't mean to shock you. Look, you don't have to give me an answer now. I understand. You probably need some time. Whatever you need, please let me know. Okay?"

Kugy still didn't respond. She was staring at him with a dazed expression, her body rigid.

"Do you need to be alone?" asked Remi as gently as he could. "I can leave for a bit. When you're ready, let me know and I'll come back."

Kugy nodded slowly. Still she said nothing.

"All right. I'm going. Please call me, okay?" Remi stood up, kissed Kugy's forehead, and left.

Then Remi was gone. Kugy ran into the house and locked herself in her room. She didn't come out again.

———

It was eleven o'clock at night when the doorbell rang. Karel hurried out of his room. He'd been living in his new house for only three months, so not many people knew his address yet. Anyone who was visiting this late was someone to be wary of.

Karel took a quick peek through the blinds. He didn't see a car. He craned his neck to the side to get a better look. His eyes narrowed, trying to see if he recognized the figure standing at the door, carrying a bag.

"Kugy?" Karel was astonished. Quickly, he opened the door. "What is it? You didn't come here alone, did you?"

Kugy turned a weary face to her older brother and gave him a pitiful look. "Karel, can I crash with you for a while?"

———

It had been three days since the incident at the ice cream parlor. Keenan still couldn't reach Kugy. He didn't know how to find out what was going on. Noni was his last hope.

"When are you coming to Jakarta?" Keenan asked when she picked up the phone.

Noni was suspicious. "The day after tomorrow. What is it? Why do you sound so tense?"

"We have to meet. There's something I want to ask you."

"About?"

"Kugy."

"What about Kugy?"

"She's disappeared. Do you know where she is?"

"No. What's with that kid? Has she disappeared again? It's a hobby of hers." Noni chuckled, remembering when Remi had called her to report something similar. "Did you call her house?"

"Yeah. It's like they've all sworn themselves to secrecy. Kugy probably doesn't want to be found."

"If that's the case, just let her be," said Noni breezily. "She must want to be alone. She'll come home soon."

"If it were only a matter of coming home, I wouldn't be worried. I'm sure she'll come home by herself. But that's not the only problem. There's something about Kugy that we need to discuss. Is that okay? The day after tomorrow?" Keenan was adamant.

Noni swallowed. She'd never heard such determination in Keenan's voice.

———

The townhouse only had two rooms and wasn't very spacious, but it was more than enough for Karel, who lived by himself. The presence of another person should have made the house feel more cheerful, especially since that person was Kugy, but it had been three days and his little sister's presence had made the house gloomier instead. Kugy was definitely different. She was quiet and brooding, and often kept to herself. She was fond of the small balcony at the back of the house, where the clothing was hung out to dry. She spent hours there. Who knew what she was thinking about.

He heard footsteps on the wrought-iron stairs. Kugy had just come down from the balcony.

"Eat some dinner," called Karel. "I bought us some fried rice."

"Not hungry," said Kugy curtly.

"It's impossible for you not to be hungry. Come on, eat something." Karel placed the fried rice, wrapped in brown paper, on Kugy's plate and got out some spoons. He began to eat. "Dig in," he urged.

Listlessly, Kugy unwrapped the rice and ate a few spoonfuls. She finished half before rewrapping the rest. Then she went back to sitting in silence.

Karel watched her. Only after he had finished his own rice did he try to start a conversation. "How long are you going to stay here?" he asked calmly.

Kugy shrugged. "Don't know. Why? Am I starting to irritate you?"

Karel chuckled. "No. That's not it. But I am getting annoyed at you not saying anything." He folded his arms across his chest. "I'll stop being annoyed if you tell me what's going on. So come on. Let's have it."

Kugy looked at her older brother. It was the look of someone begging for help. There was so much she wanted to tell him. She was tired of keeping everything to herself. "Ask me something," she said, almost whispering.

There were so many questions swirling in Karel's head. Suddenly the ring, glinting in the lamplight, caught his eye. "Did Remi give you that?"

One question was all Kugy needed. It could have been any question. It didn't matter. The floodgates were ready to burst. She just needed some help in opening them. The whole story poured from her in a steady stream—a story four years in the making, beginning with Keenan and Josh, then Remi and Luhde, and ending with the ring around her finger.

"Karel, I'm confused," said Kugy helplessly. "I'm confused by *me*. I don't understand why I reacted the way I did when Remi gave me this ring. It's not his fault. I don't understand why I got so worked up when I found out about Luhde, either. It shouldn't be like this. It should have . . . it should have . . ."

"It should have what?" asked Karel gently.

"It should have . . . made me happy. I should be glad to have someone like Remi. I should be happy he gave me this ring. But . . ."

"But?"

"But why am I here instead?" she wailed. "Why am I running away?"

"Kugy, your head will always think about how things should be. But the heart plays by its own rules." Karel smiled. "Stop thinking with your head. As clever as that brain is, you can't use it to understand your heart. Just listen to what it says."

"Karel, I'm so confused. I don't know what my heart is saying anymore." She tried to steady her voice. "The thing is . . ."

"The thing is what?"

"I don't want to hurt Remi. And I'm not willing to let Keenan hurt Luhde."

Karel nodded. "Okay. If that's really what your heart is saying, follow it. You can't go wrong." Then he stood up and patted his sister's cheek.

Kugy looked at her brother as he cleared the plates from the table. "Karel?" she asked.

"Yes?"

Kugy didn't know what to say. She went back to staring at him with that helpless look in her eyes—a look also full of urgency and confusion.

Karel put his hand on her shoulder. "There's a small river nearby. Make a paper boat. Tell Neptune everything. Who knows? Maybe he has an answer." He gave her a small smile, then headed to his room, leaving her alone at the dining table.

Karel's advice niggled at her. *If that's really what your heart is saying, follow it.*

CHAPTER 44

EVERLASTING LOVE

Noni arrived at the ice cream parlor in the Kemang area where she and Keenan had agreed to meet. Within five minutes she saw Keenan's SUV enter the parking lot. He emerged from the car and entered the parlor. He was wearing a business suit.

"Hey, Boss Boy. Looking good!"

"I didn't have time to change. I had a meeting and came straight here." Keenan threw himself down on the sofa.

Noni shook her head. "I still have to get used to the idea of you as the director of a company. It's so weird to hear you say you were just in a meeting. Very un-Keenan." She laughed.

"So what would be very Keenan?" he asked, grinning.

"Oh, you know. 'Sorry, I was up all night painting,' or 'Sorry, I just got out of a gallery exhibition.' Or if you *have* to use the word 'meeting': 'Sorry, I just had a meeting with Kugy about the future of the East Jakarta branch of Alien Nation.'"

At the mention of Kugy's name, Keenan's expression changed. "Speaking of which, what's going on with Kugy? Do you know something?"

"I haven't spoken to her all this week," Noni replied.

"It's not just about this week. I feel like something's been going on for longer than that." He looked out the window, and his mind returned to that evening. It had been in this very place, at this very table, when Kugy had suddenly run away and hailed a cab. There had been no news from her since. "Eko told me you and Kugy didn't talk for almost three years. What happened?"

Keenan's request startled Noni. She remembered the gift wrapped in blue paper that Kugy had left at the boarding house. She remembered the birthday card. "So . . . you really feel something's not right between you two?" Noni sounded hesitant.

"I don't know. But it would be helpful if you told me what happened. I'm not sure why."

Noni was silent. Finally, she made a decision. "This isn't easy for me to say, so I'll say it quickly: Kugy is in love with you." She shook her head. "Wrong. All wrong. Let me rephrase. Kugy is head over heels in love with you."

Suddenly, Keenan found it difficult to breathe.

"It started when she was still dating Josh, before you met Wanda. And I'm sure she still feels the same way today."

Keenan couldn't speak.

Noni continued, "I don't know what happened to make her disappear like this. But you're right. It probably has something to do with everything I just told you."

"How's her relationship with her boyfriend?" asked Keenan.

Noni shook her head again. "I don't know the exact details. It seemed like she was in love when she told me about him. But who knows? Anything can change." She was quiet for a while. "And anything can change because there are a few rare instances in this world where things are impossible to change," she added thoughtfully.

"I wonder where she is." Keenan went back to gazing out the window.

Noni was quiet as well. Suddenly, her eyebrows shot up. "We're so stupid. We should ask her boyfriend!"

"You know him?"

"Yes, I have his number."

"Then call him!"

"Ah, that's the problem," Noni said. "I ran out of minutes."

Keenan couldn't help but smile. "We're not stupid, you're just broke. No wonder you weren't picking up when I tried calling you just now."

"Just call him from your phone. But let me talk to him, okay?" Noni looked for the number. "Here. Zero . . . eight . . . one . . ."

Keenan dialed the number, then pressed the call button. A name appeared on his screen: *Remigius Aditya*.

"Remi?" he mumbled.

"Hey, you know him?" Noni asked.

He heard the ringing on the other end. Before long, he heard a "hello." Keenan hastily passed the cell phone to Noni.

"Hello? Remi? Hi, it's Noni. Kugy's friend. Yeah, you're right, I am calling from Keenan's phone. I just found out you two know each other. Keenan and I went to university with Kugy. Yeah, we only just figured it out! Who knew?" Noni laughed. "So, here's the thing. We're looking for Kugy. And we thought you might know where she is . . ."

Keenan was deep in thought. He heard Noni chattering away in her distinctive high-pitched voice. But it was as if the sound were echoing in a void. He didn't care what Noni was saying anymore. He was alone in that void now, lost in a whirlpool of memories and fragmented recollections. Remi's words played again in Keenan's mind. *You two would definitely get along . . . she's very special to me . . . I've never felt like this before. Never.* Keenan bowed his head and closed his eyes. So Remi was Kugy's boyfriend. Remi—whom he so admired and respected.

Then Keenan was reminded of the big plans Remi had told him about. There was a bitter taste in his mouth. He replayed their conversation again, including what he had said. *If you ever need me for anything, just let me know. Who knows? I might be able to help.*

Noni thrust his cell phone at him, and with that, he was brought out of his reverie. "Remi's been going crazy looking for her, too. He doesn't know where she is. That girl!" Noni shook her head in disapproval. "By the way, how do you know him?"

Keenan suddenly remembered something. "I have to go. I'll call you later and tell you everything, okay?"

"Where are you going?"

"I need Karel's new address. It shouldn't be too hard to find. Bye!" He was gone in a flash.

"Madman," she muttered. Noni became aware of a large platter of ice cream heading her way. And she would have to finish it all by herself.

———

It was almost dark when Keenan arrived at Karel's house. Karel opened the door and looked surprised to see Keenan.

"Karel, is Kugy here?" asked Keenan. *She must be.*

Karel didn't respond right away. "You should go to her," he said at last as he turned and pointed at a door. "She's on the balcony out back, where we hang the laundry. See that door? It leads to some stairs. Climb them and you'll find her."

Keenan nodded. He headed for the stairs and climbed to the top.

The balcony consisted of a concrete ledge with a plastic chair and table. He could see Kugy's silhouette. She was sitting with her back to him, gazing up at the evening sky. Her hair was loose and hung over the back of the chair, fluttering gently in the wind.

Keenan held his breath. "Little One . . ."

Kugy turned around and saw Keenan standing before her. "You . . . How did you find me?" she asked, her voice faltering.

"Neptune radar," Keenan answered as he flashed her a smile. Then he drew near and squatted in front of her. "Why'd you run away?" he asked gently.

"Even I don't know why." Kugy shook her head. "I've spent every day here trying to figure out why, and I still don't know the answer."

"I'd like to help you. May I?" Keenan took Kugy's hand. "I've been waiting to say this for years. Kugy Karmachameleon, I love you. I've loved you from the moment we met. I love you now. And I'll love you until I don't know when. I don't see this love ever ending."

Kugy's vision blurred. Her eyes were hot from the tears waiting to roll down her cheeks, but she held them back.

"That's the first thing. But there's more." Keenan tried to steady his breath. "I already know about Remi. If I had to let someone else have you, it would be him. Nobody else. He is a very, very good man. You're lucky."

"You're lucky, too," Kugy whispered. "I met Luhde at a temple when I was in Ubud. We chatted for a while. She's like an angel from heaven. Never let her go."

Keenan was startled to hear Kugy utter Luhde's name, but he recalled his conversation with Remi once again. *She came with me to Ubud when I was in Bali, but unfortunately, she didn't visit the gallery because she was at a temple taking photos.* At last, Keenan understood—the dramatic change in Luhde's demeanor when she had come back from the temple; the change in Kugy's demeanor, too, when she had come back from Bali. Finally, it made sense.

"Luhde doesn't deserve to get her heart broken," whispered Kugy.

"Remi doesn't, either," Keenan answered softly.

Kugy bowed her head and shut her eyes. Her eyes were so full of tears she almost couldn't see anything anymore. The sky grew darker. The wind blew more gently. The pain in her heart grew sharper.

"There's so much I want us to do together," whispered Keenan.

Kugy looked up, and tried her best to smile. "We can do it. Of course we can. We're still going to make that book together, right? And I can still be your friend." She almost choked on that last word. She knew friendship was just a last resort—that it could never contain all her feelings for Keenan—but it was all she had left. Oh, how vast was the ocean of her feelings—how wide! But she restrained herself.

"Yes. We can still work together. And we'll always be best friends." Keenan swallowed. How hard it was to utter those words—especially when his whole heart rejected them. But he remembered the promises he had made, to Luhde and to Remi. If this truly was the help Remi needed, then just as he'd helped him once, so Keenan would help him in return.

"Keenan . . ." Kugy squeezed his hand, her voice tender. "There's so much I want to tell you. So much I want to give you. But never mind. It doesn't matter. It's not meant to be. We're not meant to be. Go back, Keenan. Go home."

Keenan nodded. There was nothing more that needed to be said. Anything else would only further wound his heart. "Don't stay too long up here either, Kugy. It's getting late." Keenan touched Kugy's cheek for a moment. Slowly, he turned to go.

Her tears flowed then, and her vision cleared, though all she could see of Keenan was a black shadow retreating into the distance. "Keenan!" she called.

"Yes?" Keenan turned around.

"Ten, twenty years from now, I don't want to feel this pain every time I think of you." Kugy pressed her hand to her heart.

Keenan choked. "You won't. If I can do it, so can you."

"And you're sure you can?" Kugy sobbed.

"I'm sure . . ." Keenan's voice trembled, filled with hesitation, confusion, and fear. But he would not back down. He climbed down the steps, one by one, and vanished from Kugy's view. *We can do this. We have to,* he thought. *If not . . .* Keenan couldn't remember when he had felt such sorrow.

Kugy cried. She made a promise to herself. This was the last time she would cry over Keenan—and of all the times she had cried over him, she had never been in as much pain as she was now. She was happy and brokenhearted all at once. Now she knew beyond a doubt that they loved each other—and also, that they could never be together.

CHAPTER 45

THE SHADOW HAS A NAME

The next day, Kugy decided to come out of hiding and return home. And the very first person she called was Remi.

One phone call was all it took to bring him straight to her house.

He came armed with a thousand questions. But the second he saw Kugy, they all vanished. Instead, he took her in his arms and held her for a long time. He could only ask her one thing. "What's wrong?"

Everything that Kugy wanted to say also melted away, crystallizing into a single request. "Please forgive me."

Remi loosened his embrace and took Kugy's left hand. The ring was still there. He breathed a sigh of relief.

"Remi, I'm ready," said Kugy firmly. "Your proposal caught me off guard, but I'm all right. I'm prepared to go through anything with you. Starting now."

Remi gazed into her eyes, looking for certainty there. "Are you sure?"

Kugy took a deep breath. "Positive," she answered with resolve.

Remi kept looking into her eyes, still searching. "Kugy, I appreciate what you're saying. But I'm not going to lie. I need more reassurance."

His tone was heavy. "Your decision to disappear surprised me. And, to be honest, I'm still confused. But I also promised to respect the fact you needed to process things. I'm not going to force you to talk or tell me anything before you're ready. But again, I need more proof. I'm not sure I can face this kind of situation again."

Kugy swallowed. She understood what Remi meant. "So what can I do? What can I say to make you believe me?"

Remi shook his head. "I don't know. You're the only one who knows."

Her mind and her heart flew into a frenzy. But she knew that in this new chapter of her life, she didn't have much of a choice. She knew the decision she would have to make in the end. It was as clear as the diamond sparkling on her finger. And she didn't want to waste any more time.

"I want to give you something," she said, her heart beating faster. "Wait here." Kugy went into her bedroom. She opened the top drawer of her nightstand. It was something that had recently been returned to her—something that had been gone for years. And now she was going to part with it again. *I hope it will be in good hands,* she prayed.

Then she returned to Remi and handed it to him. She closed her eyes for a moment. *It's time.* "Remi, fairy tales mean everything to me. Writing them is my greatest dream, and this is the closest I've ever come to achieving that goal. I still have to make my books by hand, but hopefully someday I'll be able to share an actual published copy with you. Until then, this is the most valuable thing I own. It's never changed hands—not once." Kugy swallowed again. "But today, I want to give it to you because I also hope to share the rest of my life with"—Kugy felt she couldn't go on. Her chest tightened—"you. And only you," she said at last.

Remi was quiet for a long time. He couldn't remember anyone ever saying anything so beautiful to him. He was only brought to his senses when he saw Kugy's tears. "Why are you crying? I can't bear to see you cry." He pulled her to him.

Between sobs, Kugy whispered, "It's not because I'm sad."

He stroked Kugy's hair. "Whatever the reason, I'm here for you. Thank you for this book. Thank you for sharing the most valuable thing you own with me. Thank you for giving me this reassurance."

It was true Kugy wasn't crying because she was sad. But she also wasn't crying because she was happy. She didn't know the reason herself.

———

It had been six months since Keenan had returned to Jakarta. His father was completely transformed. The man had become living proof that miracles could happen. He had been completely paralyzed, and the doctors predicted he would suffer irreparable damage. Now that same person had recovered and was functioning as well as he had before. He had abandoned his wheelchair. He was even doing light aerobic exercise every morning, just as he had done every day before the stroke. Things were almost as they had been. Almost. He hadn't gone back to work yet. It was the one thing the doctor still advised against.

Everybody knew Keenan's departure had been the cause of his stroke—but his return was also the antidote that had made this miracle happen. Not only did he keep his father company whenever he was able, Keenan also took his father's place every day in the office, ensuring the family's economic affairs could continue to run as normal.

Yet Keenan also knew this moment would come—that one day he would have to confront the miracle and be honest about how things stood. And it was impossible to know who would come out the winner.

Cautiously, Keenan opened the door to his parents' bedroom. He found his father sitting by himself in bed, reading a book.

"Dad?" he asked.

"Come in. What is it?" Adri put down his book and took off his reading glasses.

Keenan sat down beside his father. "Dad, I have to talk to you about something."

"Is something wrong at the office?"

Keenan swallowed and shook his head. "It's not that. It's just that I—" He stopped for a moment. Every day he had held these words in check. Every day he had delayed saying them. But he couldn't contain them anymore. "Dad, I want to go back to painting."

Adri tried to comprehend his son's words—tried to understand what would happen as a result of them. "You want to stop working at the company?"

Keenan gave a heavy nod.

"But if you don't run things, who else—"

"I'll continue to carry out my duties until you've fully recovered. Or until someone else can take my place. My point is"—Keenan swallowed for the umpteenth time—"I can't keep working there forever. I want to paint again."

"Why? What's wrong?" Adri protested.

"Do you really need an answer?"

Slowly, Adri shook his head. "I know you've always wanted to paint. I've just found it difficult to accept."

"Why, Dad?" blurted Keenan, finally asking what he'd wanted to ask for years. "What's wrong with painting? Painting is my life—I've been trying to prove that to you ever since I was little. But you always thought of it as a wall, an obstacle. You shut your eyes and covered your ears and acted as if everything was okay. And I've never understood why."

Adri didn't know where to start. It was an old story, rusted over with age. But it had haunted him for decades. Art. The world of art was what kept Lena connected to her old love—that love, which didn't seem to know the meaning of the word "death." Then the world of art had made a reappearance, to bring his son into contact with someone whom he wanted nothing to do with. Maybe it was because he felt guilty. Maybe it was because he felt jealous. Who could say? And he had been made so blind by all of it that he had tried everything in his power to kill Keenan's artistic potential. But how could he tell Keenan any of this?

"It's all my fault," said Adri instead. "I'm the one who never tried to understand you—who tried to keep you locked up and never gave you the freedom to be yourself. You, on the other hand—you've been so brave, sacrificing your dreams to come back here and take care of our family."

"And I'll keep doing it as long as I need to," Keenan declared. "Given the situation at the time, coming home wasn't a matter of choice. I didn't think of it as a sacrifice, either. But now, I would like to be able to choose."

Adri smiled. "In my eyes, it's just the reverse. Painting has never been something you've chosen. It's who you are. And it's who you always will be."

Keenan found it difficult to breathe. "So . . ."

"You can stop working at the company whenever you want to," said Adri gently. "Don't worry about anything. I'll find a way to handle it. I'm positive." He sighed heavily, but he felt a weight lift from his chest. It was as if letting Keenan pursue his artistic dreams had set Adri free, healing the rift between him and Wayan, and putting his guilt to rest. Who knew that Keenan—in some ways, the cause of all this—would end up being the cure as well. He never thought he would say this, but . . .

"You can even go back to Bali, if that's what you want."

Keenan could feel his heart pounding. Never had he dared to imagine his father giving his consent like this—not even in his wildest dreams. He leaned forward and pulled his father in close for a hug. For the first time in years, he felt they understood each other, and that the things that were sometimes left unsaid didn't matter anymore. Keenan didn't feel the need to demand any further explanation. This was enough. At last, Keenan could feel the love, the affection, and the freedom that had finally sprung from their relationship.

———

The weekend was almost here. Keenan had finished packing. He checked the front pocket of his backpack again to make sure his plane ticket was there.

He was resolved. He was going back to Bali—back to Lodtunduh in Ubud. He didn't know how long he would stay, but he did know he would find a new beginning there. There was nothing tying him down here anymore.

Before he got into the taxi, he turned around. His father, mother, and Jeroen stood behind him, waving good-bye. They were smiling, genuinely happy for him, without exception.

He spread his wings. There was nothing stopping him anymore. He was free.

———

Remi was up late figuring out the places he and Kugy were going to visit the following day. There was a bridal show, and several very promising potential venues. He didn't know when the final plans would take shape. He hadn't dared press Kugy about them. But there was no harm in looking around and learning about different options. In the last text message she had sent him, she had even agreed to tomorrow's agenda. He smiled with satisfaction.

Close to midnight, Kugy sent him another message:

In the immortal words of the great Rhoma Irama, "Lie awake? Don't lie awake." Especially if you're just surfing the Web. I'm not a famous *dangdut* singer, but let me offer my own humble counsel: "Go to bed. Just go to bed." But before you do, don't forget to read the fairy tales. That's why I gave them to you, you know! Sweet dreams, darling. See you tomorrow.

Remi chuckled. He turned off his laptop, which he had indeed been using to surf the Web. Then, casually, he picked up the book of fairy tales Kugy had given him.

He didn't usually read fairy tales. But at every page, Remi was moved by the beautiful illustrations, by the stories so full of life, and by how much love Kugy had poured into creating every square inch of it all.

He reached the last page—the back cover. It was blank. But there was something sticking out from inside it. It was the corner of a white sheet of paper. Without thinking, Remi pulled it out. It was an envelope. Suddenly, he felt apprehensive. Remi wasn't sure it was meant for him.

At the same time, he felt the urge to open it. He took out the card and frowned. *Happy birthday?* Remi turned the envelope over looking for a name. There was none. His uneasiness grew. The book wasn't a birthday present. Who was this card for?

Then Remi read what was written inside, line by line, all in Kugy's hand, the words in neat rows like ants in single file. Every now and then a word would send him reeling. *Illustrations . . . sharing . . . only with you.* Finally, he saw the date. January 31, 2000. *That date. That year.* He recalled his last conversation with Noni and how suspicious he'd felt. Now he was sure.

Suddenly everything became clear: Kugy's reaction when he told her about Luhde, her strange behavior of late. His head slumped forward. It was all too bitter and painful for him. But at last he understood the shadow that hung over their relationship—that he had never been able to touch, that he had never been able to name.

Now everything was clear. The shadow already had a name. *Keenan.*

CHAPTER 46

THE HEART DOESN'T NEED TO CHOOSE

The whole family had been acting funny all morning. Some were smiling, some were giggling, some were whistling for no apparent reason. Kugy was conscious of all this, but she didn't know how to respond.

An hour before Remi was supposed to pick her up, her sister Karin blurted out, "So I heard you're going to a bridal show!"

"Nothing too fancy, okay, kid?" her father added as he walked by. "Keep it simple. As long as it's meaningful—that's what counts."

"Dad? Wha—" Kugy protested.

Kevin chimed in. "No need to get a wedding planner. Just go in-house. I have my own planning committee and everything! Can I do it? Can I do it? Can I do it?"

Kugy looked around for Keshia. Only her youngest sister hadn't said anything yet. *Don't tell me she's in on this, too . . .* Keshia was sitting on the sofa, a mischievous look in her eyes. "Now Keenan belongs to me!" she exclaimed.

Kugy's face turned bright red. "Mom!" she called out. "What is up with the people in this house? Talk about obnoxious!"

"Are you going to wear a traditional *kebaya* or a Western-style wedding gown?" her mother said. "If you're going with a *kebaya*, my friend Ms. Sugianto makes beautiful ones. And they're not expensive, either."

Kugy's mouth hung open. "Not you, too!"

"What's wrong? We're all being supportive!" answered her mother.

"Supportive of what?" asked Kugy.

"Oh please," said Karin, rolling her eyes. "As if you didn't know. Besides, if anyone should be upset, it's me. How do you think I feel, knowing that my little sister is planning to beat me to it?"

"Of course Karin's upset!" Kevin added. "Of all the people in this house, she's spent the most on her appearance, yet the scruffiest person has found her soulmate first."

Kugy's cell phone rang. It was Remi. She let out a sigh of relief—saved just when the hot potato had landed in Karin's lap. She fled into the living room.

"Hey, are you almost here?" Kugy asked.

"Not yet," said Remi. "Sorry, but I can't pick you up. Would you mind if I just met you somewhere?"

"No problem. I can drive myself. Are we meeting at the bridal show?"

"Do you mind if we pass on the show today?" asked Remi.

Kugy was startled. "So . . .where do you want to meet?"

———

Kugy would never forget that place—that swing, that New Year's Eve. This was where everything had started. She took off her sandals and let her feet graze the sand. A warm sea breeze blew on her skin, sending her long skirt fluttering. A cluster of dark clouds hung overhead. It looked like it was going to rain.

"Kugy!"

Kugy turned around. Remi was walking toward her. He had a faint smile on his face, and in his right hand he carried a paper bag. There was something strange about all this, but she wasn't sure what.

"Why are we meeting here?" she asked.

Remi didn't answer. He took her hand and slowly sat her down on the swing. Gently, he began to push her, swinging her forward, then backward, without saying a word. All she could hear was the squeak of the iron hinges on the swing set and the sound of the waves lapping against the seawall at their feet.

Finally, Remi spoke. "I've known you for almost a year now."

Kugy's feet, which had been dangling, suddenly planted themselves in the sand. The swing stopped. Kugy spun around. "Remi, please tell me. Why did you want to come here all of a sudden?"

Remi let go of the swing and knelt in front of Kugy, bowing his head. And he was silent—long enough to make Kugy even more concerned.

"Remi. What is it?" Kugy asked.

"I . . ." Remi spoke with great difficulty. "I . . . want to give this back to you." He picked up the paper bag he had propped against the swing set.

Kugy took it from him and looked inside. It was the book she had made. She was confused. "Why are you giving it back?"

"Because . . . of this." Remi handed her the envelope.

Kugy felt everything come to a stop. All time. All life. All sound. All motion. All she could do was stare. She had almost forgotten about it. But she hadn't forgotten about it completely. A second was all she needed to recognize the card—to remember what she had written inside and for whom.

"This book was meant for Keenan, wasn't it?" Remi's voice was gentle. "Kugy, Kugy . . . why did you run away?"

Kugy felt as if everything had gone mute, except for Remi's voice, which was speaking to her, as softly as the wind.

"Did Keenan ask you to give him this?"

Kugy couldn't speak. All she could do was shake her head.

"Why did I have to ask before you gave it to me?"

Something moved, breaking through the silence and stillness holding her in place. A single tear.

As if he were touching a porcelain doll, Remi held Kugy's left hand, which bore the ring he had given her. "Did you ask me for this ring?"

A second tear. Kugy shook her head again.

"So why did I have to ask you to wear it?"

Kugy could barely breathe. She tried as hard as she could to suppress her tears, but it was no use. Now the slow sobs broke through the silence and stillness as well.

Remi slid the ring off Kugy's finger with the same gentleness, and with great care. "Kugy, if things were different, I would never stop asking you to love me. You've done everything I've asked you to do. But love isn't about asking. Now go. Find the person who'll never ask you for anything, but whom you'll want to give everything unasked."

Kugy couldn't bear it any longer. Her shoulders began to shake. "But that someone is you," she gasped, between the sobs and the tumult filling her chest. "I've never asked you for anything. But you've given everything to me . . ."

"I know." Remi nodded as he wiped the tears from Kugy's cheeks. "You've found your someone. I'm the one who hasn't." His voice began to tremble. "I'm the one who hasn't . . . ," he said again, almost whispering, as if he were saying it to himself.

Then Remi stood up, embraced her, and walked away.

The stillness and the silence had been obliterated. Everything looked dark and overcast; but something had thawed between them, had been set flowing. They had been truthful to one another. As if in agreement, drops of rain began to fall. What had remained unsaid for so long had finally burst, splitting open. And the earth dissolved along with it.

Two nights had passed since Keenan had arrived at Uncle Wayan's house, and that evening, Luhde returned from Kintamani. To her surprise, she found Keenan there, waiting for her in the *bale*.

Upon seeing her, Keenan sprang to his feet. Beaming, he stretched out his arms, waiting to embrace her. But Luhde didn't move. She stood there smiling, and greeted him with a polite nod.

"Luhde, I've come back. I'm going to live in Ubud." He spoke cheerfully. "I'll move here in stages. I'm going back to Jakarta tonight, but starting next week, I'll be staying for longer and longer, until finally"—he cupped her face in his hands—"I'll never have to leave you again."

Luhde's smiled broadened. "I'm glad, too."

Keenan sensed something wasn't quite right. "What's wrong?"

Luhde looked down as if gathering her strength. When she raised her head, her gaze had transformed. "I have to know. Why do you want to be with me?"

Keenan hadn't expected this at all. It took a long time for him to answer. "Because . . . I've chosen you."

Luhde's entire body felt weak. It took all the strength she had to remain standing. But deep down in her heart, she had known that would be his answer. "Keenan, wait here," she said softly. "I have to fetch something from my room."

Soon she was back. In his confusion, Keenan tried finishing what he had started saying before.

"I want you to come with me to Jakarta. Stay with me while I get things sorted out. Then we can return here together. What do you think?"

Again, Luhde only smiled. And slowly, she shook her head. "I'm not ready to go with you, Keenan." She spoke firmly but gently. "Tonight I'm going back to Kintamani."

"All right. So when will you be ready? I'll wait for you," he said.

The smile didn't fade from Luhde's face. Her tone grew firmer. "Keenan, you're wasting your time."

"Luhde, all my time is yours. Who else would I waste it on? The idea of wasting time doesn't apply here." Keenan sounded exasperated.

"You should go back to Jakarta. It would be better that way. What you're looking for isn't here."

Keenan stared at Luhde, trying to comprehend what signal she was sending, because he really didn't understand. "Luhde, what do you mean? Don't you want me here?"

Carefully and almost tenderly, she said, "I want you to go, before we argue and end up hating each other. Or before we realize we don't love each other. Do you understand?"

Keenan had never seen her so determined. So unflinching. "Luhde, please—"

"Keenan, I'm the one who's pleading. Please take this back." It was something she had longed for very much—something she had asked for and that, eventually, he had given her. But Luhde now realized a wooden carving of a heart was all she would ever own.

Keenan shook his head with a frown. "It's yours. I gave it to you. You should be willing to keep it at the very least. Please."

Again the same smile appeared on Luhde's face. "Even the name you carved on it isn't mine," she whispered. "But it was very good of you to lend it to me. Thank you."

Keenan didn't know what else to say. Every path he tried was a dead end. "If you really want me to go, I will," he said, choking up. "But please tell me, why?"

"I've learned from someone else's experience. The heart doesn't choose to love. Love chooses the heart. So you see, when you say you've chosen me, you will never be able to truly love me. Because the heart doesn't need to choose—it always knows where to set down anchor and rest." Luhde held Keenan's hand for a moment. "What you're looking for isn't here."

Keenan was quiet. He heard the wind whistling and suddenly his mind was pulled back into the past. Back to the night when he heard the wind making a similar sound, shaking the bamboo *kentungan* hanging from the roof of the *bale*. The night when he had made his choice. What Luhde said made him realize something. He had decided to give Luhde the wooden carving, but that was all he could give her. The feeling that had compelled him to make the carving—that he could never give. Keenan squeezed his eyes shut. It was all too bitter for him to swallow. And yet, it was the truth.

"Forgive me . . . ," whispered Keenan. He was trembling. His eyes were filled with tears.

Luhde didn't answer. But a warm smile spread slowly across her face. Her gaze was clear and pure, like a fresh spring. There was no vengeance. There was no sadness. There was nothing to apologize for. Then she turned to go, her black hair fluttering down her back, and bade him farewell.

Keenan gazed after her. A single tear rolled down his cheek. Slowly, he wiped it away. And then he left.

From a distance, someone was watching them. Wayan felt as if he had been broken in two. Part of him was devastated, as Luhde was. And the other part was immeasurably happy for Keenan. Now, Keenan had an opportunity that he himself had never had those twenty-some years ago—an opportunity to be chosen by love, and to surrender himself to its current. Where would it take him? *The heart will know,* thought Wayan. It always knew.

July 2003

Keenan got his backpack ready—the maroon one with the letter *K* that he had been using ever since university. He put it in the front passenger seat of the car and got behind the wheel. For a moment, he looked at the bright morning sky.

Now there was nothing tying him down anywhere. Not here. Not Bali. For the first time in his life, Keenan got a taste of what freedom really meant. He decided he would drift with the wind. The wind always knew where it was headed in the end.

———

It was evening when Keenan arrived. This was the third time he had come back, but there was no better place to be. He parked his car on top of the cliff, and waited in anticipation for the bats in the cave below to stir.

The crash of the waves roaring and breaking beneath him was unnerving and soothing all at once. Keenan lay on his back and watched the heavens until they began to turn orange. It was so quiet. He felt like he could stay there forever, just nature and him. He had no plans.

Suddenly, his vision darkened. A backpack dropped on the ground next to his head. Keenan's eyes narrowed, trying to make out the person standing above him.

"Password?" she asked.

Keenan smiled. "*Klappertaart.*"

"What? A fart?"

"Banana."

"Okay. You can pass."

"Why are you here?" asked Keenan.

"I should be asking you the same thing. But I think we both know the answer."

"Neptune radar." Keenan grinned. Suddenly, his heart burst into bloom—and how brightly it blossomed, and kept on blossoming, as if there were no end.

His view was unobstructed once again. Kugy was now lying beside him. And Keenan couldn't remember when the sky had looked so beautiful.

EPILOGUE

In the middle of a calm blue ocean, two hands appear from the side of a fishing boat to set a paper boat adrift. Not from a reservoir. Not from a stream. Not from a small river. This time, she wants to set it down in the middle of the ocean. It is her last letter to Neptune.

> *Nep,*
> *It's been years since I've written. Don't be mad, but I would like to resign. I have no more secrets to tell you, or dreams—because we're living those dreams. Now. And forever.*
> *K&K*
> *(And a little K on the way)*

The paper boat drifts all alone. The wooden boat leaves it behind and heads slowly back to shore, where Kugy jumps out with a splash. Where Keenan is waiting for her with open arms, ready to embrace her before hoisting her into the air.

ABOUT THE AUTHOR

Dee Lestari is one of Indonesia's bestselling and critically acclaimed authors. Born in 1976, she began her writing career with the serial novel *Supernova* in 2001. The popular series achieved immediate cult status with Indonesian readers.

Dee has published ten books in total. The original version of *Paper Boats, Perahu kertas,* was the first digital novel in Indonesia that readers could subscribe to from their mobile phones. It was printed in 2009 and was made into a movie that became a national blockbuster and marked Dee's debut as a screenplay writer.

Dee also has had an extensive music career as a pop star in Indonesia and has released several albums. In her spare time, she writes songs for other renowned Indonesian artists.

For the latest information about Dee's releases and future books, visit www.deelestari.com. Chat with her on Twitter @deelestari.